THE HAUNTING

OF

MELMERBY MANOR

A SPOOKIES STORY

DAVID ROBINSON

A VIRTUAL TALES BOOK

The Haunting of Melmerby Manor

Cover Art © 2008 Jeff Reitz (http://www.jeffreitz.com)

Edited by Karen Anne Webb

A Virtual Tales Book
PO Box 822674
Vancouver, WA 98682 USA

www.VirtualTales.com

ISBN 0-9801506-6-3

First Edition: October 2008

Printed in the United States of America

9 7 8 0 9 8 0 1 5 0 6 6 7

❧

THIS BOOK IS DEDICATED TO

CAROL, FOR HER PATIENCE

❧

To Sue

Best Wishes

David Robinson

John 2009

✥

Coming Soon From David Robinson:

The Man in Black A Spookies Story

HTTP://WWW.FREEWEBS.COM/DWROB

✥

1

Three men stared down at the battered body on the concrete floor. Blood poured from an open head wound and smeared the stone.

"That was a stupid thing to do," said the tallest of the trio surrounding the inert body. "He can't tell us anything now, can he?"

The leader shrugged and dropped the baseball bat with which he had done the damage. "I pay you to do as you're told, not to hassle me." He opened the cold room door. "Get him in there for the time being."

The curly-haired, shorter henchman sneered. "Great. Rack him up with the frozen pies."

"It's a cooler, not a freezer." The leader grinned. "It'll keep him nice and fresh until we can get rid of him. Now move it. We don't have all night."

Reluctantly, the two men bent to the grisly task. Suddenly, the blood-streaked corpse groaned.

"Hey," complained the taller thug, "he's not dead yet."

"Think positive," said his boss. "The cold room might keep him alive a bit longer." He slammed the cooler door on the dying man. "We can move him later."

❧

At 16 Rossington Terrace, the curtains were closed; the TV, DVD player, and the electric fire were all off and disconnected from the mains. In the rear kitchen, the appliances were switched off and the only noise was a slight rattle from an old, inefficient refrigerator.

Upstairs, in the back bedroom, 6-year-old Damon Bilks slept soundly beneath a single duvet printed in the red and white of the Arsenal soccer team. All around him, the stars of his favorite Premier League Club plied their skills in stylized pictures, watching over him, standing sentry on one of their most avid fans.

It was house at peace.

Almost.

In the double bed of the front bedroom, Angie Bilks could not match her son's untroubled slumber. Waking for the fourth time, she checked the clock. 2:00 a.m. and Bilko was not home.

Not that she was afraid of being home alone through the night. It was anger that disturbed her sleep. Her errant husband had rung at nine and promised he would be home as soon as he had settled a bit of business. Five hours gone, and where was he?

She knew. Knew that he must have concluded his business, meaning he had money in his pocket, meaning the call of the bar and the wink of the waitress would be too strong for him to resist. Angie also knew that when he came in, he would be smashed out of his mind, and her irritation would have to wait until the morning before she could properly vent it.

And when she got her hands on him...

She took a sip of water from a glass on the bedside cabinet, turned over and closed her eyes.

It was just too bad of him to do this. He knew Damon had school in the morning, he knew she had to be up early to get their son ready and take him there, and yet he persisted in staying out till all hours. He was a selfish, lazy, good-for-nothing...

It was only the slightest tinkle of glass or china, coming from downstairs, but it was enough to bring Angie fully alert. She knew her house, knew the noises it made, and the sound of breaking glass or pottery was not on the list. Bilko had a key, so he wouldn't be breaking in, although, if he was full of booze, he might well be staggering in. Angie knew better. If he was drunk, he'd have made a lot more noise coming through the front door. It was not Bilko.

As if to confirm her assumptions, there came a bump from downstairs. Anger fuelling her courage, she threw off the duvet and marched out of the bedroom.

On the landing, she met her 6-year-old son.

"Mum, there's someone downstairs and he's been in my room."

Her anger turned to absolute fury. No one disturbed her son—not if he valued his neck.

"Go back to bed, Damon. I'll deal with it."

She tromped boldly down the stairs and at the bottom glanced to her left, into the kitchen. No one to be seen. A noise from her right directed her to the front room. The door was closed. Odd. She always left it open.

Angie crept first into the kitchen, checked the worktops, picked up a rolling pin, thought better of it, and instead took a long meat knife. No point messing about. Threatened properly, the intruders might learn some manners.

Adrenalin surging through her bloodstream, she hurried back to the living room, to find Damon sitting on the bottom step.

"I told you to go back to bed. I'll deal with it."

"But Mum, he's torn my wallpaper."

About to charge into the front room, Angie paused. "What?"

Damon held up his hand with a strip of wallpaper about 20 centimeters long, showing two feet in football boots, a ball between them. "Look."

Angie put her most disapproving face—the one her son knew so well. "What have you been doing, Damon?"

"It wasn't me. Honest. It was *him*."

"Who?

"The old man."

Angie clucked. The imaginary old man had plagued Damon on and off since they first moved into the house a year ago.

"Damon, I won't tell you again. Go back to bed."

The boy made no effort to move, and another noise from the living room distracted Angie. She gripped the doorknob, threw open the door and burst in.

"Right, you—"

A china nymph flew through the air and silenced her protest. It missed her by millimeters and shattered against the wall alongside her head. She flicked on the light. It promptly flicked off again, but in that fleeting second, she could see that the room was as devoid of burgling scum as the kitchen had been. She was alone in the room.

She had to duck to avoid a second ornament: a regency woman by *Capo di Monte*, which she remembered Bilko stealing from some house up near the Memorial Park, flew at her and she had to duck to avoid it.

The confidence with which she had entered the room evaporated instantly. Now her heart pounded with fear. She turned to leave; the door slammed shut. She yanked at it, but it would not open. Across the room, the TV set wobbled on its stand, lifted a few millimeters, and dropped down onto the carpet; the cable, already disconnected from the electricity supply, squirmed behind it like an angry snake. Angie dragged at the door again. She whimpered, suddenly terrified for her life. A large drinks cabinet, filled with cheap spirits Bilko had bought from one of his dodgy mates, toppled and shattered into a thousand pieces.

"Let me out, let me out!" she cried, hammering on the room door. She hit the light switch again. The lights came on, flickered momentarily, then went out again. Electric blue flashes circled the ceiling, lighting the chaos. "Damon!" she screamed. "Get out, Damon! Get Mrs. Armstrong! Tell her to call the police!"

A small vase of flowers smashed into the wall above her head. Filthy water showered her. An armchair bean to move, swiveling from side to side on its castors.

Angie stared frantically around for a means of escape. Dull light from street lamps came through the closed curtains. The window. She looked around. Alongside the smashed drinks cabinet, from where it had fallen, was a model truck. Bilko had stolen it from a secondhand market. It was made of metal. She picked it up, tested the weight, and made for the window.

The moving chair swiveled before her. She dodged right; it followed. She dodged left; it followed. From somewhere came the sound of booming laughter. She leapt on the chair, rode it like a bucking bronco as she reached over to snatch at the curtains. The chair yanked her away. She clung to the drapes, and they tore from their hooks. The chair threw her off. She landed midway between door and window. Scrabbling to her feet, she hovered on the edge of total panic.

Got to get out, got to get out.

The door? The window? *Got to get out, got to get out!* The door creaked open few centimeters. She raced towards it. It slammed shut! She stood by the door, unable to react, tears streaming down her face, her body shaking. She was no longer a rational human being. She was a puppet, dancing on the strings of panic-driven, nervous impulses, unable to think, unable to act.

Through the all-consuming terror, a chink of logic shone through. The curtains were gone. The window was exposed. She still held the die-cast model. *If I can't get to the window, I can still get this thing through the window.*

She threw it.

It struck the glass in the center and bounced off.

"That's not how you do it," cackled a maniacal voice. "*This* is how you do it." The telephone flew from its table under the window and smashed cleanly through the glass. The damp chill of a late autumn night flooded into the room.

As Angie leapt for it, the chair moved in front of her again. Behind her, the door flapped open, and then closed once more. She stared back at it, the sweat of fear running down her face. It closed, opened and closed again! She ran for it, praying it would carry on flapping. It slammed shut! Her heart sank. It opened again; she leapt through. It slammed, catching her arm. She yelled in furious pain. In the hall, her son was straining to reach the deadbolt. Angie snatched him into her arms, fumbled with the lock, snapped it back and yanked the door open, and then tumbled out into the rainy street, away from the pandemonium.

❦

Fishwick looked down on the serene face of Scepter Rand and felt something close to peace. As long as the mistress was safe, he could relax.

It had been a busy night. This time of year in the Northern Hemisphere, it was always busy. There was the usual crowd passing over from the cold and damp weather, drunks celebrating Christmas a month early (and some of them stupidly driving home), the ever-increasing violence of the streets—all conspired to form a steady stream making their way over, but as long as Scepter was not one of them, it was all no concern of his.

The Light was there. The Light was always there, in the background, twinkling, warm, inviting, calling to them, calling to *him*. Most of the Incoming understood The Light and went straight to it, on to the next world. There were times when he yearned to go into The Light, but he could not. Not while she needed him.

Suddenly, he realized, a newcomer had arrived, and he, too, was ignoring the silent call of The Light. The undulating energy form was gripped by an uncontrollable rage, rushing, dashing everywhere. Fishwick had never seen such anger.

"Calm down, me old sparrow," Fishwick urged.

The spirit's only response was an almost incomprehensible roar.

"Sounded like 'wigwam,'" Fishwick muttered to himself as the spirit flew off. Fishwick checked on Scepter again, and, satisfied that she was fine, he followed.

He watched in dismay while the furious interloper wrought havoc on the little terraced house, and decided that it was time to intervene. But there was a complication. Another spirit nearby. An old man. This would need handling from both sides of the Great Divide.

Fishwick returned to Scepter's room. "Modom," he called. "Modom, there is a crisis and I think you may be needed."

Scepter stirred. "Fishwick? Is that you, Fishwick, or am I still dreaming?"

"No, Modom. You're not dreaming. We have a situation."

She sat up and rubbed the sleep from her eyes before checking the clock. "Fishwick, do you know what time it is?"

"Time has little meaning for me, Modom, and it has no meaning for those who would harm others. You are needed, Modom."

She yawned. "Oh, very well, Fishwick. Where?"

"16 Rossington Terrace. I suggest you take Mr. Brennan along. He may be needed, too."

Fishwick left his mistress' bedroom, allowing her to dress in private. Discretion was one of the prime requirements of a butler. It had been drummed into him when he first entered service with the Rand-Epping family. The mistress must have her privacy. Fishwick had forgotten none of his training even though he had been dead for 90 years.

❧

Police constable Dave Robb pushed his cap back and scratched his forehead as he read his notes.

Like most of Ashdale's police, he knew Bilko—Steven Bilks, to give him his proper name. A small time wheeler-dealer, general thief and fence with a liking for strong beer and even stronger spirits, he had a record as long as a Philip Glass double album, and one that was just as repetitive.

The trouble was, Robb knew Angie, too. A hard-faced, hard-fisted woman, more than capable of tackling burglars, and if she said there was someone hiding in number 16, moreover someone who was so violent he had persuaded Angie to run for the sanctuary of a neighbor's living room, then Robb had to take it seriously.

She sat now in the Armstrongs' living room, still wearing her nightie, with a mug of tea in her shaking hands, seriously afraid. WPC Smedley sat alongside her, and young Damon sat in his mum's lap.

"Right Angie," said Robb, "I'll go take a look in your place. You want to wait here?"

Angie shook her head. "I need to see who it is."

"I don't need you in the house while I'm trying to collar the burglar," Robb objected.

"I'll wait on the pavement," Angie said, and Robb gave up trying to persuade her.

He led the way out, thanking Mrs. Armstrong, and with Smedley, Angie and Damon immediately behind him, stepped into the street.

Some of the neighbors had already come out, attracted, like flies, by the flickering blue beat of his car's emergency lights. Robb noticed that behind the shattered window of number 16, there were more flashes of light, but they were not simply reflections of his car. There was definitely something going on in there.

Urging Angie and Smedley to wait there, he stepped cautiously into the hall, riot stick in one hand, his torch flashing nervously ahead.

He felt irritated. He'd had no plans for anything major on a wet and windy November Thursday night, other than parking up near the Memorial Park and chatting up WPC Smedley, inviting her out to a football match at the weekend. He'd been sweet-talking WPC Smedley for the last two years, and he was sure he was making slow progress.

When the call came through and he recognized the address, he felt certain they would find Bilko drunk and the disturbance to be nothing more than Angie venting her anger on him. Even when he saw the flashes of cool blue and angry red light coming from the house, even when he spoke to Angie, he was still convinced that Bilko would be behind it all.

Making his way along the hall, stepping around Damon's bike, he tried the light switch. Nothing. With a shrug, he passed on, peered into the living room and watched in amazement as the armchair jiggled left and right, twisted and turned like a whirling dervish high on a cocktail of illegal substances.

He couldn't see anyone, and no explanation readily presented itself, so he assumed that the Bilks had been fooling around with some kind of electrical apparatus.

He stepped out of the room again, and a jar of marmalade flew past his head. He ducked back into the room, and other jars followed him, missing his head by millimeters. From the kitchen came the sound of papers being strewn across the floor. Robb could not see anyone. He glanced at the chair, which was now doing a passable imitation of the Twist, then made for the kitchen once more. As he reached the doorway, the oven door opened and a voice boomed from within.

"BOO!"

Robb turned and fled.

2

In the rear seat of Pete Brennan's estate car, Scepter watched rows of high density, terraced housing pass by. The casual observer would have considered her calm, serene, but beneath her placid features excitement and anticipation coursed through her. Tonight was the start of a new chapter in her life.

Aged 27, she had been born into privilege, but circumstances had compelled her to live in the real world. After the North Yorkshire family seat of the Rand-Eppings was sold to the nation to pay off family debts incurred by her gambling grandfather, she and her mother had moved into more modest accommodations in York. Her father had died when she was a child, and at the time of her mother's untimely death in an automobile accident, Scepter became the Countess of North Yorkshire, but there was no family fortune. All that remained of her distinguished lineage was the useless title and a butler dedicated to their service even in his afterlife.

Coming out of university with only a small amount of money from the sale of the house in York, she was appointed as a tutor in history at Ashdale College of Further Education. Scepter knew that teaching teenagers was not her vocation. The job was part-time and lacked challenge, but it provided her with a meager income, sufficient to support her until she could reach her true calling: bringing peace to the bereaved by contacting the spirits of their departed loved ones.

Soon after moving to Ashdale, she answered an advertisement for a third person to share an apartment, and met Kevin Keeley in a pub to discuss terms. When she learned that her potential flat mates were both male, she almost walked away, but Kevin's gift for persuasive chatter soon convinced her that she was safe, and if Pete had never let up on his efforts to charm her into his bed, he was easy to hold at arm's length.

Kevin was more interested in the profit potential of her psychic powers. Ghost hunting as a team had been his idea. He could supply the technical know-how, Pete would handle security, and Scepter would provide the view from the Other Side. Somewhere along the line, he had also promised to think up a name for them.

"Something catchy," he had promised her, "something people will remember."

"Something like 'Numpties 'a' Us?'" Pete had asked.

Kevin had dismissed his best friend's cynicism, assuring Scepter that he had contacts in the TV industry. Scepter begged leave to doubt that Kevin could be so persuasive, but he would not be put off by her doubts. He was confident that if they could put together a good enough presentation, he would be able to land them a lucrative contract with one of the cable or satellite channels.

"We need good footage of spooks in action," he told her. "Noises, bumps, bangs, things moving around by themselves. You know the kind of thing I mean."

Intrigued by the idea, caught up in his enthusiasm, she gave Fishwick instructions to monitor the astral comings and goings in and around Ashdale. Tonight was their first call out. It was exciting, exhilarating, and not a little nerve jangling.

She wondered whether Pete and Kevin felt the same mixture of emotions. Pete appeared calm enough as he braked sharply and turned into Rossington Terrace. In the front passenger seat, Kevin, too, appeared cool and collected fiddling with the settings on his digital camcorder.

Up ahead, Scepter could see the flashing blue light of a police vehicle and a small crowd of people on the sidewalks. Pete pulled his car into the curb and climbed out, moving immediately to the rear of the vehicle. Kevin also left the car, but he was now engrossed in fitting a halogen spot-lamp to his camcorder.

Scepter paused a moment before getting out, her eyes fixed on the open door of number 16. That was where her future, all their futures, lay.

A police officer, dressed in a heavy, quilted, high-visibility overcoat, came rushing out of the house followed by a flying glass vase that shattered on the pavement. From inside the house came a fearsome roar and flashes of electric blue light.

Getting out of the car, she muttered, "Fishwick, are you there?"

"Right here, Modom."

"Check the house."

"Very good, Modom."

Scepter zipped up her coat and crossed the street, peering into the narrow hall, catching occasional glimpses of a child's bicycle illuminated in the intermittent flashes of light. She had had regular contact with Fishwick since childhood, but she had never seen, nor experienced any other form of manifestation from the spirit world. Indeed, she had never *seen* Fishwick. She had only communicated with him, and that was limited to his voice in her head.

"There are spirits, Modom," her butler had once explained, "who will readily manifest themselves, but such apparitions can be unnerving, and I prefer to concentrate my energies on assisting, not frightening you."

Further along the street, kept back by the police patrol cars, neighbors had turned out in various states of dress and undress, to see what was happening. On the pavement close by, with Police Constable Sandra Smedley for company, Angie stood shivering in her nightie, looking drawn and afraid, young Damon hiding in her nightdress. The sight evoked Scepter's sympathies. This woman needed help.

While Kevin aimed his video camera into the house and began filming, Scepter addressed the police officer who had just run from the house: his jacket identified him as PC Robb.

"Good morning, constable," she greeted. "I believe you're having trouble with a restless spirit?"

Robb looked her up and down. "Just keep out the way, luv, there's a good girl." He made a move as if to head for his car.

"I," she declared grandly, "have come here to put matters right, and kindly do not speak to me like that again. I'm not a child." Scepter's tone, as stern as the dowager duchess who had instilled them in her, coupled with her air of aristocratic authority, had Robb nonplussed. He stopped dead in his tracks and looked her over as if assessing her, his frown indicating that he was wondering how to deal with her.

He adjusted his tone from patronizing to practical. "Listen, missus, we don't know what's going on here, but whoever's in there has just chucked a bloody great vase at me, so if you value your nut, keep out of the way."

Scepter dismissed him with a contemptuous, aristocratic snort and turned her attention to Angie. "Is it your house?" She waited for the woman to give a forlorn nod, then declared. "I am an expert in these matters, and I'm here to help." Scepter made the claim with a lot more confidence than she actually felt, but she was pleased to see Angie show the faintest sign of relief. It was no more than a tiny adjustment in her withdrawn stance, a slight turn towards Scepter, as if pleading for someone to end the insanity. Scepter gave her a smile of encouragement. "Tell me what happened."

PC Robb tried to intervene again. "Now look, luv—"

"All right, Dave?"

At the sound of the new voice coming from behind, Robb twisted to his left. His face ran through a rapid series of emotions: irritation, recognition, contempt, and outright anger. "Well, well, well. Detective Constable Brennan. Ex-Detective Constable Brennan, I should say." Robb's voice oozed cynical pleasure as if he were anticipating something nasty about to happen. "What are you doing here?"

Pete nodded at Scepter. "I'm with her."

"I might have known. If anyone was capable of ferreting out the loons at this hour, it'd have to be you. Well, there's nothing here that need concern you, so push off before I run you in."

Pete smiled easily. "On what charge?"

"I dunno," shrugged Robb. "How about interfering with the police officer in the course of his duties?"

"You're the one who should be arrested—for impersonating a police officer—and so far, we haven't interfered with you. Seems to me you ran out of the house under your own steam."

Robb glared. "One more crack like that, Brennan, and I *will* run you in. Nobody likes a bent cop, remember."

"Yes, and nobody likes cops screwing around where they shouldn't do, so just watch that your boss doesn't find out about that tramp on the Cranley estate you've been jumping for the last five or six years."

Scepter looked sharply at Pete, as if asking, "Huh?" Pete frowned and gave the slightest shake of his head, indicating that he would explain later.

He turned back to Robb. "Cut the empty threats, Dave, and let Scepter sort this out."

"Sort what out?" PC Robb looked wildly back into the house. "We don't even know what's going on. Angie called us for a burglary, we turned out, and the place was in chaos. I went in, couldn't see anyone, and suddenly a jar of jam comes flying at me. Next it was salad cream, then salmon paste."

"Midnight feast in the dorm?" chuckled Pete.

"Knock it off," sulked Robb. "When I legged it, that bloody vase came after me. Honest, Brennan, I don't know where the burglar is, but he's in one helluva mean mood."

"Then let us have a go?" Pete suggested.

"Tough guy, huh? I'm telling you, Brennan—"

Scepter, who had been following their debate, now cut in. "Oh do shut up, constable." She turned back to Angie. "My name is Scepter Rand. I'm a psychic medium. Would you like to tell me what happened tonight?"

Angie looked to Robb for support, but the police officer merely tapped the side of his head to indicate his opinion on Scepter's sanity. Angie then looked to Pete, who smiled, and then to Kevin.

"Trust me, Angie," he reassured her from behind his lens, "Scepter knows what she's talking about."

Scepter glanced sharply up at Pete, checking his reaction to Kevin's assertion, but he simply shrugged at Angie and smiled again, as if encouraging her to take it all with a grain of salt.

Kevin, his eye still pressed to the viewfinder, panned the camera between Scepter and Angie.

Frowning, shielding her eyes from the dazzling spotlight, Angie spoke to Scepter, but her voice was edged with uncertainty. "We were in bed when suddenly all hell broke loose. We came downstairs, found the furniture moving on its own, the TV thrown on the floor, ornaments and stuff smashed, and I guessed we'd been broke in, so I brought my son out and belled the filth –er—law on my mobile." She held her cell phone up to the camera as if giving evidence.

"And you can't tell me anything else?" asked Scepter.

Frightened and bewildered, Angie gave a shrug. "What's to tell?"

Ignoring Kevin and his intrusive filming, Scepter chewed her lip and looked at the house. It seemed peaceful enough at the moment. Turning back to Angie, she asked, "Has anything like this ever happened before?"

Angie shook her head. "Damon's always telling us about an old man, but you know how kids are, with imaginary friends. But we do know that the bloke what lived here before us was in his eighties when he died."

"There you are then," said Scepter with a degree of satisfaction. "It sounds as if something may have disturbed him. I'm going in to see if I can calm them down."

Robb opened his mouth to protest, but Pete beat him to it.

"Hold on, Scepter." He, too, questioned the frightened householder. "Angie, where's Bilko?"

Her face creased. "I don't know, Pete. Honest," She begged as if he were still a police officer seeking explanations. "He rang me earlier from Flutter-Bys, but the little sod still hasn't come home."

Scepter was perplexed. "What's Flutter-Bys?"

"Night club off Yorkshire Street," Kevin reported from behind his lens.

"And who is Bilko?"

"Her husband. Steven Bilks. Small-time villain." Kevin still did not take his eye from the viewfinder.

There was a moment's silence while Scepter considered her options. "Fishwick, are you there?"

Around her, the police and householders looked on with amused amazement as she entered into what was for them a one-way communication with her butler. Unable to see or hear Fishwick, PC Robb leaned close into Pete and asked, "Who's she speaking to?"

Pete grinned. "Her great-granddad's butler."

Robb looked around at the night. "So where is he?"

"He died in 1916."

Robb gaped. "Oh. So she's a real fruitcake?"

"Fully qualified," Pete agreed.

◈

The conversation between Scepter and her deceased butler continued. "Can you add anything to what we have heard, Fishwick?"

"A little, Modom," replied her butler. "There are actually two spirits in the house. One is the original owner who, it seems, crossed over about five years ago. He's the old man the little boy has talked about. The other is newly deceased, and he's very angry. He's the one doing most of the damage."

"Do we know who this newcomer is?" Scepter asked.

"No, Modom," said Fishwick. "He's too angry to respond. All he can say is what sounds like 'wigwam'."

The comment was a puzzle to Scepter. "And is he a North American Indian?"

"I don't think so, Modom."

The flat, matter-of-fact manner in which Fishwick delivered his responses irritated Scepter. "Then it makes no sense, Fishwick."

'No, Modom," agreed her butler.

Scepter put aside the question of the violent spirit. "What about the old man?"

Fishwick replied, "The ravings of this newcomer have awakened him. As near as I can make out, he did not realize he was dead until the newcomer arrived. As a result, he's only just realized how annoyed he is that the new owners have put up Arsenal wallpaper. He tore some of it off."

"Arsenal football team?" Scepter puzzled over this "Why should that annoy him?"

"He was a devout Manchester United fan, Modom."

"I understand," said Scepter, even though she did not. "Can you do anything with him?"

"Difficult to say, Modom," Fishwick confessed. "As soccer hooliganism goes, ripping the wallpaper off is mild, and he does have a point. I prefer Manchester United, too. They play the game like it's supposed to be played."

Scepter disapproved of his levity. "Your preferences do not enter into the debate, Fishwick. Do you have any recommendations?"

Her butler reverted to his pragmatic self. "It is impossible to get any sense out of the furious spirit, Modom, while the old man is with him. We need to get rid of the old chap so we can concentrate on the newcomer."

"And how do you imagine we should do that?" demanded Scepter.

"We should try get the old fool to go through The Light, Modom, and that, I believe, is where you come in."

She was satisfied. "Thank you Fishwick. Stand by."

She could almost imagine Fishwick saluting as he responded, "Very good, Modom."

❦

Scepter terminated the conversation with her butler and, ignoring the bemused stares of those around her, addressed Robb. "I'm going in there, and this time, I mean it."

The policeman tried to assert his authority. "Now listen, chicken, I can't let anyone in there. Not even a well-meaning nut like you—"

Scepter's patience, which had been wearing thin ever since she first encountered Robb, finally snapped. She drew in her breath, squared her shoulders and faced him at her imperious best. "I've warned you about addressing me in such a casual manner. I am not your love, nor your darling. Neither am I a missus, nor a fool. I am Lady Concepta Rand-Epping, Countess of North Yorkshire, and I know what I am doing. Now kindly stand back. I am going in there." She snapped her fingers. "Peter, Kevin. With me, please."

In the face of her tyranny, Robb acquiesced and stood back to let them in.

⚜

Scepter stepped cautiously over the threshold with Pete at her shoulder and Kevin, still running his camcorder, right behind. "What was that you were saying about his superior learning of his affair with some woman?"

Her question was aimed at Pete, who explained, "A police officer is responsible for his conduct both on and off duty. Robb's bit on the side sleeps around. If she whispered a few sweet nothings in the wrong ears, she could compromise Robb's position."

"What an appalling way to describe a lover. A bit on the side," Scepter disapproved. "Do you mean she could blackmail him?"

Pete nodded. "Not necessarily. But if she's sleeping around, she may be jumping convicted felons and passing on information on Robb, his beat, his movements, and so on. If she's in cahoots with a burglar, for instance, the burglar could pay her to keep Robb busy, while he rips off the local liquor store. You get the picture?"

"I think so."

Her curiosity satisfied, Scepter turned her attention to the task at hand and stared around the hall. The power was off, yet light from an unknown source flickered from the living room, lighting the faded, yellow wallpaper and dismal floor covering.

Just ahead lay the staircase to the upper floor and, beyond it, the kitchen entrance. Both were quiet: it was the living room, the first door to her left, that was the source of the disturbance. Angry lights in blue and red flashed and sparked; rumbling, grumbling noises came from within.

Scepter edged into the room and surveyed the scene. The TV, as Angie had said, lay face down on the carpet; the armchair had stopped its dancing and, along with its twin, had been upended and dropped onto the couch. The overall effect was that the suite had been made ready for the moving men. Like the hall, the walls were covered in flock wallpaper, which was hanging off in places. Above the fireplace, an Arsenal banner hung from a single drawing pin, as if someone had ripped the other end down. As she watched, the message *Man. U. 4 Ever* appeared across it as if sprayed by a hand wielding an invisible can of paint.

"Crikey," said Kevin, following her in, his eye still pressed to the viewfinder. "What a mess. It looks like our place after a party."

Ignoring him, Scepter spoke to the room in loud, authoritative tones. "Spirit, I command you to go into The Light and cross over."

Her announcement was greeted with a loud raspberry.

Taken aback, Scepter called upon her butler. "Fishwick, did either of the spirits understand me?"

"The old man understood, Modom," said Fishwick. "His reply was not very pleasant."

"I had suspected as much, but do tell me, Fishwick."

"Get stuffed."

Her butler's words annoyed her. "Fishwick, are you merely being impertinent, or was that his answer?"

"His answer, Modom," Fishwick assured her with implacable calm.

Scepter considered her options. Lacking any previous experience of helping a spirit cross the Great Divide, she had arrogantly assumed that the old man would obey her the way household servants had obeyed her mother. She had read of other mediums ordering spirits to go into The Light, and the spirits meekly obeyed. This old man would need more determined handling.

She injected more force into her voice this time. "Spirit, I will not tolerate your impudence. I *command* you to go into The Light, to cross over."

Immediately in front of her, a ghostly body took shape, its empty eye sockets trained upon her, the lean body shimmering in the darkness. Scepter's heart beat rapidly, but she stood her ground. As she watched, the face changed, the jaw dropped, the mouth opened wide, and, taking on an almost lupine appearance, great jaws projected forward, snapping shut just centimeters from her face, bellowing loudly, the blast of its fetid breath blowing her hair back.

Scepter reached down to the carpet and picked up the evening newspaper, then proceeded to fan herself nonchalantly with it.

"You really should see a dentist," she said. "Your breath smells terribly." She gave a deliberate yawn of disinterest, and faced the ghastly apparition. It was time, she decided, to teach the old man just who he was dealing with. The Rand-Eppings had been stalwarts of the British aristocracy since the Civil War, and she was not about to be beaten by an obstinate old football fanatic. "Now listen to me. I am not afraid of you. I am not going away; I will be here as long as you are. You will tire of the game before I do. There is peace, comfort and as much Manchester City football as you can watch for eternity, if you go through The Light."

Her announcement was greeted with another furious roar.

"It's Manchester United, Modom," said Fishwick urgently.

"What difference does it make?" Scepter demanded, her patience wearing down.

"It is the same difference as you asking me for strawberries and ice cream, and me delivering steak and kidney pudding, Modom" her ephemeral manservant explained.

Completely at sea, Scepter protested, "I don't like steak and kidney pudding."

"I do," interjected Kevin from behind his lens.

Ignoring the interruption, Fishwick said, "The old man doesn't like Manchester City, Modom. The only thing a Manchester United fan loathes more than Arsenal is Manchester City."

At a loss for anything else to say, Scepter announced, "I apologize, spirit. I meant Manchester United. Now be a good chap and go through The Light."

⁂

Immediately behind Scepter, Pete viewed the scene with amusement. He could see nothing of the apparition she saw, and he could hear only Scepter's side of the two-way conversation between her and Fishwick. Deciding that she was safe enough with Kevin and her imaginary butler, he drifted out of the living room and turned along the hall towards the kitchen.

Scepter was a strange woman. A slender—some would say anorexic—green-eyed redhead, she was not beautiful, merely attractive. There was an upper class naiveté about her that appealed to Pete. She viewed the world with an almost childlike simplicity, and, despite his best efforts to persuade her otherwise, she persisted in her belief in some invisible nether world from which her great-grandfather's butler watched over her. It was amusing—and frustrating. Pete preferred women who put their faith in *him*, not in a man who had been dead for nigh on a century.

Not that he doubted her sincerity. Unlike Kevin, who would jump on any bandwagon at the slightest sniff of a profit, Scepter truly believed in her supposed abilities, but Pete was convinced they had more to do with Kevin's glib tongue than anything else. When Pete originally agreed to go along with them on their ghost hunts it was with the idea that she would need someone to keep her feet on the ground. He also figured it would be fun: a distraction from bad debt collections and gathering divorce evidence that were the routine fodder of the private investigator.

Despite Dave Robb's disparaging opinion of him, Pete had been a good police officer, an *honest* officer, part of a small town force where a sizeable proportion of the team was anything but honest.

His integrity did not endear him to his colleagues, many of whom regarded him with suspicion, and when he made the one error of judgment for which he was disciplined, he had gotten the impression that there was a lot of silent cheering in Ashdale Police Station. It was while he was going through that disciplinary process that he named those crooked officers. A few days later, during a particularly unpleasant interview, he lost his temper and punched the investigating officer in the nose. Soon after, he was summarily dismissed.

He could not complain. Even when he had attacked his superior, he had known what he was doing, had known it could get him fired, and it had come as little consolation when the men he had named were also fired.

His thoughts turned to Steven Bilks, a man well known to the police. A thief who had been in and out of prison ever since his school days. The opportunity to go through the house of a scumbag like that while there on legitimate business—acting as security for Scepter and her ghostly games—was too good for Pete to pass up.

"You're not really prying," he told himself as he entered the kitchen. "Just looking for the intruders causing the ruckus."

The room was furnished with a cheap dining set consisting of a table, four chairs, and the usual array of kitchen appliances. All of them had that air of use common in a family house: one of the control knobs was missing from the cooker, a threadbare hand towel hung over the washing machine door, which was slight ajar. To the left of the chimney was a computer workstation hemmed into the corner by a large, drop-leaf cabinet.

Pete lowered the door of the cabinet and examined the contents as best he could in the dim light coming from the outside world. It was full of run-of-the-mill stuff: a sheet of A4 paper detailing the school holidays for the coming year was taped to one side, while the shelves were littered with routine correspondence, bills, a threat of court action for non-payment of Council Tax. A couple of DVDs in their plastic cases lay amongst the papers. Pete studied the front cover of *Dr. No*, the first-ever Bond movie, and put it down again.

The second DVD was more interesting. The twisted face of an insane woman dominated the predominantly dark blue cover. The title read *Mind Games III*.

"Now then, Bilko," he said to the empty, darkened room, "what are you doing with the DVD of a movie that doesn't get released to the cinemas for another month?"

Noises from the next room reached his ears. Abandoning the idea of searching further, he tucked the DVD into the rear waistband of his tracksuit bottoms and made his way back to the living room.

⚜

In front of Scepter, the ghastly apparition had calmed somewhat, looking a little more human than bestial, although the eyes and mouth were still no more than empty spaces through which the bare walls and the ghostly message denigrating Arsenal in favor of Manchester United was fading.

The phantom now gave the appearance of wearing a puzzled frown.

"You will find," said Scepter, "that Fishwick, my butler, is standing quite close to you. He will help you through The Light."

"He's already aware of my presence, Modom," Fishwick announced.

The ghostly figure now looked to its left, almost as if it were waiting for Fishwick to do something.

Scepter took advantage of the calm to press home her control of events. "Now, my man, if you were to go through The Light, you would find the soccer heaven where you should have gone shortly after you passed over."

There was a brief silence before Fishwick's voice came to her once more. "Modom, he doesn't believe you. He wants me to go with him."

"If you go into The Light, Fishwick, you can never come back. You can't go with him... unless you want to, of course."

"If I wanted to, Modom," he assured her, "I would have done so long ago."

"In that case, let's defeat him with logic," suggested Scepter. "Ask him where he thinks the great footballers go when they pass on."

After a brief pause, Fishwick reported, "Accrington Stanley and Stockport County, Modom."

Scepter was puzzled. "What?"

"He insists that all great footballers go to Accrington Stanley or Stockport County when they can no longer play in the Premier League. If I may make so bold, Modom, you do not know about football. Accrington Stanley and Stockport County play in a lower division than Manchester United and Arsenal, and when footballers like David Beckham and Pelé get older, they go to play for smaller teams."

Scepter was still puzzled. "Correct me if I am wrong, but David Beckham has gone to play in the United States."

Another few moments of silence followed. Eventually, Fishwick reported, "The old man says it amounts to the same thing, Modom."

Scepter rolled her eyes to the ceiling and puffed out her cheeks. "Fishwick, I'm beginning to tire of this nit-picking. Explain the situation to him properly."

There was another lull during which Scepter looked around the room. The carpet, an old and worn beige Axminster, had suffered having a bottle of salad cream, salmon paste and what she hoped was only a jar of jam splattered over it. It would, she guessed, be the Devil's own job to get the stains out. She did not know for certain because throughout a 27-year life of aristocratic indolence, she could not recall ever having had to remove stains from a carpet. When she was a child, the household staff had always handled such matters, and later on, at school, in the dormitory, there were no carpets, while during her university years, her student roommates did it for her. It was their way of acknowledging her titled superiority... and making a few pounds a week out of her.

"I think, Modom," Fishwick said at last, "that he's got it. I took the liberty of telling him that The Light is a floodlight from Bloomfield Road and that, at this moment, Stan Matthews and Stan Mortensen are taking on the deceased from the Manchester United 1957 title winning team. I'm going to guide him to The Light."

"Good," Scepter approved. "Whatever it takes, Fishwick."

There was a long silence, punctuated only by the sounds from the outside world: fresh police cars arriving and the babble of conversation from somewhere just beyond the front door where more neighbors had come out to sympathize with Angie Bilks. Around Scepter, lights flickered, tiny sparks of electromagnetic energy, flashing on and off, drifting momentarily through the supercharged air before winking out, illuminating the room for the milliseconds of their existence, before plunging everything back into a darkness ameliorated only by the flickering police car lights coming through the windows.

Scepter became aware that some time had elapsed since Fishwick had last contacted her. She glanced at her watch. How much time? A minute? Two? There was nothing strange about this. Fishwick initiated contact most of the time, and many hours could go by without word from him. Scepter remembered when her mother died. Fishwick was busy for hours on end afterwards, trying, so he reported, to locate her spirit amongst the steady stream of souls going through The Light. So even when there was a crisis, it was not unusual for him to be away for some time.

She looked at the wall, where the ghostly message, *Man. U. 4Ever*, now barely visible, still hovered. She looked around the living room and the upturned furniture. The old man and the angry spirit had already demonstrated their ability to interact with the material world in no uncertain terms. Even with Pete and Kevin present, the situation was risky, and Fishwick would not usually leave her this long if there was potential danger.

"Fishwick?" Calling her butler caused Kevin, who had been filming the mess on the floor, to swing his camera towards her.

The first doubt began to nag at her, and for one ridiculous moment, she wondered if the worry showed on her face.

Pull yourself together, girl, she ordered herself. *Remember who you are.*

It was no use. She just knew that something had gone wrong. Fishwick would not be silent for this length of time when he knew she needed him.

"Fishwick? Are you there, Fishwick?" Even to herself, her voice carried a note of anxiety.

Fishwick could not go through The Light. If he did, she would never be able to contact him again. He had been with her so long that she could not imagine a life without him.

"Fishwick. Answer me, Fishwick." Her iron, aristocratic front crumbled. She was close to tears. Her limbs trembled and her worst fears welled from deep within. Had the old football fanatic haunting this house and so determined, even in death, to support his favorite football team, taken her faithful retainer with him to the next world?

"Fishwick." Her voice was shaking, angry. "Please, Fishwick! Don't desert me!"

Scepter checked her watch again, and her heart sank. She resigned herself to the inevitable. For most of her 27 years, Albert Fishwick, whose life had been lost during the terrible summer of 1916, had been at her side to encourage and assist her, and now he was gone. Gone through The Light, starting the next life. The tears welled, and trickled from her eyes, down her cheeks. She could not believe that Fishwick was no longer here. *After all these years*, she thought miserably. She looked for somewhere to sit, but both armchairs were still upside down and on the settee. Instead she slumped back against them and tried to control her emotions.

"I'm right here, Modom."

Relief flooded her at the sound of her manservant's voice in her head. She stood upright, once again the proud aristocrat. "Fishwick. Thank God for that."

"It was a close call, but I managed to persuade him that he should go on alone." There was a brief pause before Fishwick went on. "You were obviously worried, Modom, that I may have deserted you. I have told you many times that I will never leave your side as long as you need me."

Scepter relaxed visibly, her shoulders slumping as the tension left her. "Thank you, Fishwick. How did you persuade him?"

"He was leaning forward looking into The Light, trying to see the football match I'd told him about, when I booted him up the backside and kicked him through." Fishwick sounded angelically innocent as he related the tale. "He'll thank me for it one day."

Scepter turned to face Kevin and Pete, who had just entered the room. "We've dealt with one spirit." As she spoke, a cheap, triple-light chandelier flickered into life above them. Scepter frowned. "Fishwick, I thought there was another spirit here. An angry one."

"There was, Modom," reported her butler. "He, too, seems to have left."

"He hasn't gone through The Light?" Scepter wanted to know.

For once, Fishwick lacked certainty. "I don't think so, Modom, but I will make an effort to find out."

THE HAUNTING OF MELMERBY MANOR—21

While Fishwick went off to look for the spirit, Scepter explained to her partners what had happened and concluded, "Fishwick's gone to look for him, but I think this part of it is over."

Pete laughed. "You do talk some twaddle, Scepter."

Scepter's eyes blazed with a determination just short of anger. "I can readily explain everything that's happened here tonight. Can you?"

He checked his watch and gave a casual yawn. "It's turned three in the morning and I'm not at my best, so I'll need to think about it. Whatever it is, I don't believe it has anything to do with ghosts. Ask me again, tomorrow lunchtime."

Kevin stopped his camcorder. "Pete, you're such a septic."

"The word is skeptic."

"I know what I mean."

Pete narrowed his eyes at his best friend. "Do you reckon Scepter will nurse your cuts and bruises?"

Kevin's brow furrowed, causing Pete to comment aloud on a documentary he'd seen concerning gorillas.

"Cuts and bruises?" said Kevin, "I don't have any cuts and bruises."

Pete spat on his knuckles. "The night's young yet."

Cautious footsteps sounded along the bare floorboards of the hall. Pete leaned his head back out of the door and smiled a welcome. "Oh look, it's PC Plod. Where's Noddy?"

"I saw the lights come on," said Robb.

Pete waved him forward. "Well, you can come in now, Dave. Scepter's chased all the ghosties and ghoulies away."

Robb entered the living room and stared around at the devastation just as Scepter got into conversation with her butler again.

"Modom?"

"Yes, Fishwick?"

"Finding this spirit may take a little time, but that kind of angry energy leaves its mark wherever it goes. I'll contact you the minute I find him."

"Thank you, Fishwick." Terminating her conversation, Scepter concentrated on the bemused police officer and Angie Bilks, who had just stepped nervously into the room. "My spirit guide tells me that it's all calm now." She reached into her purse, took out a pen and a piece of paper and scribbled her number on it. Passing it to Angie, she invited, "If you have any more trouble, ring me. I only live on the Cranley Estate, with Pete and Kevin."

Pete tapped Angie on the shoulder. "I've checked the place over, Angie, and there's no one here—"

"No one human," Scepter interrupted.

Pete frowned at her, and spoke once more to Angie. "We've scared 'em off. Tell Bilko that's one he owes me. Robb and his chums will help you sort out the furniture. You two ready?" He shot the last question at Scepter and Kevin, who both nodded. He led them out into the street, followed by the protests of PC Robb.

"Hey, what am I supposed to tell my guv'nor?"

"Tell him I'll send him a bill," Pete called back as they crossed the street to his car.

⚜

Pete climbed behind the wheel and Scepter settled into the passenger seat, half turning to speak to Kevin as he got into the rear seat.

"I'll want to see that footage, Kevin," she said.

"Some good stuff on it." Kevin chuckled with delight. "That copper, Dave Robb, was scared out of his wits when we got here."

"I'm more interested in the paranormal stuff," Scepter admitted with a jaundiced glance at Pete. "If only to try and convince our skeptical friend here."

Shuffling in his seat, Pete removed the uncomfortable DVD from the waistband of his joggers. "And I have my own agenda. Like, how come Bilko had hold of this?"

Kevin leaned over his shoulder and whistled. " Geez! That thing won't be officially released for another month. It must be a pirate."

"Yep, and there's only one man in Ashdale with the wherewithal to produce pirates as good as this." He ran a hand over the cover. Looking at Kevin through the mirror, he grinned, and Kevin returned the gesture.

"Jimmy Tate."

Pete nodded. "Precisely."

Kevin was practically drooling. "If the recording is as good as the quality of the cover, it'll make for some good viewing."

Scepter felt like a child left out of a school prank. "Who's Jimmy Tate?"

Pete fired the engine, slotted the car into first and pulled away. "Remind me to tell you sometime."

⚜

Time and distance had little meaning on the astral plane. For Fishwick, locating the angry spirit was as simple as looking around for the outburst of emotion and then moving toward it. He could be 10 kilometers or 10,000 kilometers away, it made no difference to the old butler. He would be able to detect the spirit and be with him in an instant.

He found the spirit hovering above an old manor. "Now then, how are you doing, me old mucker?"

"Wigjam!" roared the spirit.

"What's tha doing here? Git outta my house."

The interjection came from another spirit, one that communicated with a broad Yorkshire accent. The newcomer had roughly the shape of a stocky, broad-shouldered man. There were no facial features to distinguish him from any other of the millions of spirits who never went through The Light, but Fishwick was able to identify them all individually. His mistress had asked how he was able to do so, and he did not know. There were no visual clues, such as facial features, on the spirit plane, but he just *knew*.

In contrast, the angry one was a ball of blazing energy, glowing red and orange, like the fires of the sun. He darted hither and thither, unable to make sense of this half-world, unable to make sense of himself.

"It's not your house anymore, is it, chum?" Fishwick argued with the new arrival. "Not been your house since you passed on."

The figure glowed purple with indignation. "It belongs ter me and my family, now git on with thee."

Fishwick ignored the order. "Who were you?"

"Sir Henry Melmerby." The announcement came with a degree of hubris. "In life, I was thy better, so think on and show some respect."

Fishwick's training as a manservant compelled him to take a deferential step back. "So what are you doing hanging round here, Sir Henry?"

"I told thee, it's my house. And *she* keeps me here." The putative head of the spirit form jerked in the direction of another spirit, a sadder one, hovering nearby, its attention rooted on the property below.

At Sir Henry's mention, the woman drifted to them. Her form, like that of all females on the spirit plane, had a gentler, curvier shape about it. She glowed a dull, mournful blue, but flashes of red appeared as she spoke to Sir Henry. "Tha done me, you old bugger," she complained. "Aye, and tha wouldn't own up to it, would tha? Tha'd rather see me swing."

"Aggie Devis," Sir Henry explained. "There were a bit of a misunderstanding between us."

"That were no misunderstanding what tha did to me. Tha knew what tha were doing." Aggie bristled vermilion with anger. "Aye, and not only ter me. There were all them others an' all."

Fishwick backed off and left them arguing. He turned to the angry spirit, its fiery energy blazing now to crimson. "And what's your story?"

"Wigjam!" roared the spirit.

"A disgruntled housemaid, a randy squire and an incomprehensible lunatic." Fishwick sighed to himself. "It's going to be a long night."

3

Originally built to accommodate lower income families, the Cranley Estate sat on the northeastern outskirts of Ashdale. A maze of narrow streets encircled by an access road, it was owned and managed by the local council, and like many such estates up and down the British Isles, it suffered from neglect born of under-funding, over-population and inappropriate letting. Anyone considered a "problem tenant" was housed on Cranley.

Many of the properties were boarded up, awaiting repair and renovation so they could be re-let, but council employees willing to work on the estate were thin on the ground, would only go out in teams of three or four, and then only in daylight.

Pete and Kevin had been joint tenants of 63 Nineveh Crescent for five years. The arrangement and area suited both. Cranley had a couple of good pubs and a small shopping area, which dealt with their day-to-day needs. In addition, Pete's fearsome reputation ensured that they were never hassled. Unruly teenagers, who often congregated in certain areas of the Estate, gave them a wide berth. Loan sharks and drug dealers, who flourished in the general lawlessness of Cranley, kept their distance. For Kevin, the unwillingness of the police to venture onto the Estate meant he could cook up his occasionally dodgy deals in comparative safety.

The day began just after noon when Pete finally crawled out of bed and met Scepter in the kitchen where she was preparing a cup of chamomile tea.

"I know where the spirit went after leaving the Bilks' place," she declared.

Pete, still tired from the night's exertions, merely grunted and made himself a mug of strong, sweet tea.

They made their way into the living room and sat at the table beneath the windows, where he scanned the sports pages of the previous day's *Ashdale Evening Chronicle* and Scepter sat, warming her clasped hands on her mug. "Fishwick came back to me just after four this morning and told me he'd tracked the spirit down to Melmerby Manor. It's not difficult for him, apparently. Better than that, he says there are other spirits there."

She narrowed her gazed at Pete, who continued to take in the news of alleged discontent in the ranks of Ashdale Athletic Football Club.

Scepter raised her voice. "Pete, I'm talking to you."

He put the newspaper down. "So what do you want me to say? Hurrah, old Fishy's found the poltergeist hassling Angie Bilks? For God's sake, Scepter, I don't even believe in Fishwick."

"Then how do you explain last night?" she challenged.

"I told you. I need to think about it. Whatever it was, I don't believe it was ghosts." He picked up his newspaper again.

Scepter pressed him. "All right then, how do you explain my knowledge of an emergency at 16 Rossington Terrace?"

With an angry sigh, Pete tossed the newspaper on the settee and scanned the room. His eyes fell on Kevin's computer workstation by the rear wall. Like everything else to do with Kevin, it was untidy, the work surfaces littered with books, bills, letters, overflowing ashtrays, empty cups and empty cigarette packs. To one side of the computer sat a portable radio. Getting to his feet, Pete crossed to it and switched it on. There was a hiss of static and for a moment, nothing else. Then came the voice.

"Control from delta-four-zero, we have an r-t-a on Shambles Island. A trucker's lost it on the approach, rammed up the back of a Jeep. Over."

"Delta-four-zero from Control, you need the paramedics? Over."

"Er, negative, Control. You could get it out to Radio Ashdale, avoid the area for the next hour or so. Over."

"Roger, wilco, delta-four-zero."

Pete switched the radio off again and rejoined Scepter at the table. "Kevin's always monitoring the emergency wavelengths. He could have left that on last night, you heard it while you were asleep, and it registered on your consciousness."

"Nonsense," Scepter declared. "There were two doors between that and me, both of them closed. There's no way it would have registered with me."

Pete forced patience on himself. "We know less about the abilities of the human brain than we do the surface of the Moon. When we sleep, we're theoretically aware of everything that goes on a round us, but we choose to disregard most of it. That's how new mothers always know when their babies need them. Now if you were halfway between waking and sleeping, a radio broadcast like that, which your mind would be tuned to, could become a dream. You would have dreamt that Fishwick told you when in fact it was the radio."

"Pete, I did not dream it."

"You say that," he placated her, "but your dreams can be remarkably real, you know."

Scepter raised her voice to a shout. "I didn't dream it."

"All right, all right." With a grin, Pete crossed his two index fingers and held them forward. "Pax, pax."

Scepter fumed for a moment. From the bedrooms came the sound of Kevin moving around. "Now look what you've done."

Pete checked the clock on the DVD recorder. "Turned noon, time he was up anyway." He rejoined Scepter at the table.

She took a sip of tea and, as he picked up his newspaper again, she asked, "You have heard of Melmerby Manor?"

Pete sighed and raised his eyebrows above the newspaper. "Come again?"

"It would help," Scepter complained, "if you put down the paper and listened to me. I asked have you ever actually heard of Melmerby Manor."

With a weary sigh, Pete dropped the paper again and leaned forward, resting his forearms on the table. "Yes, I have heard of Melmerby Manor. Ashdale's only genuine stately home, open to the public from April to October, owned by some bigwig in London who never shows up there except to collect the takings at the end of the season."

The hall door opened and Kevin wandered in wearing only a pair of baggy underpants. "Who turns up at the end of the season to collect the takings?"

Kevin's habit of turning out in his underwear had troubled Scepter when she first moved in, but time had acclimatized her to his less savory habits. But that did not mean it did not still unnerve her.

"I do wish you would dress before you come out of your room," she reminded him.

"I haven't got anything you haven't seen before," Kevin complained.

"You don't know whether I've seen it before or not," Scepter pointed out, "and even if I have, it's usually presented in a better format than you." She stared pointedly at his baggy undies. "You usually reserve floppy discs for your computer."

Kevin took instant offense. "I don't need snide remarks from you."

"No," grinned Pete. "He gets enough from everyone else."

Kevin scowled. "At least when they talk about me, they use my name."

Now Pete frowned in anger. "And what's that supposed to mean?"

Scepter could see an argument brewing. Determined to head it off, she asked, "Talking of names, I thought you were supposed to be thinking up a business name for us, Kevin."

With a glower at Pete, Kevin replied, "I've been working on it. How about Exorcists Unlimited?"

Scepter's face fell.

"What, you don't like it?" Kevin sounded offended.

"You make us sound like a bunch of rogue church officers," Scepter pointed out.

"So you want me to have a rethink?"

Scepter did not reply, but looked to Pete for support. He just shook his head.

"All right," said Kevin, huffily, "I'll go back to the drawing board. In the meantime, who turns up at the end of the season to collect what takings?"

Both Scepter and Pete looked puzzled. Kevin reminded them, "You were talking about someone collecting money at the end of some season."

"Oh, that." said Pete. "I was talking about the rich bitch that owns Melmerby Manor."

"Oh, him." Kevin's interest waned and disappeared. He wandered into the kitchen.

"Him? I thought Melmerby was a woman." Pete directed his question at Kevin's disappearing back, but it was Scepter who responded.

"Whatever gave you that idea?" she asked with a smirk.

Pete shrugged and finished his tea in anticipation of Kevin bringing a refresher. "When I was a cop, I was once sent out there to investigate a break-in at the back gate. They didn't have it properly secured. Anyway, I ended up talking to Lady Clarissa Melmerby. An old bat worth more money than the three of us will ever see in our combined lifetimes, and she was moaning about the time it had taken us to get out there."

"Lady Clarissa is Sir Jonathan Melmerby's wife. He happens to be a millionaire financier. Works in the City, and do you know something else?"

"What?"

"I know him."

Whatever grand effect Scepter hoped to produce with her announcement, it did not work. Pete merely gave a sigh and asked, "Why doesn't that surprise me? All you top nob families feed from the same trough, don't you? I supposed mummy had you earmarked as a bride for Melmerby's eldest son?"

Scepter ignored his cynicism. "No. As far as I'm aware, the Melmerbys are childless. Sir Jonathan was a great friend of my mother's, and that's proved very useful this morning."

"How so?" asked Pete.

Scepter could hardly contain her excitement. "I rang him, and he's given me permission to investigate Melmerby Manor and its hauntings."

Kevin returned with a single mug of tea and sat between them. "Who's given us what permission to investigate where?"

Pete rattled his mug on the table. "Where's my tea?"

Kevin scowled. "You know where the kettle is. After the way you called me, you can get your own. Now, since you woke me up, the least you can do is bring me up to speed."

Scepter looked at Kevin's computer set up. "You know your laptop? Can you rig it to drive EMF sensors, video cameras, microphones and whatnot, from a distance?"

Kevin gave a tubby shrug and a gaping yawn. "I'd need to get the gear and the software, but yeah, I have enough memory to work with. Why do you want it?"

"Melmerby Manor." For their benefit she reiterated her earlier conversation with Fishwick and then detailed her phone call to Sir Jonathan Melmerby.

When she had finished, Kevin stroked his chin thoughtfully. "So you wanna set up the cameras, audio feeds, magnetometers, infrared motion sensors, and maybe a few PIRs to eliminate mice and stuff, and drive it all from the computer."

"Seven out of ten for comprehension," said Pete giving him a mock round of applause.

Kevin ignored him and focused on Scepter, whose mouth was hanging open in an expression of horror and revulsion.

"Eliminate mice and stuff?" she gasped. "What are these PIR things? Laser beams? We're ghost hunters, Kevin, not exterminators."

"I didn't mean kill them," Kevin yelped in his own defense. "A PIR is a passive infrared sensor. It needs both heat and movement to trigger it." He could see she was no nearer understanding. "Look, your bog standard ghost is cold, isn't he? If he walked past, he'd trigger an infrared motion sensor, but he wouldn't trigger a PIR. So if you use a PIR and it triggers, you know you've got something alive, like a mouse, rather than something dead."

Scepter calmed down. "Oh. I see. And you can set all this up?"

Kevin nodded. "Yeah, it's no sweat. All we have to do is get all the gear and the cables to run it back to a modem." Kevin moved to his desk, picked up his cigarettes, lighter and a ballpoint pen. Returning to the table, he lit a cigarette and had his first coughing fit of the day, causing Pete to comment on his habit. Refusing to rise to the bait, Kevin tore the flip top from the pack and began to list the items he would need. "We'll want a couple of fifty-meter drums of mains cable, audio/video feeds and a distributor board."

"Kevin," said Scepter, interrupting his train of thought, "you know you said these PIRs only detect movement *and* heat?"

He stopped writing. "What about it?"

"We need to detect movement, so they'll be no good."

He sighed with enforced patience. "That's why I said we need both infrared motion sensors *and* PIRs. If the motion sensor triggers and the PIR don't, you know you're dealing with a spook. Geddit?"

"Oh. Right." Scepter watched a moment as he went back to his list.

"I'll need the motion sensors too, and magnetometers with auto triggers, couple of ion counters, one or two direct-reading thermometers, EMF meters. Hand-held are the best—"

"Kevin," Scepter interrupted again.

"What?" His irritation at the interruption was beginning to show.

"How do you know all this?" Scepter wanted to know. "Have you been on a ghost hunt before? Only you never mentioned it."

"I just know it, right?"

Pete laughed. "He's watched so many ghost hunters at work on the Sci-fi and Living channels, he knows exactly how they work."

"*You* watch them, too," Kevin pointed out. Addressing himself to Scepter, he went on, "I know about electronics. I know how the gear works, and it's all about using a bit of common sense, isn't it? Ghosts are some kind of energy form, so you need equipment that will register energy. If you can fit it with auto triggers, they'll kick the video and audio equipment in when they're triggered. But you have to make sure you're not triggering this stuff with mice, spiders and what-have-you. Hence, the PIRs."

Scepter nodded her understanding and chewed her lip. "Is it going to be expensive?"

Kevin gave an easy shrug. "You're looking at three or four grand, but I know a face who'll let me have it all on hire and I can screw the price down to the ground. We'll get away for under five ton."

Pete's features darkened. "Which face?"

"Benny Stringer."

Pete's face screwed into a mask of disdain. "Bent Benny? He's hookier than you."

Scepter's pretty face registered surprise. "What a curious nickname. Bent Benny. Who is he?"

"Runs a shop over on Chapel Road," Kevin explained, "and he sails a bit close to the wind now and then."

"Now and then?" Pete's voice dripped scorn. "Put it this way. If it's electrical and it's not nailed down or bolted to the wall, it'll be for sale in Bent Benny's shop the next day. He's one of the biggest crooks in Ashdale." He jerked a thumb at the DVD recorder. "He sold that to Kevin and swore blind it hadn't fallen off the back of a lorry."

"Well, it hadn't," Kevin defended his contact.

"No," said Pete. It never even *made* it to the lorry. He nicked it straight from the factory in Birkenhead."

"Look, Pete," Kevin urged, "beggars can't be choosers. Have you got three, four grand to spare? No. In that case we're down to hiring from Bent Benny, like it or don't. And trust me, I'll be able to make enough money to pay Benny for the hire." Kevin stubbed out his cigarette and lit another.

"How?" asked Pete.

Kevin glared. "I asked you to trust me." Turning to Scepter for support, he said, "Benny is an electronics genius. He'll have everything we need and I won't have to explain it in words of one syllable." Returning to his list, he ran through it with his pen. Looking to Scepter, he asked, "How many cameras? Three? Four?"

"As many as we can afford," said Scepter.

"Go for four and we can use mine too, which makes five. We'll need an 8MB modem at least or the stuff will take ages to download. Whose phone will we be using?"

Pete and Scepter exchanged a glance that was almost telepathic, each telling the other that Kevin had not understood their intentions and someone would have to break it to him gently.

"Phone?" asked Pete.

"Yeah. You know. It's that thing you make phone calls with." Taking in their puzzled stares, Kevin flicked the ash from his cigarette roughly in the direction of the fireplace and missed, spreading it across the threadbare carpet. "Look, if you wanna drive these things from the computer here, you need a fast Internet connection. Half a meg, even a full meg, is too slow considering the speed we may need to react. To run it, we have to hook up a phone connection and leave it open while the gear is running. Geddit? That lets the cell phone out. Lose the satellite and you break the connection, leaving you up the creek. For me it has to be the landline..."

His voluble flow dried up as he realized they had turned first puzzled and then sympathetic eyes on him. Nervously he flicked the ash from his cigarette again.

Scepter reached across and took his other hand, squeezing it gently, a gesture of support and encouragement. Her smile was the sort one usually reserves for someone lost in an alien environment, or someone in deep shock. Kevin's suddenly worried face said he was wondering which he would be when she made the announcement she was obviously going to make.

In a low, soft and infinitely compassionate voice, Scepter said, "Kevin, we can't do this from here. We'll be spending the night at Melmerby Manor."

Kevin withdrew his hand from hers, took a jumpy swallow of tea, crushed out his cigarette in his saucer and promptly lit another. "Spend the night at Melmerby Manor?" he squealed. His eyes were wide, his mouth half open as if he had just faced his worst nightmare.

"What did you think we'd do?" asked Pete. "Wait here for the spooks to e-mail us? Hope they'd text us to say they were up and about?"

Kevin's malleable features shifted rapidly. His chin jutting forward, eyes narrowing, he said, "I was just telling you what I thought we were going to do: run it all from here."

"We need to be there in case something goes wrong with the equipment," Scepter pointed out. "We need to be there when things happen so we can get to the actual location within the house."

"But the place is haunted." Kevin had shifted position again, almost pleading with her.

"If it were not," Scepter said, "we wouldn't be interested in it. I have to follow up on this poor soul from the house last night, and he has gone to Melmerby Manor, therefore I have to be there."

"Well, you'll be there on your own."

Scepter tried to encourage him. "You've seen how they do it on those ghost hunting programs; they don't work remote, do they?"

"That's TV," Kevin complained. "You're talking real life."

"Kevin, the spirits will not hurt you... well, most of them won't."

Scepter's admission did nothing to lift Kevin's flagging courage. "You mean there are those that will."

Scepter hedged. She needed to bolster Kevin's confidence, but she did not want to tell him outright lies. After thinking about it for a moment, she said, "There are those spirits who get angry when they realize their lives have been taken. Their anger can manifest itself in the physical movement of objects, but if they were to hurt you, it would probably be accidental."

"Well that's a comfort, I must say" Kevin snorted. "They kick me down the stairs, break my neck but it's no problem because they didn't mean to do it."

Across the table, Pete grinned. "Don't be such a soft tart, Kev. Look, I don't understand why we're going, either. Scepter says her spooky butler has told her to go there because the burglars who scared Angie Bilks last night are out there—"

"They were not burglars, they were disturbed spirits."

Pete pressed on, ignoring Scepter's interruption. "To me that's so much bull, but hey, it's a way of passing the time."

Kevin was not persuaded. He played with his cigarette and his eyes darted left and right, taking in his flat mates by turn. "And suppose there really are ghosts?"

"Oh, there are," Scepter assured him.

Pete scowled at her. "Kevin, there's no such things as ghosts."

Leaning on the table, Kevin took a deep drag on his cigarette and aimed his left index finger towards the computer station where the digital camcorder he had used during the night sat dormant, its battery on charge. "My footage last night says you're wrong. I filmed that message on the wall as it happened."

Pete dismissed the observation with an airy wave of the hand. "You mean you think you did."

Angrily, Kevin got to his feet, strode to the workstation and picked up the camcorder, unplugged it and returned to the table. He set it on "play" and rewound the footage, searching for the particular frames. As he did so, his brow furrowed.

"That's funny. It's not there."

Scepter looked sharply at him. "What's not there?"

Kevin passed over the camera and allowed her to run the frames. "The message on the wall, written across the Arsenal banner. It's not there now, yet I know I filmed it. I was running the camera when it appeared."

He passed the camera across and allowed Scepter to watch it. As she did, she, too, frowned. "That's impossible. We both saw it. You did too, Pete."

He shrugged. "I don't know what I saw. Besides, I was in the kitchen for a while. I have to go see Bilko this afternoon, so I'll check to see if it's still there."

While Scepter rewound the recording and watched it again and again, her puzzlement increasing with each viewing, Kevin raised an eyebrow at Pete. "You want to know about *Mind Games III*?"

Pete nodded. "I want to know where he got his hands on one of Jimmy Tate's jiffy DVDs."

Kevin checked the time. "I'll have to get a move on, too. I've a deal going down."

Pete shot him a glance. "Deal?"

Kevin rose to the challenge. "Yes, a deal. Where do you think we'll get the money for all this gear?" He took in Pete's determined and disapproving frown. "I said, didn't I? Trust me."

"The day I trust you, Keeley," said Pete, "is the day I start believing in fairies … or Fishwick."

Scepter passed the camera back to Kevin. "Don't be too long, either of you," she ordered, putting an end to their disagreement. "Sunset is just after four, it's properly dark by five. I'd like to be out at Melmerby Manor and set up before dark."

Kevin grumbled, "We're back to that, are we?"

"Oh shut up moaning," Pete chuckled. "I'll be back in plenty of time, Scepter, and if his deal is that simple, it won't take him long."

"If you're gonna make me spend the night at Melmerby Manor, my deal could take all night," he muttered.

Pete sighed. "Scepter, why don't you tell us about Melmerby Manor and calm Sir Coward de Custard's nerves?"

"No problem." Scepter gulped down her tea and stood up. "When I was at university, I did a piece on the Melmerbys, and since then, I've done considerable research on the hauntings. I'll just get my folder."

She scurried across to the bedrooms. Kevin watched her leave, then turned on Pete. "What are you playing at?"

"What do you mean?"

"You don't believe in ghosts," Kevin reminded him. "How come you're falling for this?"

Pete toyed with his empty cup and turned a benign smile on his oldest friend. "Correct me if I'm wrong, but when she first moved in and told you all this guff about her spooky butler and psychic powers, weren't you the one who said you might be able to sell the ghost hunting idea to a cable TV channel?"

"Well, yes, but—"

"How do you propose to sell it to the cable channels if you don't have any footage to show them?" Pete cut in.

"I know, but I thought—"

Pete cut in again. "And despite what you may think of them, the bods who work for cable TV are professionals. You fake it and they'll spot it in seconds. You need genuine footage, mate, and the only way you'll get it is to spend the night in a place like Melmerby Manor."

"I know all this," Kevin objected, relieved at last to get a full sentence out without being interrupted, "but I asked why *you* were going along, not me."

"Because I've nothing better to do" Pete confessed. "This time of year is quiet for private eyes. There won't be much bad debt work till after the New Year, and there won't be many divorces until February, after the party season is over. I don't fancy working security in the shopping mall, so I might as well tag along with you two."

Kevin drew deeply on his cigarette. "You mean you're trying to get into her pants."

Pete grinned. "Well, you never know your luck in a big city." He made an effort to encourage his best friend. "Come on, Kev, it'll be a lark. And no ghost worth its salt would hassle me or he'd get my boot in his proverbials. And you never know—get this right and the paranormal investigations could be a paying game, even if all you ever do is provide rational explanations for this stuff."

"On telly, you mean?" Kevin's eyes brightened in hope.

Pete dashed his wish. "TV isn't the only medium, you know. I was thinking more of explaining this stuff to those bods who claim they've got spooks in the cellar."

Kevin gave a non-committal grunt, crushed out his cigarette and got to his feet. Behind him, on a corner cabinet close to the settee arm, sat a CD player and a rack of discs. Kevin selected an Abba album, powered up the player and dropped the CD in.

Carrying a loose-leaf folder, Scepter returned from the bedrooms as "Dancing Queen" began to play softly. "Abba?" she asked. "Why is it always Abba?"

Pete smiled. "The 70s are back. Anyway, Kev has a thing about the blonde."

The remark put Kevin on the defensive again. "So do most blokes."

Pete snorted. "As if a tasty bit of totty like Agnetha would look twice at a fat, windy git like him."

"Pete, that's very insulting," Scepter scolded.

Kevin smiled gratefully. "Thank you, Scepter."

"Agnetha is not a tasty bit of totty."

Kevin pulled his tongue out at her.

Seating herself at the table, Scepter opened the folder and spent a few moments studying her neat handwriting before she spoke. "I want you to understand that this," she tapped her papers, "is not a definitive history. Even with my family contacts, I was not given access to many private papers which would have confirmed or denied a lot of what I'm going to tell you."

Pete looked down his nose. "You mean these snooty sods didn't want skeletons coming out of the closet."

Kevin looked alarmed. "Skeletons? Are there skeletons? Tell me there aren't any skeletons," he implored

"It's a metaphor, Kevin." She sighed. "Stop being such a dunderhead." She concentrated on Pete. "Old families like my own and the Melmerbys have much to answer for, Pete, but they are nevertheless very protective of their names." She gestured at Pete's newspaper, its headlines blazing with the latest scoop of a politician caught in a compromising position. "With today's media, you can hardly blame them."

Pete shrugged. "All right. Go on."

Scepter cleared her throat. "In 1612," she began, "Donald Devis arrived in Ashdale and was taken on as a shepherd by the Melmerbys. He was the son of a woman hanged as one of the Lancashire Witches in 1609. Donald had a daughter, Aggie, and in 1648 she, too, was accused of witchcraft and hanged from an ash tree within the grounds of Melmerby Manor."

"And what kind of evidence did they bring against her?" asked Pete.

Kevin tutted. "Typical copper. Always looking for incidentals like evidence. Can't you take anything on trust, Pete?"

Scepter ignored him and answered Pete with a casual air. "The usual kind; a ewe she was tending gave birth to a deformed lamb; the local farmhands were all bewitched by her beauty. At her trial, they confessed to having been forced into having sex with her, which meant they, too, were guilty, and as a result, they had their souls cleansed. It was the custom."

"Had their souls cleansed. How was that done?" Pete wanted to know. "Flogging? The stocks? Drowning them in a pool of holy water?"

"They were hanged."

Pete was appalled at the matter-of-fact simplicity with which Scepter delivered the announcement. "They were executed after she dropped her drawers and said, 'come and get it'?"

"It was the way they dealt with bewitched men," Scepter explained.

Kevin chuckled. "So, go on, Scepter. You've strung up Aunt Aggie and Desperate Donald's shepherds, what happened then?"

"Shortly after her execution, it was said that the area was being haunted by her ghost. Sir Henry Melmerby, the man who had her hanged, was killed four years later when his horse reared on the moors and threw him into a peat bog. He hit his head on something, blacked out and drowned, and when they dug him out, they found that his head had struck Aggie's skull. Having been condemned as a witch, she had been buried in non-consecrated ground on the moors."

Kevin lit another cigarette. His hands had begun to tremble at the preceding account. "And his horse chucked him at exactly that spot."

Scepter lowered her voice to a hushed whisper. "It was said that the horse was spooked by the ghost of Aggie Devis."

"I'll bet they hanged the horse," complained Pete.

Scepter stared icily at him. "No, they did not hang the horse."

"Thank God for that."

"They shot it." Scepter took in their gaping faces but pushed on in defense of the 17th century way of life. "Those were tough times, you know. Life was hard and cruel and there were hundreds of crimes for which a man could be hanged."

"Or a horse could be shot," snorted Pete. "They were barbarians."

"They were simple and superstitious people, Pete," said Scepter. "We live in a more enlightened age."

"Oh, of course." Pete's voice oozed sarcasm. "I mean if you think about it, we pick on people for much more important reasons, don't we? Skin color, religion, even the football team they support."

"Yes," agreed his chubby chum, "and I'll bet those Arsenal supporters will never forget the day you picked on them." He smiled at Scepter. "Four of them spotted his Manchester United shirt and started giving him verbal."

Scepter almost dare not ask. "Pete beat them up?"

"Put it this way, by the time Pete had done with them, two of them were auditioning for soprano choirs and the other two had decided that watching snooker was safer than watching football." Kevin laughed at the memory.

She frowned her disapproval. "Violence is the last resort of the feeble-minded."

"No," Pete disagreed. "Violence is the last resort of the Man U supporter faced with four Arsenal supporters looking for aggro."

"Can we just stick to Melmerby Manor?" She shook here head. "Get you two on about Arsenal, Chelsea and Manchester United and we'll never get anything done." She paused a moment to gather her thoughts, while across the table, her two partners looked suitably contrite. "Over the years, Melmerby Manor has been rebuilt and had bits added onto it, and there have been numerous sightings of several ghosts, but two of them appear more often than the others. One is the apparition of a woman drifting along the upper landings as if she's seeking something. The sound of a woman crying has also been heard on that landing. Most commentators believe it to be the ghost of Aggie Devis."

"Do we know what she's looking for?" asked Kevin.

"A short, fat, windy-arsed git from Ashdale," grinned Pete.

Kevin rounded on him. "Shut it, you." To Scepter, he invited, "Go on."

"No one knows," she said, "but there is a theory. Aggie was born at Melmerby Manor in 1624, and had lived a happy life there. No one knows for sure, but it's believed that she was—er—intact." Scepter blushed and Kevin screwed up his face in puzzlement.

"What, you mean she had all her arms and legs and stuff?" he asked.

"She was a virgin, you idiot," said Pete.

Scepter blushed again. "Thank you, Pete. I was trying to avoid using that word. Anyway, Aggie was a vi–what she was, and the story goes that Sir Henry raped her. If you think about that situation, the house where she had been so happy for her whole life would become like a prison: a place of great torment. It could be, then, that Aggie's spirit is seeking a way out of the house, a way out of the area. You see?"

Kevin nodded. "Makes sense to me."

"Sounds like so much drivel to me," said Pete.

Kevin waved a dismissive hand at him. "Scepter, you said there were *two* spooks at the manor."

She nodded. "The other is supposed to be the apparition of Squire Henry Melmerby, the man who hanged her. He has a habit of throwing things at people in the house. Cups, plates, knives, forks—that kind of thing."

"Knives and forks?" Kevin's terror showed through again. "And has anyone been hurt by them?"

"Not seriously, but one man was knocked off his chair by a bottle of vintage port flying through the air. Mind you, that was in 1922, and there was some debate as to who actually threw the bottle: Sir Henry or one of the guests. They were all a bit tipsy and Sir Henry had a fondness for vintage port, so even as a ghost he wouldn't have thrown a bottle owing to the danger that it might break."

Pete and Kevin smiled, certain that she was joking, but there was nothing about her deadpan expression to suggest humor.

Pete summarized the information. "So what have we got? Some Moaning Myrtle who walks about the place whining because she was topped three hundred-odd years ago, and a horny, gout-suffering wine connoisseur, who chucks the best dinner set about because he's pigged off with being dead?"

Scepter made an effort to excuse the spirits. "Some believe that Sir Henry really did rape her and that young Aggie was pregnant by him when she was hanged. Aggie's alleged rape was not the first such incident. There were others before her.

"You have to consider Sir Henry's position. Not only was he the local landowner, but a magistrate, too. He could not afford to have his reputation compromised by a young girl making accusations of rape, and you can imagine the fuss there would have been if she really was pregnant and she claimed him to be the father, so when the ewe conveniently gave birth to a deformed lamb, he took the opportunity to accuse her of witchcraft. Even in those days, every Englishman— or woman—was entitled to a trial by jury, but in the case of a rural community like Ashdale, Sir Henry may have picked the jury. They found her guilty of witchcraft, and passed sentence: death by hanging. The local community would have approved, but the actual evidence is wafer-thin. As the magistrate, he was pretty quick to get the farmhands on the end of the rope, too. The tale could be no more than scuttlebutt, but it's not beyond the bounds of possibility."

"In that case," Pete demanded, "how come the farmhands don't haunt the place?"

"But they do," Scepter assured him. "Melmerby Woods, adjacent to the manor, has many ghosts, and so do the surrounding moors."

Pete considered her response for a moment, then asked, "If this place has such a long and violent history, how come there have been no other investigations into the hauntings?"

'Firstly," said Scepter, "its history is no more violent than any other medieval manor, which is why so many of them are haunted, and secondly, other than Sir Henry's reputation for throwing things at people, which is largely anecdotal, there is nothing to suggest that the spirits at Melmerby Manor are violent. They may have lived in violent times, but spirits spending many hundreds of years on the astral plane have the capability to learn, to advance as we have advanced from those awful times."

Pete smiled. "You're rationalizing to account for the unaccountable. Anyway, I asked why there have been no other investigations."

"There were," Scepter declared, "but they were all pre-war. When the house was opened to the public in the late fifties, Sir Jonathan banned all such investigations. He was happy for the house to enjoy a reputation for being haunted, but he refused to have visitors disturbed by paranormal investigations." She beamed a smile of pure joy on Pete. "Until now. Pete, we are honored. We are the first investigators to be allowed in the house since the 30s."

He grinned. "I must make sure the glory doesn't go to my head."

Kevin had been thinking about the tale while Scepter and Pete exchanged arguments. Now he spoke up. "Surely, if Aggie was up the spout, it would have shown up at autopsy?"

Peter and Scepter exchanged a glance.

"In 1648?" asked Scepter.

"Besides which," Pete pointed out quite logically, "even if she told them at the trial, they'd have assumed that the bun in her oven was the spawn of Satan and that once the farmhands had rogered her, they were infected with the same evil."

Kevin turned his back to them as the CD player began to act up. He pressed the "eject" button, and the disc flew out. Kevin snatched it out of thin air, catching it as expertly as a desperate bridesmaid leaping for the bride's bouquet, he growled, "Temperamental sod," slotted the disc back into its case and faced his colleagues again. "I don't know if I'm happy about all this. I mean, it's one thing to set up cameras and stuff, but to go to a haunted house and spend the night there? I'm not sure about it all, but I will tell you this: the first sign of any knives coming at me, and I'll vanish, like Mister Spook going back to the Starship Booby Prize."

"You mean Mister *Spock*," Pete corrected him.

"As long as he vanishes."

4

From the inside of his limousine, Jimmy Tate watched the rain sweep down the windscreen. It seemed to him that it was coming down faster now.

The day had dawned leaden and overcast, the rain of the last three days persistently refusing to move on. With the clock reading 11:00, the temperature had dropped a degree or two, and now there were flecks of white in the downpour. It would snow before the day was out.

His brother Johnny guided the Rolls Royce Corniche up Rossington Terrace and pulled up outside the Bilks' house.

There were times when Jimmy did not know what he would do without his younger brother. Johnny was a butler, valet, confidante, protector and junior business partner. His lean and wiry six-foot frame performed all those tasks Jimmy could not. Things like shifting the gear from the house to the van, the van to the lockup, dealing with the weekly shopping... helping him put on his socks and tying his shoelaces. The simple things Jimmy could not handle because of his *disability*.

Life could be very unkind. When it came to business, legitimate or otherwise, Jimmy was a wizard. His brain moved like lightning to spot the potential in almost anything. As a result, when the world of home entertainment latched onto the DVD, Jimmy Tate latched onto the concept of pirate DVDs as quickly as he had rumbled pirate videos and computer games years earlier. His skills at breaking down security encryption to produce the pirates were what had made him a millionaire while he was still in his thirties.

And yet, if nature had been good enough to grant him a fast, technologically agile mind, it had given him a grotesquely overweight body. Other than in surprise or disgust, few women looked twice at his grotesque, 350 pound frame, and if Nicky, his second wife, had sworn her undying love for him, he knew it had more to do with his bank balance than his looks. Jimmy Tate was a man who had learned the hard way the truth behind the maxim "money can't buy happiness." It could only make you more comfortable in your misery.

Johnny killed the engine. "Jimmy, I know it's not my place to say so, but don't you think you should cut your losses on this one?"

Jimmy tutted again, this time expressing his impatience at the naiveté of younger brothers. "If I don't deliver, I drop 50 thou, not to mention the ten grand it cost me to set up. No way am I forgetting it." He stared moodily out at the Bilks' terraced home.

Someone had ripped him off. 25,000 copies of *Mind Games III* stored in his lockup in 50 cartons—on five pallets, 10 to a pallet—had disappeared, and the only lead was a call from Bilko the previous evening. Now it was time to make Bilko talk. Johnny would make Bilko talk.

But when they finally settled into the rear kitchen, it was only to speak to a tired and drawn Angie. Bilko's wife knew who he was, she knew who Johnny was—not surprising since a part of the pirate producer's living was to maintain contacts with thieves and informers like Bilko—but, despite the ominous threat of Johnny cracking his knuckles, insisted she knew nothing.

"I don't know where he is," she said wearily, her brow knitted into a frown of concern. "Something happened here last night, I don't know what, and I needed him home, but as usual he wasn't here. He rang me from Flutter-Bys, but that's the last I heard." She twisted and knotted a handkerchief around her shaking fingers. Her eyes were streaked and bloodshot from crying; to Jimmy, she looked like a woman on the edge.

Jimmy came in softer in an effort to counter the towering threat of his younger brother. "Angie, he belled me early last night, telling me he had news about a DVD. Did he say anything to you?"

She shook her head, and tears formed at the corner of her eyes. "He did have a DVD with him when he got in yesterday morning. It was in the cupboard there." She nodded at the drop down cabinet and got up to cross to it. She moved like an automaton, eyes unfocussed, steps even but automatic. She dragged down the door and looked in. "Oh. It's gone. He must have it with him." She suddenly looked genuinely scared. "Either that or Brennan took it last night."

The name rang instant alarm bells with both Tates. They exchanged worried glances.

"Brennan?" asked Jimmy.

"Yeah, you know him. Pete Brennan. Used to be filth." She sighed as she returned to her chair by the fire. "We had some sort of a disturbance here last night. Plod couldn't handle it. Then Brennan turns up with that mate of his, Kev Keeley, and this tart; Simply Randy or someone. She reckoned it were a ghost causing the ruckus, but Brennan figured it was burglars. Anyway, he went through the house and told me it was clean. He musta looked in here, and, if he found that DVD, he coulda taken it. He was iffy when he was a cop, wasn't he?"

Jimmy drank his tea, then struggled to bring his great frame to a standing position. "All right, Angie, we'll split. When you see Bilko, tell him to get in touch. There's two grand in it for him. He knows the score."

The Tate brothers came out of the house and climbed into the Rolls.

"What now?" asked Johnny.

Jimmy stared at the rain. "I don't like the smell of this. Not where Brennan is concerned." He remained silent for a few more moments, his brain ticking over, eyes following the track of the wipers across the screen. At length, he came to a decision. "Put the word out on the street. The reward is now five grand."

⁂

It was 1:00 when Pete arrived and persuaded Angie to let him in.

"Like I keep telling people, Pete, I don't know where he is," she cried. "He never came home last night. Five'll get you ten he was smashed out of his brains and is sleeping it off in some gutter."

"People?" Pete asked. "What people?"

Angie shrugged. "Just people." She avoided his eyes as she replied.

Pete considered pushing her, but she already appeared on the edge of a breakdown, so he changed tack and held up the DVD. "I found this in your kitchen last night."

Angie's eyes lit. She made a grab for it.

Pete held it out of her reach. "Naughty," he rebuked her with a grin. "If Dave Robb had found this, you'd have been in trouble. That's why I took it, and for now I'm hanging onto it. Tell me what you know."

"I don't know nothing. Honest. You know Bilko, he never told me anything. That way, if I got pulled, I couldn't tell, could I?"

Pete held the DVD between his thumb and forefinger as if he were weighing it. "This is one of Jimmy Tate's pirates. If Bilko has crossed Tate, he could be at the bottom of the river by now. If he gets in touch, Angie, tell him to bell me. I'm the only thing that stands between him and street justice."

⁂

In the cellar of Flutter-Bys, Kevin heaved the last of the cartons into place and stood back, counting them. "There you go, Ronnie, 40 cases of *Old Sporran* whiskey. 25 nicker a case, that'll be two grand." He held out his hand for the money.

"Not so fast, Keeley." Ronnie Wilcox, the proprietor of Flutter-Bys, the sleaziest club in town, took a drink from the sample bottle Kevin had given him, then split open the top of the nearest case and withdrew a bottle. He checked the label against the sample. It matched. Putting the bottle back, he repeated the process four times, selecting cases at random from the stacks, ensuring they contained bottles of whiskey, not soft drinks.

While he carried out the spot check, Kevin took in the cellar, with its stacks of crates, galvanized metal beer barrels, and the great tuns of lager and ale. He would give his right arm to be let loose in a place like this for the night.

Eventually, satisfied that he was not being conned, Wilcox counted out the money and handed it over.

"Good on you, Ronnie," said Kevin, folding the stash of tens and twenties and cramming it into his pocket. "I've gotta shoot off now. Bitta business with Bent Benny."

Wilcox grinned, and cracked the cap on the sample bottle again. Taking a swallow from the neck, he asked, "What are you up to with that old scroat?"

"I told you. Business." Kevin lowered his voice even though there was no one in the cellar to overhear. "Between me, you and the gatepost, I might be going into telly. See, me and Pete—you know him, Pete Brennan, used to be a cop—anyway, me and him have this new flatmate, Scepter Rand, and she's a psychic. She's got permission for us to go out on a ghost hunt at Melmerby Manor. Bent Benny's gonna supply the gear, and when we're done, I'll sell it to the cable channels."

"And you've struck a deal with Benny?" Wilcox sounded doubtful.

"Course I have," Kevin breezed. "He just doesn't know about it yet. Anyway, keep an eye out for us on the Sci-Fi channel. Catch you later, Ronnie."

❧

Leaving the Bilks' home, Pete drove down into the town center and Bride Street, a narrow passage just off the High Street, around the side of Flutter-Bys. He parked behind a brewery lorry delivering beer to the club, climbed out of his car and rapped on the side door.

A hatch slid open and the ugly, unshaven features of Lemmy Groom, one of Wilcox's minders, appeared. He took one look at Pete, scowled, and announced, "We're shut."

Pete grabbed his hair and yanked his head through the hatch. "Well, open up before I drag the rest of you out through this hole."

Pete pushed the door partway open and released Groom. Stepping inside, he took full advantage of his greater height to intimidate the smaller man. He loomed. He scowled. Groom cowered. "Tell your boss I want a word with him. Now."

Groom skulked off along the narrow, dimly lit corridor with Pete behind him and into the main clubroom, where the chairs were still stacked on the tables, the stage was unlit, and the place sat quiet and dormant. The only activity Pete could see was behind the bar, where Tommy Lawson, Wilcox's other lieutenant, was stacking bottles on the shelves, while Wilcox himself stood reading the racing pages. Pete had been here many times in the past, usually to help quell fights, and he knew that Groom was particularly skilled at feigning acquiescence and then coming up from behind. As he ambled to the bar, his eyes moved constantly watching for the sudden attack from the unexpected angle.

Wilcox looked up from his reading. His face split into a broad grin. "Get out, Brennan. We get enough scum in here when the place is open."

Pete ignored the bravado. He laid the DVD on the bar. Suddenly, Wilcox was no longer amused, but neither was he impressed by the gesture. "I found that last night at Bilko's drum," said Pete. "Word is he rang Angie from here earlier in the evening. That right?"

Wilcox shrugged. "How should I know? Busy in here last night. You see him, Lem? Tommy?"

Groom and Lawson shook their heads.

"See?" said Wilcox. "Now do like I say and get out. Before I have my boys show you the door."

Pete laughed. "These two? Show me the door? It took Groom all of three seconds to let me in, and he couldn't show me the way out with a dog leash." He stopped smiling. "You heard from Jimmy Tate?"

"Didn't I just tell you, Brennan … YEEEEOW!"

The final exclamation was dragged from Wilcox's mouth as Pete grabbed his ear and practically dragged him over the bar.

"I don't seem to be making myself clear, Ronnie. I'm not with the filth anymore, so I don't have to play by the rules. When I ask, you answer. It's that simple. If you don't, I'll pull your ears off."

Through gritted teeth, Wilcox ordered his men. "Tommy, Lem, see to him."

Groom and Lawson came. Pete released Wilcox, blocked an incoming fist from Groom and head-butted him. As Groom reeled, Lawson launched himself over the bar. Pete sidestepped and watched with interest as the flying thug shot past and landed on a nearby table, scattering chairs across the floor.

With a grin, Pete turned back to Wilcox. "You need to hire some professional muscle, Ronnie. These two idiots couldn't take my sister's kid, and he's only ten. Now, once more from the top. Bilko rang Angie from here last night, and that DVD belongs to Jimmy Tate. So I'm putting two and two together, and I get two. Two scroats—you and Tate—rapping over the phone about this DVD. Now tell me what you've heard from Tate."

"I ain't heard nuthin' from that fat ass. And I don't see any reason why I should." He gestured at the DVD. "If that's one of his, it's nothing to do with me. And I haven't seen Bilko, either. Now get out, Brennan, before I bell your old boss and have you arrested."

Tucking the pirate DVD in his pocket, Pete pointed a warning finger. "If I find out you're lying, I'll be back, and next time, I won't be so pleasant."

5

The moors around Ashdale could be daunting even at the height of summer when tourists flocked to the area, but only the most experienced local driver would venture onto them under a turbulent and rainy November sky when the fog threatened to close in and cut them off totally from the world.

"It takes a brave man or an idiot to come this way at this time of year," Kevin commented as Pete's estate car crested Melmerby Hill and leveled off 500 meters above sea level.

Pete grunted. "In that case, why are we coming this way? You're not brave and I'm not an idiot."

In the rear seat, almost buried under a mound of cartons containing electronic equipment begged and borrowed from Kevin's contact, Scepter watched the desolate moors flying past, a serene, contemplative look on her face.

She knew, if Pete and Kevin did not, that the coming night would bring its share of nervy moments. But she had Fishwick for support, and Pete's skeptical presence would bring a sense of reassurance to Kevin. Moreover, if their investigation were really productive, if it succeeded in persuading a hard-nosed skeptic like Pete, then the possibility of Kevin's TV series might yet materialize.

Fishwick had done his share of the research from the Other Side. He maintained that there were several disturbed spirits haunting the house, but his report back to her was filled with concern. "Sir Henry, Aggie and the other spirits in the house and surrounding area are troubled souls, Modom," he had told her. "There are other members of the Melmerby family, one of them a child, still tied to the house for various reasons, and the farmhands who were hanged with Aggie are there. They want their remains moved to hallowed ground. But the biggest problem is that the spirit from last night is there. He may make your stay dangerous."

Albert Fishwick had been killed along with her great grandfather, Lord Aigburth Rand-Epping, on the first day of the Somme in July 1916, and it was not until Scepter was born that he had found a medium through whom he could communicate with the living. Communication with her ethereal butler was a strange affair. If he was about other business in the spirit domain when she called, all she could do was wait for him to return.

Scepter had been eight years old when he had first spoken to her. Not old enough to understand the implications of his contact, still young enough to be frightened, she became more and more relaxed, more and more blasé about his presence and his assistance as time progressed and she learned of him, of his history, of his absolute devotion to the Rand-Epping family.

Worse still, when talking to him she had to speak out loud.

"I could not read minds when I was alive, Modom," he would frequently remind her, "and I cannot read them now."

It often led to embarrassment, especially when she was in a restaurant or bar and forgot herself. Many times Fishwick had called her and she had responded aloud, only to receive curious stares from those around her.

But for all the problems talking to her butler brought, Scepter had never found anyone in the real world to be as utterly loyal and reliable. As long as Fishwick remained close by, the coming night held no terrors for her.

❧

Negotiating the narrow and winding Melmerby Lane, Pete glanced across at Kevin, who sat in the passenger seat fiddling nervously with a cigarette. In stark contrast to Scepter, Kevin was neither calm nor content. He was seriously scared, as the occasional whiff of methane testified. Twelve stone, barely five and a half feet tall, not exactly obese, but showing signs of a spreading tummy, Kevin was not the world's bravest man. His natural pusillanimity, coupled to a penchant for getting into trouble, were allied to a taste for curries, lager and chocolate, giving him a gastric system capable of producing the most appalling odors. Pete had often remarked that since Scepter had come into their lives with her more delicate sensibilities, Kevin should be learning the lessons of food combining.

Heavy clouds hung over the moors; the Pennine fog closed in rapidly. By nightfall, less than two hours away, the visibility would be less than a hundred meters. Already the rain had turned the windscreen into a sheet of water, and the temperature was dropping.

The entrance to Melmerby Manor lumbered up on the right; beyond the high retaining wall, the house itself could be seen in the distance, brooding and melancholy in the fading afternoon light.

Pete stopped at the gates, climbed out of the car briefly to open them, and hurried back in, shaking the drops of rain from his Manchester United baseball cap, grimacing at the turbulent skies before continuing up the gravel drive, past lawns still wearing their faded green of autumn scrub. In the center of the lawns, an ornamental fountain lay dormant, as if awaiting awakening for the far-off summer when the tourists would flock in by the thousand to this stately home.

On the far right was the tubby, round tower of the mausoleum. Scepter pointed it out as they drove past. "Most of the Melmerbys are buried there."

Kevin trembled. "Dead?"

"It's to be hoped so," said Pete as he shifted up a gear and his tires kicked gravel. "Burying people alive is against the law." He transferred his gaze to the approaching house. "This place doesn't look Tudor."

"The original Tudor house," Scepter launched into a run-down on the place, "was razed to the ground in the Great Fire of 1789, which coincidentally took the life of Arthur Melmerby. He was a sort of hick scientist and inventor, and at the time he was experimenting with a chemical match. A thin strip of wood, coated with sulfur and tipped with a mixture of potassium chlorate and sugar, which would ignite when touched to sulfuric acid."

"Worked, did it?"

"Of course it did, Pete. Unfortunately, it worked next to several jars of potassium nitrate, charcoal and sulfur, which, as any chemistry student knows, are the basic ingredients of gunpowder. Apparently, Arthur's experiment resulted in the loudest explosion ever heard before the First World War, and it actually caused the Great Fire."

Pete cruised round towards the front of the house.

Even in the afternoon gloom, the manor was a magnificent edifice, dominating the forlorn landscape. Three stories high, with subterranean cellars, it was constructed of local sandstone, blackened with age and the consistently inclement weather. The fine line of mortar between the large blocks gave the walls the appearance of a friendly, inviting checkerboard, but the rest of the front dispelled any such warmth. Mullioned windows gave it eyes to watch over its domain, and the giant, double doors of black oak resembled the maw of a leviathan waiting to devour its prey.

The car crunched to a halt on the gravel by the steps, where rampant lions carved from Welsh stone guarded the entrance. Pete looked up at the grand house and grimaced. "This place was built at the time of the Napoleonic wars. Half the country was dying for Wellington, yet toffs like this could still spend a fortune on houses."

Ignoring the reference to "toffs," Scepter said, "The wars actually started ten years after this house was built, Pete. Although," she went on as she dug out the keys from her bag, "the French Revolutionary Army did declare war on England in 1793."

"Pitt the Younger," muttered Pete as if to prove that somewhere behind his lager-fogged nihilism lurked intelligence.

Kevin looked more nervous as they got out of the car. "I didn't know he had any kids."

"Who?"

"Gene Pitney. And what a name to call a brat. Pitney Younger. I mean—"

"Kevin?"

"Yes, Pete?"

"Shut up."

Following the other two to the doors, Kevin was having third thoughts. He'd had second thoughts when Scepter told them about Melmerby Manor, and he now wished he had heeded them!

"We could be doing something a lot safer, you know," he mused.

"Like what?" asked Pete as he and Scepter got to the doors.

Kevin caught up with them. "I don't know. Tap dancing through a minefield?"

His partners ignored his riposte. Scepter came up with the keys; there was a momentary delay while she found the right one, unlocked the door, and pushed it open. It opened with a long, nerve-wracking creak, starting somewhere around a low groan and rising up the scale to an "eeeeeek" that was positively spine-chilling.

Checking the solicitor's notes, Scepter punched in the four-digit code to silence the intruder alarm, then she and Pete strode boldly into the building. Kevin followed much more apprehensively, coming to stand at Pete's shoulder in the cavernous entrance hall.

To the right lay the family's private apartments, roped off to keep out the summer visitors; to the left stood the cafeteria and kitchens. Straight ahead was the entrance to the Long Gallery, its walls dominated by paintings dating from the Renaissance, some of them originals from the likes of Turner, Stubbs and Constable. Just left of the Long Gallery's entrance sat a broad, curved stairway leading to the upper floors, its walls bedecked with portraits of Melmerby family members. The older ones at the bottom had a severe appearance about them, their eyes narrowed, features pinched, even their puritanical clothing suggesting a disdain for anyone who would dare to raise his eyes and look upon them. Later paintings from the Victorian era and early twentieth century, situated higher up the staircase, appeared slightly more welcoming. At least the subjects wore smiles.

"A set of evil looking gits, aren't they?" said Kevin, indicating the earlier pictures with a nod.

"They were squires and magistrates," Scepter reminded him, "and they had to be seen to be guardians of the law, which meant threatening punishment by their very appearance." She felt around for a light switch and flicked it. Nothing happened. "Electricity's off."

Kevin chuckled. "Me and Pete worked that out when the lights didn't come on."

"Pete and I," she corrected his English.

"No. Me and Pete. See, you said the electricity was off, so you can't have—"

"Kevin?"

"Yes?"

"Shut up."

He did not quite shut up. "Maybe it's a fuse," he suggested as Scepter flicked the switches again. There was more than a tremor about his voice.

Scepter doubted it. "They probably turn it off at the mains when the place shuts for the winter. Kevin, do you want to go down to the cellar and switch it on?"

"Me?" Kevin's tone suggested he was both amazed and appalled at the suggestion.

"Well, you know about electrics," Pete reminded him. "All that wiring that you plug into your computers."

"You don't need an expert! You've only gotta pull a bloody lever." Kevin shouted his complaint, and the word "lever" bounced off the interior walls of the grand house. "*You* go down in the cellars."

"Stop being a tart, Kev, and go turn the power on."

"Pete, you're the ex-cop, not me. You're the big hero type."

Pete finally agreed with a shrug. "All right. I'll turn the power on, and you can unload all the gear from the car."

Kevin's dread of manual labor overcame his fear of dark basements in haunted houses. "Which way's the cellar?" he squeaked.

Scepter rooted in her bag once more and came up with a flashlight. Passing it to Kevin, she consulted the plan the Melmerbys' solicitor had given her when they collected the keys. She pointed left to the cafeteria and kitchens, telling Kevin there was a door behind the service counter.

⸎

Kevin glanced around at the laminate tables and plastic chairs all bolted to the floor as if the Melmerby family were worried that someone might steal them. From somewhere behind came the sound of Pete and Scepter carrying boxes into the house from the car.

He switched his attention to the serving area. Behind the actual counter was the kitchen where hot meals and snacks were prepared. Even though it was very dark in there, he could still hear his two friends pottering in the entrance hall. The sounds emboldened him. He noticed tall refrigerators, and pangs of hunger automatically assailed him. Pangs of hunger always attacked him when he was in a dicey situation, or when he felt sorry for himself, or when he passed a cake shop, saw a refrigerator, an oven, a plate... in fact, pangs of hunger attacked him most of the time.

"When did the season end?" he asked himself. "October," he answered himself, recalling press adverts from the Ashdale tourism office. If the staff had left any food behind, would it still be edible? If it was in the freezers, it might be. He opened the cabinet doors one after the other and learned, to his disappointment, that they were empty. He closed them again and moved quickly out of the kitchen back into the better-lit, but still gloomy, cafeteria.

The cellar door was located in the narrow alley between the service counter and the kitchen. Kevin opened it and peered down into inky blackness. As he aimed his flashlight down the stairs, his courage waned.

"Hello." His voice, not much above a whisper, quavered.

There was no reply.

He looked back at the cafeteria with its modern, pristine, spotless appearance and its panoramic windows looking out onto the Melmerby lands and misty moors beyond. He twisted his head further round and took in the stainless steel tops of the servery, with its racks of clean cups, saucers, cutlery, and glass cases—cases that were empty now but were usually filled with foodstuffs for the ever-hungry visitors.

My kind of area, he thought. *Food, drink, and I can watch life go by.*

After leaving school, he had signed on as a civilian administrator with the police. It was a safe job, one where he could watch the criminals go by without actually having to deal with them. His propensity for getting into trouble, usually a function of his desire for money and his lack of scruples over the means of getting his hands on it, soon landed him in hot water, and by his 25th birthday, the police had elected to do without him. He had not been unduly worried. By then, he had secured enough contacts to make a living wheeling and dealing, buying and selling, and if he did sail close to the wind now and then, his best friend Pete made certain that he did not become an out-and-out criminal. Like today, for example. After delivering that load of whiskey to Flutter-Bys, he had spent much of the early afternoon negotiating with Bent Benny for the hire of the equipment. That was his forte: negotiation, persuasion, cutting the deal. Not nicking the stuff, not breaking and entering, just trading.

A life on the edge, however, had not changed his basic desire to sit on the sidelines watching life go by, and that was the trouble with cellars. You couldn't watch life pass by in a cellar because there was no life there, and no windows onto life outside. Cellars were where you stored defunct matter: old mangles, washing machines, rustic workbenches and rusty tools. Cellars were the graveyard of those things you no longer needed in life. Cellars were graveyards, full stop.

Summoning his courage, he began the descent. To his relief, the steps were made of stone, so at least they wouldn't creak like the front door had done. Creaking gave him the creeps. Tramping hard on each step, deliberately clomping his weight down and making a lot of noise, as if he hoped to scare off any potential ghosts, goblins, vampires or tramps who might have wandered in for shelter from the inclement weather, he made his slow way down to the cellar. As he reached each step, he paused, listening to the darkness ahead. His courage evaporating faster than a pan of water boiling away, he began to whistle tunelessly, his quaking muscles producing a staccato trill that many trumpeters spent years of triple-tonguing practice to achieve.

Outside, the light had been fading quickly into dusk; a deep, late afternoon gloom had settled over the cafeteria and kitchen. In the cellars, that gloom became the total blackness of a night so dark that it was the heart of a black hole, sucking in everything and everyone in its vicinity, including Kevin Keeley.

His torch beam cut through the impenetrable darkness like an angry Pete Brennan cutting through a gang of football hooligans, picking out strange, angular and elongated shadows on stark, whitewashed brick walls. He reached the bottom of the steps and the cold, stone, cellar floor. A low, arched ceiling hung above his head, and tall wine racks created a labyrinth of narrow aisles ahead of him. His hand shook; the torchlight wavered and the shadows quivered in time to the trembling. He flicked the light here and there, seeking anything that looked like a mains fuse box or electrical isolator switch, but all he could see were bottles of wine in tall, wooden racks, and dark, narrow alleyways between them.

There was no sound save for the click of his heels as he eased his way along the constricted lines of floor-to-ceiling racks. At the end of one aisle, he came to another at right angles and worked his way along. The comforting noise of Scepter and Pete unloading the car, chattering softly to each other, was gone, lost somewhere behind and up above him.

He moved further along, found a gap in the rack, made his way through it and found more racks. The silence began to prey on his nerves.

"Can't even hear the wind and rain anymore," he said to the wine racks.

But then, as he reminded himself, he wouldn't, would he?

"I'm two to three meters below ground level, the same depth as they bury coffins in a ceme—"

Kevin cut off the thought before it could properly mature and flashed his torch back the way he had come, seeking the bottom of the steps, only to learn that he could not see them anymore, only racks and racks of wine.

"Now, did I turn left and right or right and left? Or was it left-left-right, left-right-left, right-left-right, right-right-left, right-right-right-right, or left-left-left-left?"

He cursed softly.

"In the place less than ten minutes and I'm lost already." He paused, deliberately trying to calm his mind. "Take it easy Kev. There's no need to panic."

The moment he uttered the words into the void, his mind rebelled.

"No need to panic? There's *every* need to panic!" His words sliced into the darkness. "I'm on my Jack Jones in a pitch-dark cellar with nothing for company but an unpublicized liquor store and a couple of ghosts. And one of them likes chucking knives and bottles of plonk at visitors."

Silence engulfed him; the complete silence of a funeral director's chapel of rest, broken only by his short, sharp breathing and the thrumming of his pounding heart. Upstairs, outside—in the sane world of drug dealing, murder, famine, the ever-present threat of annihilation by nuclear weapons or rogue comets, and race, religious and economic wars—there were three CB handsets nestling comfortably in a box in Pete's car, quite content not to go anywhere. If he had used his head and brought one with him, at least he could have called for help. Now, he dared not even shout out. There was no guarantee that Pete and Scepter would hear, and any shouting might disturb the ghost of Henry Melmerby.

He pressed on. He was sure that at some stage, he would encounter a wall, and when he found it, he would stick to it, follow it until it brought him back to the steps, the electricity switch or both.

Disturbed thoughts jumped into his mind. Didn't Anthony Perkins keep his mother in the cellar in *Psycho*? He recalled watching it on late-night TV one night when his parents were out, and how scared he was when Vera Miles turned the decaying old woman round and the cameras gazed into the hollow eyes, fastened on the festering, unrecognizable skin and...

Once more he closed his mind to the images. That was fiction. People didn't do things like that in real life... did they?

Frantically, he searched his anxious mind for the good things that happened in cellars. To his terrified dismay, he could not think of any. Everything that happened in cellars was bad, dark or dirty, including the delivery of coal in the dim and distant past. When Buffy got into a fight, it was always in some subterranean crypt or vault, and Christopher Lee had spent half his working life in these places before he moved on to cutting people's arms off with his light saber and sending Orcs to waylay them.

Kevin pressed on, almost tiptoeing so his footfalls would not disturb the phantoms in that black hole.

From somewhere in the distance came a scrabbling. Convinced that it was a figment of his imagination, Kevin stopped and held his breath, ears pricked, listening. There it was again. That was no auditory hallucination; he knew enough about the strange sounds that sometimes emanated from headphones and microphones to know the difference, and this was for real. A scratching, scraping sound, and it was not far away. His aural sense of direction was poor, thanks, he maintained, to all those times when the school had compelled him to sit by the speakers during morning assembly. He couldn't locate the direction from which the sound came, but there was no mistaking it. A scratch-scratch, scrabble-scrabble, as if something was trying to get in—or out—out of its coffin.

Then came the tiniest of squeaks, leaping into the darkness, and that was enough for Kevin. He ran. Heart thumping painfully, he ran blindly along the narrow aisles between racks, flashlight waving erratically in front of him. He tripped, rattled heavily into a rack, heard a crash, wondered vaguely if the wine bottles were coming to life to pursue him, accelerated his pace just in case.

He turned right, ran some more, turned right, ran some more, turned right, ran some more and finally had to stop to catch his breath, the years of smoking and crummy diet catching up to him, denying him the strength to get out of that dark, forbidding vault. He gained some control over his heaving chest and listened. There it was again. *Squeak, squeak, scratch, scratch.* Something clawing its way towards him. He looked at the torch.

"Maybe the light's attracting it," he whispered to himself.

He flicked off the lamp... and promptly flicked it back on again. Less than a second of utter darkness produced terrifying visions far worse than anything he had ever seen in the movies, much more terrifying than the notion of a vampire trying to give him a love bite.

He ran again. Where were those rotten steps? Sod the electricity. Pete could come down and switch it on. He was bigger than Dracula anyway. Bigger and stronger. And so thick-skinned, the vampires would need a hammer drill to get through his neck, never mind fangs.

Ahead, he made out the whitewashed walls, that he knew lay near the steps where he had first come down. He was moving so fast he almost crashed into the wall. He flashed the torch right and left, and still couldn't see the steps. All he could see was more whitewashed wall, running off in both directions. The scrabbling was coming closer. Consumed by panic, he tried to decide which way. *Eeny, meeny, miny, moe.* He turned left and hurried along. Ten meters away, another wall sat at right angles to the one along which he was tearing. He reached it, turned left again and—

Suddenly the entire cellar was flooded with light and there, straight ahead of him, was the tall, gaunt figure of a man.

He let out a terrified scream.

༺❦༻

Up above, Pete had found the mains switch in a cupboard, just inside the double doors at the entrance, and flipped it on. Seconds later, he heard Kevin's shout.

Pete looked urgently at Scepter. "What the hell...?"

Scepter ran for the cafeteria. Hurrying after her, Pete called out, "Scepter! Wait!"

"Kevin's in trouble," she called over her shoulder.

Pete caught up, grabbed her arm and stopped her. "Leave this to me."

Scepter shrugged her arm free. "He may need help."

She turned away, determined to go on, but he caught her arm once more. "You don't know who or what is down there."

Scepter scowled defiantly. "I'm not afraid. Fishwick is with me."

"I never suggested you were," Pete told her, "but even if I believed in Fishwick, I wouldn't trust him further than I could throw Kev." Scepter struggled to free herself of his grip. "Scepter, this is my thing. The car's unloaded. You only have to unpack the gear. I'll get Kev."

Scepter nodded reluctantly and Pete hurried off, running through the cafeteria, to the cellar and down the steps. Looking into the maze of wine racks, he could see nothing of his chum, but from the far side of the catacombs came the sound of running feet.

"Kev? Can you hear me, Kev?"

From a location to his left came Kevin's weak and frightened whine. "Pete, there's someone down here."

"Yes. Me and you."

"No, you dork. Someone else. He was coming for me. A vampire."

Pete's noticed that Kevin's voice was steadier on that last. "Your terror's evaporated faster than a car thief hearing a police siren. Now, keep talking so I can work out where you are."

"He's round here somewhere, Pete. Big evil git, wearing an overcoat and hat. Watch he don't sneak up on... aargh!" Kevin cried out a second time as he ran into Pete around the end of one of the wine racks.

"Kev, what's going on?"

Kevin shook with terror as he replied. "I heard him getting out of his coffin, so I ran for it, and then I saw him. Standing by the wall somewhere back there." He waved a frantic hand toward the depths of the cellar. "He's a vampire."

"There's no such thing, you soft tart."

"Yes, there is," Kevin insisted. "I mean, who else scratches his way out of a coffin?"

Pete snorted. "You've been watching too much Sci-Fi Channel."

"Pete, I—"

"Shh." Pete cut him off and they both fell silent, listening intently to the scratching and scrabbling, louder now than when Kevin had first heard it.

Kevin's voice was a frightened whisper. "See. Now his mates are getting up."

"Those are mice and rats looking for food, you idiot." He made to head butt Kevin, but stopped centimeters short of his forehead. "Now where's this bloody burglar?"

"He's not a burglar, Pete. I'm... aargh!"

"This way," said Pete, grabbing Kevin by the ear and dragging him deeper into the cellars.

As they made their way through the maze, they came upon the red pool spread across the flagged floor. Kevin shrank nervously back from it. "Blood."

Pete crouched down, dabbed his finger it and sniffed. "It's wine, you dipstick." He looked to the right and located the shattered bottle beneath the rack. Pulling the fragments forward, he examined the label. "Marvelous. Just marvelous. Chateau Mouton Rothschild '82."

"Supermarket plonk, huh?" Kevin was more hopeful than confident.

"Only about fifteen hundred bills a bottle," said Pete with a sad shake of the head. "I hope our insurance will cover it."

"What's it got to do with us?" Kevin wanted to know.

"You must have broken it." Pete stood up. "It's freshly broken and since we're the only ones in the house and you're the only one down here, it has to be you."

"I don't remember," Kevin declared, adopting his usual position when caught out doing something he should not have been doing. More honestly, he murmured, "Mind you, I was pretty scared. I wouldn't have noticed if I'd knocked over a pallet of champagne." He gave a nervous titter. "Could we not blame it on Sir Henry? Tell everyone he was chucking the bottles about again, like he did at that party Scepter told us about?"

Pete glared. "Come on. We'd better find this guy. I left Scepter alone near the doors, and I don't want him hassling her on his way out."

It took almost five minutes for them to find the stranger, in the far corner of the cellars from the steps, and when they did, all Kevin could do was stare sheepishly at the stone floor.

Hanging on a hook on the wall were a dark overcoat and hat.

⁂

While Pete and Kevin were busy in the cellar, Scepter moved the cartons into the cafeteria and began to unpack their equipment. Having Pete along was a godsend. Kevin was a computer wizard; a talker, a persuader, but Pete was a doer—a man of action who would not hesitate to walk into Hell if he had to. Despite her half-lies to Kevin, she knew there were those spirits who sought to vent their evil on the living, and Pete would be better able to deal with such occurrences. The speed with which he had gone to Kevin's assistance, the determination that it was his place to do so, spoke of a man who cherished old-fashioned values, and those values said walking into danger was no job for a woman. Scepter was certain that his courage would be tested tonight. He did not believe in the supernatural, so whatever happened, he would seek the rational explanation, such as intruders, and he would probably wander the house alone in search of them.

Kevin's cry from the cellar confirmed for her the reality of entities within the house. Pete had gone to help a friend, but she was sure they would find no earthly presence down there. As Pete disappeared down the cellar steps, she called for Fishwick, only to receive silence in response.

She knew her butler would return when it was convenient, and while she waited, she busied herself unpacking the EMF sensors and bundles of cables, carefully laying them out on the laminated cafeteria tables. Kevin had pulled off a real coup with his contact, and secured no fewer than eight video cameras. Those, too, needed to be placed. Scepter passed the time consulting a mental plan of the house, deciding where and how they would be deployed.

"You called for me, Modom?" Fishwick's voice came into her head.

"Ah. Fishwick. Pete and Kevin are down in the cellar. Kevin has apparently been frightened by something. Is there anything down there they need to worry about?"

"No, Modom. As I said before, there are a number of spirits attached to this house and the grounds, but none haunts the cellars."

"Thank you, Fishwick."

Left alone again, her confidence took a dip. If there were not spirits in the cellar, what had Kevin encountered? Tramps or teenagers hanging out in the hall who had perhaps rushed for the cellar when they heard her and her friends enter?

"Impossible," she said to herself. "The doors were locked and the alarms had not been disturbed."

She cocked an ear, listening to the hall. She could hear the wind and rain, but she could hear nothing of Kevin or Pete. They must be in trouble!

She was about to ask Fishwick to check it out when she heard the sound of their footsteps on the cellar stairs, and of Kevin's voice. True to form, he was arguing with Pete.

❦

Emerging from the cellars ahead of Pete, Kevin was considerably calmer now that he was out of the frightening darkness. "But who switched the lights on?" he wanted to know.

Pete grinned. "I did. We found the main switch in a cupboard inside the main entrance."

Kevin's features assumed a look of indignant thunder. "So you sent me down there for nothing?"

Scepter shook her head in amusement as she attached a heavy-duty battery to a CB radio. "Well, at least it's exposed you to the vagaries of your imagination."

Pete sniffed the air. "Judging by the smell, it's exposed his underpants to the vagaries of his gastric system, too. Kev, have you ever thought of bottling all that gas and selling it? I'm sure you'd make a fortune."

Kevin stuck out his tongue. "If I did, I wouldn't give you a cut of the profits."

"Right," said Scepter, cutting off their banter and becoming more business-like. "The rules of the night. First off, mobile phones. Switch them off. We can't afford to have any distractions here tonight."

Kevin was aghast. "Switch off my moby? It would be simpler to cut off my right arm."

"Kevin, I do not want the night ruined by your cell phone receiving a text message during a manifestation. Switch it off." She held up one of the handsets. "CB radios. When we split up, make sure you take one with you. We're on channel one, so don't change the channel, and make sure that it's switched on at all times when we're apart."

Pete was clearly amused. "You think these ghosts may be mob-handed?"

"Peter, we've just had Kevin scared out of his wits in the cellar—"

"By nothing more than a few rodents, and a hat and coat hung on a hook. Get real, Scepter. There are about as many ghosts in this place as there are foot-ball supporters at a cricket match. In other words, none."

"Fishwick informs me that there are several unhappy spirits here, and some of them are rather displeased, if not actually malevolent. We can't afford to take chances, and besides," she pressed on as Pete opened his mouth to interrupt again, "it doesn't matter whether what scares us is real or imaginary, it still has the potential to give us a heart attack. If we have the CB radios, we can call to each other, can't we?" She smiled sweetly, challenging him to overturn her logic. "So when we split up, we carry a radio. Okay?"

Both men murmured muted agreement, and that satisfied Scepter. "Right. Shall we take a walk around the house before it gets properly dark?"

Kevin groaned. "Must we?"

"Scepter's right, Kev," Pete confirmed. "We need to suss out the place before dark in case we have to move quickly later in the night."

"Listen," said Kevin, following them out of the cafeteria, "the only quick direction for me will be back to your car for the drive home."

"Trust me," Pete insisted, "I've been on this kind of stakeout before, and when you're fumbling in the dark, it's easy to trip over coffee tables."

"It depends who you're fumbling," Kevin muttered.

They ambled out of the cafeteria, into the main entrance hall, now lit by one bulb in three, which gave sufficient illumination to pick out the somber reds and grays in portraits and furnishings; when they entered the Long Gallery, they could study the exhibits in display cases and the light was still sufficient to let them read small, printed signs explaining the contents.

While they wandered around the vast room, Scepter cast an approving gaze over the paintings decorating the walls. "A lot of money in those," she remarked, then indicated another set of double doors at the far end of the gallery. "That exit will lead us to the rear courtyard and the stables. It's the only part of the original Tudor building that survived the Great Fire."

She passed a digital thermometer from side to side ahead of her as they walked the long gallery; it read a constant 7° C.

Following her, Pete, too, studied the paintings on the walls: horses, people, a watercolor of the house and surrounding lands rich in purple and ochre, a lavish Stubbs original of a magnificent stallion, several watercolors in the style of Turner and one by the painter himself.

Kevin chuckled. "This reminds me of when we were kids at Durban Street School. Remember? We used to do finger painting and the best ones were pinned up on the walls in the corridor."

Pete waved a protesting hand at a watercolor of the Thames at low tide. "Kev, that's a Turner original."

"Is it?" Kevin sounded impressed. "I didn't know she could paint."

Pete cocked his eyebrows. "She? Turner was a man."

It was Kevin's turn to be surprised. "Well, you could have fooled me. She's not the best-looking chick in the world, but she's all woman."

"Are we talking about the same Turner?" Pete asked.

"Aren't we?" Kevin echoed. "I was on about Tina."

"Look at this." Scepter's excited voice drew their attention. She stood close to the rear doors, through which they could see a cobbled courtyard hemmed by low outbuildings. Scepter passed her thermometer from side to side. As it passed the double doors, the temperature dropped quickly from 7° C to 5° C. "I think we're onto something here."

Pete checked the doors. They were composed of large panes of glass set into wooden frames, and when he bent to examine them more closely, he found sufficient space between the frames to flash his light through. "Yes. I think we're onto needing a carpenter."

A glint of mild annoyance came to Scepter's eyes. "Pete, a drop in temperature may mean we've located a paranormal entity."

He smiled, her irritation heightened and he laughed. "You may be right," he agreed. "And it may also mean we've located a door that's so warped it doesn't meet the other one properly and lets in a blast of wind that could freeze Hell." Once more, he shone his light at the five-millimeter gap and illuminated the worn inner frames of the two doors. "Give me the keys."

Sheepishly, Scepter handed them over, and he spent some moments finding the right one before opening the door and leading the way out into the courtyard.

The cobbles were uneven and treacherous, partly overgrown with grass and moss. Ten meters away were the outbuildings, and at the far end were large, wooden, double gates, open so the moors were visible beyond and leading out onto a dirt path surrounding the house.

At a nod from Pete, Kevin walked to them, and peered out onto the wild moors, across a patch of mossy grass to Melmerby Woods fifty meters away, a copse of tall trees and ground-level thickets. For a brief moment, he thought he saw a shadowy figure disappear into the woods. His heart leapt. Hadn't Scepter warned them that the farmhands haunted the woods? He opened his mouth to call out, but then he remembered the embarrassing incident in the cellar and thought better of it. Scepter already had him earmarked as a coward, and Pete's patience would not last forever.

He closed the gates, pushing home a large, metal bolt. Alongside it was a small, sliding hatch. Slightly larger than a man's hand, it was not large enough to stick his head through, and Kevin wondered briefly about its purpose. He slid it back and peered through to a view of Melmerby Woods again. Again, he thought he saw movement in them but dismissed the idea as another figment of his anxious imagination. Still, he had solved the mystery of the sliding hatch. It was there so those on the inside could look through and see who was on the outside.

He turned to rejoin his colleagues.

Scepter and Pete had gone into the ramshackle stables. With thoughts of the cellar and shadows lurking in the woods beyond the grounds dancing through his mind, Kevin hurried to catch up to them.

Scepter was just explaining the stables' current use to Pete. "They keep one stable going in the summer and have the staff dressed in period costume running it, but the rest, like this one, are warehouses for catering supplies."

To Kevin's relief, Pete pressed the switch by the entrance and flooded the place with strong, fluorescent light.

They could see instantly what Scepter meant. There were huge freezers—empty when Kevin checked them—a large racking system containing half-pallets of toilet paper as well as odd, catering-sized cans of fruit, vegetables, tea and coffee. There were stocks of cleaning materials, and in the center of the floor, five pallets of new, unmarked cartons, with a forklift standing by.

While Scepter moved to different corners of the room, checking with her thermometer, Kevin studied the cartons. "Wonder what's in these?"

Pete gauged the size of the boxes. "Paper towels, I'll bet."

Kevin tested the weight of one box. "Too heavy for paper towels."

"They pack a lot in them... Kev, leave 'em alone." Pete's protests fell on deaf ears.

Kevin dragged one of the cartons from the pallet and slit it open with a pocketknife.

"You are a rotten tea leaf, Keeley."

Kevin waved away Pete's protest. "Ex-coppers. Who'd have 'em... Hey! Look at this. They're DVDs." He grinned broadly. "*Pirate* DVDs. More copies of *Mind Games III.*"

His interest aroused, Pete joined his pal and opened another case to find that it, too, contained the same title. "What price Bilko got his copy here?" He made a quick count of the cartons and pallets. After some mental arithmetic, he murmured, "What's 50,000 quids worth of pirate movies doing here?"

Slipping a copy into the inner pocket of his fleece, Kevin made ready to leave. "Maybe the stately home business doesn't do so well and the Melmerbys top up their income with a bit of warehousing work."

Scepter snorted derision. "Rubbish. Jonathan Melmerby, the present earl, is a millionaire financier. He wouldn't get mixed up in criminal activity."

"Interesting that I should find one of these last night, and now a load more turn up here," said Pete. "Still, it's nothing to do with tonight's efforts, so hadn't we better get the gear set up?"

Kevin was ahead of him, almost out of the door already.

"Hey." Pete had a gimlet eye on the square bulge of the DVD in his pal's pocket, "Put that back."

Kevin grinned. "I will. Just as soon as I've watched it."

6

For the next hour or so, they were far too busy to watch DVDs. Under Scepter's direction, they began to set out their equipment at key locations, concentrating particularly on the upper landing and master bedroom.

"This is where Sir Henry Melmerby was laid out after his death on the moors," said Scepter, "and it's reputed to be one of the most haunted rooms in the house. That bed," she gestured at the giant four-poster, "has not been used since Sir Henry was laid out there."

After setting up a digital video camera and EMF sensor, she led them back out onto the dark, oak-paneled landing, through a side door up to the top floor, and the cold attic rooms where servants had slept during their years of service at the house. On entering each room, Scepter checked the area with her thermometer, magnetometers and EMF sensors before backing out.

In one room they found a cache of toys.

Using her flashlight to study the plan more closely, she announced, "This, apparently, used to be a servants room, and Aggie Devis slept here. Later, it was divided in two and this half became a nursery."

At the far end of the room, Pete tapped on the walls; instead of the usual, solid thud associated with bricks, the sound was hollow and resonant. "Wall boards," he said, "used to create a partition."

Scepter pushed a rocking horse so that it swayed gently. "The spirits of children often come back to haunt their old rooms, and Fishwick told me there is the ghost of a child here, so we'll set up some equipment in this room, and because Aggie used to sleep here, we'd better set up next door, too."

While Kevin set up another EMF sensor and an infrared motion sensor, Pete asked, "How do you know all this stuff, Scepter? I got the impression you've never been here before."

"I haven't. I told you, I did a piece on the family when I was in university, and I've done considerable research since, albeit from third party sources. Books on notable ghosts, and so on. Sir Henry and Aggie may be the best known ghosts in this mansion, but there are many others here and in the immediate area."

"Like the woods," Kevin commented as he set up a video camera.

"Correct," said Scepter. "At least you were listening earlier. Well done."

Kevin blushed and returned to setting up the camera.

"What's wrong with you?" Pete asked. "Why so shy? Was there any other reason you remembered the ghosts in the woods? Have you seen one?"

Kevin blushed again. "No. I—er—I've been to Melmerby Woods before. When I was a teenager. With a girlfriend."

Scepter pursed her lips in disapproval. "I'll bet she wasn't frightened by a ghost." She focused on Pete again. "I learned the history of the house at university, I followed up with various books that included tales of Melmerby Manor, and naturally, Fishwick has confirmed many of them."

"Oh. Right. I forgot Fishy." Pete shook his head in mild amusement. "All I can say, Scepter, is make sure you're living in the real world if anyone hassles us tonight."

She smiled back. "You'll see, Pete. Mark my words, that rocking horse will move tonight."

Night had come down over the moors as they moved back through the attics, down the stairs to the first floor landing, trailing cables behind them. Near the top of the staircase, Kevin busied himself, hooking the cables into a complex switchboard, while Pete worked back along the landing, tucking the cables close to the wall.

Scepter watched them. Kevin, working without a diagram, connected a complex series of color-coded wiring with the practiced ease of a computer engineer. His intense concentration and the swift, accurate movements of his hands reminded her of nerdy college kids she had seen solving Rubik's Cube. Further along was Pete, the professional policeman, the safety expert, almost hiding the cables in the tight joint of floor and wall, running them behind items of furniture or, ensuring that they were kept out of harms way so that they would not trip over them, his skilled eye tracking back and forth along the narrow bundle to make sure the cable did not move out of place as he worked along its length.

The landing was a jumble of dark shadows interspersed with pools of light from the wall-mounted lamps. Scepter's eyes strayed frequently from her colleagues to the darker recesses, seeking signs of activity. Was that the hulk of a man standing at the far end, or just a trick of the poor light? A blink, and the looming shadow had become the body of a bear; another blink, and it was no more than a shadow.

Focus, Scepter, focus. Tonight was too important to let her senses start deceiving her.

Once Kevin was happy with the landing, they worked their way down the staircase, under the mean eye of the Melmerby family lineage, Kevin playing out cable from a 50-meter drum, Pete carefully taping it to the walls at stair level.

When they reached the cafeteria, Kevin set a large control board on a table and hooked his various video and audio feeds into it. Finally, he linked the panel to his laptop computer, booted the machine up and ran the specialist software. The computer's main screen was divided into ninths: one small view from each piece of equipment and a centrally located control menu giving access to data coming from any of the motion, temperature and magnetic sensors. In addition, he could drive and monitor the performance of any piece of their equipment anywhere in the house.

"Where did you learn all this stuff, Kevin? Really?" Scepter wanted to know.

"I'm self-taught, mostly," he replied, running the mouse across the screen and testing the various pieces of hardware, "but I took a college course a few years back to fill in the gaps." He smiled cheekily. "I'm the best there is. Trust me."

"If you're trusting him," Pete observed, "keep a careful eye on your purse."

Satisfied that everything was fine, Kevin sat back. "There you go. Everything's tickety-boo. I can do whatever you want now: focus a camera, start and stop it recording, start up an audio recorder. We're just waiting for something to happen." He left the computer and crossed to another table, where he plugged in his CD player and inserted an Abba disc. "Nothing wrong with a bit of music, is there?" he asked when the other two frowned at him.

"Something a bit less noisy, Kevin," Scepter suggested.

"They don't come much quieter than Abba."

Scepter reached into her own bag and withdrew a whale song CD. "Put that on. It's more soothing."

Kevin took the disc. Huffily, he crossed to his CD machine and pressed the eject button. There was a momentary delay, after which the drawer snapped open and flipped the Abba CD into the air, where he caught it. "Bad-tempered piece of junk. One of these days, I'll dump it in the canal."

He inserted Scepter's CD, and presently the room was filled with the soothing sound of whale song augmented by the gentle rush of the ocean.

The evening dragged on. Kevin dozed, Pete dozed, Scepter read, then Scepter dozed while Pete read and Kevin dozed, then Scepter read, drinking occasionally from a bottle of apple-flavored water, while across from her, Pete and Kevin dozed. The CD player continued to pour its mournful cries into every corner of the cafeteria: a simple song that surrounded and immersed them in a sea of ambient sound, inducing Kevin and Pete to doze some more, and making Scepter's eyelids heavier and heavier until she too began to drift...

⚬❧⚬

"Modom?"

Scepter woke and became instantly alert. She checked on her colleagues, both still sound asleep, and in deference to them, kept her voice down.

"What is it, Fishwick?"

"Modom, the presence is here," her butler said.

Scepter's heartbeat increased. "The one from last night?"

"Yes, Modom. He has only been on this side a short time, but his fury is giving him the strength to manipulate matter. He may very well vent his anger on you."

"Thank you, Fishwick." She checked her watch and read 10:00 p.m. "Time for work, boys," she announced.

Across from her, Pete and Kevin stirred.

"We should take another tour of the house." She chuckled at Kevin's obvious display of fear and held up a battery-operated lantern. "We'll carry lights for all those dark corners."

Kevin's face grew paler. "Can't we just let Pete do it?"

"While you sit here snoring your head off?" Pete demanded with a yawn. "I was never too keen on this gig in the first place, but if you're gonna make me do all the work, I'll go home now."

"And if you remember, I didn't want to come here, either. I could have driven it all by remote from home."

Scepter made an effort to calm the argument down before it could gather steam. "It's all right, Kevin, we'll stick together this time."

Kevin did not think it was all right. "This place gives me the willies. I didn't imagine all that in the cellar, you know. Even if they were rats, they were still scratching to get in." He continued to mutter as they left the cafeteria for the entrance hall. "And rats are just as bad as ghosts. Go for your throat, they do. Don't..."

"Shut up Kev," snapped Pete, "I..."

"Quiet," Scepter interrupted urgently. "I thought I heard something."

With the total blackness of a foggy night on the outside and the meager lighting on the inside, the hall had taken on a new, more sinister aura. Faces on portraits lining the grand staircase had developed a Baskervillian air, as if they were ready to leap from their frames and tear out the living hearts of anyone foolhardy enough to pass. At the top of the curving staircase, distant lamps cast elongated shadows of banister rails, like the grotesque bars of a supernatural prison that held unspeakable horrors for the unwary inmate. Silence hung in the tense air: a spine-chilling stillness, broken only by the cry of the moorland wind and the sound of whale song from Kevin's CD player.

Then, into the night came a distant bump that might have been a rumble of thunder, or the movement of furniture closer to home.

Pete strained his ears. "Will you shut that row up?"

"I haven't said anything," Kevin protested.

"Not you; that crap on your CD player."

The immensity of the entrance hall, its age, grandeur and dark corners—particularly its dark corners—gave Kevin the jitters. Glad to be out of it, he hurried back into the cafeteria and made for the CD player. He was halfway there when the machine ejected the CD and threw it across the room at him like a razor-edged discus, its polished surface glittering in the half-light of the room.

"Aargh!"

"Now what?" asked Pete as he and Scepter hurried back in.

They found Kevin cowering near the cash register at the end of the service counter.

"What's up?" asked Scepter.

"Th-the C-C-CD. It came out of the machine and nearly cut my head off."

Pete picked up the disc. "Well you always said that machine was a bit iffy."

"I was nowhere near it," Kevin cried. "It was as if someone picked it up and threw it at me like a Frisbee."

Scepter was delighted. "Sir Henry! The poltergeist!"

"What?" Kevin demanded, taking instant umbrage. "He doesn't like whales? Maybe I should have left Abba on. Maybe *he's* got a thing for blondes with big boobs, too. Or maybe he just didn't like my face, and decided to cut my head off!" As he spoke, his voice became wilder, closer to the edge of hysteria.

In an effort to calm him down, Pete pointed out, "It's a CD, not an axe."

Kevin scowled and held up his hand. "I've cut my finger on them before today."

His best friend began to lose his cool. "Well, if he did cut your head off, at least you'd lose twenty pounds of unsightly fat."

"Will you two shut up?" snapped Scepter. "You're like children fighting over an ice cream." She concentrated on Kevin. "Tell me exactly what happened."

"I just told you," Kevin insisted. "I came through the door. The music stopped, the CD ejected and flew at me. What more can I tell you? It only just missed me."

Scepter raised her eyebrows at the doubting Pete, who shrugged his broad shoulders and said, "I think he's talking out of his backside, as usual. It makes no sense. I think that business in the cellar and things going bump in the night are getting to him. He was never the bravest man in the world, and this place is giving him the heebie-jeebies."

Scepter mulled Pete's words for a moment. "You think Kevin ejected the CD himself?"

"Yes."

"Pete," Kevin pleaded, "I tell you, I was nowhere near it."

"You think you weren't," said Pete, "but I think your imagination's playing you up."

"Quiet, the both of you." Scepter's authoritarian tones cut them off. "I shall consult Fishwick." She paused a moment and then called into thin air, amusing both men. "Fishwick, are you there?"

"Here, Modom."

"Fishwick, there has just been an incident here in the cafeteria, with a compact disc. Was it anything to do with any of the entities here?"

"I don't know Modom, but it's possible. There are several spirits abroad right now. I was at the other end of the house when I heard you call."

"Thank you, Fishwick. I may need you, so I'd be grateful if you could stay close by." Scepter brought herself back to the real world and confronted her partners' stupid grins. "Fishwick doesn't know what happened here. He was at the other end of the house."

"Well, that's it, then," chuckled Pete. "If old Fish Slice doesn't know, who does?"

"Pete, your skepticism is becoming tedious."

"Scepter, your games are becoming dafter."

"You could try to be more constructive," she suggested.

Pete remained obdurate. "I'm trying to be realistic."

The computer emitted a loud beep and ended the argument. They rushed to it and studied the display, where a red warning was flashing *ACTIVE, ACTIVE*. Kevin clicked on it, and the main menu came up, highlighting zone four.

"Sensor triggered," he said, studying the other menu items, all of which remained passive. "It's in the master bedroom."

"Check the video image," said Scepter.

Kevin shifted the mouse to zone four and a view of the old bedroom. When he clicked on that quadrant, it shifted to the center of the nine images, replacing the menu, and expanded to fill two-thirds of the screen.

"Pan the camera around the room," she ordered.

Kevin moved it left, then right, and found nothing. "Something must have triggered it."

Pete pointed to leaves on a tree branch beyond the windows. "What about them?"

"This is an EMF sensor, Pete, not a motion sensor. It needs a change in the electrical field to trigger it. The windows are shut. You wouldn't get any electricity registering from those plants, so it wouldn't trigger."

Pete sucked in his breath. "Well, there's one way to find out. Come on."

Kevin's mouth fell open. "You're going up there?"

To Pete there was no debate. "Of course I am."

Kevin waved back towards the CD player. "And suppose he's there? Henry the whale worrier?"

Pete snorted. "Stop talking crap."

"Wait, Pete," urged Scepter. "Let me contact Fishwick again, and see if he can tell us anything."

"Scepter, you can contact directory assistance for all I care, but I'm going upstairs. If you're too scared, stay here."

"I am not scared. I just prefer to rely upon Fishwick."

Pete ignored her and marched irritably out of the cafeteria.

Scepter tutted impatiently. "Fishwick? Are you there, Fishwick?" Her question was greeted with total silence. "Oh dear, he's gone AWOL too. And I specifically asked him to stay close by." Kevin trembled and Scepter tried to reassure him. "Pete's big enough to look after himself, and so is Fishwick."

"It's not Pete I'm worried about, nor your butler: it's us. With them two gone, any spook that comes in here has us by the short and curlies."

"Oh don't be so silly, Kevin. We're in no danger. Now listen, with Fishwick out of the picture, I'm going to try meditation, and see if I can make direct contact with some of the spirits in the house, so don't disturb me."

Kevin blanched. "Please. Carry on. Don't mind me." He turned his back and put two fingers to his forehead, pulling an imaginary trigger.

Scepter ignored him and sat down, closing her eyes. She breathed in through her nose and out through her mouth, loudly, quickly. Despite his levity over her announcement, Kevin found that her actions caused him to recall images from movies like *Carrie, The Amityville Horror* and *The Exorcist*—especially *The Exorcist.*

He turned from her and studied the computer, its larger, central square still showing the master bedroom, a vast four-poster dominating the fish-eye view. Light flooded in, and presently Pete could be seen searching the room. Eventually, finding nothing, he turned to face the camera and his voice came over the CB radio.

"Nothing up here, Kev," he reported. "I'll kill the lights on this landing as I come back."

Kevin felt his face pale again. In front of Pete, a foggy, murky shape was coalescing into roughly human form. He snatched up the CB. "P-P-Pete. There's summink b-b-behind you."

On screen, Pete looked around before he spoke into his radio. "There's nothing here."

Kevin frowned. He could still see the figure there, and yet... "Pete, it's right in front of you. Looks like a foggy mass. I can see right through it."

Pete fiddled in his pocket, came out with a tissue and wiped the camera lens. Almost instantly, the ghostly apparition disappeared. "Condensation," he reported. "Colder than a penguin's butt up here. I must have fogged it when I opened the door and came into the room. I'm on my way back."

Pete disappeared from the camera view.

Kevin glanced at Scepter, who was now sitting stock-still, her eyes wide open, gazing vacantly into space, her breathing shallow but rhythmic. Happy that she had not witnessed his near panic over a fogged camera lens, he was nevertheless unnerved by the realization that he was totally alone. With Pete still upstairs and Scepter off on some pie-in-the-sky astral journey, he was every bit as isolated as if he were on the Moon. He looked around, forcing himself to take in the darker areas of the badly lit cafeteria, the deeper recesses where something or someone, such as the shadowy figure he had seen disappearing into the woods, might be hiding.

He would be the first to admit that he did not have the same reserves of courage as his best buddy, but then he had never needed them; he'd always had Pete to look after him. But that was out in the real world where the problems were physical, not this strange half-world where it was hard to decide what was real and what was a figment of a frightened imagination.

"What's up with her?"

Pete's arrival made Kevin jump. "Hell's bells, Pete, don't sneak up on me like that."

The other chuckled. "You're scared of your own shadow, Keeley. So like I say, what's with Scepter?"

Kevin shrugged. "I dunno. Meditating or something."

Pete snorted. "Looks to me like she's drunk."

Kevin held up her apple-flavored water. "On this?"

Pete shrugged, and was about to speak when Scepter suddenly began to talk. Her voice was not normal. Instead it was deep, like a man's—slurred, guttural, and carrying the strong lilt of old Yorkshire/Lancashire.

"Wha's tha doing in my house? Gitoutta meh house."

"Drunk as a skunk," said Pete.

"No," Kevin argued. "She's contacted one of her spirits."

"Yeah, like the spirit of vodka."

Kevin scowled. "Just get the camera and film her."

"Why, what you gonna do?" asked Pete. "Post it on You Tube? Or are you expecting her head to spin round and her tongue to turn green, spitting pea soup?"

"She's the one who understands this guff. She'll want to look at the recording later."

Pete turned the nearby camera to face her. "The things I do just to keep you two happy," he grumbled as he adjusted the focus.

Kevin tapped the computer keyboard to kick in the digital recording software. "You mean the things you'll do to get a girl's knickers off," he muttered.

"Speak to me," Scepter said in her normal voice. "Tell me what troubles you."

Almost instantly, she sat bolt upright and her voice went back to the garbled, deeper growl. "*Tha's in my house. Leave. Gitoutta my sadness.*"

"We haven't seen his saddles," said Kevin in a low whisper.

"Sadness," Pete corrected him.

"*Leave me with my sorrow,*" ordered the male voice.

"I dunno who she's supposed to be, but she's not cheering me up," Kevin complained.

Scepter's shoulders slumped a little, and her voice changed again. It was still a deeper pitch than her natural one, but this time unmistakably feminine.

"*Tha done me. Tha done me and tha's paid for it.*"

"*I seen thee swing,*" said the guttural male.

"*Aye, tha did. And I weren't t'only one.*"

Scepter's eyes suddenly snapped open, and she took a deep breath. After a momentary disorientation, she smiled. Taking in Kevin's total bewilderment, she explained, "Fishwick told me they were here and I asked them to channel through me. An interesting experience." She looked at the camcorder. "Did you get it on tape?"

"Most of it," Pete agreed.

"It was Aggie Devis and Sir Henry Melmerby." Her eyes burned with compelling enthusiasm. "I'm sure of it. The impression I got was that Henry definitely raped Aggie, and as she said, she wasn't the only one. He took more than his share of the local women, most of them by force. Most of them wouldn't dare complain, but Aggie did, so he cooked up the charge of witchcraft to cover his crime, had her hanged for it, and now their spirits haunt this hall still troubled by their earthly problems."

"So they chucked a CD at me?" asked Kevin indignantly.

"Oh, shut up, you." Pete was still puzzled. "It seems to me that the only trouble Sir Henry might have had was gout. And if Aggie's bones were dug up after they managed to kill him, why is she troubled?"

"Remember, Pete, her spirit caused the horse to rear and throw Sir Henry. Effectively, even though she was already dead, she took his life, and that is still a sin."

"And you remember, Scepter, her spirit causing his horse to buck was a theory, not an established fact... like the bottle of port." Pete shook his head. "Why do I get the impression that this is all so much twaddle?"

"Believe what you will, Pete, but I'm glad we came." Scepter stretched and yawned. "This is going to be an exciting night. I can feel it."

"I can feel the need of the lavatory," moaned Kevin.

❦

Beep-beep-beep… beep-beep-beep… beep-beep-beep.

Kevin jumped at the noise.

Pete woke, stretched, smiled at Kevin's apprehension and reached his right hand across to silence the alarm on his wristwatch. "Midnight."

Kevin looked even more anxious. "Midnight? But isn't that when all the ghosts come out?"

"You've been reading too many horror stories," Scepter reproved him. "Ghosts can be seen at any time, night or day."

"In that case, we could have come during the day," Kevin argued.

"No," Scepter countered, "because we didn't get up until noon." She looked to Pete for support. "Pete, will you tell him there is nothing to fear?"

Pete gave a shrug. "It's my experience that the only things we need to be concerned with are those we can touch and take possession of. I'll worry about ghosts when I become one. Now, don't you think it's time to split up and take another tour of the house?"

Pete's final suggestion was so practical that Scepter agreed with a nod; Kevin, on the other hand, did not.

"So far, everything that's happened has focused on me," he complained, "and you wanna split up, leaving me alone. I mean, I've set all the video equipment to night vision. Why do we need to leave the café?"

Scepter encouraged him gently. "The equipment we've set out doesn't cover the entire house. If we split up, we stand a better chance of witnessing whatever may happen, and we're all in touch, remember." She held up her CB radio. "Pete can be with you in a minute. Besides," she encouraged him with a broad smile, "the spirits won't harm you."

"No?" Kevin snorted derisively. "Old Henry didn't do a bad job with that CD, did he? And next time it might be something worse than an album of whale song."

Pete grinned. "The Bay City Rollers?"

"Get stuffed, you." Kevin waved at the house in general. "There are swords and stuff all over the place, hung on the walls, attached to suits of armor. Suppose he chucks a scimitar at me? I don't fancy being turned into a kebab."

Pete had heard enough. "Kev, stop being a wimp. Scepter, why don't you take Sir Coward de Custard with you and check out the ground floor? I'll do the upstairs and the attics."

She agreed with a nod and stood up, preparing to leave. "If you're sure you can manage. It's a large spread."

Pete shrugged. "You've got your radio and you can come back to the café every so often to check the computer and let me know if you get anything."

Kevin gave Pete a mock round of applause and made no effort to leave his seat. "Best suggestion you've made all night, but here's a better one. Why don't me and Scepter stay in the café and you can have a roving brief all over the house?"

"You really should get something done about your broken arm."

"What broken arm?"

Pete glared. "The one I'll give you if you carry on winding me up."

CB's in hand, they left the café armed with torches and sensing equipment. Pete disappeared up the broad staircase while Kevin and Scepter headed for the Long Gallery.

"This isn't the bit that's haunted, though, is it?" Kevin asked as they entered the room.

"Oh, yes." To his disappointment Scepter sounded positively thrilled. "There've been sightings of Aggie in the gallery, wandering the aisles, sobbing, even throwing a tantrum once." Scepter gestured at a large display case, containing pots and pans from the 17th century. "She smashed the glass on that case two days after it was set up."

"Getting her pots back, eh? Obviously wanted to get on with dinner on the Other Side." Kevin grinned, but the last thing he felt was cheerful.

❧

Pete approached the first floor landing with a sense of caution.

Something had been going on ever since they arrived. He'd known Kevin a long time, and while he wasn't the bravest man in the world, he wasn't totally soft. Neither was he stupid. Whatever was happening, Pete didn't believe it was supernatural. He was convinced that there was someone else in the house, playing games, trying to scare them off by concentrating on Kevin as the weakest link. But that begged the question, why would anyone want to scare them away unless it was to do with the pirate DVDs?

Unlike his portly pal, he was not afraid, but with no more than the sparse house lighting and the beam of a small torch, there were too many shadows for his liking. Anyone or anything could jump out of them. Anticipation prepared him for the unexpected.

He made his way warily along the upper floor. As he approached each door, he pressed an ear to it, listening for sounds from within before opening it and casting his light about, trying not to disturb the sensors in those rooms where they were located.

When he reached the door to the attic staircase, he paused even longer, ears cocked for the slightest noise.

Let caution be your watchword. The words of his old instructor at the Police Academy rang through his head. "Common sense, Brennan," he said to the empty stairs. "You're going up, he's coming down. He has the high ground."

He placed a foot on the bottom step and climbed.

Stop and listen. You're in no hurry.

Like his father before him, he was glad of the police training.

He climbed another step. It creaked noisily. Pete froze, his senses on high alert. If there was anyone nearby, they must surely have heard.

He relaxed. Nothing. No one. He climbed the remaining steps, his mind awash with images of Kevin's reaction to creaking steps. He couldn't picture his best friend's face, but he could certainly imagine the smell.

The rooms on the topmost floor were smaller than those lower down. The gables and steep pitch of the various roof sections provided awkward angles and created ungainly shadows. Bursting into Aggie's room, where Scepter had set up motion and EMF sensors, he found his heart leaping, pouring adrenaline into his system when the silhouette of a man leapt out at him. A flash of the torch beam made him grin at a teddy bear seated on the rocking horse.

He cast his beam about the room. There were toys everywhere: a spinning top, the rocking horse and teddy bear, dolls, marbles, model cars. He had not noticed them before, because he was concentrating on explaining the room's reconstruction to Scepter. But now, even to his untrained eye, it was obvious that many of them were antique, and he guessed there was a fortune stored here.

But toys were all he could find. There was no trace of anything else, human or otherwise.

It was the same in the other rooms. Some beds were turned down, others made up, and the dust of long disuse covered them all, but there was no one to be found, dead or alive.

He returned to the first floor and continued checking the bedrooms and bathrooms, all of which, he noticed, were fitted with plumbing and furniture that spanned the centuries from the period after the English Civil War of the 17th century up to the late 19th century. It caused him to wonder where the modern installations were. "The private apartments," he said to himself. The one area of the house kept from them.

By now, finding nothing to interest or excite him, he began to get bored. It had been a long day: calling on Angie, calling at Flutter-Bys, driving them out here, Kevin's contretemps in the cellar and the event—or non-events—in between had taken their toll on his reserves of stamina. He suddenly felt tired.

He wandered into the master bedroom and stared at the four-poster. Scepter said the bed hadn't been used since the day of Henry Melmerby's funeral. All records had to come to an end, and he figured 350-plus years was long enough for any bed to go without an occupant.

⚜

Given the choice, Kevin would much rather have spent the night in the bar of the Rose & Crown than this spooky old house. As he shuffled slowly down the Long Gallery towards the rear door, his heart beat loudly, and his teeth would have chattered if his jaw hadn't been set so tight. He and Scepter squatted on the floor of the great hall under a Stubbs original of a horse called Mombassa, their torches switched off, and all he could see were dim paintings on the walls, display cases between them and the entrance hall, and the outline of the rear doors several meters away, the stables beyond them backlit by a thin winter moon.

Scepter began to speak in a soft, sibilant voice. "Show yourself."

Assuming her words were directed at him, Kevin said, "What? Here?" He shrugged, and a silly grin came to his face. "Well, if you're sure..." Kevin began to unbutton his shirt.

"I'm talking to the spirits," she whispered urgently.

He smiled sheepishly. "I knew that, really."

Scepter suppressed a smile and rolled her eyes upward. "If you're frightened, why don't you get on with thinking of a business name for our efforts?" Once more she raised her voice, speaking to the room. "Show us who you are, tell us what you want. We're not here to harm you, only to understand."

"Shh," Kevin whispered. "Don't encourage them."

She frowned him into silence and continued talking to the room. "Give us a sign."

She fell quiet, and suddenly silence was the only thing around them. Outside, even the wind and rain had ceased.

"Give us a sign," she repeated, her voice not much above a stage whisper.

Nothing happened. Kevin picked up the CB, saying, "I wonder how Pete's getting—"

"No, don't," Scepter interrupted, snatching the handset from him. "The spirits can be shy, you know. Some will turn out only when they're confident no one will hurt them. If we're quiet, they may appear."

"Great," Kevin grunted. "One spook who doesn't like whales and another hiding behind the curtains."

Scepter ignored him again. "We mean you no harm. Just give us a sign that you're here. Give us just a tiny sign."

SLAM! From somewhere beyond the gallery came the boom of a door whamming shut.

7

It was a distant noise, reverberating around the great hall, as if the large double doors leading to the outside world had been hurled shut. The noise startled Scepter. Alongside her, Kevin paled, and he gave an *"eek"* of total alarm. She guessed that his heart had skipped a few beats and was now rushing to catch up.

Scepter sat taut and silent, rigid, on high alert for further sounds. She thought about Pete. He was alone, upstairs somewhere, but he could take care of himself. What she and Kevin needed to do was to pin down the location of any spirit activity. She leapt to her feet. "Come on, we'd better check the computer." She stood up.

Kevin did not move. "Can we not just stay here?"

"*You* can," she told him. "I'm going back to the cafeteria."

The prospect of being left alone obviously terrified him even more. He struggled to his feet and hurried to catch up with Scepter as she walked quickly away.

The brilliant pinpoints of their twin flashlights danced across the floor, lighting their path as they moved quickly through the Long Gallery and entrance hall and scurried into the café. Kevin hit the keyboard, bringing the computer out of its screensaver mode. His face a portrait of amazement, he tried to take in all of the messages from the screen.

On the control panel, several alerts flashed. Kevin brought up the main menu and found a host of signals indicating sensors had been tripped all over the house. "Master bedroom, Aggie's attic room, the Long Gallery, the café. The place is lit up like Trafalgar Square at Christmas."

They looked at each other.

"The café?" Scepter's voice was not much more than a whisper.

Kevin tried to talk up his meager courage. "It must be us."

"Yes. It must be," Scepter agreed. "Let me just check with the expert. Fishwick. Are you there, Fishwick?"

"Right here Modom."

"Fishwick, is there anyone here in the cafeteria with us?"

"Yes, Modom. Sir Henry is in the corner, by the soft drinks display machine. He appears to me as his energy form, but you should see him as he was in life."

Scepter trembled with nervous excitement, anticipation and—she had to admit it—some anxiety. But it was the angst associated with widening comfort zones. Like the first kiss, the first physical encounter with a man. Like exam nerves; walking into a room full of desks, knowing that she could easily pass the test, but worried that she might fail.

Get a grip on yourself, girl. She sent the mental order to her mind and body. *You've spent weeks, months telling your two friends that there is nothing to fear, so confront this spirit.*

"Remember the old man at Rossington Terrace, last night, Modom."

Fishwick's encouragement leaping into her head startled her. "I thought you couldn't read minds, Fishwick."

Alongside her, Kevin remained intent upon his computer, too terrified to look round, but he obviously thought she was talking to him, and asked, "What?"

"I'm talking to Fishwick," she reported. "Well, Fishwick?"

"I cannot read your mind, Modom, but I guessed from the length of time in which you hadn't moved that you were becoming nervous. You saw the old man at Rossington Terrace. Sir Henry is no different."

Scepter said nothing. Sir Henry was different. The old man haunting the Bilks' place didn't even know he was dead. And the best he could do was turn himself into a wolfman. Sir Henry had been hanging around this house for over 300 years and was considerably more dangerous. If Kevin were to be believed—and Scepter had no reason to doubt her partner—the former squire had already demonstrated his ability to manipulate the physical environment. To turn and face him was not simply a step outside her comfort zones or a walk into an examination room—and it was not a first kiss. It was a confrontation with a very real, possibly dangerous spirit.

Still putting off the moment, she checked on Kevin. She would get no help there. He was frozen into immobility and had even stopped playing with the computer. Pete was away upstairs somewhere. She was the only person who could face Sir Henry.

Scepter took a deep breath and turned sharply to her left.

The room was as dark as the rest of the house, lit only by a few thin, overhead lamps. The drinks dispenser was several meters away, dark and dormant without the power to make it work, just a bulky shape without depth or definition. Sir Henry stood alongside it, a grim figure, dressed, so it appeared, in knee breeches and a high-collared coat. Scepter could not be certain, but she had the odd feeling that he desired her the way he had wanted Aggie Devis. But that was nonsense, and she knew it the instant she thought it. A product of her knowledge of Sir Henry Melmerby and his rapacious appetites. Once more she recalled the old man of Rossington Terrace. She had not flinched before him, and she would not back away from Sir Henry Melmerby.

She took a step towards him. He promptly disappeared.

Startled and irritated, she spun the tripod-mounted camcorder round, trained it on the general serving area and switched it into record mode.

"Well?" Kevin's voice brought her back to reality. When she turned, he was still staring at the computer screen, too frightened to look anywhere else.

"Well, what?"

"It's us, isn't it?" Kevin wanted to know. "We triggered the alarms in here, didn't we?"

She absorbed his look of fear, felt his need for reassurance, and acquiesced. "Yes, Kevin, it's us. *We* set off the alerts."

He let go a sigh of relief. "Thank God for that. For a minute there, I thought the old whale hater was back."

Scepter did not reply. Her eyes were fixed on the glowing monitor and its eight video camera images.

"Look," she croaked. "The master bedroom. There's something in there."

❧

His finger shaking, Kevin tapped the mouse pad, directed the cursor and brought the mini-screen up to fill the monitor. The camera lens was fogged again. Someone or something had opened the door and created a temperature differential, but on the bed was something unmistakable: a huge, human form.

Scepter scrabbled for the CB. "Pete. Pete! Where the hell are you?"

On screen, the large form began to move.

"He's wearing fashionable gear, isn't he?" Much of Kevin's fear had gone with the belief that the phantom, which he had convinced himself was here in the cafeteria, was now on the upper floors, and between it and him was the formidable obstacle of ex-Detective Constable Pete Brennan. "I mean, look at those trainers. They're Reeboks, aren't they?" He looked at Scepter. "Can they do that, ghosts? Pick up modern clothing and stuff?"

She did not answer. In exasperation, she clicked and clicked the transmit button of her handset. "For God's sake Pete, will you pick up your radio? We need you."

The figure groped around the bed. "Randy old git, isn't he? Been dead all them years and he's still after the chicks."

Now the form had picked something up.

"Wonder what that is," muttered Kevin.

"We'll have to go up there," said Scepter.

Kevin suddenly realized he had been talking to himself, holding a parallel, but not linked conversation with Scepter. Upon her final suggestion, he suddenly hopped from his track to hers.

"For all we know, Pete could have been overcome," she said.

"Yes," said Kevin, "and there are fairies in my window box. Any ghost taking on Pete Brennan wants its paranormal head seeing to, and if you think I'm going anywhere near that—" He gestured at the screen. "—you've got another think coming."

"We can't just leave Pete up there alone," Scepter protested.

Kevin did not hear. He watched the apparition bring the object it had picked up to its mouth.

"Looks like a bar of chocolate," said Kevin, and pangs of hunger attacked him.

"What do you want?" Pete's voice burst from the radio.

Scepter's relief showed in her voice. "Thank God. Pete, we were worried about you. The whole house has gone mad and there's something moving in the master bedroom."

There was a brief pause. On screen, the phantom figure looked around its immediate environment.

"Well, I'm *in* there, and I can't see anything," Pete replied.

Kevin's alarm reached new heights. "It's on the bed. We're watching it."

Pete was seen to look around. "That's me, you idiots! I was having a bit of kip."

"Oh."

"Oh."

In the ensuing silence, Kevin and Scepter exchanged a sheepish glance. Kevin chuckled. "I thought those trainers looked new."

Scepter focused more on the business at hand. "We have a sensor registering in the attics, Pete, and a temperature drop on the third floor corridor."

"I'll check it out and get back to you."

The dim shape moved. Pete polished the camera lens once more, until they could see him clearly, and then he left the room, appearing almost instantly in a nearby mini-screen as he emerged onto the landing.

Still hungry, Kevin turned his back on Scepter, digging into his bag for a bar of chocolate. She moved the mouse and transferred the corridor mini-screen to the center of the display, and almost immediately, the camera lens fogged. On her instruction, Pete wiped it and made his way to the attic entrance. As he reached it, a faint glow of light moved rapidly along the floor behind him; almost instantly, the lens fogged again.

Scepter was breathless with excitement. "Did you see that?"

"No," Kevin admitted. "I wasn't watching."

"An orb," she enthused. "No one knows what they are, but one theory is they're the precursor to a manifestation. It's like a tiny ball of light wandering along the corridor."

"That's all we need," grumbled Kevin. "We're in the dark with just a couple spooks for company, and now we've got a ghost tenpin bowling along the top floors."

Scepter ignored his cynicism and flicked the screen to the attic, and the nursery, where the rocking horse was silhouetted under the single skylight.

Kevin watched over her shoulder as Pete's huge frame entered the room and the lens misted up. He wiped it clean, flashed his torch at all corners and reported, "Nothing here, Scepter. I'll come back down."

Kevin turned away to eat his chocolate. He heard the door close over the audio connection. It was followed by a gasp from Scepter.

"Look!" She cried.

Kevin groaned. "Do I have to? Can't I just shut my eyes for the rest of the night?"

"The rocking horse," Scepter breathed. "It's rocking."

Kevin glanced over her shoulder. "Rocking horses tend to rock. It's what they're designed for. That's why they're called rocking horses"

"Yes, but there's no one there to start it up."

Kevin looked over her shoulder again. "Maybe it was Pete."

"It started after he left," she assured him.

Kevin grunted and turned away.

Much calmer now in the knowledge that the rocking horse was two floors away, and that the beast in the master bedroom and the alarm in the cafeteria had been explained, Kevin wandered behind the counter and switched on the kettle. "You want a cuppa?"

"Please."

"I'll make one for Pete as well. It's freezing up there, and he was sleeping on top of the bed instead of under the blankets." He reached to an overhead shelf and took down three cups. "And, you know, if it hasn't been slept in for all those years, it'll be damp too, so maybe... where's the sugar?"

With an almost silent swish along the metal surface, the sugar appeared at his right hand.

"Cheers, luv," he prattled on. "My old mum always says there's nothing like a cuppa when you're in trouble. You got any milk there?"

There was another swishing sound as the milk slid along the surface.

"Thanks, Scepter. You know, this ghost hunting lark isn't..."

"Pete, can you hear me Pete?" Scepter's voice coming from the computer, ten meters away, cut Kevin off.

"What is it?" came the testy voice of Pete over the radio.

"We've had alerts from the Long Gallery," Scepter told Pete. "Could you take a look as you come back down?"

"Wilco," Pete's voice came back. "Meantime, check on Kevin's underpants. There are more ghosts there than here."

Kevin felt his face drain of blood again. His eyes were riveted on the sugar and milk. They had both slid along the polished metal counter from his right. He'd thought that Scepter had passed them, but she was at the computer, 10 meters away to his left, and the radio conversation confirmed that Pete was still upstairs.

Slowly, Kevin turned to his right, but his head never got to ninety degrees. At about a third of the way through, a teaspoon fell from somewhere up above him, clattering onto the surface near the cups. He almost fainted.

He gripped the edge of the range to prevent himself falling. He felt an urgent need of the lavatory, but he was too terrified to move. Anyway, making for the staff toilets at the rear of the kitchen would have meant being alone, out of sight of his friends—and right there and then, he did *not* want to be alone, nor did he imagine that Scepter would hold his hand while he visited the dunny.

"S-S-Scepter," he stammered, "tell me you've just chucked a spoon at me."

"Hmm?" Scepter studied the computer images.

"Teaspoon," Kevin repeated. "You've just thrown one, right?"

"No sugar for me."

He now turned his head frantically left and right and was relieved to see nothing and no one there. He whipped round, mouth gaping and saw her concentrating on the computer screen. "Scepter, someone's just passed me the milk, sugar and a spoon."

"Just a little milk please," she said, her concentration honed on the computer.

Kevin raised his voice to a shout. "Scepter, you're not listening."

At last she looked up, frowning irritably. "Kevin, I'm trying to concentrate here. What do you want?"

"The milk and sugar and a spoon," he told her. "Someone's just given them to me and if it wasn't you, who was it?"

"Oh, Kevin, you really have got the shakes tonight, haven't you?" It was the kind of tone usually reserved for naughty schoolboys.

Kevin's resentment swelled and he raised his voice even further, giving vent to it. "I have not got the jitters. Well, I have, but I'm not imagining it. I asked for sugar and it arrived, I asked for milk and it arrived, I didn't ask for the spoon, but that arrived anyway. All on its own."

"Well, whoever gave you the milk and sugar," Scepter said tartly, "would know that you needed the spoon." Her sarcasm getting her nowhere, she turned to her butler for support. "Fishwick?"

"Modom?"

"Have you been passing milk, sugar and spoons to Mr. Keeley?" She was just as irritated with Fishwick as she had been with Kevin.

"No, Modom," said her butler with implacable calm, "but it's possible another entity may have done. I've been up in the attics where the child has been playing with a rocking horse. However, there are no spirits here at this immediate moment."

"Thank you, Fishwick." She faced Kevin again. "You imagined it."

"Now listen—"

Scepter never got around to listening to Kevin. The computer beeped again and a temperature sensor recorded a drop of five degrees on the first floor. She snatched up her handset. "Pete, is it cold up there?"

Pete's voice echoed through the ether. "Put it this way, I've just seen a penguin thumbing a lift to warmer climes."

Scepter checked the readings from various locations throughout the house. "It's five degrees colder where you are than it is anywhere else in the house. That could indicate paranormal activity."

"It could also indicate," Pete argued across the ether, "that someone left a few windows open."

"And have they?" she demanded.

"I don't know," he replied, "because I didn't take any notice."

Scepter fumed. "Pete, if we are to be professional, we can't skimp. We need to check and eliminate every possibility. Why not check again and ensure that all the windows in all the rooms are shut?"

Pete's reply carried exactly the right amount of sarcasm to let her know what he thought of her demands. "Yes, boss."

Satisfied, Scepter turned to Kevin again. "Now Kevin, what can we do to allay your fears?"

"You can start by taking me seriously for a start," he snapped. "I might look like a fat joke with a windy backside, but I'm not a total loon. That sugar bowl, the milk jug and spoon arrived by themselves."

Chewing her lip, her features set into an expression of analytical thought, Scepter crossed the cafeteria and moved behind the counter to join him. Sugar bowl and milk jug and spoon were all manufactured from stainless steel, as was the metal top of the counter.

"Before we assume it was one of the ghosts in this place, let's eliminate all other possibilities," she suggested.

'You just said Fishwick told you I was imagining it."

"I was being economical with the truth." Kevin scowled and Scepter explained, "I was trying to calm you down. Now come on. Let's check other possible explanations. Magnetism?"

"No," Kevin disagreed. "Pete's the one with the magnetism."

"I'm talking about real magnetism," Scepter pointed out, "not Pete's theoretical charms. Let's check the counter for magnetic variations."

"And how do we do that?" he demanded. "Rap three times on it and see if it takes the rings off my fingers?"

Scepter held up a magnetometer. "With this." Switching on the detector, she wafted it backwards and forwards across the counter and studied the readings. "Nothing." As if to dispute her findings, the needle suddenly leapt to the top of the scale and back again. "Wait. I got something then."

Kevin pointed at the electrical outlet on the tiled wall, where the kettle was plugged in "Yes. You got the wall socket."

"That's plastic, not metal," she pointed out.

"Scepter," he said with enforced patience, "I don't remember much of what they taught me at school, but I do remember that electricity and magnetism are almost nearly the same thing, only different. Where you get electricity, you get *magnicity*."

"Magnetism," Scepter corrected him. "Why do you do that, Kevin? Come across as an idiot when you're not?"

He smiled childishly. "I was trying to lighten the mood."

❧

"Did one of you pass the sugar and milk to Mr. Keeley?"

Sir Henry and Aggie greeted Fishwick's question with an air of false innocence.

"Well?" demanded Fishwick.

"Listen, thee," snapped Sir Henry, "don't forget that when tha were alive, tha were a lot lower down the social scale than me."

"But now that we're all dead," Fishwick pointed out, "we're all equal."

"He asked for sugar, so I give it him," said Aggie, "he asked for milk, so I give it him."

"He didn't ask for the teaspoon," Fishwick objected.

"No, but like that strumpet said, that lass o' thine, he couldn't stir without a spoon, could he?"

Unable to refute Aggie's logic, Fishwick left the hall's resident ghosts to themselves.

❧

"You know," said Scepter, "a lot of tonight's events have centered on you."

"I've been saying this since I came out of the cellar," Kevin pointed out. "You think this Henry the tea-making whale hunter has got it in for me personally?"

"It's possible," Scepter agreed, "but unlikely. Sir Henry probably never made a cup of tea in his life. It was probably one of the servants."

"Great," whined Kevin. "Now they're all after me."

"We could try hypnotic regression with you tomorrow. See whether you knew the Melmerbys in a past life." She thought a little more. "On the other hand, it may be that you're an unconscious telekinetic."

Kevin took instant offense. "I'm as sane as Pete."

"Who's as sane as me?" asked Pete as he entered the café.

"She's just said I'm a subconscious telly frenetic, Pete."

"Is that the same as an imbecile?" the ex-cop wanted to know.

Scepter shook her head. "First the CD, now the sugar bowl and milk jug. I think Kevin has the unconscious ability to move objects without touching them. He seems to be the focus of much of what is happening."

With an air of calm composure, Pete asked what had happened. Kevin explained in detail and concluded by adding, "Not only is Henry whats-his-name after me, but so are his servants. You watch. They'll be chucking the furniture around soon."

Pete looked up above the area of the counter where Kevin had been preparing the cups. There was another metal rack half a meter higher up.

"That's probably where the spoon came from," he muttered.

"And the milk and sugar?" demanded Kevin. "I suppose they just hopped on a number 37 bus and made their way to my right hand?"

"No. The 37 doesn't come this way." Pete grinned. "I think it's the 24 that comes this far out of town."

"Pete…" There was a dangerous edge to Kevin's voice.

"You got them yourself, Kev. They were obviously closer to hand than you thought."

Kevin opened his mouth to protest. Scepter did likewise.

Pete held up a hand for silence. "You're scared, Kevin. You've been crapping yourself since we got here. I think your fear is producing lapses of concentration and memory."

"We will find out," Scepter declared. "Fishwick!"

"Right here, Modom," her butler's voice came into her head.

"Fishwick," Scepter demanded, tartly. "Have you solved the mystery of the milk, sugar and teaspoon?"

"I have, Modom," Fishwick reported. "Aggie passed them along."

"Thank you, Fishwick. That will be all for the time being." With a triumphant gleam in her eye, Scepter turned back to her living colleagues. "Aggie passed the milk, the sugar and the spoon to Kevin. Fishwick has just told me." "And you expect me to take Fishwick's word?" asked Pete. "I can't see him, I can't hear him, so I don't believe in him, and I won't believe what you say he says."

"Well, we'll know tomorrow," Scepter affirmed. "We've had video recorders in here all night, and I turned that one—" She indicated the nearby tripod and camera. "—to face the service counter about ten minutes ago, when Sir Henry appeared by the drinks machine. We can check the playback tomorrow."

Kevin suddenly became very angry. "When Sir Henry appeared by the drinks machine? You said we'd set off the alarms in here."

"You were frightened, Kevin," Scepter excused herself, "and I didn't want to scare you any more, so I lied."

"Well thanks for—"

"Let's all calm down," Pete cut Kevin off. "I've checked all over the house and there is nothing and no one here but us three."

"Then who set the rocking horse going in the attic?" asked Scepter, explaining what she had witnessed. "Fishwick assures me it is the spirit of a child."

Pete snorted. "Bloody Fishwick. I wish he'd bugger off and open a fish shop. It was probably me that set the horse in motion when I left the room. Closing the door set up a movement of air in the room and it caused the rocking horse to move."

"This entire house has been causing a movement of air in me," complained Kevin.

"So we've noticed." Scepter faced Pete. "There is no way that closing the door could have made a heavy, wooden rocking horse move like that. Face facts, we have paranormal activity here."

Pete accepted a cup of tea from Kevin and warmed his large hands on it. When he spoke, it was in the patient voice of one addressing a child.

"Scepter, you're very sweet, but you're very naïve, too. You believe in ghosts, I don't. I'd like to, but I'm an ex-copper, and I need proof. For everything that's happened, there are alternative, logical explanations." He pointed an accusing finger at Kevin. "This dipstick has mistaken *me* for a ghost twice. Once in the cellar and once in the master bedroom, where you, too, thought I was a spook. Now get ghosts off the brain and employ some logic. Look for the supernatural *after* you've discounted everything else, not before."

Scepter turned away, angry and disappointed. Kevin stood up to his old friend. "Now look what you've done."

Pete waved him away and turned to Scepter. She looked forlorn, hunched over the computer. He sat beside her and took her hand, gave her an encouraging smile and said, "I'm not putting you down Scepter, just trying to keep our feet on the ground."

She kissed him on the cheek. "I know you are, but even you must be puzzled by some of the..."

BOOM!

The noise echoed around the cavernous building and cut Scepter off. All three held their breath for a moment, waiting. When nothing happened, Pete and Scepter turned their attention to the computer.

"Nothing. There's no indication." Scepter's voice was incredulous.

"I thought we had the entire house covered?"

"We do. All except for..." Scepter's pretty features became strained.

"What?" asked Kevin. "All except for what?"

Scepter did not answer. Once more her face became strained, as if she were listening.

"It's Fishwick. He's warning me of something happening in the stables."

❧

Pete and Scepter ran for it; Kevin followed, his less athletic body straining to keep up. They burst into the rear courtyard. Pete stared around, his eye settling on the partly open gates.

"Kev, I thought you closed them."

"I did," wheezed Kevin.

"Then how come...?" Pete eyed the warehouse opposite, where the door was also open. He marched to it. More wary, Kevin and Scepter hung back.

"Damn." The curse came from Pete in the warehouse.

Slowly, cautiously, Scepter and Kevin stepped in.

Pete stood in the middle of the floor. The five pallets, which had been there less than nine hours earlier, were gone.

Kevin was distraught. "The whole lot gone. I knew this place was haunted."

"Oh, yeah?" demanded Pete. "And what the hell are Aggie Devis and Sir Henry Melmerby gonna do with 25,000 pirate DVDs? Hand 'em out to the other spooks as Halloween presents? And how did they get 'em away? You figure these ghosts have access to a ten ton truck?"

Alongside him, Scepter became suddenly intent as she listened once more to her butler. When she spoke, it was with extreme distress. "Pete, something terrible has happened here."

"Yes. Someone's been taking the mickey with us all night." He pressed his hand to the engine of the forklift truck. "Warm. They must have loaded these things onto a lorry while we were fooling about in the house."

"And we didn't hear them?" Kevin did not believe it.

"We wouldn't, would we?" Pete snapped. "We were too busy chasing ghosts. And all the time, they were creating those ghosts. One of them was wandering about the house, keeping us busy."

Kevin objected instantly. "That doesn't make sense, Pete. Scepter saw that orb on the landing and I nearly saw the rocking horse, and how did they chuck the spoon at me? Besides, you said there was no one in there but us."

"I was wrong. They've been clever, that's all. And when I get them …"

Scepter's brow furrowed with worry. "Fishwick says this place holds a terrible secret."

"Stuff Fishwife."

"Fishwick."

"Whoever," growled Pete. "I'm looking for the thieves who—"

"Pete, will you shurrup and listen to her?" Kevin pointed at Scepter.

Scepter was trembling now, near to tears. "Fishwick feels the pain of others because of what happened to him on the Somme. Pete, I'm scared. Something awful has happened or is about to. There's another spirit nearby. The one from last night and he's angry. Very angry. So angry—"

"Yes, well, he's not the only one, is he?" Pete interrupted

"Pete, I'm being serious," Scepter wept. "Something evil has happened here."

Terrifying visions from every horror movie he had ever seen filled Kevin's thoughts: vampires, werewolves, mummies, and grotesque monsters walked across his fertile imagination. He could not help it. With a loud raspberry he broke wind. Pete and Scepter frowned and gave him disapproving stares. To get away from them, Kevin wandered into the narrow alleys between the racks while Pete and Scepter continued to argue.

"Pete," Scepter cried, "angry spirits will try to vent their frustration on the living. We have to calm this spirit down, bring him peace, or he'll turn on us."

Pete glared at her. "Scepter, you might fool Kev and a bundle of no-hopers in the mission hall with your act, but don't pull it on me. The only spirit we need to be concerned with is the spirit of petroleum."

She frowned. "What?"

"A gallon of gas," he said furiously, "which I'm gonna use to torch the buggers when I get my hands on them."

⁂

Trying to ignore their argument, Kevin wandered through the racks, which had held the supplies Melmerby Manor used in its day-to-day business of catering for visitors. He was not looking for anything in particular, just something to alleviate the sense of loss he felt at having the DVDs nicked from under his nose.

He found nothing of interest, other than the same stuff he had noticed on their earlier visit. Farther along the alley, he found half a dozen one-gallon containers of floor cleaner, a few mop heads, a few kitchen towel rolls which might save him a few pennies the next time he visited the supermarket, several pairs of meter-long metal tongs for picking up litter.

Kevin hefted a pair of the tongs in his hands. He tried to calculate their value on the black market and dreamt of new uses for them: picking up socks to save wear and tear on his back, reaching for the TV remote control when he couldn't be bothered moving, stealing sweets from his local shop when the counter assistant wasn't looking.

He noticed a heap of sacking on the floor at the end of the aisle, close to the rear wall. There was only one reason people dumped sacking on the floor: to cover something up which they did not want anyone else to find, usually something valuable, like... like... well, he couldn't think of anything offhand, but there was one way to find out.

Playing with the metal tongs, he hooked the end of the Hessian with them, peeled it back—and almost threw up.

There under the sacking lay a young man, and he was dead. Kevin knew he was dead. No one could still be alive with such a large crater in his head and his face covered in such a mass of congealing blood.

8

Kevin cried out. Scepter and Pete promptly abandoned their argument and rushed down the narrow aisle from which the cry had come, and found Kevin cowering back against the metal racking.

"H-he's d-d-dead," stammered Kevin, pointing a shaking finger at the corpse.

Pete bundled his best friend into Scepter's arms, and she led him away.

Left alone with the body, Pete looked it over. The corpse was a man in his early twenties with a head of cropped, fair hair just beginning to grow after it had been shaved, and a large, bloody dent in the side of his head where someone had struck him. There wasn't much point, but Pete reached gingerly out and touched his neck, feeling for a pulse. The skin was icy cold to the touch, and there was no trace of a heartbeat.

Satisfied that the man was dead, Pete studied the battered face, compared it to a database in his brain, and identified him as Steven Bilks. He dug into his pocket for his mobile phone, switched it on and strode back along the aisle while he waited for the instrument to boot up.

He found Scepter perched on one raised fork of the truck, her arm hugging Kevin who sat trembling beside her. She eyed the phone in Pete's hand. "Ambulance?"

He shook his head. "No point. Police."

"Pete, you can't do that. They'll think we did it."

"Scepter, if this was just a break-in, I'd ring them anonymously from a public phone, but Bilko was murdered. We have to tell the law." He punched in the number and jammed the connect button. "Whatever you do," he said while waiting for the connection to be made, "don't touch anything else. They'll want our dabs for elimination."

"They've already got mine," wailed Kevin, regaining some of his color. "They're all over this house, and the minute they set the dab men to work, they'll wall me up for life."

Tears welled in Scepter's eyes. "I told you something awful had happened, didn't I?"

"Yes, you did. Hello, Police? Give me CID. Tell 'em it's Ex-Detective Constable Brennan."

There was a delay before a gruff voice came on. "Brennan? What do you want?"

"Nice to speak to you, too, Chief Inspector Locke."

"Cut the crap," ordered Locke, "and tell me what you want."

"To report a murder," said Pete.

"Now listen—"

"No, you listen," Pete interrupted. "I'm in the stables at Melmerby Manor with my two business partners, and we've got a fresh stiff in here. Bilko. Get your people out here and we'll wait for them." He closed the connection and looked Scepter grimly in the eye. "I told you there was something going on here didn't I? While we've been fooling around chasing ghosts, someone dragged a lorry up here, took all those pallets of DVDs and left us Bilko instead."

Scepter pulled herself together. "You ...you're sure it's him?"

Pete nodded. "It's Bilko all right. Kev and I have known him for years."

Kevin shuddered. "I saw someone." Suddenly he had their full attention. Once more he drew in his breath to steady his nerves. "Earlier. When you asked me to shut those back gates. When we first got here. I saw someone running into the woods."

Pete's features darkened. "Why the hell didn't you say so?"

Kevin raised his voice to a defensive wail. "Because we'd just had that do in the cellar, and Scepter had told us the woods were haunted. If I'd told you, you'd have said I was imagining it."

He was right, but that knowledge only irritated Pete all the more. Angrily, he snatched up his torch and walked out of the stables. Directing the light towards the ground, he picked up the heavy tire tracks of the forklift truck. Judging from the tracks, it had made the journey from the stables to the rear gates and back many times. Instead of stopping at the gates, however, it had then turned towards the manor house's front and the exit to Melmerby Lane. Recent, heavy rain had turned the path alongside the house to a mud bath; there in the mud, he could see the impression of lorry tires meeting those of the forklift about five meters from the spot where the forklift had angled off. He could also see a variety of footprints: boots, shoes, even a pair of lady's high heels, enough to suggest a team of four or five. He estimated that even working as a team, it must have taken the thieves 30 to 45 minutes to load the lorry, but he and his partners had been so busy chasing round the house that they had heard nothing.

Making his way back to the rear gates, he flashed the torch across to the trees fifty meters away, but the beam was too weak to pick out any individual features. All he could see was a solid mass of bushes. Even if Kevin had been right about seeing something over there, that something, like the lorry, would be long gone.

He returned to the rear yard looking grimmer than when he left. "Tire trucks, footprints in the mud outside, but no sign of anyone. There was a woman with them, wearing high heels, of all things. You wearing them?" Scepter pointed to her feet and flat soles. "Thank God for that."

"Why?"

"If you'd been wearing them, the police would have fingered us straight off. And trust me, it wouldn't matter if you were wearing spikes and she was wearing blocks, Locke would still accuse you."

There was a moment's uneasy silence in which none of them quite knew what to say to the others. Kevin fiddled with his mobile phone, Scepter made a minute examination of her fingernails, and Pete paced slowly back and forth just in front of them. Each of their thoughts centered on the gruesome find under the Hessian, just a few meters away, and the terrible way in which Steven Bilks had died.

Time passed.

Scepter cleared her throat, as if she were going to say something, then changed her mind. Kevin took out a notebook and began to work on the problem of a business name. Pete continued pacing like some caged animal, constrained by the space in which he could move, urgently needing to get out and broaden his domain.

More time passed.

"How long does it usually take them to get out here?" Scepter's innocent question broke the spell.

"Twenty minutes in an emergency," Pete reported. "But I know Locke. He won't consider it an emergency until he gets here and sees the body."

"We should check the computers," said Kevin. "Get them dismantled and stuff, because the plod won't do it."

"You can't," Pete told him. "You must leave everything as it is."

"Pete—"

"Kevin," Pete interrupted, "this is now a murder scene. If we change or move anything—anything at all—you could be charged with tampering with evidence. Just sit here and wait it out. They won't be long." Pete paced some more. At the warehouse door, he paused and looked out at the open gates. "They were the very reason I met Lady Melmerby."

Scepter started from her reverie. "What?"

"The back gates. Remember, I told you I'd been here before to advise them on security after a break-in? Well, that gate was the way the burglars came in. There's a sort of hatch in it and all anyone has to do is slide it open and they can reach in and pull the bolt on the gate. I advised them to nail it shut. Obviously, they didn't follow my advice."

"Yes, but—"

Pete cut Scepter's protest off before she could utter it. "Kev just told us he shut the gates earlier. How do you think they got in to steal the DVDs?"

"Through the hatch in the gates," said Kevin nodding in agreement with Pete.

Another long silence fell, until it was broken once more, by Scepter. "Fishwick knew."

"What?" Kevin asked.

"Fishwick. He knew. He said something was going on in the stables."

"Great. Now we have testimony from a ghost." Pete's frustration was getting the better of him.

"Pete—"

"Scepter," he cut her off, "it will never hold up in court. And whatever you do, don't mention Fishwick's testimony to Locke when he gets here."

"He's a non-believer, too?"

"He's a practical man," Pete advised her. "And he's a bad-tempered sod, too."

❦

When Detective Constable Andrea Keynes arrived at Ashdale police station, she took the passenger seat of Chief Inspector Locke's car for the drive out to the manor. As Pete had described him to his colleagues, Locke was a gruff man in his mid-fifties. Five feet ten, with a balding head and a ruddy complexion, a man with a distinguished career in the police service, he had a voice that had once been likened to that of a town crier. His challenging manner upset everyone, colleagues and criminals alike, but no one could ever doubt his efficiency: his success was reflected in his unrivalled clear-up rate.

After receiving Pete's call, he had ordered a scene-of-crime team out immediately and waited at the station for Keynes' arrival.

"Don't rush," he told her as they drove out of the station. "There's nothing we can do at Melmerby Manor until the SOCOs have done their initial assessment except make life miserable for Brennan and his chums."

"Detective Constable Brennan?" Andrea asked. "Pete Brennan, isn't it?"

"What about him?" asked Locke, stopping at a red light.

"Is it right that you fired him?"

"Correct," Locke confirmed. "And I'll tell you something else, when we get out here, we charge him with whatever's happened."

Keynes was puzzled. "Chief, he wouldn't have called us if he was guilty."

"What difference does that make?" Locke accelerated away from the lights. "Listen to me, Brennan is bad news, and that mate of his, Keeley, is as hooky as they come. They're obviously not guilty of this, but they'll be mixed up in something crooked, so just throw the accusations at them. All right?"

'No it's not all right,' protested Andrea. "We're supposed to uphold the law, guv, not break it."

"Just do as I say," Locke insisted. "They're up to something, even if it's not murder, and the simplest way to find out what is to throw the murder charge at them. Especially Keeley. He'll grass on his own grandmother to avoid having his collar felt."

DC Keynes shrugged. "You're the boss, but when the crap starts to fly, I'll tell the inquiry you ordered me to do it."

Locke and Keynes got to the manor just after three in the morning, by which time Scepter, Pete and Kevin were feeling their lack of sleep. Locke promptly accused them of the killing.

Pete refused to be browbeaten by the Inspector. Instead, he promptly retaliated. "We found him, you numpty. We didn't kill him."

"What were you doing here in the first place, Brennan?" Locke jabbed a finger at Scepter. "Breaking and entering with her? Or breaking and entering her, while Keeley hung about keeping watch and waiting for the leftovers?"

"I resent that, Inspector," Scepter complained. "My relationship with Pete and Kevin is strictly professional."

It was not the wisest thing she could have said, as Locke's next words confirmed. "So you charge for your favors, do you?"

Scepter turned vermilion with rage. She clenched her fists so hard her nails bit into her flesh.

Concerned that she might actually lash out at the Inspector, Pete stepped in to try calm matters down. "Insulting Scepter won't get you anywhere, Locke. We are here on pukka business."

His words had the desired effect. When Locke next spoke to Scepter, he dropped his acerbic veneer. "It's *Chief* Inspector," he told her, "and you may be working with Brennan and Keeley, but you don't know them like I do. They are bad news."

"If you don't watch it," Pete warned, "it'll be Chief Inspector with a busted nose... and not for the first time. Or have you forgotten the last time we fell out?"

"No, I haven't," Locke responded. "Have you forgotten I said I'd wall you up for good if I ever got the chance?"

Now Pete began to lose his cool. "You are not railroading me again. We found Bilko right where you see him."

"We'll see what forensic has to say about the time of death," Locke declared, "and then look into your alibis. And by the way, no one railroaded you last time. You put one on me."

"Well, just watch you don't give me cause to do it again," Pete advised.

Locke ignored the threat and took out his notebook. "So, what's this business you've got here?"

"We're ghost hunting. Or didn't Dave Robb tell you about Rossington Terrace last night?"

"I read his report, Brennan," Locke admitted, "and I remember thinking that it's another con."

Feeling aggrieved, Kevin muscled his way into the little clutch of people. "We're not ripping anyone off," he snapped. "We weren't getting paid for that gaff."

Locke laid a glare on Kevin. "I'll speak to you later, Keeley. Alone."

"Not without my brief, you won't," Kevin assured him.

Deciding that the time had come for frankness, Scepter stepped in. "Chief Inspector Locke, I am Lady Concepta Rand-Epping, Countess of North Yorkshire. My family can trace its history back to Oliver Cromwell. The mere idea that I, or anyone connected with me, could be party to murder, is absurd."

For the first time since his arrival, Locke smiled, but it was the sort of smile one reserves for someone several slates short of the full roof. "Is she for real?"

His question was directed at Pete, who nodded. "One hundred percent."

Scepter pressed on through their cynicism. "My mother was a personal friend of Jonathan Melmerby, which is the very reason we were given permission to investigate the haunting of this manor. And you can check that with Sir Jonathan."

"Oh, I will," Locke assured her. "In the meantime, tell me what you know."

Aware that Scepter would give Locke the plain truth, Pete got in first. "We were checking out the building for spooks when we came across Bilko's body in the warehouse. Simple as that."

"Not that simple," Scepter disagreed. "It was my spirit guide who warned us to stay away from the stables."

Locke's features, already doubting, turned to a mask of disbelief. "Your spirit guide?"

Pete laughed at Locke's dumbfounded confusion. "Scepter's ghost even warned us about you. He said there was something nasty in the stables, and here you are. Isn't it nice to know the reputation of Chief Inspector Deadbolt has spread to the next world?"

The slight on his surname caused Locke's color to rise again. "I want the lot of you down the station, pronto, in separate cars."

His announcement wiped the grin from Pete's face, and immediately, Locke was buried in a chorus of protest from all three.

Scepter's voice got through above the clamor. "And what about Pete's car and our equipment?"

"Forensic will need to look it all over. It'll be impounded while we examine it."

Pete fumed. "For the last time, man, we had nothing to do with it!"

Locke smiled again: a smug smirk of evil satisfaction. "In that case, you won't mind us checking that out, will you? *Keynes!*"

The final word was shouted, and the three ghost hunters frowned at the apparent irrelevance of it, until the smartly-dressed officer came into the building.

"This," Locke announced, "is Detective Constable Andrea Keynes."

Pete almost fell over laughing. "I don't believe it," he chortled. "Locke and Key. If you get married, will your kids be padlocks? Hey, Keys, your first name isn't Dora, is it? D'yer gerrit? Eh? Dora Keys. Door keys."

She narrowed her dark eyes at him. "Watch it, Brennan. I've heard all about you and I'm not impressed. And it's Keynes, not Keys. K-E-Y-N-E-S."

"Andrea," Locke said, "take them down the station, and keep them in separate interview rooms, no visitors." He focused his satisfied features on Pete. "And if they ask for a lawyer, arrest them… on suspicion of murder."

⊰❦⊱

Led from the station cells, up a short flight of stairs and along a narrow corridor, Scepter glanced into an office and took in the gray daylight breaking through the far windows. All her possessions had been taken from her, including her wristwatch, but a wall clock told her it was just after 7:30 a.m.

A uniformed female officer escorted her to a cramped, tiny interview room where the Chief Inspector was checking through Scepter's possessions—her purse, her watch, the keys to the hall—and replacing them in a large, buff envelope as he finished with them. Alongside him, Keynes was busy filling out fresh forms. On the table, along the wall, stood a double cassette recorder. As Scepter took her seat, Locke pressed the start button and stated his name for the record. Keynes followed suit, after which Locke turned a benign smile upon her.

"It's Miss Rand, is it?"

"Rand-Epping," Scepter corrected him softly.

Her eyes followed Locke's pointing finger to the cassette recorder.

"You'll have to speak up, so we can record your responses."

Scepter cleared her throat. "My name is Lady Concepta Rand-Epping. My friends call me Scepter Rand."

"Unusual name," he chattered.

"When I was a child, I couldn't pronounce Concepta, so I shortened it to Scepter, and the name stuck." Now that Pete and Kevin were not here, the Chief Inspector seemed friendly enough.

"Part of the landed gentry, eh?" he asked.

Scepter began to wonder whether her friends had pegged Locke wrong. He was, after all, a civil servant, just doing his job.

She smiled, signaling her recognition of his interest. "The title is largely meaningless these days."

The smile faded from his ruddy features. "Damn right it means nothing. Not when I'm investigating a murder. I don't give a hoot if you're the Queen's niece, you'll answer my questions."

Perhaps, Scepter reflected silently, Pete was right after all.

Locke calmed a little. "You're the head ghost hunter, huh?"

She felt her temper rising. "I am not," she snapped primly. "I am a psychic, in touch with the Other Side."

"Yes," said the Chief Inspector, "so am I. The Other Side of human nature. And I want to know why you three killed an innocent young burglar like Steve Bilks."

"We didn't kill him," she argued. "He was dead when we found him."

Locke said nothing; Keynes, who had been noting down the main points of the interrogation, now paused and along with her superior, gazed expectantly across the table.

Scepter cleared her throat again. "My spirit guide told me something awful had happened and I was worried. Pete and I began to argue, Kevin got fed up and wandered off. That's when he found the poor boy."

"Your spirit guide?" asked Keynes. She sounded slightly less disbelieving than her chief, but her voice was still colored with doubt.

"My spirit guide is an old family retainer, Albert Fishwick," Scepter explained. "In life, he was butler and batman to my great-grandfather. He died during the first battle of the Somme, in 1916. He has been my constant companion since I was about eight."

Locke and Keynes exchanged cynical smiles.

"You really believe this stuff?" asked Keynes. Again there was the doubt, but it was tinged with a little more sincerity than Locke's sneer.

"It is not 'stuff,'" Scepter insisted. "It is reality. I work with Pete and Kevin, and Fishwick guides me."

The reality of her predicament wormed its way into Scepter's consciousness. She had heard of people pressed into admitting murder charges and then being invited to plead insanity, and for a terrible moment she believed that was the way these two officers were heading. They had a dead body, and they needed to clear it up quickly. What better way than accuse a woman who claimed to be in touch with her great-grandfather's dead butler?

Locke's next words quelled her immediate worries. "We know all about Brennan, and we're aware of the things Keeley gets up to," he grumbled. Before Scepter could challenge him, the Chief Inspector went on, "Wasn't 3:00 in the morning a strange time to be looking for ghosts?"

"No more absurd than one in the afternoon or during the rush hour, or do you imagine we have to wait until they're up and have had breakfast?" retorted Scepter. With the feeling that she had made her point, she went on, "I spoke to Sir Jonathan yesterday, and he authorized us to be at the hall anytime during the next few days." She pointed at the envelope containing her possessions. "That's how come I have the keys to Melmerby Manor."

"And Bilko interrupted you, did he?" demanded the Chief Inspector.

"Bilko?" Scepter disapproved. "Shouldn't you use his proper name, show a little respect for the deceased?"

"Leave the lessons in etiquette to Emily Post and answer my question," Locke demanded.

Scepter sighed. "No, he didn't interrupt us. We went out to investigate the stables and found him. The DVDs had gone missing and instead, we found him."

She saw Locke's ears prick up at that. "DVDs? What DVDs?"

⚜

Pete's biggest worry was that Scepter would do something stupid and tell Locke the unfettered truth.

His experience of the police force told him that when being interviewed it was better to say nothing at all rather than lie. Lies could be uncovered; no comment remained no comment.

His worries centered on the pirate DVDs. Knowing Locke as he did, he knew that if the Chief Inspector learned of the contraband, he would put two and two together and come up with five—five years each for Kevin and Pete, with a few added on for Scepter.

His worries came to a head when Locke and Keynes dragged him into an interview room and the Chief Inspector went immediately on the attack. "I've got you now, Brennan. Your friend Septic told us that you were guarding a truck-load of DVDs when Bilko walked in."

"Her name is Scepter."

Ignoring Pete's correction, Locke pressed for an answer. "Well?"

Pete would not be moved. "I just told you, her name is Scepter?"

Keynes butted in to prevent Locke's temper exploding. "Just admit it all, Brennan," she suggested. "You'll feel better."

Pete yawned. "Admit what? That her name is Scepter? I just did."

"Just shut up about her bloody name," Keynes demanded, "and tell us about the DVDs."

Pete heaved a sigh. So much for staying silent. "For a start, we weren't guarding them, we found them. And when we went back later in the night, they were gone, and so was Bilko —to La-la Land."

Locke ignored much of Pete's cynical response. "So what were these DVDs? Porn? Pirates?"

Pete had cause to revise his earlier opinion. There was a time to lie and this was it. "Dunno."

"Liar," Locke bit the accusation off.

"Prove it," Pete invited.

"I will when we study your video gear." Locke appeared to Pete as a man both triumphant and totally in control of the situation. "I always said I'd get you, Brennan, and now I have. Copyright infringement, production and selling of illegal recordings, and murder."

In for a penny, in for a pound, thought Pete. "You missed out assaulting a police officer."

Locke was overjoyed. "I didn't even know about that."

"Because," Pete spat on his knuckles, "it hasn't happened yet." He pointed at the door. "That lump of wood has more brains than you. It's there to do a job and it does it. It opens and closes when we want it to. Now why don't you start doing your job before I knock your head against the door and see if I can drill any of its intelligence into you?"

Locke ignored the threat and carried on with his list of potential charges. "There's also trespass—"

"We were authorized to be at Melmerby Manor," Pete interrupted.

"You were authorized to go looking for spooks according to Speccy Brand—"

"Scepter Rand," Pete corrected.

"Whoever," Locke snarled. "You weren't supposed to be ferreting round the warehouse seeing what you could nick. Who did these DVDs belong to? Jimmy Tate?"

Pete decided a lie was in order yet again. "Dunno. I was gonna follow it up when we got home, this morning, but Bilko's body persuaded me I'd better ring you instead. And let me tell you something, Locke, you're gonna look a total idiot when your forensic boys tell you I never touched Bilko, and you have to stand there with your broken arm, apologizing to me."

"I don't have a broken arm."

"The door will soon put that right." Pete sat forward, leaning on the tabletop. "Now get your brain in gear, man, and let us out of here so we can all start looking for the real killer."

Locke pointed a shaking finger at Pete. "*If* I decide to let you go, you will mind your own business."

"While you carry on accusing me?" Pete sneered. "Not likely."

Locke drummed irritable fingers on the table. He looked at Keynes, who raised her eyebrows and gave a half-shrug of defeat.

"The trouble with questioning ex-cops, guv," she pointed out, "is that they know the form."

Pete gave her a round of applause. "There's a girl with sense. You could go far, Ms. Keynes. Especially if you have dinner with me."

Andrea ignored his suggestion, and asked, "You never saw Bilko all night?"

"Not until we found him in the warehouse," Pete confirmed.

"Even though you had the place covered with video cameras?" she pressed.

"We didn't have the stables covered." Pete waved at the stack of papers in front of her. "You have all this in my statement. I've nothing to add to it."

The two police officers went into a hurried and whispered discussion. Pete knew what they were doing: deciding whether or not to release him. A moment later, Locke focused on him. "All right, you can go... for now. But I'm warning you, Brennan, you learn anything, you bring it to me."

⚜

Heavy clouds, coupled with low temperatures, threatened snow over the town when they finally emerged from the police station just after 9:00 a.m.

Scepter yawned. "I need some sleep."

"Breakfast first, I think," suggested Kevin.

"The Germ Factory?" asked Pete.

Kevin grinned broadly. "The Germ Factory."

Pete hailed a taxi, which swerved violently into the curb alongside them. He opened the door and let Scepter in, and Kevin nipped round the far side to join them on the back seat.

"The Germ Factory," Pete ordered the driver.

"How is it everyone knows it by that name?" asked Scepter as the driver pulled away. She had become a regular at the place since moving in with them, but she had never taken a taxi in Ashdale and had not realized that even the cab drivers knew the place by its sobriquet.

Pete laughed. "It's always been The Germ Factory. Even when I was a kid."

The Germ Factory was the affectionate name for Wilf's Café, situated on the ring road surrounding the Cranley Estate. Wilf Mannion ran the joint with his wife Sheila, and, as Pete explained, he was known for his easy approach to life. Even when Environmental Health prosecuted him for trying to pass off dog food as stewing steak, he simply claimed he bought the cans without labels as a job lot from an unnamed source.

Kevin had good cause to be grateful to Wilf on that occasion, since he was the unnamed source in question.

"I actually helped him unload the boxes from his van into the café." Pete smiled at the memory.

Scepter disapproved. "Kevin, how could you sell dog food as fit for human consumption?"

"I didn't," protested Kevin. "I thought it was stewing steak, too."

"So you mean the tins had no labels when you bought them?"

"Exactly," affirmed Pete, still chuckling. "Mind you, it says something for the stomachs in this area when Wilf's homemade meat and potato pie, containing the finest horsemeat this side of a Grand National aftermath, was the most popular dish on the menu, and nobody twigged until the nosy-parkers from the health department took a few tins away for analysis."

The rush hour was over, the roads were free and clear, and the taxi made rapid progress to the Cranley area. Scepter stared out at the leaden sky. Working class cafes were a world away from garden parties and afternoon tea on the lawn.

Bringing herself away from memories of a contented childhood, she asked, "Pete, what's the story with you and Locke?"

His features clouded. "I'd rather not talk about it."

Scepter smiled encouragingly. "We're supposed to be business partners. It would be nice to know where one's partner is coming from."

Pete did not answer, but instead stared grimly out at the rain, lost to his memories just as she had been.

The taxi driver pulled into the curb outside The Germ Factory, where Kevin handed over the fare before they climbed out and hurried into the café, out of the rain.

Pete and Kevin had been regulars at The Germ Factory for years, and since moving in with them, Scepter, too, had become known to the proprietor, who had even gone to the trouble of stocking health foods for her.

"At least they look like health foods," Pete had once commented. "Knowing Wilf, they could be rabbit food, and I wouldn't know the difference unless I saw Benjamin Bunny nuzzling the packet."

Wilf looked surprised, but was, as always, pleased to see them. "You're not normally up until lunchtime."

"Long story, Wilf," said Pete. "Remind me to tell you about it some time. We'll have two bacon sandwiches for me, a full breakfast for Kev and a bowl of muesli for Scepter. Kevin'll pay."

Wilf passed the order through a hatch to his wife, then began to pour tea for them.

"How come it's always my turn to pay?" Kevin complained

"You're the only one with any money," Pete reminded him, "and I don't think Wilf'll give me credit."

Wilf confirmed it. "I trust in God, but everyone else pays cash." He passed the mugs of hot tea across the counter and took Kevin's money. "Sit you down, I'll bring your food over when it's ready."

They took a table by the window. Kevin picked up one of Wilf's complimentary newspapers and puzzled briefly over the sports headlines on the back pages until he realized it was the previous day's. "Hey Wilf, what happened to today's papers?"

"Nobody's left any behind yet," the proprietor called back.

With a grunt about tight-fisted businessmen, Kevin skimmed through the newspaper. "Look at that," he said suddenly, pointing to a small article on one of the inside pages. "Some bloke has set a record by eating twenty-seven meat pies at one sitting. Amateur. I bet I could have gone to thirty."

Neither of his colleagues was listening. Scepter toyed with a menu while Pete continued to stare moodily through rain-streaked windows.

"I'm sorry," Scepter said suddenly to Pete.

Her apology brought him out of his thoughts. "Huh?"

"My question about you and Chief Inspector Locke. I didn't mean to upset you."

"Oh, right," said Pete. "You didn't upset me. You just reminded me, and when I think of it, I always get angry."

She smiled encouragement. "Want to talk about it?"

He gave a heavy sigh, took a swallow of tea and shook his head.

Kevin studied Pete and thought better of opening another can of worms. To distract Scepter's attention from Pete's antipathy for Chief Inspector Locke, he asked, "What are we gonna do about getting our gear back from plod?"

"Stop worrying about it," Pete advised. "We'll get it back when they've finished all their tests."

"Well," said Scepter, in agreement with Kevin, "our investigation won't go much further without it all, and we need to go back to the manor later this week to concentrate on those areas we may have missed."

Kevin shook his head. "If you think I'm going anywhere near that place again, you've another—"

The arrival of their food shut him up.

"By the way, Kev," announced Wilf as he placed their orders before them, "had a mate of yours in yesterday. Asked me to ask you to call on him when you had the time."

Kev tucked heartily into his bacon and eggs. "Who?"

"Ronnie Wilcox. Summat about some whiskey."

Kevin blanched and almost choked on his food.

Pete glowered at him. "Whiskey? What are you doing selling whiskey to Ronnie Wilcox?"

"Who's Ronnie Wilcox?" asked Scepter.

Kevin chewed on his food again. "Just a bitta business, Pete."

"Tell me more," Pete ordered.

"Who's Ronnie Wilcox?"

"I got hold of this consignment of whiskey from Latvia," Kevin ploughed on over Scepter's question.

"Scotch? From Latvia?" Pete sounded dubious.

Kevin nodded. "Old Sporran it was called. 50 cases, 40 quid a case. Two grand. Easy money. Ronnie was made up with the deal."

"Who's Ronnie Wilcox?"

"So why does he want to see you?" This time it was Pete who rode over Scepter's question.

Kevin swallowed a large bite of sausage and laughed nervously. "Well, see, the whiskey might have passed through a light shower on its way across from Latvia."

Pete stared in disapproval. "You mean it was watered down?"

"It says 40 proof on the label," said Kevin with a glum nod. "I think they might have added one zero too many. It was more water than whiskey."

"And now Wilcox wants his cash back."

Scepter came in forcefully as the conversation flagged. "Will someone tell me who the hell is Ronnie Wilcox?"

Pete bit into a bacon roll. "He runs Flutter-Bys, Ashdale's premier night-club-cum-dump, and has a nice little sideline in anything and everything that's crooked, including knocked-off booze, hooky betting, loan sharking and pimping. And oddly enough, I was there yesterday."

"Nice class of person, in other words," commented Scepter. "And is he really anyone to worry about?"

"Everyone is scared of him but for one man," said Pete, aiming a finger at his own chest. "Me." He swallowed half his mug of tea. "When I was a DC, I lifted him and his goons more times than you've had your knickers—"

"Thank you Pete, I get the picture. And now you say he wants his money back?"

Kevin agreed. "Seems likely. Pete, will you see him for me?"

Scepter reached across and touched Kevin's hand. "I'll come with you if you want, Kevin. Talk to him. He can't be that bad."

"Can't he?" demanded Pete. "If he doesn't get his money back, Wilcox is likely to have Kev concreted into the next motorway bridge."

"Yes, but it's two grand Pete," Kevin whined.

"So take it out of the bank and pay him back," Pete suggested.

"It never went in the bank. I used it yesterday to pay Bent Benny for the gear we used at Melmerby Manor."

Pete shrugged. "In that case, take it out of one of your secret accounts and give him it back."

"Aw, Pete—"

"No arguments. When we've finished breakfast, we go to the bank, you draw the cash, and we go see Wilcox. I want a word with him anyway. Flutter-Bys is the last place Bilko was seen alive."

9

From The Germ Factory, they took a taxi home. The two men left Scepter to catch up on her sleep, while they took Kevin's van down to Flutter-Bys. When Groom let them in, they found Wilcox cleaning glasses, while Lawson and Wilcox's wife Sylvie were generally helping to ready the place for opening.

Once upon a time, Wilcox's wife had been a good-looking woman, but her lifestyle of booze and unsociable hours had taken its toll, leaving her with a large girth, narrow shoulders, and spindly legs. A large scar on her cheek, picked up in a fight, hadn't helped, either. It had left her with the face of a professional boxer, and a lazy eye that looked like a boxer's after 10 rounds. It was an acceptable analogy for most people because Sylvie was equipped with fists like a boxer's as well, and she packed a punch many a welterweight would envy.

On Pete and Kevin's arrival, all work ceased, and the pair found themselves hemmed in near the bar. Groom and Lawson kept out of range of Pete's long arms, while Sylvie moved in close, keeping Kevin between her and the ex-cop.

"Well, if it isn't Little and Large," laughed Wilcox. "Again."

Pete was in no mood for Wilcox's usual bravado. "Shut it, nurk, or I'll make it so you'll be checking the beer barrels from the inside."

"Tough talk, Brennan, but you're outnumbered again. And as if that's not enough, you brought this tub of lard with you. You must like testing the handicapper."

Pete was tired of the constant, immaterial threats. "I've warned you once, this is twice, don't push me a third time. You were asking for Kevin at The Germ Factory?"

Wilcox held up a bottle of whiskey. The label showed a piper in jacket and kilt. Above the image was the label, *Old Sporran*. "He sold me forty cases of this crap." Wilcox pointed an accusing finger at Kevin. "I've drunk cola with more clout. I want shot of all those bottles of water, and I want my money back."

Pete snapped his fingers, and, choking back a sob, Kevin handed over the money.

"I was saving that money for my old age," Kevin complained.

"Try to screw me over again," Wilcox warned, "and you won't have an old age."

"Don't make threats you can't back up," Pete advised as he handed the money to Wilcox. "There's your cash back. Do what you like with the bottles. We don't wanna see them again."

"Hang on, hang on," protested the other. "It's not that simple, is it? I took that booze in good faith. He's had my cash, he's used it, now I want it back... with interest."

"Okay," Pete agreed, and Kevin looked momentarily more worried. "Here's my offer. You take your money back, you get to keep the bottles, and I don't rip out your jawbone and use it as a novelty can opener."

If Wilcox was worried, he didn't show it. Causally, he lit a cigar and leaned on the beer pumps. "Get this straight, Brennan. Unless I pick up another five hundred, the filth might get to know about the alleged booze he flogged me."

Pete was as unworried as Wilcox. "If they do," he promised, "they might also get to know about the loaded roulette wheel and marked cards in your gaming room. You take your money and shut it."

Wilcox's face turned a deep shade of red as his temper rose. He looked at Groom and Lawson. Groom's forehead still showed the marks from his meeting with Pete the previous day. He decided not to press his luck till his keepers were back in form. "I won't forget this, Brennan."

"You'd better, because if you don't, I'll try out the world's first brain transplant and *make* you forget." Wilcox pocketed the money and Pete went on, "Now, you recall I asked about Bilko yesterday? Well, I found him. Or rather, Kevin did."

"I'm happy for you," scowled Wilcox. "Give him my regards."

"He's dead."

Groom, Lawson and Sylvie exchanged haunted glances. Wilcox merely shrugged. "And?"

"Ronnie," suggested Kevin in an effort to counsel the club owner, "I wouldn't upset Pete if I were you. We've had a bad night, he hasn't had much kip, and he might just take it out on your place." He looked around the dimly lit, shabby room. "I mean as dumps go, it's never been the best, but you do keep a nice beer."

"Well, thanks a lot, Keeley," sneered Wilcox. "I really must get you to work on my publicity."

"Cut the cackle," Pete snapped. "Someone was fooling us around last night, Ronnie, and I wanna know who."

Wilcox held up his hands, palms upwards, as if demonstrating his innocence. "Why should that have anything to do with us?"

"Because whoever it was used a heavy van, like yours, and one of them wore high-heeled shoes, like hers." He pointed at Sylvie's feet and the pair of spiky heeled shoes she was wearing. "Only not like hers. These were more block heels." He looked over Groom and Lawson. "Does either of your muppets go in for cross-dressing?"

The two men appeared outraged; Wilcox merely sneered in silence. Sylvie examined her nails, then leered at Pete. "It's not wise to make accusations, Brennan. It could get you a good kicking."

Pete looked at her and winced. He had dragged corpses from wrecked cars that were better looking. "You know something," he said, "my worst nightmare is getting drunk and waking up next to you or Kev. At a pinch, I'd say Kev would be is the lesser of two evils. And as for you and the Two Stooges here giving me a good kicking, dream on. Push me and I'll hammer the three of you." He ran his eyes over her face, which reminded him less of a horse than of a buffalo. "Normally, I don't hit women, but I'd make an exception in your case because I'm not sure you *are* a woman." He turned back to Wilcox. "Well?"

"I told you yesterday, I don't know nothing. Now get outta here."

Pete pointed a threatening finger. "You hear anything, you call me. If you don't, I'll come back, and the only way you'll get away is to pre-book your ambulance. Come on, Kev. I don't like the smell in here."

❦

When Pete got up just after four that afternoon, it was to find Scepter watching TV.

"Pete," she called, "when do we get our computers and cameras and so on back from the police?"

He went to the kitchen to make tea. "I told you, later today or, looking at the time, probably tomorrow." He returned to the living room, placed a beaker of weak tea before her, and a stronger mug for himself. "They need to check everything, especially the videos, to see whether we caught Bilko and his killers on them by chance. What's the rush, anyway? They're not gonna show anything."

Scepter promptly disagreed. "There's the orb on the upper landing as you entered the attics, the rocking horse, and I'd like to get a look at the business with Kevin when he was making tea. The video camera in the cafeteria was set on wide angle and I'm sure we'll have caught it."

Pete grinned. "Which is more than Kev did with the spoon. Scepter, I've told you what happened."

"No," she disagreed, "you've told us what you *think* happened."

Not disposed to argue, Pete changed the subject. "Have you told Kev we have to go back there for another night?"

"I mentioned it in passing, if you remember, when we were at the café, but I haven't pressed it. I didn't want to scare him. We can work on him together when he gets back."

Pete chuckled. "He was always the same. I've seen puppies with more bottle." He sipped his tea and glanced around the room. "Where is he, by the way?"

Scepter shrugged and drank her tea. "He went out about half an hour ago. Said he had to see some man about some money."

Pete looked sharply at her. "Which man?"

"I dunno. Tate or someone."

"Jimmy and Johnny Tate?" There was a sense of urgency about Pete's words.

"Yes. That's them."

Pete's face became worried. He reached for his jacket. "I'd better get over there."

"What? Why?" Now Scepter was worried.

"I've just saved him from one gangster, and he's gone out to see another. Tate and his brother will kill Kev if he tries to take them for money."

❧

Kevin had been brooding all afternoon. The police may well have found the *Mind Games III* DVD he had nicked from the warehouse, although neither Locke nor Keynes mentioned it when they questioned him. He had left it on the table near their computer equipment. Well, if his copy was gone, Pete still had Bilko's in the flat and he and Pete were best buddies. Pete wouldn't mind him borrowing it for a few hours. Just long enough to prize a reward from the Tates.

Booting up his cell phone, he had found an unread text message. When he opened it, he read a single word, *WGJAMW,* and puzzled over it for a moment. He checked the source number from which it had been sent and did not recognize it.

"Damned spammers," he had cursed, and deleted it. "What the hell does it mean anyway? Wigjam? Doesn't make sense."

The instrument's directory was filled with contact numbers, amongst which was Jimmy Tate's. Kevin made a quick call and a few minutes later hurried out the door, making his excuses to Scepter.

The journey from the Cranley Estate to the more exclusive suburbs of West Ashdale would normally take about ten minutes, but a combination of Kevin's aging van and rush hour traffic doubled that time, and it was quite dark by the time he pulled through the electrically operated, wrought iron gates.

The house was a large, rambling place at the top of a long tarmac drive, surrounded by well-tended lawns and shrubbery. Pulling up in front of the faded brown door, Kev noticed that, for all its location on the main road out of Ashdale, he could see and hear very little street sounds. It did not trouble him. He understood that for a man who had made himself a millionaire turning out pirate copies of blockbuster movies and computer games right here in this place, privacy was vital.

When he rang the doorbell, it was opened not by Jimmy but by his younger brother, Johnny, dressed in jeans, trainers and tee shirt. Johnny had a reputation for being fast with his temper and fists.

"Keeley?"

"The same."

"Follow me."

Johnny closed and locked the door after them, and as they passed along the narrow hall, it occurred to Kev that if Jimmy Tate really was a millionaire as he claimed to be, he certainly didn't live like one. The walls were covered with cheap wallpaper, which had been painted pale green to match the outer door, the floorboards, which creaked as they walked along, were covered with a dirty, threadbare carpet, and the only lighting came from a naked, overhead, 60-watt bulb. Kevin glanced into the front room as he passed and saw it littered with computers, video and audio equipment, some still in the manufacturer's boxes, while the walls were lined with CDs in racks. That was obviously where the pirate copies were produced 20 or 30 at a time.

They passed into a rear dining room—and Kevin promptly changed his mind about how Tate lived. It was as lavishly furnished as Melmerby Manor. A huge copy of Constable's Salisbury Cathedral hung above an ornate fireplace; there was a polished mahogany occasional table which gleamed like a mirror and two, three-seater divans. Jimmy sat on one, and Kevin noticed that he took up almost all of it.

A big man in every sense of the word, he was dressed in a pair of blue shorts and a huge red tee shirt and had a three-day growth of beard. Even reclining, he had a waistline that called to mind the M25: slow moving, enclosing London, and likely to take all day to get around. Men of such a size always left Kevin feeling comfortable with his own weight. He had promised himself that he would do something about his increasing waistline long before he got close to Jimmy Tate's league.

"Decide whether you're going to get our guest a beer, Johnny," Jimmy invited, and the younger, slimmer brother moved behind Kevin. "Sit down, Keeley."

Kevin took a seat on the armchair opposite. "I think you know a mate of mine. Pete Brennan."

Jimmy gave a fat chuckle. "Detective Constable Brennan?"

Kevin's eyes lit, and he smiled broadly. "That's him. We go way back, me and Pete. In fact, we're in business together. Ghost hunting."

Kevin became aware that Johnny had never left the room, and that there was no sign of his beer.

"So Brennan's involved in this rip-off too?" asked Jimmy.

Kevin began to worry. "Rip-off? I dunno what you mean."

Abruptly, Jimmy brought up the subject of business. "You mentioned *Mind Games III*?"

Nervously, Kevin nodded. "Any danger of that beer?"

"Johnny hasn't moved, so he hasn't decided yet," said Jimmy, "but we'll get to it in good time; when we get thirsty. Now what about *Mind Games III*?" When Kevin did not answer, Tate strained to heave his giant frame forward in his seat. "See, Keeley, I didn't get to be one of the biggest pirate producers in the country by being taken for a mug by cruds like you. In my book even *knowing* about *Mind Games III* makes you guilty. There are only a select few people who know about it. You're not one of that select few, so there's only one way you coulda got to know about it. You stole my DVDs."

Jimmy struggled to get to his feet. It would take time for that blubbery frame to bring itself erect, and when it did, Jimmy would give the order to pound him. Kevin calculated that he had only a minute or so before they began to beat him up. Before he could make a dash for it, Johnny, who was still standing behind him, placed his hands on Kevin's shoulders, pressing him more deeply into his seat and effectively pinning him. Kevin began to sweat. Not for the first time in his life, he had got himself into a spot of bother, and this time there was no Pete Brennan to help him out of it.

But Jimmy held off on the order. "Two days ago," he said, finally getting all the way out of his seat, "some thieving git nicked those DVDs from my warehouse. I want them back, and if you know where they are, you're gonna tell me."

Unable to get out of his seat, Kevin trembled with fear. "Well, there must be a reward out for finding them."

"There is," Jimmy agreed, blocking out the view behind him. "You tell me where they are and you get to stay in one piece."

Kevin weighed his options. He was trapped, without his hero chum to help him, and he had no weapons. Correction. He had one weapon. Summoning up as much energy as he could, he broke wind.

"For God's sake..." Johnny's complaint trailed off. He released Kevin and turned away, his stomach heaving at the foul stench.

Jimmy Tate, too, backed off to avoid the smell, and Kevin launched himself, head-butting the elder Tate in the gut. He almost disappeared into the huge, bloated belly. Jimmy fell back onto his settee, and Kevin ran for it.

He did not get far. Johnny stuck out a foot, bringing Kevin crashing to the carpet, banging his head on the corner of the coffee table. The last thing he saw before he blacked out was Jimmy's huge frame towering over him.

❧

Pete drove Scepter's Fiat Punto up to the closed gates of the Tates' house, told Scepter to get into the driver's seat and to bring the car in when he opened up. Then he climbed the tall iron gates, dropped nimbly down the other side and yanked them open.

"Why didn't you open them from the outside?" she asked.

"They're electrically operated from the house," he explained, getting into the passenger seat, "and Tate would never open them for me." He let Scepter drive up to the door and park behind Kevin's van, and, with a nod, indicated that she should kill the engine.

"Jimmy has every way in and out of the house covered with CCTV," he said, gesturing up at a camera above the door. "They'll be watching us now, waiting to see which door I go for. I'll ring the bell, and Johnny Tate will come to lock it. While he's doing that, I'll leg it round the back and catch them there. Give me a minute and follow me to the back."

She nodded; he climbed out of the car, walked to the front door and rang the bell. A second later, he heard the chain being applied. He ran for the corner of the building, zipped round the side and arrived at the back door just as Johnny was trying to lock it.

Pete burst in, grabbed the younger Tate by the shirt and forced him back into the house. There was a momentary tussle while Tate tried to break Pete's grip, but although they were of similar height, Johnny's physique was slimmer, Pete's more powerful. He swung Johnny round and slammed him into the wall. "Where's Kev Keeley?"

"I dunno—"

Pete silenced Johnny's denial with two sharp slaps across the cheeks. "Listen to me, Tate, your rep as a hard man doesn't cut any ice with me. Kevin's van is outside the front door. It may be a piece of crap, but he loves it and wouldn't even park it in a scrap yard unless he had business there. Now either tell me where he is, or I'll tear you into strips and feed you to the your own fish." He nodded at large fish tank on the side wall.

Behind them, Scepter ambled in through the open door. Johnny cast a glance in her direction. Pete glanced, too, then realized it was a stupid thing to do when Johnny took advantage of the distraction to throw a punch.

Pete raised his left arm and stopped the blow. With a smile, he head-butted the younger Tate, sending him crashing to the floor.

Shaken, his aplomb gone, dragged back to his feet by Pete, Johnny conceded defeat and led the way through to the palatial living room where the obese Jimmy stood over the unconscious Kevin.

One look at his friend and Pete's normally placid features became a mask of fury. The huge mass of fat and hair that was Jimmy Tate backed off, looking worried.

"You're dead meat, Tate!" Pete screamed, removing his windjammer to bare his powerful arms and fists. "I'll sell that blubber as cooking fat."

"Cool it, Brennan," said Jimmy. "It wasn't us."

"Honest," Johnny seconded. "Your mate got worried, legged it and fell."

"Why was he worried?" Pete demanded. "Because you threatened him, Johnny? Well now *you* can worry, because you're dead." Pete smacked one fist into his open palm.

Jimmy Tate forced calm onto his fat features. He smiled. "You watch it, Brennan. Remember, I still have that tape of you and Nicky."

The air of false confidence did not fool Pete. Beneath it, he knew, both Tates were seriously worried for their safety.

"Won't work, fat man. I got fired a year ago and Locke didn't need your help to do it." He was satisfied by the way in which Jimmy's slobbery mouth fell open, like a man suddenly faced with the barrel of a loaded gun, confronted with the awful realization of his own mortality. Pete flexed his biceps. "Now, say your prayers, Tubby, you're about lose some weight."

Jimmy succumbed to total panic. He looked to his younger brother, but Johnny was transfixed with fear, his eyes fastened on Pete's furious features and larger frame. He turned and ran for it, but his huge body would not permit him to go at more than a fast waddle. In abject terror, Jimmy shuffled towards the door. Pete ran after him. Snapping out of his trance-like state, Johnny moved between them. Pete hurled him out of the way, carried on to catch Jimmy at the door and slammed the fat man up against the frame, which shook in protest. Pinned against the wall, Jimmy Tate could do nothing but tremble and sweat.

"Detective Constable Brennan," came a new voice. "Long time since you and me have seen more of each other." Pete turned to see Nicky Tate ambling down the stairs and flashing him a seductive smile.

Jimmy's wife was many years younger than her husband. A pert and sexy former actress, she had a way of carrying herself that made every movement of her body, from the wiggle of her hips to the deliberate pout of her mouth, seem like an invitation to dalliance.

Pete wasn't buying it. "Forget it, whore," he snapped. "Say goodbye to your old man. I'm about to top him."

Behind Pete, Scepter sized up Tate's wife and then ran her gaze over Pete, as if she were working out what had happened between the two in the past, especially in light of Jimmy's reference to a tape, which he had made sound like an instrument of blackmail. She focused on her business partner. "Pete," she suggested gently, "let's calm down and listen to what Mr. Tate and his brother have to say."

Looking disappointed, Pete did not immediately posture down. All day he had been seeking an outlet for his frustration at having been arrested and questioned by the police.

Scepter smiled sweetly. "If you're not happy, you can always beat them up afterwards."

At that, her partner relaxed sufficiently that Jimmy was able to free himself from Pete's grip. Relieved that the immediate heat had been taken out of the situation, he looked her up and down with an appreciative, eye, and licked his lips. "Well, hello, my honey," he purred. "A heavenly bit of totty like you could be living with a millionaire this time next week."

Scepter took in his bloated frame and shuddered. "Thank you, but no."

Nicky scowled. "You're already married to me, Fatso, or had your forgotten?"

Jimmy chuckled. "Sorry, Nicky. Only joking."

On the floor, Kevin stirred. Scepter knelt beside him. His eyes flickered open. He gazed into hers and smiled as if he were being confronted by an angelic vision.

"Am I in Heaven?" he asked dreamily.

"You'll be in Hell when I get you out of here," Pete warned. The smile faded quickly from Kevin's lips as he realized more people than Scepter were in the room.

"Now I remember." He sat upright and glared at Jimmy, then at Johnny, then stared in surprise at his partners. "Pete, Scepter, how did you get here?"

"We beamed down from the Starship Enterprise," Pete grumbled. "How do you think we got here, you clod?"

Scepter stroked Kevin's brow with gentle fingers. "We were worried about you, Kevin. Pete thought you might have been walking into trouble."

Kevin's face wobbled indignantly. He glowered again at Jimmy. "You were gonna beat the crap out of me, Tubby."

"Tubby?" said Johnny with an eye on Kevin's expanding waistline. "That's smart, coming from you. Talk about the kettle calling the pot."

"Calm down," Scepter urged and turned to Jimmy. "Mr. Tate, Kevin came here to talk to you about a load of DVDs we found last night at—"

Kevin put a finger to her lips to shush her, and stared at Jimmy. "How much for me to keep my gob shut, Jimmy?"

Pete was on the point of losing his temper again. "Will someone tell me what's going on before I wreck this place?"

Jimmy sat down again, the settee groaning under the load. Nicky sat next to him, almost invisible in his giant shadow. "You mean you genuinely don't know?"

"I wouldn't be asking, if I knew, would I?" Pete pointed out.

Jimmy eyed his younger brother. "Johnny, get some beers, will you?" To Pete he said, "Sit down, Brennan, and I'll tell you a story."

"I don't wanna hear your stories, Tate."

"Pete," Scepter soothed, "let's hear Mr. Tate out."

Pete conceded; Johnny returned, handed out cans of lager, and the fat man began.

"I've just finished producing the *Mind Games III* copies, right? I've got 25,000 advance orders, which means a clear profit of 50 thou'. The entire load is stashed at my lockup, all ready for shipping out. Then, a coupla nights back, someone raided my drum and nicked the flicking lot."

"You didn't have them insured?" Scepter wanted to know.

Jimmy looked at her with a strained expression on his chubby features. "Where do you get insurance on a lorry load of illegal pirate movies?"

"As opposed to legal pirate movies," riposted Kevin.

"Surely your drum was alarmed?" Pete asked.

Jimmy hedged. "Well... after a fashion."

Pete understood immediately. "You mean a dummy bell box?"

Scepter frowned. "What's a dummy bell box?"

"A dummy bell box," Kevin explained, "is what it suggests. You have an alarm box on the outside wall of the building, but no works inside it. The place looks as if it's alarmed, but it isn't."

"I did have security on the job," Jimmy defended himself. "Sherlock's."

Pete groaned. "Tony Holmes?"

Jimmy slurped his lager. "That's him. Worked for one of the pukka companies before he set up on his own."

"He served time four years back," Pete said. "The only reason he could set up in security was because Kevin here and Wilf Mannion between them cooked up—no pun intended—a false background for him."

Jimmy's face fell. "Oh," was the only comment he made.

"Well, I must say, Jimmy," commented Kevin, sipping his beer, "for a businessman, you've got all the acumen of a total berk." He placed a finger to his temple and turned it several times, indicating his opinion of Tate's sanity. "No alarm on your lockup, and you use an out-and-out crook like Sherlock for security."

"He was cheap, right? I didn't become a millionaire by throwing money about." Jimmy gulped down the rest of his can and cracked another.

"Did you not report the theft to the police, Mr. Tate?" Scepter asked.

Jimmy looked at her, then at Pete. "Where do you get them, Brennan?"

"Scepter is a cut above me and you, Tate. She's a real Countess."

"Well, my naïve little bit of upper crust totty, how interested do you think the law would be in a load of stolen pirate DVDs? They'd do me for producing them." He turned once more to Pete. "Anyway, the minute it all went missing, I put the word out on the street. Five grand to whoever can turn it up. But I only let the—er—*right* people know. The underground bods. That's why, when *you* turned up, Keeley, I knew you shouldn't have known, and that's why I figured you'd nicked them."

"A few nights back, Bilko rang us," Nicky took up the story, "and he said he had a lead on them, but we haven't seen him since."

"You know what a mouth almighty Bilko is," said Johnny. "You can't always trust him, and I figure he was just mouthing off. He wanted the reward money, and he didn't know nothing."

Jimmy summed it all up. "If you tell me where they are, the reward money is yours."

"Bit difficult," Pete admitted, having finally calmed down. "We know where they *were*—Melmerby Manor—but they disappeared again. And by the way, Johnny, you're wrong. Bilko must have known something because he was topped." Pete paused briefly to let his words sink in. "We found his body at Melmerby Manor, and whoever left him there took the DVDs."

Johnny displayed no emotion; Nicky looked shocked and Jimmy disappointed.

"Tell me you're joking," groaned the fat man.

"Would I joke about something like that?" Pete demanded

"Probably. You used to be plod, and you coppers always have an odd sense of humor."

Pete ignored the jibe. "Bilko must have found something because the DVD Kevin brought you didn't come from Melmerby Manor. I found it at Bilko's drum the other night."

Jimmy scowled. "Angie mentioned you'd been there."

"Bilko didn't give you any clues as to what he knew?" Pete wanted to know.

Jimmy shook his head. "Nicky told you, I put the word out on the street, he rang and said he'd heard whispers in Flutter-Bys. Other than that, I know nothing, but the deal still stands: you find them and the five grand is yours."

❧

From the Tates' house, they drove back to the flat, where they left Kevin's van, and using Scepter's Fiat, drove to the Crown and Anchor, and spent much of the evening discussing the turn of events until they called it a night at 10:00.

"I can't drive," objected Kevin, unwrapping a bar of chocolate. He broke off a large chunk and put it in his mouth. "I've had three lagers," he pleaded in the light of their disapproving glances.

"So have I," complained Pete.

"Yeah, but you've got friends on the force."

Scepter took the keys from them. "I'll drive," she said and climbed behind the wheel. "It's my car anyway."

She climbed behind the wheel, Kevin got in the back and Pete sat himself in the passenger seat, next to Scepter. "Pete," she asked as they drove away from the pub towards the Cranley Estate, "when you were arguing with Jimmy Tate he said he still had the tape of you and Nicky, and you said it wouldn't work because you'd been fired. I presume he was blackmailing you."

Pete's features darkened at the memory. "Don't ask."

Scepter clucked. "There's a lot about you that you're not telling me."

"How do we go about finding the DVDs?" asked Kevin to change the subject.

"Easy peasy," said Pete, happy for the distraction. "I was a detective, you know."

Kevin snorted at Pete's assertion. "According to Locke, you couldn't detect a smell in a bunged up lavatory."

"Neither can you with a broken nose."

Kevin fell for it once more. "I don't have a broken nose."

"Yet."

Kevin swallowed the last of his chocolate and reached for a cigarette. Lighting it, tossing the pack on the seat, he gave a disdainful sniff. "Okay, Hercules Parrott, where do we start?"

"We call on Sherlock, the most crooked security guard in town."

Silence fell, punctuated only by the uneven purr of the engine and the swish of wipers on the screen. Scepter peered through the rain, concentrating on her driving.

Light began to grow in her rear view mirror. She checked and saw a pair of headlights gaining on them with a speed that dizzied her. Scepter eased her speed and tucked in tight to the curb to give the car room to overtake. The lights grew larger as the car approached, but the driver made no effort to pass.

"Damned tailgaters," she cursed. To take her mind off the erratic driver, she said, "May I remind you that we still have a haunted house to deal with?"

"Frankly," Kevin said, "I'm glad to be out of the place."

"We have to put our findings together, Kevin. Run through all the videos, see what we can see, and then—" She took a deep breath. "—We have to go back." She glanced in the mirror. The vehicle behind hung dangerously close to her bumper. Scepter wound down her window and irritably waved him round.

The combination of shock and his cigarette caused Kevin to have a violent coughing fit. Getting his breathing under control, he gasped, "Go back? Scepter, let *me* remind *you*, that Henry Melmerby had it in for me, and I told you before, no way am I going back to that place."

"Kevin—"

Scepter never finished what she was about to say. The lights of the car behind, which had been growing steadily brighter, suddenly blazed on high beam, and there was a tremendous bang as it rammed them.

She struggled with the steering wheel. "What the—?"

The car rammed them again. Scepter's head snapped back and she emitted an angry cry of pain.

"What's he doing?" cried Kevin.

"Maybe he doesn't like Scepter's bumper stickers," Pete said while she fought a battle with the steering wheel. He reached across and steadied it for her. "Swap places!" he ordered. Still gripping the wheel, he half stood. Scepter sneaked under him, wriggled over the gear lever and settled into the passenger seat, drawing the seat belt across her midriff. Pete, meanwhile, dropped into the driver's seat, changed down a gear and hammered the gas pedal to the floor. Behind them, the crazed vehicle came with them, its bumper ramming theirs and giving them another sharp jab in the back.

"Do something!" Kevin panicked. "Wave him round."

"I'd have to wind the window down and it's too cold," snapped Pete, his sarcasm lost on Kevin.

They came into the residential area of the Cranley Estate, the street lined with houses on both sides. Pete's mind was ahead of the game. Residential property meant parked cars, even if they were only parked on one side of the road.

Even as he thought of it, a parked lorry appeared in the dim street lighting a couple of hundred meters ahead. The rogue vehicle backed off, then pulled out, accelerating rapidly until it came alongside. Now he could see it was a stout pickup truck. Pete slammed the brakes on in an effort to make it overshoot, but it slowed too, sideswiping them, its front corner pushing on Pete's door, pressing him into the curb. The parked truck came nearer. Pete pushed the wheel out, trying to force the pickup over. There was a tussle as they careered along the road. He braked again, but the pickup forced him along.

Scepter crouched in the passenger seat, too terrified to look. Kevin half lay on the rear seat to protect himself from the impact. At the last moment, the pickup broke free and accelerated away. The parked wagon was just meters ahead. Pete hit the brakes. There was a squeal of protest from the tires, sliding on the wet road. He let go of the steering wheel and threw up his arms to protect himself as they smashed into the lorry.

10

Pete came around quickly. He heard the horn blaring and realized his head was resting on the steering wheel. He looked out, saw flames and smoke coming from under the bonnet, and then glanced across at Scepter. She was unconscious, her head slumped back against her headrest. Pete realized that on impact, she must have jerked forward, probably hit her head on the dashboard and bounced back. For a horrible moment, he worried that her neck might be broken. He put a finger to her throat, felt a pulse and breathed a sight of relief.

Smoke seeped into the Fiat's interior. In the back, Kevin groaned and sat groggily upright.

"Get out, Kev," Pete ordered. He yanked his door handle. It would not open. He shouldered the warped door. No good. The compact Punto was smaller than his estate car, and there was insufficient room to get any force behind his movement.

"Pete…"

"Get out, Kev. Now."

"But Scepter…"

"Get out. I'll see to her."

Kevin shouldered the rear door open and leapt out. Pete reached across and past Scepter's inert form to try forcing her door. That, too, was so badly battered it would not move. He pressed her seat belt release, but it refused to work.

The smoke began to sting his eyes and choke him; his lungs felt like they were on fire. He threw himself over the seat and followed his old friend out into the fresh air, gulping it in to relieve his tortured lungs. He briefly studied the damage, seeking a way of getting Scepter out. The Fiat's nose was smashed in; its engine was pushed back, buckling the doors, making them impossible to open. The clouds of smoke colored with orange flame he had noticed coming from under the bonnet were now creeping backwards, the flames igniting anything that would burn. There was only one way to get her out: through the window.

He removed his jacket, wrapped it around his fist, and hammered it against the passenger window. The result was a set of bruised knuckles and no effect on the window. He cursed the invention of safety glass.

The flames were climbing higher. Soon they would reach the gas tank at the rear, where the deadly mixture of air and petrol would ignite and then… boom!

He looked around. Even a stone ornament would have done as a hammer to smash the window, but the houses all had gardens with only neatly trimmed hedgerows, and there was nothing of any use to him. Ahead of him, Kevin was rooting through the back of the lorry, seeking anything that might help. Alongside him, the flames took hold.

⚜

Inside, Scepter came to her senses and hammered at the window. Tears streamed down her face, and her pretty features turned to a mask of terror.

"Fishwick!" she screamed, fighting frantically to release the door.

"Be calm, Modom," came Fishwick's voice. Suddenly, she felt the seat belt release jiggling.

⚜

Doors opened along the street. Neighbors rushed out, some of them yelling, others simply staring. Wearing only pants, a vest and carpet slippers, the owner of the truck appeared, a short, tubby man, thinning on top, wearing a pair of gold-rimmed glasses. He stared, appalled at the damage. "What have you done to my truck, man?"

"I don't like bright yellow wagons, so I thought I'd try ramming yours off the road," retorted Pete. "Now stop asking stupid questions. Have you a fire extinguisher?"

"Oh naturally, I keep one in my back pocket," said the driver. "And you accuse me of asking stupid questions. I'll get you a hammer."

"Make it snappy. I've got to get her out before the smoke kills her."

The truck driver ran to the front of his vehicle, reached into the cab, came out with a carpenter's hammer and rushed back to Pete.

"Lean over, out of the way," Pete ordered Scepter. "Cover your face and eyes."

Scepter obeyed. Pete smashed the hammer into the Punto's window. It cracked. He drove it home once more and the glass shattered in a crystal shower. Pete reached in. Almost instantly, he began to cough. The air was thick with black, choking smoke, rich with toxic chemicals released from the burning and melting plastic of the dashboard and upholstery. He grabbed Scepter under the armpits and hauled her back. She was trapped by the seat belt. Leaning back out into the fresh air, he called for a knife, and the lorry driver rushed off to his cab again.

He returned a moment later and handed Pete a carpet knife. Pete leaned into the car and sliced at the belt. The knife bit into it, but he knew it was too slow. Scepter would be dead long before he could cut through eight centimeters of reinforced webbing. Throwing the knife out, he leaned in once more, trying to ignore the poisonous heat. Scepter gagged and began to lose consciousness. He slipped his hands under her armpits again.

"I'm gonna try drag you out through the belt," he said and pulled.

Immediately, she cried out as the belt caught on her hip.

"Bear with it," he told her and pulled again.

And then the seat belt came free, the tongue sliding out of the anchor as if the release had been pressed. Without stopping to question how it could happen, Pete yanked her out of her seat and through the window, to the pavement, where she stood, sobbing, burying her face in his chest.

"Look out!" yelled Kevin. He pointed to the underside of the car, where the flames, driven by fierce winds, were licking back to the gas tank.

Dragging Kevin behind him, followed by the truck driver, Pete threw himself and Scepter over the hedgerows into the truck driver's garden.

"Get down, you nutter," Pete warned the truck's owner. He covered Scepter with his body.

People ran in all directions; the truck driver threw himself to the ground next to Kevin. The Fiat exploded in a ball of flame, a huge pall of black smoke billowing into the night sky. As the charred remains continued to burn, people began to come back to watch, and there came the distant blue lights and wail of a fire engine.

Kevin and the truck driver emerged from the garden and stared, hypnotized, at the wrecked car. Pete and Scepter returned, too, and all three watched the shell of their vehicle blazing away. Around them, people were scurrying to put out the small blazes ignited by flying debris from the explosion.

"Great," complained the lorry driver. "You've smashed up my truck, wrecked my hedges, broken my carpet knife. What are you gonna do next? Go in the house and beat the wife up?"

Pete ignored him. "That was a close call."

Kevin nodded. "I'm stunned. How could I be so stupid?"

Pete and Scepter were puzzled. "It wasn't your fault," said Scepter, still coughing up smoke from her lungs. "You didn't invite that moron to run us off the road."

"It's not that," said Kevin with a broad, half-drunken grin. "I left my cigs on the seat. They've just gone up in smoke."

৩৩৩৩

Her face lit by the flashing blue lights of the fire engines, DC Keynes surveyed the scene with dismay. It looked like a small disaster area. The burned-out remains of Scepter's car were covered in foam, thick hoses covered the road, firemen were everywhere, ensuring the smaller blazes were properly extinguished, and at either end of a fifty yard stretch of road, uniformed police officers directed traffic away from the area. Nearby an ambulance stood, its doors open, the attendants drinking coffee and smoking under the disdainful eye of the fire chief.

Keynes turned back to Pete. "So your car was insured?" she asked. "That's a first for you, isn't it Brennan?"

Pete shook his head. "I'll have to get myself a publicity agent. I've got an appalling image."

"Yeah," agreed Keynes. "The cons don't like you because you used to be a copper, and the cops don't like you because you were bent."

He looked her in the eye. "The cops don't like me because I grassed them up for taking graft. Do *you* take graft?"

"Let's concentrate on your accident, shall we?"

"That's an interesting description, Keynes," said Scepter. "Accident. Is that the official term for attempted murder? And by the way, the car was mine, not Pete's."

The strobe lights of the fire appliance, made Keynes appear more irritated than she was. "Listen, Septic—"

The same flashing lights gave Scepter's face an ice-cold appearance that was genuine. "Scepter. In fact, only my friends call me Scepter. You may address me as Lady Rand-Epping, or My Lady."

Keynes ignored her aristocratic haughtiness. "*You* say attempted murder, I'm inclined to think drunk driver."

"At this hour?" protested Scepter, pointing to her watch.

Keynes made a point of sniffing Pete's breath, and he scowled. "Come on, Keynes, Scepter was driving. I only took over when that nutter rammed us. And you're wrong. He was no drunk. He hit us deliberately."

Keynes was not prepared to discuss it. "Are any of you seriously hurt?"

"No," said Kevin, and nodded at the foam-covered remains of the Fiat Punto, "But Scepter's car ain't well."

Keynes ignored him. "I have your statements. Leave it to us, Brennan."

"Oh, of course … if I never wanna hear any more. Let me give you some advice, Keynes. Make an effort to find him, because if I get to him first, there won't be a lot left for you to interrogate."

Without waiting for her to answer, Pete turned away and began the 500-meter walk home. Scepter and Kevin hurried to keep up with his longer stride.

"What will we do without transport?" Scepter asked. "My car's out, the police still have yours, Pete, and I have reservations about Kevin's van."

"Kevin can hire something for us," Pete replied.

"Great," moaned Kevin. "I've already had open wallet surgery to pay back Ronnie Wilcox, and now I've got to stump up for a hire car. What's wrong with my van?"

Pete dismissed the idea. "Like Scepter, I don't like it, and I'm not running round in your old wreck unless you get the heater fixed. Anyway, you're the only one with any money, and you can have it back when we pick up the reward from Jimmy Tate."

Now Scepter turned on him. "Pete, we formed ourselves as a team of ghost hunters, not private investigators."

"And, in case you've forgotten, I *am* a private eye. Besides, there's not a lot of difference, except that we're more likely to get results as private eyes."

"And less likely to get the TV series Kevin promised me."

Pete snorted. "Tell you what I'll do. You wait for Kev's TV series, I'll wait for you to drop your knickers for me, and we'll see who gets there first. My money's on me."

"Are you saying Kevin was daydreaming?" Scepter demanded. "He said he had contacts in television and that he may be able to get us a series on cable and satellite."

Pete forced patience on himself. "Scepter, Kev has more contacts than a printed circuit board, but the only contact he has in TV is Bent Benny, who, aside from loaning out audio-visual gear, also happens to supply knocked off cable and satellite boxes."

"That's not true," yelled Kevin as his cell phone buzzed for attention. "I do have other contacts in TV. When I worked in admin for the police, I processed the drunk driving charge against George Booth, and he was a freelance TV director. Scepter, I stand by what I said. If we can get a result at Melmerby Manor, I'll have a word with George, and see if we can get something on satellite."

He took the phone from his pocket and studied the menu. "Text message," he said, pressing the connect button. He watched the message appear and his brow creased. *WGJAMW*, read the message. "That's twice I've had this message. What the heck does WIGJAM mean?"

Pete leaned over his shoulder. "Gobbledygook. Weather screwing up the satellites, I'll bet. Who's it from?"

Kevin fiddled with the keypad and read the source number with a mutter. "Means nothing to me. That number is not in my address book."

Scepter shushed them as they turned the corner of the street, a hundred meters from their apartment "Fishwick is trying to talk to me. Yes, Fishwick?"

"Modom," said Fishwick, "there is an angry spirit in your apartment. I think it's the spirit of the murdered young man at the manor. Steven Bilks."

She dropped her voice to a whisper. "Can he harm us?"

"I'm not sure, Modom. I can manipulate matter, and he can too."

"Speaking of which, thank you for releasing the seat belt back there, Fishwick."

"It's what I'm here for, Modom. To take care of you."

Scepter turned her attention to her partners. "Be careful. Fishwick has told me there's something terrible waiting for us in the flat."

Pete glared at Kevin. "Have you left a curry going cold in the microwave again?"

"No, I haven't," said Kevin.

"That's not what I meant," said Scepter irritably. "Fishwick tells me there's a lost soul in our flat. He's violent and angry. He may do us harm."

"You mean a burglar?" said Pete and stared across at their ground floor flat. The place was exactly as it should be with the front door closed and the place in darkness. "You're crazy."

"I do not mean a burglar and you know perfectly well that I do not," snapped Scepter. "I mean Steven Bilks."

Kevin, too, stared. His chubby features turned pale in the street lighting. "No, Pete, she's right. Look. There's a face at the window."

Pete studied the windows. "I can't see anyone."

"It's gone," wheezed Kevin, "but I swear I saw it."

"Scepter, every time you talk about your spirits, you send his brain into orbit."

Scepter waved an angry hand at their front door. "Pete, there is some... *thing* in our flat. Fishwick is never wrong about these matters."

"All right. Let's find out what." Pete marched up the door and tried it. "Locked," he declared. "Considerate little burglar, isn't he, locking the door behind him so he won't be disturbed by insurance salesmen?"

He took out his key and let them in.

Natural caution made them creep into the hall, where Kevin picked up the *Ashdale Evening Chronicle* and read the headline: *Telescope Powerful Enough to see Matchbox on Comet.* Kevin tutted irritably. "Which untidy sod left the matchbox on the comet in the first place?"

Pete recognized Kevin's attempt to cover his fear with humor but shushed his best friend. "We don't wanna disturb Casper, the Housebreaking Ghost."

Suddenly reminded of his fear, Kevin backed off and let Scepter pass him as she softly closed the front door.

"Has Fishcake told you where to look?" Pete asked, pressing an ear to the living room door.

"Behind that door," she whispered, "and it's Fishwick."

Kevin gave her a sickly smile. "Ladies first."

Pete gripped the door handle, prised it slowly, quietly down, then heaved the door open and rushed in, followed by Scepter.

Kevin stayed where he was.

Presently, he could hear them shuffling about in the living room and kitchen and suddenly realized he was just as alone in the unfurnished hall as he had been in the cellars at the mansion. Fear got the better of him, and he stepped into the living room, and then through to the kitchen, where Pete and Scepter were waiting for the kettle to boil. He could hear them arguing again even before he opened the door.

"I don't care what you can sense, or what Alf Fisherman tells you, there's no one here," Pete was saying.

"His name is Fishwick, not Fishcake, Fishwife or Fisherman, and you're wrong, Pete. There is a presence with us. A distressed soul. The same soul we encountered at Melmerby Manor. Steven Bilks."

"Right, so Bilko's a mobile distressed soul, is he? What does he drive? A Rolls Royce Silver Ghost? D'yer gerrit? Eh? A Silver *Ghost*?"

"I wish you two would shut up," said Kevin, reaching into a cupboard above the radio for cups. "This whole scene is giving me the ab-dabs."

His hand knocked a cup, which fell out of the cupboard, knocking into the radio before falling to the ground and shattering. Immediately, the radio came to life with a hiss of static.

"Damn," complained Kevin and made to switch the radio off.

"Leave it on, Modom," urged Fishwick.

"Wait," Scepter ordered Kevin. "Fishwick is telling us to listen."

"I'm getting sick of the Fishmonger. I wish he'd clear off to Grimsby," Pete groaned.

At Scepter's insistence, they strained their ears. All they could hear was the hiss of a radio tuned to nothing.

"Is it that symphony?" asked Pete. "You know. Four minutes of total silence."

Irritably, Scepter yanked the volume up full and static filled the room. But there was something else, something underneath: the faintest whisper of a voice.

They all leaned into the radio to listen. Eventually Kevin, who had been bent over, listening carefully, straightened up. "What's he saying?"

Pete listened a moment. "Sounds like wigwam."

Scepter hurried from the kitchen and returned a moment later with a cassette recorder. She plugged in the extension microphone, held it close to the radio and started recording. She allowed the tape to run for a minute, then stopped it.

In a businesslike manner, she faced Kevin. "This TV repairman you know, could he enhance the recording? Eliminate the white noise?"

"Bent Benny? Suppose so. He's into all that kind of thing."

"Could we go see him tomorrow?" she asked.

Kevin nodded. "Sure."

"Well, before you do," said Pete, "don't forget we need wheels, and Locke won't let Scepter have her car back until he's checked it seven ways from Sunday."

11

A gray dawn brought a light dusting of snow on the ground, and a heavy fog enshrouded the town.

"I think I nudged the cup and made it fall, but how did it manage to hit the radio and switch it on?" asked Kevin, as they waited for their food at The Germ Factory.

"Perhaps it was our traveling ghost," Pete suggested, breaking off from the football pages. "Bit of a bummer, though. He comes all the way from Melmerby Manor and all he can do is turn on the radio. You'd think he'd do something more spectacular, like the Ultimate Wedgie: pulling Kev's underpants up over his head."

"Very funny. You should be on the TV."

Pete frowned. "TV?"

"Yeah," said Kevin. "You'd look good next to the picture of my mum."

"Your skepticism is depressing, Pete," said Scepter before a proper argument could break out.

Wilf delivered Pete and Scepter's plates. Pete looked with dismay at his poached egg on toast.

"Wilf, what the hell is this?"

"Our new cook, Pete." Wilf beamed with pride. "He's fully trained, you know."

Kevin stared glumly at Scepter's bowl of oatmeal. "Trained as what? A bricklayer? This porridge looks like cement."

"It's good for you," said Scepter.

"Now listen, you two," Pete said as Wilf wandered off, "this whole business is getting out of hand. The other night it was milk, sugar and a spoon at Melmerby Manor, last night it was a cup and the radio. Was this ghost in catering when he was alive?"

"Cynic," snapped Scepter.

Pete was not to be sidetracked. "Look at it logically. So Kev knocked a cup off the shelf and it hit the radio. There are a thousand possible reasons why it happened, and none of them are likely to be anything to do with Bilko's ghost. He might have *nicked* the radio when he was alive, but he wouldn't switch it on to find out if it was working now he's dead." He drank from his cup and swallowed a mouthful of poached egg.

Scepter chewed thoughtfully on her oatmeal. "And what about the signal on the radio?"

"Scepter, you should have studied psychology."

"And you did, I suppose?" she demanded tartly.

"I did a bit of it, yes. All police officers do. It helps when dealing with people in distress."

Wilf returned with Kevin's much larger plate. "Now, this is what I call a breakfast!" Kevin enthused as he shoveled all the components of a full English breakfast into his mouth at once. "People in distress?" he said around the mouthful of food. "I don't understand."

"We'd just been run off the road. That's attempted murder in my book. Scepter, particularly, could have died in that car. We were hyped up, nerves on edge. You should know: you're the one who thought you saw the face at the window."

"I *did* see it," his pal retorted.

"You *think* you saw it. Kev, you've been seeing pink elephants and purple dinosaurs as long as I've known you."

Kevin chewed on a sausage and swallowed it quickly so he could come in with his next point. "Everybody sees them when they're drunk... pink elephants and purple dinosaurs, I mean. But not everybody sees faces at windows."

"They do when they're stressed out," Pete went on patiently. "What I'm saying is that over the last 36 hours, we've been under severe stress. The ghost hunt and all the things that happened at Melmerby Manor, finding Bilko's body, the smash last night. It fooled Kevin into thinking he saw a face at the window, it fooled the lot of us into thinking that we heard something on the radio: wigwam."

"Wig*jam*," Kevin corrected.

"Whatever."

Scepter had listened carefully to the brief exchange between the two old friends. "And what of Fishwick's warning to me?" she asked.

Pete smiled benignly. "I don't believe in Fishwick."

"He doesn't believe in you either," Scepter said, trying to lighten Pete's mood.

"Scepter—"

"Pete," she cut him off, "there's one thing you're missing out in all this. Suppose Kevin goes to this Benny character and he enhances the tape and we really do find a voice on it. What will you have to say then?"

Pete put down his cutlery and sighed. For a moment, he stared through the windows at the wintry weather, while his mind ticked off ways and means of easing his frustration. "Here's what I'll have to say. When the cup knocked the radio on, it dropped onto the frequency used by a radio ham somewhere in the States and his call sign is W-J-A-M."

"Radio hams don't use AM or FM." Scepter's own frustration was obviously getting the better of her. She rattled her spoon into the porridge dish. "What will it take to convince you?"

"A damn sight more than you've come up with." Pete swilled down the last of his tea. "Let's apply a little paranormal logic, if that's not a contradiction in terms. Your average, streetwise ghost tends to haunt his favorite place when he was on earth, doesn't he?" He did not wait for an answer. "So far, Bilko has shown up at his own house, Melmerby Manor and our bloody flat." He threw Scepter a challenging glare. "Explain that."

Finished with her breakfast, Scepter pushed her bowl to one side. "You are entertaining a popular misconception. An unhappy spirit will, indeed, haunt the place where he was happiest or saddest in his life, or he may haunt the place where he died. In Bilks' case, I think he's also trying to channel through Kevin, and in life, he knew where you lived. He may not recall how he knows, but he knows to visit our flat because he's trying to tell us something."

"And Melmerby Manor?" demanded Pete.

"I believe that is where he was killed. If not, it's certainly where those DVDs were left, and he was strongly attached to them in real life, wasn't he?" She paused to let him take in her words. "Pete, there is nothing strange about ghosts turning up at many locations. How do you think mediums can channel on a stage in, say, London, and contact the spirit of a man from, say, Manchester? How do you think Fishwick keeps up with me? It's some years since I left our ancestral home, which is where he was in service with the family."

"I don't account for either of them," Pete replied, "because I don't believe in Fishwick and I believe all mediums are con artists. Scepter, you're asking me to take something on trust or faith, and I won't. Give me concrete evidence. Give me Fishwick, right in front of me. Let me hold a conversation with him. Let me see him. Let me eliminate every other possibility, and then I'll believe. Until you can do that, you stick to the pie in the sky and I'll look for other explanations."

"You," Scepter grumbled, "are totally impossible."

"Yes, but I'm sweet with it." Pete grinned at her scowl, and then checked his watch. "Right, if you're fit, Kevin, get me some wheels, then you go on to Bent Benny's, try to sort out Radio Spooksville, while I'll go see Ronnie Wilcox."

Kevin put on a pained expression. "Aw Pete, do I have to? I mean, hire cars are so expensive. Can you not use my van?"

Pete said nothing. He allowed a grimace to do the talking.

Scepter frowned. "Pete, are you sure it's wise, going to see Wilcox? Facing him alone, I mean."

"Yeah," agreed Kevin. "Shouldn't you tell Padlock and Chain?"

"You mean Locke and Keynes? No. I don't have enough evidence to interest the filth. All I know is, Wilcox told me he hadn't seen Bilko for yonks and yet

Jimmy Tate told us that Bilko rang him from Flutter-Bys." Pete set his features into a determined grimace. "Don't you worry about Wilcox. I can deal with him and his goons."

❧

Leaving his hired Ford in the car park, Pete stepped into Flutter-Bys to find the cleaners finishing their morning's work and Wilcox at the bar with his wife and two minders.

"Brennan," grinned the proprietor, "if you show up much more, I'll have to insist on you becoming a member."

"I don't come here by choice, Wilcox. This is business... again"

Seated on a high bar stool, Sylvie turned her brutal face on him and blew cigarette smoke into his eyes. "We don't do business with your sort."

"According to what I've heard, you'll do business with anyone willing to pay, but sad sacks who are totally blind and stupid are thin on the ground."

She put down her cigarette and moved off the stool, her fists clenched.

Pete turned a threatening, gimlet eye on her. "Watch it, Mighty Mouth, or I might be tempted to jam your head up Ronnie's jacksey and let you check out his colon." Sylvie backed off and Pete leaned on the bar, turning on Wilcox. "I've laid a bet with my bookie. I've bet him that I can find the moron who ran me off the road last night and wiped out my partner's wheels, all before lunchtime today. He's given me eight to one on Chief Inspector Locke, threes on Jimmy and Johnny Tate and guess who came in at even money?"

Wilcox's tone was calm and matter of fact. "Wasn't me. If I'd run you off the road, you wouldn't be here talking about it now. Besides, Sylvie don't drive and last night I was too drunk."

"What about Groom and Lawson?"

"Tommy doesn't drive," Wilcox said, "and Lemmy is a professional. He does a proper job."

"Funny that, Wilcox," Pete commented. "I'm a professional too, and I do a proper job, and right now, I'm gonna do a proper job on you, your goons here, and your club unless you start to talk fast. You ran me off the road last night and cost Scepter her car."

"Now look, Brennan, I've told you once, it's nothing to do with us. You say one more word, I'll call my lawyer and sue you for every penny you've got."

Pete grinned. "And how far will you get on 68 pence?"

Wilcox raised his voice. "For the last time, we had nothing to do with your accident. You think I'm the only one in this town with a beef against you? There are lots of people out there who'd like to see you snuffed, and I'm only one of them, but unlike the rest, I don't have time to bother with slime like you. I'm too busy running this place. Now get out before I call the filth."

Pete showed no inclination to move. "And how many of that anti-Brennan brigade own a dark-colored pickup truck?"

"Not me for one, and I don't know of anyone else. As far as I'm concerned, anyone who rids us of you should be given the Queen's Award For Industry." Wilcox reached for the phone. "You've got ten seconds before I bell the law and have you arrested for harassment."

Puzzled and irritated, certain that it had been Wilcox and his crew, Pete backed off. For once, Wilcox's words had a ring of truth about them. "If I find out you were linked to it, you'd better book your seat on the next flight to nowhere, because I'll come gunning for you." He drew in his breath as Wilcox put down the phone. "Let's change the subject, shall we, and I'll ask again about Bilko."

"I told you yesterday, I haven't seen him for months, now push off."

Pete made no effort to move off. He played with a glass dish full of peanuts. "I have it on the best authority that Bilko made a telephone call from this place the night before he was killed. You say you haven't seen him for months, and yet he was in your bar the night he disappeared. That doesn't sound right to me."

If Wilcox was worried, he did not show it. He gestured at the large room, chairs and table neatly arranged in a semi-circular pattern, centered on the small stage.

"Do you know how many guys we get in here of a night? Hundreds. Bilko could have been here and I wouldn't notice because I'm too busy. Busy working, Brennan. You know what I mean by work, don't you? I mean actually getting something done instead of harassing law-abiding citizens."

Pete did not rise to the bait. He cast a glance at Groom and Lawson. "What about your two clowns?"

Groom particularly took umbrage at the insult. "Just give us the word, Ronnie, and we'll teach him some manners."

Pete laughed with genuine pleasure. "You? Take me apart?" He traced the outline of the bruise on Groom's forehead, fading now after a couple of days. "You have short memories, don't you? Less than 48 hours ago, I showed you how easy it is to fly … off the end of my fist. Now what about Bilko?"

"We never saw him, right?" insisted Lawson.

Pete detached himself from the bar. "I find out you're lying, any of you, and I'll be back. And next time, I start to take this place, and you lot, apart piece by piece." Without glancing back, he marched out of the room.

⁂

From the Germ Factory, Scepter and Kevin climbed into his van for the journey to Benny Stringer's shop across town. He started the engine and as they drove off, Scepter asked, "Have you come up with a suitable name for our business venture, yet, Kevin?"

"I've had ideas," he assured her, turning right out of the end of the street. "Banish Your Banshees?" He glanced at her to judge her reaction. Scepter's face told him all he needed to know. "All right, how about Poltergeist Punishment Pack?"

"Kevin, I appreciate—"

He cut her off. "Scepter, I said before, if you want to be a success, you have to find something that people will remember. What about The Ghost Gang?"

She chuckled. "You make us sound like a mob of children. Keep it simple, Kevin. Have you considered something along the lines of Brennan, Keeley and Rand, Paranormal Investigators?"

Kevin gave a disdainful sniff. "Bit boring." A light came to his eyes. "You've given me an idea, though. I'll get back to you."

He concentrated on his driving, taking them off the Cranley Estate and up towards Ashdale town center, but before they got there, Kevin turned off into an area of terraced housing. Eventually they reached a secondary road, a shortcut between two main arteries. He turned left onto it and, a hundred meters farther on, pulled in outside Stringer's Electrical.

Wire-grilled windows protected a stock of TVs, satellite and cable decoders, hi-fi's and a range of accessories from headphones to jacks, antennae to blank videotapes. When they entered, they found the wall displays littered with mobile phones, portable radios, cassette and CD players, while glass stands showed off his latest range of quality electrical apparatus.

Bent Benny looked up from the morning's racing pages as they came in. A hunched, middle-aged individual with a wizened face, he wore a pair of narrow reading glasses that added to his weasel-like appearance. He smiled up at Kevin: a smile of avarice. "Kev. Again. Nothing wrong with the gear I supplied, was there?"

"It's fine, Benny."

"What can I do you for, then?" Benny rubbed his hands together, as if warming them to accept money. "How about a nice new satellite dish with a smartcard by-pass? A hundred quid to you, no subscriptions, no questions asked."

"And no guarantee, I'll bet."

Stringer grinned. "It didn't fall off a lorry, if that's what you're thinking."

"No? Nicked direct from someone's house, huh?" Kevin declined the offer and got straight down to business. "We need a favor, Benny."

The electronics man shrugged. "Bit short this week. Had to pay the missus her child support."

"I said a favor, not a loan."

"We need an audio tape enhancing," Scepter said, announcing her presence.

Benny gave her a hungry smile. "We?"

"This is Scepter Rand, my partner," said Kevin.

Benny was surprised. "What's a gorgeous dolly like you doing with this Teletubby?"

"We're business partners, nothing else."

Benny perked up, his face twisting into a leer. "Oh right, so there's hope for me yet?"

Scepter looked him up and down and suppressed a shudder. "I shouldn't think so." She held up the audiocassette. "Can you enhance this recording?"

Benny dropped the wolf act when confronted by his true love—electronics. Taking the tape, he placed it into a cassette recorder, hit "play" and listened to the hiss of white noise and the faint whisper somewhere in the background. His eyes narrowed, and his brow knitted in concentration. Eventually he came from behind the counter, crossed to the shop entrance, dropped the lock, and turned the sign around to read "closed."

"Come into the office," he invited, leading them into a rear room where a mass of electronic equipment, computer-driven multi-deck tape machines, equalizers and mixer boards lined the walls and workbenches.

Stringer shifted the cannibalized innards of a CD player from the bench, sat before his array of machinery, and switched everything on with a single flick of a wall socket. Dropping the tape into a slot, he began to play it, watching the LED displays dance before him.

"You'll be able to help us?" asked Scepter.

"By the time I've finished," he boasted, "you'll be able to hear two flies having it off on the ceiling."

"As long as we can hear the voice," said Scepter primly.

Benny's eyes focused on the oscilloscope and graphic equalizer readings.

"Definitely something there," he muttered. He fiddled with switches, slides and dials, and the white noise filling the room began to fade into the distant background. He turned up the gain, and there came the unmistakable sound of a human voice, but flat and phased as if generated by a synthesizer.

"Can you bring that voice up?" asked Scepter.

Benny fiddled with more knobs. Suddenly the voice came through clearly.

"WIGJAM... WIGJAM... WIGJAM... "

Kevin's brow creased. "See. Wigjam again." He smiled at Benny's puzzlement. "I keep getting this as a text message, too."

Benny looked up at them. "Wigjam? New pop group, is it?"

"This," said Scepter proudly, "is a voice from beyond the grave. Make a recording of it, please, Mr. Stringer." Scepter turned a smile on Kevin. "We need to think about this before we go back to Melmerby Manor."

Kevin gulped audibly. "I'd rather think about a cozy night in with a bacon slicer."

"Don't be such a baby," Scepter smiled. "The spirits won't harm you."

"I dunno," said Benny, slotting a fresh cassette into the recording deck. "You should see me after a night on the rum and Cokes."

Kevin did not find Benny's remark amusing. "You keep telling me this," he reminded Scepter, "but the spirits don't seem to be doing a bad job of making you look a total liar."

Before they could get into a proper argument, Benny started the machinery again, and once more the eerie voice filled the room. "From beyond the grave, eh?"

"Electronic voice phenomenon," said Scepter, "There are many documented cases of EVP, not always associated with hauntings, either."

"Wigjam," said Kevin, ignoring both her and Benny. "That reminds me of something, but I can't think what."

Scepter, too, pondered. "I've heard it somewhere before, too. But where?"

Benny handed over the two tapes, Kevin handed over £10, and the investigators left.

⚜

The moment he had let them out of the shop, Benny dropped the locks again, removed a second copy of the mysterious voice from the machinery that had been surreptitiously running in the background, and grinned to himself. He picked up the telephone and dialed.

"Mike McKinley," he demanded when he was put through. "Hello, Mike? It's Bent Benny. You looking for a story?"

At the other end, McKinley sounded skeptical. "As long as it's kosher, Benny."

"This is the real thing." Stringer chuckled greedily. "How much will you pay for your first recording of a voice from beyond the grave?"

⚜

Tony "Sherlock" Holmes saw Pete's car pull up and tried hurriedly to lock the door, but Pete got there first and forced his way in.

Slightly shorter than Pete, Sherlock was a rangy, skinny individual with shifty eyes and a nervous habit of running a hand through his untidy, dark hair.

"Morning Pete. Can't hang about, mate, gotta go out." He glanced anxiously at the door.

"Not just yet, Sherlock." Pete kept his voice deliberately friendly. "You're the man I've been looking for. Let's have a little chat, huh?"

"Sorry chum. Like I said, I've gotta dash. I've—"

"You've gotta find five minutes for me, Sherlock. That's what you've gotta do." With a friendly but unbreakable grip on Sherlock's arm, Pete led him back to the desk.

The front of the premises looked like any other shop on the row, but the interior was set up as an office. The walls were adorned with photographs and one or two diplomas. When Pete checked the photographs, they were all of Sherlock. Sherlock shaking hands with the mayor in front of the town hall on the day he was awarded the contract for guarding the Housing Department's material stores. Sherlock with the chairman of Ashdale Athletic FC. Sherlock with the Director of Ashdale Coliseum Theatre. The diplomas were all NVQ certificates in security, and all bore Sherlock's name.

"Doing well for yourself, pal," Pete commented.

Sherlock glowed in the praise. "Well, you know. Busy, busy, busy. Always been the same, Pete."

"So you have," Pete agreed with a judicious nod. "And all thanks to Kev Keeley."

With a couple of convictions for theft in his younger days, Sherlock had served a six-month sentence as a welfare chiseler, and when he came out, Kevin had cooked up a false background, and Wilf Mannion provided an accommodation address, both of which helped Sherlock secure a job with a well-known security organization. Two years down the line, Sherlock cut loose from his employer and set up on his own. Now, two years further on, he was well established in the town.

But he disagreed with Pete's analysis. "Kev? All he did was give me the references, Pete. I did the rest myself."

"True, but without those references, you'd never have got a job in the first place, and your trusting employers wouldn't have paid for all those training courses you took. So you do owe Kevin, really."

Sherlock's face turned to a look of determined anger. "Now look, if you're after the inside info on some joint so Keeley can rip it off, you can forget it. I've too much at stake to give it away casing joints for you."

Pete laughed, but there was no humor in his voice. "You know me better than that, Sherlock. I just need the answers to a few questions, buddy. Like, what do you know about 25,000 missing pirate DVDs and a dark pickup truck running me off the road?"

Sherlock swallowed hard and checked the door, assessing his chances of getting out. He decided it would be backing a loser. "I'd like to help you," he wheedled, "but I can't stay, I've gotta—"

"Answer me Sherlock, or I might lose it."

"No, look, I'm due at—"

"Forget the excuses, just answer me."

"I dunno what you're talking about."

Pete pushed him back, round the desk and into his chair, then perched on the edge of the desk. Leaning menacingly over his suspect, he drove his fists hard into the chair arms. Sherlock began to sweat.

"Let me spell it out. You were paid to keep an eye on Jimmy Tate's lock-up where these hooky DVDs were stored. They went missing and subsequently turned up at Melmerby Manor, before going AWOL again. When they disappeared for the second time, Bilko's body turned up in their place. Someone had caved his head in. Me and my partners were accused, released and then run off the road, and the only lead we have is Tony "Sherlock" Holmes because he was the one paid to guard the lock-up where the DVDs were stored before they went walkabout."

Sherlock was silent for a moment. When he spoke, his tones were friendly and interested. "So how did you get on at Melmerby Manor? Find any ghosts, did you? Only I heard—"

"Sherlock," Pete snapped, "you're not with it, are you? This is serious stuff. I've got Locke and his new sidekick, piano tuner—"

"You mean keyboard."

"Keynes," Pete corrected. "I've got them breathing down my neck, and you know what Locke is like with me. He has a special rope in his office, with my name attached to it, and if he can, he's going to hang me for nailing Bilko. Then, as if all this is not enough, some berk ran me off the road and burned out my partner's car."

Holmes gave a sympathetic tut. "Some drivers, eh?"

"Exactly," agreed Pete. "I get the feeling that people don't like me and that makes me so sad, I get angry. Now I wanna know what happened to the DVDs."

"I don't know," yelped Holmes. "Honest, Pete. I don't have a fixed guard at Jimmy Tate's lock-up. It's checked every half hour by patrol, and on that night I covered the patrol myself."

The admission only made Pete more suspicious. "I figure it must have taken them at least an hour to load those DVDs onto a lorry, and that must account for two, maybe three calls, so I have to ask myself what happened to the regular calls during that time?"

Sherlock blushed. "Well, they—er—kinda got missed. I had a flat tire."

Pete said nothing. He continued to stare Sherlock in the eye, patiently waiting for the rest of the tale.

For his part, Sherlock felt the pressure of the silence more keenly than if someone were leaning on him. He looked around, looked out onto the street where pedestrians passed by, muffled up against the cold, drab, dreary weather. He checked the door again, but he had to lean over and look round Pete to see it and he knew that looking at it was as close as he was going to get.

Running a sweating hand through his hair, he turned once more to pleading. "Aw, come on, Pete, you can't expect me to grass a guy up."

"I do."

Holmes stared at the walls, seeking further inspiration. His eyes fell upon a photograph of him and his wife on their wedding day. He smiled secretively. "Tell you what. The wife. She's always fancied you. I'll send her round to your drum and you can—"

Pete cut him off. "I'm not interested in your wife. I'm not saying she's ugly, but The Elephant Man would have run away from her. Now I'm getting tired of this dithering, so let's have it all before I turn nasty."

"All right, all right." Holmes' face was a picture of dejection. "Jimmy Tate's place was on a thirty minute schedule while the DVDs were stored there. One night, early last week, I gets a call. Skip two checks and I cop for five hundred sovs."

Pete worked out the schedule. "So the place was unguarded for an hour and a half while they loaded them onto a truck?"

"Yes. When I got there, the job had been done and the doors were left open for me to find."

"And of course, you never called the law."

"What? To let 'em know that 25,000 pirate DVDs had been lifted?" Sherlock sounded shocked. "I might be stupid, but I'm not an idiot. Can you imagine what Jimmy Tate would have done to me?"

Pete accepted the explanation. "So what did you do?"

Sherlock shrugged. "I belled Tate. What would you expect me to do?"

Pete nodded. It was logical enough. "And he had the standard screaming fit at you?"

"And how. I told him about the flat tire and why I couldn't make it, and he asked why I hadn't put another guard on to cover the calls. Well, on the money he was paying, I couldn't afford it. That's why I covered the job myself. It was the only way I could make a profit." Sherlock's voice lowered to an angry grumble. "He never paid me for that night's work, either."

"Well, you can hardly blame him, Sherlock," Pete commented. "You're paid to do a job and you didn't do it and he lost his DVDs as a result. Besides, you picked up £500 for not doing the job, didn't you?"

Holmes fiddled with a ballpoint pen. "Granted, but with Jimmy refusing to pay me, I barely broke even on the night. I wish I'd never agreed to do it."

"In that case," said Pete more persuasively, "you won't mind telling me who paid you to turn a blind eye."

Sherlock was diffidently evasive again. "Come on, Pete, you know the form. No names, no pack drill."

"Not the first time I've heard that in the last couple of days," said Pete, "and it's not good enough, Sherlock. I want names before Locke locks me up. Either cough or I'll redecorate this place with your brains."

Holmes looked wretched. "If he finds out, he'll kill me."

"It might be preferable to what I'll do." Pete stood up and ambled around the office, helping himself to a cup of water from a cooler by the door. "You've done well for yourself, Sherlock, but how many of your contracts will duck out when they learn that you did six months after claiming welfare for three kids who never existed?"

"Come off it, Pete, you wouldn't grass on me, would you?"

"*I* wouldn't, no, but Scepter Rand might. She's as honest as the day is long and she disapproves of any form of criminal activity, no matter how trivial. Now tell me, who paid you?"

It was a long time before Sherlock spoke and when he did it was in total misery.

"Ronnie Wilcox."

Pete absorbed the information with satisfaction. So it *was* Wilcox who had nicked the DVDs. All he needed now was confirmation.

He beamed at Sherlock. "Good boy. You know it makes sense. I'll leave you with it. Let me remind you that Ronnie won't hear a word from me, so if I learn that he's found out about this conversation, I'll be back, and it won't be a social call next time."

Satisfied with his morning's work, Pete came out, climbed into his hired Ford and considered his next move. He could either go back to Flutter-Bys or check on Kevin's progress. He glanced back at the windows of Sherlock Security where Sherlock stared back at him, looking unhappy. Pete grinned back, and Sherlock returned to his desk.

"Check on Kev, I think," he said to his car, and fired the engine.

As he pulled away, his mobile rang. He tutted irritably and pulled back into the curb, killing the engine. Taking out the phone, he made the connection.

"Brennan."

"It's DC Keynes. If you'd like to come to the station, you can have your car, your computer and video stuff back. There was nothing on any of it to give us a clue what happened to Bilko."

Pete had known all along that their equipment would reveal nothing, but he refrained from saying, "I told you so." Instead, he said, "I'll pick up Kev and we'll come right there. Any news on the pickup that ran me off the road last night?"

"We found it at midnight in Alexandra Park," Keynes reported. "Not a pretty sight. It was stolen from outside the owner's home an hour before it connected with you, and when the driver had done with it, he torched it. Forensic are working on it right now."

⚜

Scepter rolled from the bed, where she had been taking a nap, crossed to the window, and parted the curtains to look out on the street. Both Kevin's van and the pale blue, hired Ford Pete was using were absent. Pete had rung earlier, and she guessed that Kevin had gone out to meet his friend to collect the car and equipment from the police station.

Persistent rain poured on the untidy street, and the window was covered with condensation. As she looked out, something began to happen to the condensation. A line appeared, then another, and another.

Scepter was not afraid. Fishwick had been at her side too long for much to frighten her. But she was intrigued.

As she watched, the lines began to form letters, and the letters a word.

W... G... J... A... M... W.

WGJAMW, or WIGJAM as Kevin pronounced it. Again.

What did it mean? First the text messages, then the radio, and now written by an unseen finger in the condensation on a window. She knew it was important, but it had not yet clicked into her place in her mind.

"Fishwick?" she called to the room.

He replied promptly. "Yes, Modom."

"Is there another spirit nearby?"

"Yes, Modom. It is the same aggrieved spirit we have encountered so often over the last few days."

"And you can't yet confirm his identity as Steven Bilks?" Scepter asked.

"I feel certain, Modom, that it is the soul of Bilks, but he's so angry that he cannot remain calm for long enough to remember much of his earthly existence."

"And yet he can deliver mobile telephone messages," Scepter pointed out firmly. "He can get his voice carrying on radio waves. How is he doing that?"

"I do not know, Modom. *He* does, but he is not calm enough to tell me."

"I see." Scepter mulled the information for a moment. "And do you know what this strange message, W-G-J-A-M-W means?"

"No, Modom. He is trying to tell you something, but I don't know what, and once again, he is not calm enough to explain."

"Thank you, Fishwick." Scepter broke the communication and wiped the window with a towel so she could see out again. "But at least I remember where I've heard wigjam before."

⚜

After dropping off the hire car and getting his deposit back, Kevin ran them to the police station to collect their equipment. As they drove through the busy streets, he listened to Pete's account of his morning.

"So it *was* Wilcox," said Kevin worriedly. "What are you gonna do?"

Pete looked smugly satisfied. "I was gonna see him today, but we have to be back at Melmerby Manor tonight, so I'll give him a day to stew, then go see him tomorrow."

"Pete, he's already run us off the road! If you tackle him head-on over this, he won't be so gentle."

"Relax," Pete breezed. "I'll persuade him."

"I know your idea of persuasion—breaking fingers instead of heads. But it won't work with Wilcox and his mob. They're dangerous, and if Sherlock's rung him—"

"What do you mean, *if*? You know Sherlock. He'll have been on the jelly bone ten seconds after I left him. You leave Ronnie Wilcox to me and concentrate on the ghost hunt." Pete smiled in anticipation of busting a few heads.

Kevin shunted his van into the rear yard of the police station and switched the engine off. "I don't know which is more frightening—Wilcox or Melmerby Manor... or even you."

"In that case, think about setting up a business name." Pete gave his pal a jaundiced stare. "You do recall you're supposed to be thinking up a suitable name for us."

"I'm on with it, I'm on with it," Kevin squeaked.

They hurried from the van, through the rain to the rear reception and announced themselves. The officer on duty made a brief call, then allowed them through to the interior, where Keynes met them outside the property room. Pete greeted her with a warm smile.

"You're looking very pretty, Ms. Keynes."

"That's DC Keynes to you, Brennan. Just get your gear and your car keys and go." She gestured into the room.

Kevin followed her pointing finger with his eyes; Pete made no effort to move but leaned against the doorpost. "I feel we got off to a bad start. How about having a night out with me? Or a night in if you prefer." Pete gave her his most charming smile.

"No thanks," she shook her head. "I told you, I don't like bent coppers."

He gestured vaguely at the corridor and its many offices. "You won't like working here, then. Did Locke ever tell you how many bent cops I pointed out to him?" His eyes narrowed. "*I* was screwed for a single error of judgment. There were men here who had been taking graft for months. For *years*."

Keynes looked uncomfortable. "Yes, well, you weren't the only one screwed, were you? What about the chick you were supposed to be bringing in?" She turned away from him. "Just get your belongings and scram."

As Kevin came out carrying a laptop and its cables, Pete moved into the room and picked up one of three cartons. "Any progress on the drunk driver?" he called over his shoulder.

"I told you," she replied, "we found the truck. Forensic are still working on it, but I wouldn't bet on them finding anything."

Pete came out of the room again, carrying the carton. "Ah, it's so comforting to know that when the chips are down, we can still rely on the filth to bugger the job up altogether."

"Just get a move on," Keynes snapped.

They took the hint and got a move on.

Ten minutes later, their equipment loaded into Kevin's van and with Pete settled comfortably behind the wheel of his estate car, they pulled out of the police station and back into the afternoon traffic.

"I notice you didn't tell her about Wilcox," Kevin said when they pulled up outside the flat after a further ten minutes.

"Tell her what?" asked Pete. "That Wilcox carried out a robbery the police know nothing about, and stole 25,000 copies of a DVD that, legally, don't exist? Talk sense, Kev."

"Pete," complained his chum as he opened the rear doors of the van, "it's odds on that Wilcox killed Bilko, and we know he nicked the DVDs. Plod should be told."

"I agree," said Pete, "but we have no evidence other than the say-so of a known liar—Sherlock. If you were plod, would you do anything on Sherlock's word? Not likely. You might drag Sherlock in for questioning, but that's about it. As a private eye, I can do a lot more. I can wind Wilcox up, push him, twist his arm, *break* his arm if I have to. I've told you already, leave Wilcox to me. When I have enough evidence, I'll see Padlock and rattle his chain."

It was just after two by the time they unloaded the van. Kevin set up the computer for Scepter, who began work immediately, studying the video images from their night at Melmerby Manor. Behind her, Pete and Kevin continued to argue, bringing a frown of disapproval from her.

"I wish you two would keep the noise down," she complained.

"Why?" asked Pete. "Listening for the phantom playing the organ, are you? A selection of haunting melodies?" He grinned. "D'yer gerrit, eh? *Haunting* melodies."

Kevin stared blankly at him. "No."

"These are ghosts, right? Ghosts haunt, and if he was playing the organ he'd be playing haunting—"

"There wasn't no organ at Melmerby Manor. And anyway, the tape from Bent Benny has him talking about wigs and jam, not playing no organ."

"I'm trying to concentrate," said Scepter. "The things I'm looking for are so tiny, so fleeting, they're easy to miss."

"Yes, well, the things *we*'re looking for actually *went* missing," Pete pointed out, "and if we can get them back, we can still pull five grand on the deal, and help Wilcox to get where he belongs: the nick."

Scepter gave a frustrated sigh. "Gentlemen. The noise. Please. Anyway, I need you both to see this."

They came to look over her shoulder, and Scepter ran the video clip. It showed Kevin at the cafeteria counter, making tea. As they watched, the sugar bowl slid along the counter to Kevin's elbow, and he made use of it. They heard him ask for the milk, and it too slid along the counter. Scepter's voice, closer to the camera and its built-in microphone, drowned out other sounds, but shortly after she had finished speaking to both Pete and Kevin, a spoon, hidden away on the upper shelf where the camera high above the level of the camera's lens, suddenly appeared and dropped to the counter.

"There you are," said Scepter, triumphantly. "Explain that."

"I can't," Pete admitted. "Well, I can, but you wouldn't like my explanation."

Both she and Kevin laid suspicious eyes on him. "Go on," Scepter invited.

"This machine has been with the filth for the last 24 or 36 hours. They could have fooled around with it." Pete paused a moment to see if they would react. When they did not, he went on, "I was a cop, I know what they're like."

"Crap," said Kevin. "I know the cops have CGI experts on call, but they couldn't put that together so quickly."

Scepter gleamed victoriously. "That is exactly as it happened. Kevin will swear to it."

"Of course he will," said Pete, as Kevin nodded in further agreement with Scepter, "but would you take Kev's word for it? He's like Sherlock, the man we were discussing on our way from the police station. Kev is well known as a man who will do anything to make a fast buck, so no one would believe him, and if you try presenting that as evidence, every skeptic in the world will swear it's been done by camera trickery. Even I think it has been."

The doorbell put an end to the argument. Kevin went to answer it. Pete and Scepter could hear muted voices from beyond the front door. Kevin returned a moment later with Mike McKinley at his side.

"Look what the cat dragged in," Kevin declared glumly.

Scepter glanced up. Pete noticed a sudden, unmistakable light of interest in her eyes, and his features darkened. "What do you want, McKinley?" he grumbled.

The reporter matched Pete's height and good looks but was almost ten years older. Wearing a quilted coat and flat cap to keep out the weather, he gave the impression of a football commentator looking for a post-match interview. He held up a cassette tape. "Rumor has it you've been listening to Radio Cemetery."

While Scepter shut down her work on the video images, McKinley ignored the daggers of ice the other aimed at him and slotted his cassette into Kevin's player. He hit "play" and jacked up the volume. They all listened to the huge hiss of white noise and the faint voice in the background.

"What's that he's saying?" asked McKinley. "Wigwam?"

"WGJAMW," Scepter struggled to pronounce it.

McKinley poised his pen over a notebook. "How do you spell that?"

Kevin grinned. "I-M-B-I-S-E-A-L."

The reporter studied the word. "That's not how you spell imbecile."

"There you are, then," said Kevin, "don't ask me to spell wigj... wojo... whatever the tape says. We prefer to think of it as wigjam."

McKinley paused his scribbling. "So you didn't find anything at Melmerby Manor?"

Pete scowled. "Yes, we found Bilko's body, but the police have it now."

"Oh yes, I heard about that," McKinley commented and made a note. "You've been questioned, I believe?"

Scepter frowned at her partners. To McKinley, she said, "It's nothing to do with us. We're only concerned with the hauntings at Melmerby Manor, and we're going back tonight."

McKinley's eyes lit up enthusiastically. "That's great. How about having a reporter there, on the spot, to note down anything that happens?"

"Like a reporter suffering a terminal thump to the head?" demanded Pete, and Scepter stepped in once more to prevent a riot.

"Pete," said Scepter with a good deal more enthusiasm for the idea than her colleagues would have preferred, "we need the publicity. We'll be there by 5:00, Mr. McKinley, before it gets dark, and we'll be happy to have you along, as long as you're prepared to be objective."

Kevin chuckled. "Oh, he's objective. I've been objecting to him for years."

"Look, Keeley," protested McKinley, "just because I chose to expose a few of your scams and—"

"Business propositions," Kevin corrected, with forced aplomb.

"Scams and rip-offs," McKinley reiterated. "Just because I exposed you as a con man and went public on your mate Brennan as a bent copper, you don't have to take it personally. If this ghost hunting stuff is pukka, I can do you a lot of good."

Kevin looked to Pete for guidance and Pete shrugged. "If nothing else, Sir Henry might hate McKinley as much as he does you, and chuck the cutlery at him instead."

"I'll go for that," agreed Kevin cheerfully. "Five o'clock then, at Melmerby Manor, McKinley, and don't be late. I'd hate for Sir Henry to be kept waiting."

McKinley frowned puzzlement. "I thought the owner of the hall was *Jonathan* Melmerby."

Much to Pete's irritation—he would have preferred to throw McKinley out—Scepter stepped in to explain, and from his point of view, she appeared even more enthusiastic. Pete could not fathom whether it was talking about her work or cozying up to McKinley that made her appear so happy.

"Sir Henry died in 1652," she said, "but his spirit haunts the place to this day. He's a poltergeist. He throws things at people he dislikes."

"Whereas Pete just throws *people* he doesn't like... especially reporters." Kevin grinned at McKinley.

The reporter ignored the jibe and put his notebook away. "Until later, then." He, too, smiled. "I'm gonna enjoy this. An on-the-spot report from the Next World. Could be a prize-winner." He grinned broadly and gave them a thumbs up. "Mike McKinley, the hack who knows how to hack it."

12

Kevin watched McKinley and Scepter leave the room as she showed the reporter out.

With the media representative gone, he turned to Pete. "What are you gonna do about Wilcox?"

Pete stretched, yawned and flexed his biceps. "I'll go there tonight and beat his brains in," he promised nonchalantly.

"I admire your subtlety," said Kevin flatly. "Why not just dynamite his club?"

"My fists are cheaper."

"Pete," protested Scepter as she came back into the room, "I thought we were going back to Melmerby Manor tonight."

"You two can go on ahead in Kevin's van," Pete replied. "I'll catch you up after I've dealt with Ronnie and his chums."

Scepter and Kevin exchanged concerned stares.

"Don't tell me you're scared. Crikey, you're a good pair of ghost hunters, aren't you?" Pete nodded at Kevin as he spoke to Scepter. "I can understand *him*. He's always been a coward."

"That's what I love about you, Pete," said Kevin, "the way you bolster my confidence."

Pete ignored him. "I'm surprised at you, Scepter. If you're really in touch with the spirits, you shouldn't be scared."

Scepter tutted impatiently. "I am not afraid of the spirits, but there was someone else at the manor the other night. Someone human, and they killed this poor man. It pains me to admit it, but I would prefer you to be there in case they come back."

Pete grinned. "With Mike McKinley along, the biggest danger you face is being made to look a total fool in that excuse for a newspaper he writes for. I'm going to see Ronnie Wilcox, and after that I'll come along to Melmerby Manor." He gave her a hug. "Just to make sure you're safe."

❧

Pete arrived at Flutter-Bys just after four and found Wilcox in a cheerful mood as he prepared his club for the evening opening. As usual, Groom and Lawson, his minders, stood close by, along with his dumpy wife, but now a gaunt, middle-aged man wearing an oversized pinstripe suit had joined them, and he was the source of Wilcox's good cheer.

"This, Brennan, is my lawyer, Arnold Gillibrand."

Pete turned a sour eye on the fifty-something with flowing gray hair and baggy suit. "Gillibrand? Weren't you a German politician?"

"That was Willy Brandt," said the lawyer.

"If you say so." Pete made sure they understood he was not impressed. "Well, it's nice to meet you, Mr. Gillibrand, and I'd love to compare notes on law and order, but I've come here to bang your client's head against the wall until he tells me all about the DVDs he knocked off and stored at Melmerby Manor."

Gillibrand fished in his pocket and came out with a single sheet of A4 paper. "This, Mr. Brennan, is a restraining injunction, preventing you from harassing my client any further."

Pete took the document and read it. It appeared to be a list of long and complex numbers, each with a price attached. It had him completely mystified, until he saw the labor charges added at the bottom. "This, Gillibrand, is, in fact, a bill for repairs to a boat called The Legal Ass." He handed it back. "It seems your legal ass has a hole in it." He smiled. "Actually, looking at the bill, the hole should have been transferred from the boat to your wallet."

Confused and embarrassed, Gillibrand dug into his pockets once more and came out with another piece of paper, which he read to ensure it was the correct document before handing it over. "I think you'll find that in order."

Pete checked it. He had seen enough restraining orders in his time as a police officer to know that it was not only the correct document this time, but also valid. He passed it back and shrugged. "Okay. No problem. I'll just go see Padlock and Chains with my evidence." Without waiting for a reaction from Wilcox, he turned his back on them and walked away.

At a signal from Wilcox, Groom hurried after Pete and grabbed him by the wrist. The results of this hasty action astonished everyone, especially Groom. Pete shrugged the hand off, turned and landed a single punch. Groom staggered back into a table, rolled over it, landed on a chair, and came to rest with his arms and legs splayed, eyes shut and his mouth open, snoring his head off.

Pete marched back to the bar. Gillibrand moved in front of him. Pete shoved him out of the way, reached across the bar and grabbed the front of Wilcox's shirt. Half dragging the hapless club owner across the bar, Pete lowered his voice to a dangerous hiss.

"That's twice you've sicked your goons on me plus several threats of grievous bodily harm. One more time, Wilcox, and I don't care how many court orders or boat repair bills you come up with, I'll jam my fist down your throat and rip out your tonsils. You understand?"

Shaken, his composure gone, Wilcox could do nothing more than nod vigorously.

"Now, what went down with Tate's DVDs?" Pete demanded "And before you give me any more crap, let me tell you, I have a witness who swears you ripped off Jimmy Tate's lockup. I came here to discuss it amicably, but since you decided to start the rough stuff, you leave me no choice. Either tell me what happened or I go to the filth... but only after I've rearranged your features to match your wife's ugly mug."

Pete released him and Wilcox looked suitably miserable, while Gillibrand flapped uselessly in the background. Across the floor, Sylvie and Lawson tried to bring Groom round with light taps to his cheek, but the thug continued to snore.

"Do you ever stop to wonder why people hate you so much, Brennan?" Wilcox wanted to know.

Pete shook his head. "Nope. I've a thick skin, and anyway, I know where I'm at with hate. It's love that confuses me. Now tell me what happened."

Wilcox sighed and, with a shaking hand, poured himself a Scotch. "Okay," he said. "About a month ago, I got a call. Guy called himself Jay. Asked me to plan the heist. There was five grand in it for me if I did it. The job was straight-forward. All I had to do was turn up with a big truck, which I already had, and the manpower, and I had to arrange for Sherlock to turn a blind eye. We carried it out a few nights ago. Sherlock did as he was told and skipped a coupla calls, we loaded the truck and shipped the lot up to Melmerby Manor just as we'd been told to. That's it, that's all I know."

"Why Melmerby Manor?"

"Because it's shut for the season. No one there, and that guy what owns it, that Jonathan Melmerby, he doesn't live there, does he?"

Pete found the explanation reasonable. "And the other night you went out there and shifted it all again, killing Bilko into the bargain."

"That wasn't us," Wilcox insisted. "I was at my mother's bedside that night." He grinned as if daring Pete to challenge his tale.

"Your mother's doing five for corruption," Pete snarled.

"I meant my grandmother."

"She's been dead ten years."

"I meant her graveside." Wilcox smiled again. "Come on, Brennan, I'm trying to lighten it here. You've got what you wanted, haven't you? I don't know anymore. The other night, while you were hunting spooks, we were here."

"Then how did you know we were ghost hunting?"

Wilcox shrugged. "Your mate, Keeley. He told me all about it when he dropped that hooky scotch off."

Pete considered the pros and cons of this for a moment, then asked, "This Jay. What do you know?"

"Nothing. Half the cash turned up the day before the hit, the other half was on the doormat the day after. Straight up, Brennan, that's all I know." Wilcox's craggy features begged Pete to believe the tale.

"Who killed Bilko?" Pete asked.

"I don't know!" Wilcox yelled in frustration. "How many more times do I have to tell you, it wasn't us?"

"Then who took the DVDs back from Melmerby Manor?"

"I don't know. It was probably this Jay character. I just told you, Keeley was mouthing off about your ghost hunting efforts and if one of my people—" Wilcox gestured at his team still trying to bring Groom to his senses, "—opened their mouths in here and someone overheard, the word could have got back to Jay. If he dumped Bilko at Melmerby Manor, he'd be worried that you'd rumble the DVDs and the body, so he decided to take them back. It was probably him what scared you and your mates that night."

"He might have scared Kev, but he didn't scare me." Pete paused a moment in thought, working out his next question. "Who hit my car?"

"I swear I don't know. Honest, Brennan, I don't. You need to find this bloke Jay. He's behind it all."

"So, again, I ask—what about this Jay?"

"I know nothing. All contact is by phone. I've never met the guy." Again Wilcox resorted to pleading. "Come on, Brennan, you know me. He asks, he pays up front and in cash, I do. No names, no pack drill. Jeez, for all I know it might by Jimmy Tate himself, trying to screw his insurance company."

Pete laughed, humorlessly. "Insurance? On jiffy DVDs? Do me a favor." He detached himself from the bar, ready to leave. "You'd better be telling it like it is, Wilcox, because if I find out there's more, I'll be back." He cast a mean eye on Gillibrand. "And you know where you can stick that court order."

Deep in thought, Pete stepped out into the darkening afternoon.

Wilcox's story did not sound likely, but there was the remote possibility that he was telling the truth, and it would serve no purpose beating him and his idiots up, getting himself locked up while Bilko's killer and the DVD thief remained at large. Much better to chew on the facts, play out a bit of rope, and let Wilcox hang himself. In the meantime, he needed bait to try and bring this mysterious Jay out into the open.

❧

Kevin could see McKinley's BMW waiting for them at the main gates to the manor as they approached it. The reporter was in the car, reclined in his seat, smoking a cigarette.

With her car demolished, Scepter sat in the passenger seat of Kevin's van. Throughout the journey from Ashdale, she had sat in quiet contemplation in the passenger seat, but her eyes lit with more than a passing interest when she, too, saw the reporter's car.

Kevin's lip curled in contempt. "Get involved with him, and he'll only break your heart."

"Kevin?"

"Yes, Scepter?"

"Mind your own business."

Kevin responded to Scepter's stern tone with meek acquiescence. "Yes, Scepter."

As he brought the van to a stop by the gates, Scepter asked, "Have you got a name for us, yet?"

"I'll have it by tomorrow," he promised.

Scepter was satisfied. "Good. With Mr. McKinley doing a piece on us, we need a name."

Spiteful thoughts crossed Kevin's mind as he got out to unlock the gates, but he kept quiet as McKinley joined him.

"The big hero not with you, Keeley?" the reporter asked.

"Pete has other business to attend to. He'll be along shortly." Kevin pushed open one gate and nodded at the other, inviting McKinley to open it.

Both vehicles drove through and stopped. The two men got out, closed the gates behind them, leaving them unlocked for Pete, got back into their vehicles and continued the drive to the front entrance. When he opened his door, Kevin noticed that Scepter had left his van in favor of McKinley's car. The move irritated Kevin. It didn't help matters when McKinley gave him a cheery grin as drove past. In fact, at that point Kevin felt as if the EMF sensors in the cartons behind him should be bleeping to in time to his bad vibes and the infrared detectors should be reading the steam shooting out his ears.

He had no illusions about himself or his appearance. His girlfriends tended to be of the plain variety. Pete was the man who hit on the good-looking women, and normally they flocked to the ex-policeman's side, but he had been trying with Scepter ever since she moved into the flat—without success. She resisted all his charms and his chat. Yet she had obviously fallen for McKinley in a matter of minutes. It was a mystery to Kevin. He figured Scepter would have yielded to Pete before now, but there was no accounting for taste.

He stopped outside the main entrance and reached across to the cup holders where Scepter had left the keys to the manor. Climbing out, he noticed that Scepter and McKinley were smiling and chatting as they got out of the reporter's car. Kevin's lip curled again. He ignored them, marched up the steps and unlocked the door. He would love to give Scepter a piece of his mind and boot McKinley back up the drive, but that kind of confrontation was not his forte. Instead, he vented his irritation on the door, slamming it open before marching in. Their team was three-handed, and if they ever needed a fourth, it should not be scum like McKinley.

He stopped dead. In giving in to his annoyance, he had committed a grave error. He had walked into the hall alone. After what had happened two nights previously, he felt it a near-suicidal move.

The electricity was off, and, in the rapidly approaching dusk, the manor had taken on its familiar, sinister air. Kevin remained frozen just inside the entrance. The silence assaulted his ears; his eyes took time to get used to the gloom, and during that acclimatization, he was sure he spotted dark shapes moving quickly, stealthily through the shadows, secreting themselves to watch his activities.

A huge boom sounded around the hall. Kevin's heart leapt. He swiveled and found the other two standing behind him. McKinley had just slammed the front doors.

Kevin let go a large sigh and a lot of wind. "Don't do that," he protested, "You scared the Hell out of me."

As on their previous visit, Scepter switched on the mains electricity and flicked every other light switch, illuminating one bulb in three, barely lighting the severe portraits and silent exhibits.

She frowned. "The alarm wasn't set," she commented.

"The police," Kevin told her. "They're always bleating about taking care of your property, but they're the worst of the lot. I wouldn't trust 'em to look after my granny's pension book."

With a quick glance at her watch, Scepter became brisk and businesslike. "We have only about half an hour before it gets properly dark so we have to set up quickly," she ordered.

Kevin, visions of manual labor filling his mind, readily agreed. "You two get the gear set up, I'll put the kettle on."

"Kevin—"

"Look, Scepter," interrupted Kevin, "physical bits and pieces are not my strong suit. Pete normally handles it, but he's not here, so McKinley can help you carry the cameras and stuff up to the other floors and I'll get the computer set up *and* have a cuppa ready for you by the time you get back." He beamed ingratiatingly. "You do seem to be getting on famously."

Scepter did not rise to his jibe. She turned to McKinley. "Do you mind?"

He smiled. "Of course not."

"All right, Kevin," she agreed, "we'll do it your way."

"You know it makes sense." Smiling broadly, Kevin wandered off to the cafeteria. As he reached the door, Scepter called to him.

"Oh, Kevin." Her tones were sweet and mischievous.

He paused, turned and faced her. "Yes?"

She smiled impishly. "Watch out for sliding sugar bowls, falling teaspoons and flying CDs won't you?" She gave a girlish giggle and left.

❦

Leaving Kevin setting up his computer control center, Scepter and McKinley quickly unloaded the rest of the equipment and carried the cameras, sensors and cable drums to the first floor landing and corridor.

Fifteen minutes later, while Scepter angled a camcorder along the corridor outside the master bedroom, McKinley leaned against the wall watching her. "What's a good-looking girl like you doing hanging around with a pair of losers like Brennan and Keeley?"

Scepter did not answer immediately. She studied the screen display on the digital video camera, recalling the track of the orb a few nights previously and ensuring that the wide-angle lens would catch any movement in the corridor. She inserted the power jack and then plugged it into a cable socket, which would run back to the main power drum at the head of the stairs. Having done that, she finally turned to face him.

"I'm beginning to see why they don't like you," she said. "They are *not* losers."

"Oh, come on," McKinley protested. "If it's not nailed down or welded to the floor, Keeley will nick it, and Brennan's more interested in scoring with the chicks than anything else."

"Not with me, he isn't." Her response was clipped and disapproving.

Putting the finishing touches on the setting up of the camera, Scepter asked herself why she was suddenly being so defensive. McKinley was not the first person to assume that her living arrangements with Kevin and Pete were more than platonic, and she would not normally put the rumor down so brusquely. Somewhere at the back of her mind was the feeling that she had snapped because she was afraid of yielding to the reporter, and she had more important concerns.

"Sorry," she apologized. "Everyone thinks there's something between Pete and me, and it's not true."

He shrugged. "No sweat."

Content with the camera's aim, she led the way up the stairs to Aggie Devis' attic room where the rocking horse had been so dramatically active two nights previously.

Carrying a box full of equipment, McKinley struggled to keep up with her.

"So, you're living in the same flat as Keeley and Brennan and you're not—er—you know—with either of them?"

"No, I am not. Please, Mr. McKinley, can we get on with the work?"

McKinley smiled and put the box down. "Well if you're not getting on with them, how about... " He leaned forward, took her shoulders, turned her to him, and kissed her. "By the way, the name is Mike." He kissed her again.

Scepter broke the kiss and put down the camcorder and tripod. She turned back to him, reached up and put her arms around his neck, pulling him to her so their lips could meet again.

Her thoughts were a jumble. She had never given way this quickly with any man and yet... Was her heart beating so fast because she was afraid of the physical contact, or...

You widened your comfort zones with Sir Henry the other night.

Scepter yielded just a little, relaxing in his arms. McKinley caught the signal. His hands began to wander. She brought them back. They wandered again, further this time. She brought them back, but not quite all the way. Her breathing came faster. She broke away from him and whispered into the night. "Fishwick?"

"Modom?"

"Take an hour off."

"Very good, Modom."

⚜

In the cafeteria, Kevin busied himself setting up the command computer, keeping one wary eye on the kettle. After the events of their previous visit, he had prepared cups, sugar, milk and spoons before even switching the appliance on and told himself that he had prevented any shenanigans from the resident spooks.

All the same, he was jittery when he returned to the computer, booted up and ran the control software.

"Pull yourself together, Kevin," he muttered to the empty room. "There's nothing here that can harm you."

He listened briefly to the silent hall. Nothing. Not a sound. Not even the sound of Scepter and McKinley moving around upstairs, but there wouldn't be, he told himself. The upstairs here was not like the upper floor of a normal house. It was meters and meters, maybe hundreds of meters away.

He could hear nothing but the noise of the wind outside and his own breathing. In... out... in... out... out... in... in... out... out...

"That can't be right," he said to himself. He didn't breathe in and then in again, then out and then out again. Given the amount of tobacco he consumed, he was incapable of moving such volumes of air into and out of his lungs.

He drew in his breath and held it. The noise of his heartbeat was loud in his ears, but there was something else. The noise of someone breathing... and it was coming from right behind him.

He was frozen by the kind of hypnotic terror that grips small animals caught by snakes. He was absolutely petrified, his heart pounding, while that terrible breathing grew louder and louder and louder as whatever creature lurked behind him drew near. The hairs on the nape of his neck stood up. His heart rate increased to painful proportions. There was some... some... thing there, with him, in that room; it was just behind him and he dared not look. His mind was filled with terrible visions of Bilko's battered head in the stables, of the sugar and milk sliding towards him, of the overcoat and hat hanging in the cellar. He risked a glance to his right, and in the far corner of his eye he could just make out the black maw of the cellar door, wide open. Hadn't he closed it the other day when he and Pete came out of there? He knew it! Hadn't he warned Pete that there was something down there? And hadn't Pete ignored him, and wasn't he now alone, with whatever it was coming to get him?

Somewhere beneath the horrible images filling his mind, the panic alarms were ringing, telling him to get out fast, but his scrambled brain, re-running every horror movie he had ever watched, could not get the message through to his muscles, and he remained immobile, waiting for fate to strike, unable to do anything about it.

Beneath the dread, he recalled his happy life and wished that he had never heard of Scepter Rand, never thought of ghost hunting. If he could have his time again, he would lead the blameless life of a saint. He would retreat to a monastery, take holy orders... on the other hand, maybe he would pass on the whole church thing. There were plenty of monasteries kicking up and down the country, and they all had their fair share of ghosts and goblins and demons.

The breathing was so loud now that it sounded like it was only a matter of centimeters from his ear. It was so close, he should be able to feel the hot breath on his neck, but the hair there was tingling so much he probably wouldn't feel it if an executioner's axe sliced through the air to take his head off.

The mere idea of an executioner's blade sent fresh tremors through him and he broke wind. He had to do something or he would be past the need of a lavatory soon, and more in need of a shower and a change of clothing.

The breathing was louder in his left ear. He tried to force his head in that direction, but it would not move. Fear held him so tightly in its grip that he could not move a single muscle.

He sucked in as large a lungful of air as he could to charge his muscles with oxygen and forced his neck to turn. It began to turn, but slowly, unwillingly, like an old carousel whose parts had not been oiled for years. His head seemed to click round in stages like a rusty cog, and if it had been a door—like the one at the front of Melmerby Manor—he was sure it would have creaked.

He kept his eyes wide open as he turned to face his tormentor, and whatever horrible shape it had assumed. He slowly turned full circle, passing the serving counter, the kettle boiling happily away, the checkout, the open cafeteria doorway, then round to the windows, beyond which lay the late afternoon gloom, the drinks dispenser, the cellar door and kitchen access and back to the service counter. And throughout his tortuous procession, he fully expected the visions to materialize.

But there was nothing.

Kevin breathed a huge sigh of relief and let out a near-hysterical laugh. Once again, it was all in his imagination. The moment he faced up to his terrors, the breathing had stopped and all he could hear was silence.

Abruptly, into that silence came a huge, deafening voice, its message booming across the house, echoing around the cafeteria.

WIGJAM!

Kevin's heart leapt, stalled, restarted, and pounded in his chest. Once again, mindless terror seized him, but this time, his muscles had no problem obeying the panic-stricken messages from his brain. When it said "run," his legs obeyed.

He hurtled blindly from the cafeteria, letting loose a shriek of pure horror, whizzing towards the front door. As he reached it and snatched it open, a massive, menacing shape loomed before him, blotting out the last shreds of daylight beyond the threshold.

Kevin cried out again and cowered before the massive body, whimpering like a whipped dog. He went down onto his knees begging for mercy, praying for forgiveness for his life of sin.

He went further down, burying his face in the heavy-duty carpet of the entrance hall. Face close to the floor, eyes shut, arms spread before him in total surrender and subjugation, he babbled the word over and over again as if it were some incantation designed to placate an evil spirit.

"Wigjam, wigjam, wigjam... "

13

Pete was astonished to find Kevin kowtowing like some Egyptian slave from the days of the Pharaohs. "Kevin, what the hell are you doing?"

Kevin ceased his supplications. He looked up, eyes level with the toecaps of a familiar pair of scuffed and untidy trainers. He raised his head higher, taking in the tight jeans, the Manchester United football shirt hiding a massive, muscular torso—and Pete's surprised features staring down at him.

The tubbier half of the pair struggled to his feet, composed himself and turned an angry face on his buddy. "Don't do that," he yelped.

"Do what?"

"You scared the bejeebers out of me."

"How?"

"Breathing in my ear like that."

Pete was nonplussed. "If you were a woman I might breathe in your ear, but—no offense, Kev—you're not my type." Pete stepped into the hall and headed for the cafeteria. "So what were you doing on the floor?"

"I—er—oh—I was—er—y'know—just checking the—er—acoustics. Right. Yeah—just checking the acoustics. That's what I was doing. Making sure there were no extraneous noises coming through the wood."

Pete gave him a doubtful eye. "Like termites having a little community sing-along? Where are Scepter and that muckraking git, McKinley?"

"Upstairs."

"Doing what comes naturally?"

Now Kevin poured scorn on Pete. "Not everyone's like you, you know. At least I hope not. They're supposed to be setting up the cameras and sensors."

As if on cue, noises came from the staircase. Scepter came down the stairs, her features businesslike, McKinley behind her, playing out the power cable from a drum. Pete wondered whether it was his imagination or whether there was an air of tension between her and the reporter. Certainly, when Scepter turned back and told McKinley to tuck the cables tight into the wall, she did so in clipped tones like a schoolmistress instructing a recalcitrant pupil in some simple task.

She left the reporter and turned her attention to her business partners. "Hello, Pete. What's all the noise about?" she asked.

"Termites," said Pete as he continued into the cafeteria.

"Termites?"

"Warbling the national anthem, so I'm told." Pete moved behind the counter and flicked the switch on the kettle. "Ask Kev. He was the one checking the floorboards." Pete examined the kettle and found it almost empty. He held it under the tap, refilled it and put it back on the worktop, switched it on once more. "Must have been important, too, to let the kettle boil almost dry."

Scepter turned, meaning to raise inquiring eyebrows at Kevin, but he had not followed them into the cafeteria.

They found him in the hall arguing with McKinley.

The reporter had run the cable back to Kevin's central connection point where four, three-pin sockets were rigged on a cable drum capable of carrying high voltage. McKinley had been about to plug his cable into the drum when Kevin intervened.

"This is precision gear," Kevin argued, "and I don't want your ham fists mucking about with it."

"I'm only plugging the socket in, you tub of lard," snapped McKinley.

"Call me that again," Kevin threatened, "and I'll plug you into the mains."

"Knock it off, you two," ordered Pete.

Grateful for his intervention, Scepter turned her attention to Kevin, asking him for an explanation of Pete's nonsense.

"I heard a voice," he reported. "The wigjam voice again. Only it was louder this time. You could hear it all over the house."

McKinley dropped the electrical socket, took out his notebook and pen, and began to make rapid notes.

Scepter was beside herself with excitement. "You heard it in here?"

"No, not in here," retorted Kevin sarcastically. "It was out on the lawn while I was waiting for a bus home. Of *course* it was in here, you numpty."

She frowned. "I'm becoming very disillusioned with you, Kevin."

"Why don't you tell *me* what happened, Keeley?" suggested McKinley. "I'm sure my readers would be interested."

"I told you, I heard that voice again." Kevin bent to plug in the cable from the upstairs, and then made his way back into the cafeteria.

Pete followed quickly. "That's not what you said to me."

"Well," Kevin breezed, "I didn't wanna worry you."

"Never mind all that," Scepter put in before an argument could start. "What did you learn from Wilcox?" she asked of Pete.

"A little." Pete made tea for them, and they moved out into the cafeteria, taking a table near the computer, where he gave them a rundown of his findings at Flutter-Bys.

McKinley listened intently to the tale, occasionally making notes. Eventually, he said, "Here I was thinking I'm on a ghost hunt and I find you playing like a real detective, Brennan. What's wrong? Getting a conscience?"

Pete pointed a threatening finger. "You print one word of this, McKinley, and I'll cut you up into strips and flog them off to Wilf Mannion for his meat pies."

"Look, Brennan, news is news, and I—"

"This is serious stuff, and we need it kept under wraps until it's sorted out. You can have the exclusive when it's done, but for now, you keep your trap shut." Taking a large swallow of tea, Pete turned to Scepter. "Anything happening here? Apart from Kev having another attack of the heebie-jeebies?"

"Nothing yet." She checked her watch. "But it's still a bit early." She too sipped from her cup. "You know, Pete, I think you're being very hard on Kevin."

He laughed. "*I'm* being hard? You're the one who's just told him off for calling you a numpty."

"A woman in my position is not used to being called such names. Anyway, don't change the subject. I don't think he's imagining it. He's the focus of much of what happened here the other night, and I believe he may have channeling abilities of which he's unaware."

"No," Pete disagreed with strained patience. "He has the ability to channel stolen goods to other users, without the law being aware, but as for hearing voices, I don't think—"

"I know what I heard," Kevin interrupted. "It was wigjam. Again." His mobile buzzed for attention. He took it from his pocket and studied the menu window. "Text message," he muttered, and made the connection. His brow creased. "Funny. It's that same message as the other day." He held it forward for them to see the message WGJAMW. "I wonder who's sending it."

While the other two men crowded round Kevin to read the message, Scepter wandered off to the windows, her ear cocked to the astral plane.

"Modom," Fishwick announced, "the text messages and the voice on the radio are from one and the same source."

"And is that source Steven Bilks?" she asked.

Her butler concurred. "I have said before that I believe we are dealing with Mr. Bilks' spirit, Modom, but he cannot confirm it."

"Thank you, Fishwick."

She became aware that her one-sided conversation had attracted the attention of her colleagues and that they were watching her with inane grins on their faces.

She blushed and coughed to hide her embarrassment. "Fishwick has just told me that Steven Bilks is sending those messages, and it's his voice we heard over the radio. He's trying to tell us something, but even Fishwick cannot understand what it is."

Kevin stared open-mouthed; Pete and McKinley were incredulous.

"Techno-spooks," said the reporter with a wry grin. "I must say, as stories go, this beats the latest celebs caught with their knickers down. Ghosts sending text messages."

"Scepter," said Pete, "I can just about buy this spirit contact of yours, but ghosts sending texts and getting airtime on radio is stretching believability just a bit too far."

"Then how do you explain it?" Scepter demanded.

"Someone, no prizes for guessing who, is playing games with us." Pete took the phone from Kevin, and studied the source details of the text. "McKinley, can you trace the owners of mobile numbers?"

"Yes. Not easy, but we can do it," agreed the reporter.

Pete passed Kevin's phone over. "Get us the owner of that text source, will you? This is twice he's texted Kev, and I'd like to know who he is."

"So you don't believe he's the ghost of Alexander Graham Bell bringing himself up to date?" McKinley grinned. "Mr. Keeley, come here, I need you—to show me how to get the source number for a text from your phone."

Kevin tutted. "Bloody technophobes." He joined McKinley and began to work through the phone's menu to find the source number.

"Kev started receiving those texts after Bilks was killed," said Pete, "and I believe that someone is just trying to scare us off. You just get me the owner of that number, and I'll do the rest."

Making a note of the number, McKinley handed the phone back to Kevin. "So. What now?"

Kevin pocketed his phone. "Now we sit back and wait for the other Melmerby Manor spooks to wake up. Those who *don't* breathe in your ear and shout at you." He checked his watch. "There's a good few hours yet."

Pete shook his head as he picked up a camcorder, tripod and a cable drum. "Not quite. I'm setting up one more camera. Give me a lift, McKinley." He handed the cable drum to the reporter.

❦

Under the baleful eyes of portraits, Pete and McKinley made their way across the entrance hall and along the Long Gallery, their footsteps echoing eerily around the walls.

"So, what is it with you, Brennan?" McKinley asked. "Did you just jump on the ghost hunting bandwagon because you fancied Scepter?"

"Well, thanks to pains in the butt like you and DCI Locke," Pete grumbled, "I lost my job and had to turn myself into a private eye. There's not much doing at the moment, so I tagged along with Kev and Scepter. Nothing better to do, had I? Besides, a lot of people believe in this guff and I'm here to make sure those two keep their feet on the ground."

At the far end of the Long Gallery, they put their equipment down. Looking through the glass of the rear, double doors, Pete unlocked them and let them out into the rear yard.

"This is where you turned up the body of Bilko, huh?" McKinley wanted to know.

McKinley's use of Steven Bilks' nickname made Pete instantly suspicious. "You knew him?"

McKinley tapped the side of his nose and grinned. "I'm a reporter. I have sources, and Bilko was one of them."

He peered intently at the reporter. "Did he contact you in the last few days? Tell you anything about a big heist going down?"

"Nope, and that's not the kind of information I used to get off him. He'd tell me about crooked councilors or businessmen—" McKinley grinned again. "Or bent cops."

Pete rounded on him. "Watch it. I only have so much patience."

His threat wiped the grin from the reporter's face.

Across the courtyard, the big gates and the stable doors were covered with police "crime scene" tape in a gaudy yellow with blue lettering. The ground was littered with patches of forensic dusting powder, washed away in places by the heavy rains.

Pete waved at the nearest doors. "We had some rum goings-on here the other night, so I thought I'd set up a camera tonight."

"Goings-on? How rum?"

Pete shook his head. "Never you mind. Let's just say that they led us to Bilko's body."

Pete threw open the rear gates and checked outside. Happy that there was no one immediately visible and that the warehouses were secure, he closed the gates again and they returned to the Long Gallery with McKinley at his shoulder. Once inside, Pete locked the doors and set the video camera and infrared motion sensor on the inside, aiming them through the glass doors so that they were aimed at the warehouse entrance.

"If I set them up in here," he explained, "no one can mess with them, can they?"

With McKinley's help, he ran the cable back along the gallery, tucking it under display cases and exhibit stands to ensure no one would trip over it, and into the entrance hall, where they connected it to Kevin's central power drum.

Satisfied, Pete stood back and checked everything over with a practiced eye. "Anyone starts fooling around tonight, and I'll have 'em."

It was to be a long and boring evening. They sat in the cafeteria talking, occasionally dozing, McKinley fishing for bits and pieces of information, Scepter telling him the plain truth as she saw it, Pete and Kevin remaining circumspect, although they frowned upon her honesty.

Eventually, when Kevin and McKinley dozed off, Scepter and Pete were left alone and her interest in his past sparked again. "Pete, you never did tell me what went on with you and Chief Inspector Locke, or Jimmy Tate."

"It's not something I like to talk about," he admitted.

"You're ashamed?"

He gave a sardonic laugh. "Some chance."

"Come on," Scepter encouraged. "Tell me."

He heaved a sigh. "Oh, all right. A few cops take bribes. I didn't. I was a good cop. Honest and more concerned with law and order in this town than with what I could take for myself. My record of arrests and my courage in facing down muggers, robbers, and so on, was the reason I was promoted to Detective Constable so quickly. Then Locke sent me out to arrest a young woman on the Cranley Estate. Not far from where we live. She was—er—how can I put it? Her company did not come free of charge. She begged me not to take her in, because she'd been booked so many times before that they were sure to send her to prison this time. I fell for it. She was, shall we say, *grateful* to me. Then the rotten cow rang Locke and told him I'd offered to let her off in return for a freebie."

Scepter shook her head and tutted to show her disgust. "I'm shocked that you accepted her offer in the first place, Pete, but for her to do that is disgraceful."

"Well, Locke took the same line," said Pete picking up his tale. "There was an argument during which I told Locke just how many of his men were taking graft from the pimps and pushers. He didn't believe me, the argument got worse, he threatened to kick me all over town, and I lost my temper. Hung one on him. I was suspended, and later, fired. Not for allegedly taking advantage of a known prostitute: that couldn't be proved, and no one would have taken her word for it. At worst, I would have been suspended and got off with a warning. No, I was sacked for striking a senior officer."

Scepter took his hand and held it sympathetically. "You enjoyed being a policeman, too, didn't you? I can tell from the way you talk about it."

He sighed again. "My father was a cop. He was the last policeman in Ashdale to be killed in the line of duty. He tried to stop a gang who'd just robbed a bank getting away, and they mowed him down with their car."

A look of anguish came over Scepter's face. "Oh, Pete, I'm so sorry. You never mentioned it before."

Pete glowered at the memory. "I was nine years old and it hurt. It doesn't hurt anymore, but it makes me so mad. They were caught, tried and found guilty, and what did they get? Life. And what does life mean? The judge set a tariff of fifteen years, and they're already free. They served less thirteen, whereas me and mum... I was left fatherless and she was left without a husband and with only a crappy pension." The glaze of reminiscence left his eyes and he focused once more on Scepter. "That's why I became a cop. I never wanted to do anything else. I vowed that no one should suffer the way I did. Locke is the same kind of man. Despite what you may think of him, he believes in the rule of law, and he's as honest as the day is long. For obvious reasons, he has a blind spot when it comes to me. He'd be happy to see me rot in jail, but to be fair to him, a couple of months after I was fired, most of those men I'd named were suspended, three of them were fired and one went to jail, so he had obviously investigated my accusations, and he hated bent cops."

Scepter was silent for a moment, waiting to see if he had anything more to say. When he did not, she asked, "Have you ever thought that the prostitute was a set up? That the very men you were naming briefed her?"

Pete nodded. "Thousands of times. Trouble is, I only thought of it *after* I got fired. All I achieved was putting an end to my career. And Locke swore he would get me back one day for punching him like that."

"So he'd love to pin a murder rap on you?"

Pete shook his head. "Don't be fooled by Locke's accusations. He knows we're innocent, but you're half right. He would love to pin something on me."

Scepter allowed a sizeable pause and then asked, "What about Tate?"

Momentarily lost in his memories, Pete stared through the rain-streaked windows. Eventually he said, "Similar scenario. About four years ago, I went out to arrest both the Tates. When I got there, no one was home except for Nicky, Jimmy's missus. You've seen her. She was an actress before she married Jimbo. Anyway, we got talking, one thing led to another and—well... you know."

"No I don't." Suddenly Scepter blushed. "Oh. Right. I don't have much experience of that kind of thing."

Pete gave her a smile. "We can soon change that."

"No, thank you, Pete." Scepter removed her hand.

Pete took up his narrative once more. "That *was* a set-up, and Tate had a video camera on us. When I went back the following morning, he showed me the tape and threatened to use it. You know, send it to Locke. I'd have been fired. Consorting with known criminals."

Scepter's reaction amused him. When he first admitted that Tate had video-taped the incident, she shuddered in revulsion. Now her eyes widened in shock. "That's a little more than consorting, Pete."

"Consorting is the legal term, it's also the disciplinary term for it, and even if you don't have much experience of that kind of thing, you don't need me to draw you pictures, do you?" Once more he sighed. "It was the one mistake I ever made… apart from the tart, that is."

Scepter sympathized. "I can see the fix you were in. So, what happened?"

"The price of Tate's silence was my keeping him up to date on raids. What could I do?"

Scepter thought about it for a moment. "You could have approached your chief and told him."

Pete shook his head. "When I said, 'What could I do?' it was a rhetori-cal question. I may be daft but I'm not stupid. I told you, Locke doesn't like bent cops, and he would have booted me off the force. Anyway, Jimmy had me snookered, and afterwards, every time we raided him, we found nothing more incriminating than a chocolate wrapper telling us he wasn't sticking to his diet. I tipped him off to everything."

Scepter clucked irritably. "And of course, when you eventually did get fired, it was for the same sort of thing with a prostitute, wasn't it? Your sex addiction is a real problem. Have you never tried to do anything about it?"

"Sex addiction?" Pete raised his eyebrows in surprise. "Two mistakes in a lifetime do not make me a sex addict, and how many girls have you seen me bring home since you moved into the flat? Contrary to what you may imag-ine, I have not had more women than you've had hot dinners." He gave her a good-humored smile. "Anyway, an addiction to sex would be preferable to being hooked on chocolates and sweeties like him." Pete cast an eye over his shoulder at Kevin, who was now snoring loudly. "So now you know why I'm prepared to take Tate's money for recovering the DVDs. He cornered me into breaking the rules and took advantage of it, so if I can take him for five grand now, I will." The bleep of an alarm on Pete's wristwatch told them it was eleven-thirty. "It's time we were checking the place over." He looked at Kevin's dozing form once more, turned and kicked out at his pal's chair. "Wakey-wakey, Sunbeam, rise and shine, supper time."

Scepter got to her feet. "Time to go to walkies."

Kevin immediately became nervous. To McKinley, he said, "This is when things started to happen the other night."

"Well, tonight," said Scepter, asserting her authority as psychic-in-resi-dence, "we'll stick together, and if you sense anything, Kevin, I'll get straight onto Fishwick."

They left the cafeteria to make their way round the house, heading for the uppermost floors first, then working backward, systematically checking the darker nooks and crannies of the building. They were a small huddle of people dwarfed in the immensity of the hall's interior, the dim lighting and their torches casting long, dark and shifting shadows on the walls.

"So what's with this Fishwick character?" McKinley asked, as they returned to the first floor landing and the master bedrooms.

"He's my channel, my spirit guide," Scepter explained. "He is my contact with the Other Side."

The reporter could not help but chuckle. "The other side? You mean West Yorkshire?"

"Oh, don't you start. I have enough trouble with those two." She gazed affectionately in the direction of Kevin and Pete, who were at the far end of the corridor, checking the rooms, switching off mains lights.

As they came back down the stairs, the meager light from their lamps picked out hooded stares from portraits of those who had passed away in this grand mansion. From outside, the wind moaned and rain lashed at the building.

"As long as it's moaning and lashing the building and not me," said Kevin through chattering teeth, his fear intensifying with every light they doused.

"Wouldn't it have been simpler to knock the mains off?" asked McKinley as they returned to the cafeteria.

"We had that debate the other night," grumbled Pete, "and, as I pointed out then, it would kill our equipment too."

❧

They settled again in the cafeteria, listening to the violence of the weather outside. Kevin soon nodded off, and, shortly thereafter, so did Pete and McKinley. For a while, Scepter worked busily on her notes. But soon the pressure of the night and the many hours without proper rest began to take their toll, and her eyelids became heavy, drooping, dropping, finally closing...

She sat bolt upright, eyes staring, and gasped.

The sound woke all three men. They jumped as she let out a strangled cry. Her chest thrust out and her head snapped backward and she sat rigid on the chair.

"Did someone hook her into the mains?" asked Kevin.

Pete moved towards her. McKinley stopped him. "If she's being electrocuted, it'll kill you too," the reporter warned.

"Reporter's license again, McKinley?" sneered Pete. "Electrocuted? Do you see any wires?" He took another cautious step towards her. "She looks to me like she's having some kind of fit. We've got to get her laid flat on the deck. McKinley, give me a hand. Kev, clear us a space."

While Pete went to Scepter's aid, gripping her hands, Kevin began making what proved a futile effort to move the chairs and tables. McKinley, rather than doing as Pete had requested, took out his notebook and pen.

She still sat rigid on the chair, her eyes glazed, staring into space. Then she relaxed but began to breathe rapidly, almost panting as if she were exerting herself to her limit.

Unable to shift the furniture, Kevin looked at her and shrank back. "She scares me almost as much as the ghosts do." He looked to Pete for guidance. "Maybe she's going into a trance again. You know. To talk to her butler, Fish Slice."

"For God's sake, shut up, Kev," Pete snapped, "and get that furniture moved."

But Kevin's jitters had finally got the better of him. Tugging uselessly at the table, his face wobbled in fear and he rambled, almost talking to himself. "She said I'm an unconscious telly frenetic."

"More like a brainless telly addict," snapped Pete.

Her breathing accelerated even further. The sound escaping her lips became a rapid conglomeration of rasping rattles. Pete gripped her more firmly.

"She's hyperventilating," he said.

"She's hyperventilating, my backside," flapped Kevin as he broke wind.

Pete released her, and she began to slide from the chair. Her limbs trembled; her eyes and mouth twitched rapidly, involuntarily. Pete moved behind her and pressed her shoulders to keep her there. He glowered at McKinley who was busy scribbling in his notebook. "Never mind taking notes—give me a hand! Kevin, have you not shifted those tables and chairs yet?"

Kevin's frantic mind shifted into a hysterical overdrive. "The bloody furniture's fixed to the floor," he cried. "Do something, Pete."

McKinley knelt before her, pressing her feet down firmly to the tiled floor. Scepter shook violently, struggling for release.

Pete nodded to McKinley. "We'll carry her to the counter. There's space on the floor in front of it."

They made to pick her up, McKinley gripping her behind the knees, Pete tucking his hands beneath her shoulders.

Then suddenly she spoke. Her mouth opened. Her lips did not move, and the sound her throat emitted was tortured, guttural, unrecognizable as her own.

"*WIGJAM, WIGJAM, WIGJAM, WIGJAM, WIGJAM!*"

Suddenly her whole body tensed. Again her back arched, her chest thrust up and out. The trembling became an uncontrollable shudder. Some unseen force threw both Pete and McKinley back and away from her. They recovered quickly and tried again to move her to the area in front of the counter. For long seconds, while they struggled to control her, she bounced in the seat. Then, just as suddenly, all movement stopped. Her chest collapsed and she slid from the chair, lying completely still on the cafeteria floor.

McKinley got to her first. He put an ear to her chest. Stunned and frightened, he looked up at them.

"Oh my God, she's dead."

14

Standing by, flapping uselessly, Kevin almost burst into tears. "Do something!"

For a long moment, Pete stared at her lifeless body; then, gripped by a sudden determination, he shouldered McKinley out of the way and tore open her blouse.

"Pete, please," gasped Kevin, averting his eyes from her lacy bra. "I know you've always fancied her, but not now."

"Shut up, you idiot!"

Pete closed his mouth over hers, pinched her nose and breathed into her lungs. One, two. He left her mouth, moved down, the heel of his right hand at the base of her breastbone, left hand pressing down. One, two, three, four, five, six, seven... He returned to her mouth and breathed, one, two. Apply chest compression, one, two, three, four, five, all the way up to 30.

Standing back, feeling useless and ineffective, Kevin began to weep.

"Quit blubbing," Pete snapped, "and call for an ambulance."

"It'll take too long to get here," McKinley pointed out.

"Let me worry about that," Pete said, breaking his mouth from hers, "you just call it." Keeping up his resuscitation attempt, he shouted at her. "Damn you, Scepter, breathe, will you!"

Sweat broke out on Pete's forehead. McKinley watched in silent shock as he worked to bring her back. Alongside the reporter, Kevin fumbled with his mobile phone, his hands shaking so badly that he could hardly control his fingers.

The frustration of his fruitless efforts got to Pete. "Come on, you silly cow, breathe."

Mouth to mouth, one, two, chest compression, 5, 10, 20, 30, mouth to mouth, one, two, chest compression, 5, 10, 20, 30. He glanced at his watch. Three minutes. He watched her. Not breathing. He felt for a heartbeat. Nothing.

"She's going," McKinley whispered while alongside him, Kevin was speaking quietly but urgently to the emergency services.

"Not yet. She doesn't go until I let her." Pete lowered his mouth over hers again.

Breathe, one, breathe, two. Palm on breastbone, press, 5, 10, 20, 30. Mouth-to-mouth, chest compression, mouth-to-mouth, wipe away the sweat, chest compression.

On the far side of the house where he was communicating with the spirit of Sir Henry Melmerby, Fishwick first realized something was wrong when he heard his mistress' strangled, garbled voice uttering the incomprehensible word "wigjam."

"Don't matter how much she tries to hide her voice, I can still recognize it," he muttered to himself. He swooped back to the cafeteria. Looking down on Scepter's rigid body from his vantage point near the ceiling, he realized instantly what had happened. Steven Bilks had possessed her.

But Steven Bilks was a fresh, new spirit; he did not know how to control a live body. All he could feel was his fury and frustration.

Fishwick had known such frustration himself on the fields of Flanders. Carrying his master's body back to the British trenches, he had felt a rack of agonizing pain and, to his fury, found himself here, on the spirit plane. That anger, that blazing outrage at having his life cut short so brutally, had been the cause of his inability to communicate with any of the Rand-Epping family, and it was only when Scepter was born and he got his first sight of her angelic face that he had calmed down enough not only to communicate, but to learn to master his abilities to manipulate matter in the real world.

From Fishwick's his point of view, Scepter was one body with two spirits fighting to control it—and Bilks was winning! In his 90 years on the spirit plane, he had seen it before, and he knew that if a person was forced from his or her body, it was the devil's own job to get him back into it.

Difficult, but not impossible. Rather like firing a rifle, it was a case of taking careful aim to knock the intruder away, without disturbing the body's true soul. He had seen it done on occasion, but he had never done it himself.

First time for everything, Albert, he thought.

He calculated his move precisely and aimed not at her, but at the struggling, bitterly frustrated spirit of Steven Bilks. WHOOSH! Off he went. They struck in a shower of light. Bilks flew off across the astral plane, his fury exacerbated by the intervention, by losing the body of the one person with whom he might have communicated.

But Fishwick's own spirit was also deflected by the collision. Before he could reorient, he caromed like a billiard ball, collided with Scepter and knocked her out of her body as well.

"Oops," he said as much to himself as anyone.

⚜

A sense of surprise flooded Scepter when she came to herself. The landscape around her was unfamiliar. The sky was there, dark as it should be. But the sun was there too, shining with a steady, white light, and it called to her, beckoned her to enter. She could not hear it, but the call was there, somewhere in her being.

There were others nearby, human forms of various colors, ranging from dull and neutral whites to cool blues to high reds, and somewhere on the other side of them, a fiery ball of anger flitted across the starless night.

She looked down, and, with a shock, she understood. Pete knelt over her lifeless body, working frantically. She could not hear what he was saying, but she could see that he was trying to revive her.

I have died. This is the spirit plane.

A male form approached her. There were no distinguishing features, but she knew instantly who it was. "Fishwick? Fishwick! I'm so pleased to be with you, Fishwick." She found that, with little effort, she was able to emanate waves of love. In a sense, she thought, she *was* love.

Fishwick was less pleased. "Modom, you don't belong here. It's not your time yet." He gestured towards the real world in the cafeteria, where Pete continued in his efforts to revive her.

Scepter looked down. A sense of calm acceptance had come over her. She felt sad for Pete. Sad that he did not know the peace that she had just attained. "But I like it here, Fishwick. It's so peaceful."

Her butler put some urgency into his voice. "Modom, *that* is where you belong. With the living. Your time will come, but not for a good few years yet. And if you do not get a move on, go back to your body, soon it will be too late. Despite Mr. Brennan's efforts, your body cannot survive for long without the essential *you*."

Scepter ignored him and looked around at the other nearby figures. A steady stream of spirits soared into The Light. "Where's my mother?" she asked.

"Your mother passed through The Light soon after she came here, Modom, as I have told you many times before." Fishwick sounded as if he were reproving her. "She has moved on to the next life."

"Ah. I forgot." Scepter felt a great forlornness come over her. "How did I come to be here, Fishwick?"

Her manservant gestured at the crimson form of Steven Bilks. "He tried to take over your body."

Scepter had a dim memory of a titanic struggle in the cafeteria, but like the waking memory of a dream she could not piece it together into a coherent sequence of events. "I forgot, again," she said.

"Forgetfulness is the first sign of a spirit ready to move on, Modom." Now Fishwick was practically begging her. He waved at the spirits moving into The Light. "They have already forgotten, Modom, but you haven't yet. Your body is dying without you. You must return."

Still Scepter would not heed his words. "Should I go through The Light, Fishwick?"

"No!" The word was bitten off. "You must not go through The Light. Go back, Modom, go back now."

His insistence got through to her. "I owe you so much, Fishwick. For the companionship and guidance you have given me since I was a little girl, for your protection in times of danger. I don't want to leave you here, alone."

"I appreciate your concern, Modom, but I am all right here," Fishwick assured her. "I am not alone as long as you are with me. There is only one way you can repay me for my work."

"Yes?" Scepter was eager to show her gratitude.

Fishwick gestured to the cafeteria, to her lifeless form, and indicated Pete's desperate efforts to revive her. "Go back where you belong. Don't come here again until it is truly your time."

She understood, and with that understanding came further waves of gratitude for her butler. Had she been in her body, she would have had tears in her eyes. His concern had ever and always been only for her welfare.

She was about to return to her body when Fishwick stopped her. "Wait, Modom. I almost forgot."

She stopped. "Forgot, Fishwick?"

He stretched out an arm. "Take my hand, Modom."

Scepter reached for him. She could see no fingers on her silvery arm, but she nevertheless felt his hand close around hers. He drifted slowly towards The Light. Closer and closer they approached and, as they neared, it slowly expanded until it filled the sky. When she looked back on the cafeteria, it was like looking down a microscope, or, more correctly, a telescope turned the wrong way round. Her body and her friends were far away at the bottom of a narrow tunnel.

Scepter felt no fear, only a tingle of apprehension mingled with a feeling of wonder at the sheer immensity of The Light. She noticed that its edges were not as sharply defined as she had thought. Instead there was a hazy area between the dark of the spirit plane and the rim of The Light, an area where the two boundaries undulated. It reminded her of a photograph she had once seen of the sun. What looked like a steady, shining disc, was really a swirling mass of activity, pulsating with energy.

This, she reminded herself, was not the sun. This was the gateway to the next life. When they reached the outer edges, she looked in. It was not a consistent light. Inside, there were areas where strong eddies were at work, creating a clockwise-turning vortex. The spirits of those recently come over sped past them, hurtling into The Light until they were swallowed up by these powerful whirls, swirling and twirling their way to the next world. She tracked one or two, but in an instant, they were hopelessly lost in the brilliance.

The lure of The Light was so much stronger here. She felt an intense yearning to leave Fishwick, to allow herself to drift until the power of The Light sucked her in too.

"Why are we coming so close, Fishwick?"

"It's all about energy," Fishwick explained. "Those of us who have been here a long time have learned how to take energy from The Light. Go too close and it will suck you in, stand too far, and you will gain nothing, but get it just right and..." He reached his free arm to The Light so that it barely touched.

Scepter felt pulses of energy running through her, invigorating her, investing her with enormous power. At the same time she could feel the pull of The Light, a desperate urge to be at one with it, to go through that white tunnel and learn what lay ahead.

"When a spirit returns to its body," Fishwick explained as the energy continued to course through them, "it normally feels like hell. This infusion of energy will ensure that you are no worse than disoriented."

He yanked his arm away and drifted with her back to the area above the cafeteria. "Now, Modom, you can go back."

"Thank you, Fishwick." With a final gesture of farewell, Scepter swooped towards her body and dropped precisely into it.

⚜

To Pete and the others, it was as if she had heard, as if, just before the last spark of living energy puttered from her, the message got through. She coughed, she spluttered, a trickle of saliva ran from her mouth and her eyes flickered open.

Pete sighed in relief. "Thank God for that." He smiled down at her. "Welcome back." He slid a strong arm under her shoulders and helped her sit up.

Scepter became aware of her open blouse. Blushing, she buttoned up the garment and looked into Pete's eyes. Then she burst into tears and fell into his arms, sobbing.

Relief flooded through them all. Kevin, having finally got through to the emergency services, now told them to cancel the call. Shutting off his phone, he made his way to the rear of the service counter and made tea for them. Presently, they sat at a table and Scepter detailed her experience to them while McKinley made notes.

"I remember everything clearly," she reported, drinking gratefully from her cup. The tea restored her energy, helped calm her bubbling emotions. "Fishwick was away monitoring the far side of the house, and Steven Bilks moved in to possess me as I slept. He possessed me before I could stop him."

His mind filled with memories of her open blouse, Kevin muttered, "He's lucky then, isn't he?" He realized they had heard and blushed. "I mean, it's lucky Pete knew how to keep calm in a crisis."

Scepter gave him a prim stare, then turned her gaze to Pete. "I believe Bilks is trying to tell us who killed him. He wants to see them pay."

"Scepter," said Pete gently, "you've been through an ordeal. You're confused. Give yourself time to come round properly."

"I am not confused," she said. There was no conflict in her voice, no argument with Pete, just a simple statement of fact. Her face took on a beatific appearance. "While I was on the Other Side, I didn't remember, but now I can recall it all quite clearly. For a brief moment, Bilks and I were one and I knew what he was trying to do. This message, wigjam or whatever it is, is telling us who killed him."

"Someone who works in a jam factory and wears a wig," suggested Kevin, and McKinley made a note of it.

Pete spotted the reporter's pen wriggling across the paper. "McKinley, Kevin was joking when he said it. Right Kev?"

"I—er—yeah. Right. I was joking."

"Doesn't matter," McKinley said. "It's good copy."

Scepter brought their attention back to their purpose. "I had the impression of a keyboard linked to this wigjam."

"Like the computer?" asked Pete, waving in the general direction of Kevin's laptop.

"No, not like a computer. More like a calculator, but not like that. There's a difference between this and a calculator, but I don't know what it is."

"If you want a third party opinion—" McKinley began, but Pete cut him off.

"We don't. Just shut your trap and make up your stories, McKinley." He turned back to Scepter. "Listen luv, we can't go to bolt and solution—"

"Who?" interrupted Kevin.

"Locke and Keynes. Solution. Key. Geddit?" Pete spoke to Scepter again. "We can't go to them with testimony from a ghost. The Chief Inspector won't need much of an excuse for sending me down, and that might be enough of one. You've just had some kind of seizure and you're evidence is no good. We need something more concrete."

"Pete," cried Scepter in distress rather than anger, "will you get it into your head, this was not an epileptic fit? I was possessed by the spirit of Steven Bilks."

Pete shrugged and took a sip of tea. In deference to her obvious anguish, he placated her. "All right, all right. Just calm down. All I'm saying is, it's no use to us if all we've got is a confused message about wigs and jam, and even if we could sort it out, we'd still need more evidence before we could go to the law."

Scepter's face took on a dreamier quality. "I saw Fishwick over there. He guided me back. He infused me with healing energy so all the damage done by Steven's attempt to possess me, all the damage done by the whole episode, was healed." She smiled. "It's like I always imagined it would be. A place of peace and reflection, where life in this world can be still be viewed and where we can study the errors of our fellow humans before moving on to our next life."

"Just like you always imagined it?" said Pete.

Her features hardened again as she picked up the implications of his remark. She narrowed her eyes at Pete. "Yes. Just like I always imagined it would be, only this was no figment of my imagination. I have seen the Other Side."

A bleep from the computer ended the argument.

"Hell's bells," said Kevin. "We've been so busy I'd forgotten about it." He crossed to the console and studied the displays. "Attic," he murmured, bringing the relevant camera to the center of the screen. "Motion sensor triggered, EMF sensor going bananas, but I can't see nothing."

"Right," said Pete, with fresh determination, "let's get up there."

McKinley stood and helped Scepter to her feet.

Only Kevin held back. He squirmed under their disapproving stares. "All right," he admitted, "so I'm scared."

Pete nodded. "Fine. You wait here, Kev, and keep an eye on the rest of the house... alone."

"I'm right with you, good buddy." Kevin jumped up and scurried after them.

They hurried from the cafeteria.

Their progress up the stairs and along the landings was slow and cautious. Pete had a wary eye open for the human intruders he felt certain were in the house, while Scepter called softly to Fishwick and received only intermittent replies as her butler busied himself with events on the Other Side.

They reached the top landing. Pete paused at the door to Aggie's room and pressed his ear to it, listening for a moment. Gripping the handle, he yanked it and hurled himself in.

The place was empty.

Pete cursed. "They got away. Again."

Kevin stared at the wall. "Look!"

Across the wall, written in large, dark red letters, was the word WGJAMW.

❧

"It's writ... writ... written in b-b-blood," stammered Kevin.

Pete crossed to it and dabbed the lettering with a tentative finger.

"Whatever it's written in," he said, taking a clasp knife from his pocket, "it's dry and must have been here for a while."

Fishing further into his pocket, he came out with a notebook, tore out a sheet of paper and folded it in half. Scraping at the lettering, he allowed samples to fall into the folded paper, which he then folded over again, before tucking it gently back into his pocket.

"Scepter," he asked, "did you notice this when you set up the cameras?"

"No, Pete. It must have been written there after we came up here."

"And yet we all know that's impossible," said McKinley.

"But you didn't notice it, either?" Pete persisted. "When you were up here with her, I mean."

The reporter shook his head. "I swear it wasn't there."

"But then," Kevin pointed out, his fear momentarily forgotten, "you'd swear Arsenal were a cricket team if it sold a few extra newspapers."

For the first time the reporter reacted as if the slights on his character were getting under his skin. "I do not tell lies."

"'Course not," breezed Kevin. "Not compared to, say, politicians—or used car salesmen."

"One of these days, Keeley—"

"Shut it, the both of you," Pete ordered. "I have a pal in forensics. I'll get him to analyze this stuff tomorrow, but I think it's just paint." He shone his flashlight on it, highlighting its crimson surface. "Blood usually dries dark brown, not red."

"It doesn't matter what was used to produce the message," Scepter objected. "It wasn't here when McKinley and I checked the room earlier."

"It doesn't matter how it was produced?" Pete demanded in total amazement. "Suppose we find out it's paint? What conclusion will you draw? That Bilko's ghost nicked it from a decorator's merchant, like he would have done when he was alive? Or maybe he bumped into Michelangelo over there and asked for a loan of his paint pot."

"You know what I mean," Scepter argued. "This is Bilks trying to tell us who killed him."

"I'll reserve judgment on that until I've checked the video footage," said Pete, leading the way back out onto the landing.

"Checking the videos? What will that prove?" demanded Scepter.

Pete stopped on the landing and turned to face her. "The cameras have been running in that room for hours. If that really did materialize by some supernatural method, we'll have picked it up." He turned again and led the way back along the landing.

❧

"Modom?"

Hanging back behind the others as they made their way along the upper corridor, Scepter kept her voice low. "What is it, Fishwick?"

"The message on the wall in Aggie's room. Steven Bilks did not produce it."

Scepter quelled her surprise. "Do you know who did?"

"No, Modom, I have been busy with many matters tonight."

"Sir Henry? Aggie Devis?" She sounded more hopeful than convinced.

"Modom," Fishwick insisted, "this was not produced by any spirit.'

"How can you be so certain?"

"A simple process of deduction, Modom," her butler explained. "The raw materials are not available to him. There is no red paint in the house, and if it is blood, where did he get it? There is no blood, animal or human, in such quantities"

"Your conclusion?" Scepter demanded.

"That message was left on the wall by someone from the real world, and it was there when you arrived."

"Thank you, Fishwick," said Scepter, "I'll keep all that in mind."

⟡

"I'll say this for you guys," said McKinley as they made their way down the stairs, "you certainly provide good entertainment." He looked around at the long shadows. "And this place is seriously spooky."

"Especially for an empty head like yours," Pete noted.

"Bit barbed, Brennan. You know, I could do you a lot of good."

"Not based on past form, you couldn't."

They reached the grand hall and the entrance to the Long Gallery. Pete stopped and faced the reporter. "Why don't you tell us what you're really after?"

McKinley's ears colored red. Catching up with them in time to hear the exchange, Scepter leapt to his defense.

"Pete, why can't you accept that he may be genuinely interested in our work?"

Pete turned and carried on to the cafeteria. "Because I know him. Three hick ghost hunters? Not McKinley's bag. He'd have given it to a junior."

He moved into the servery, switched on the kettle and gathered cups for fresh tea. While he prepared them, he eyed McKinley. "Well?"

The reporter gave him a lopsided grin. "You may be right, Brennan, but I'm saying nothing. We journalists never reveal too much."

Pete had been getting steadily angrier since the exchange with Scepter in the attics. Kevin had noticed it. So, too, had Scepter, but McKinley seemed ignorant of or impervious to it. Now, the ex-policeman suddenly turned on the reporter.

"And we ex-cops have ways of making you tell."

"Don't push it, Brennan. You may impress him and her—" He jerked his thumb sideways at Kevin and Scepter. "—but it doesn't work with m—" McKinley trailed off as Pete advanced furiously towards him. "All right, all right," McKinley capitulated. "I'll tell you."

Pete stopped and waited, the other two hung in the background, also waiting for the reporter to explain himself.

"I got a call from a contact. I won't say who." He gave a weak smile. "I told you, I like to keep my sources secret. Anyway, he told me about you and the tape of a voice, supposedly from beyond the grave. When I got to see him, he mentioned that it was all linked with the disappearance of a consignment of pirate DVDs, and *that's* what I'm interested in. The police never mentioned them, but you did, and they are the reason Bilko was killed, aren't they?"

Pete turned back to the kettle. "No comment." He smiled cynically. The reporter grinned.

"I'll find out, you know."

"Not from me, you won't."

McKinley took Scepter's elbow and led her towards a table.

"And don't you tell him anything, Scepter," Pete called after them. His words fell on deaf ears, and he assumed she was still annoyed at his interpretation of her seizure.

With a wary eye on them, Kevin walked round the service counter to stand at Pete's side, and kept his voice to something just above a whisper. "Why aren't you telling him, Pete?"

Pete too kept his voice down. "Because I don't know where he's getting his information. Aside from Bent Benny, that is. Anyway, you know what a prat he is, and I hate his guts."

"Because he's scored with Scepter?" Kevin inquired.

Pete shook his head. "Judging by the look on her face when they came down the stairs just after I got here, I'd say he scored an own goal with Scepter."

Kevin looked across at the reporter and their partner, engrossed in conversation. "He seems to be doing all right now."

"Just shut up about it, Kev. I'm telling him nothing."

"But I don't get it." Kevin complained again.

Pete heaved a sigh. "Did you tell him about the DVDs?"

Kevin shook his head. "No."

"Neither did I," said Pete. "So where did he get it from?"

"You said it," Kevin pointed out. "Bent Benny."

"And did you tell our Mr. Stringer?" Pete pressed.

Kevin shrugged. "Can't remember. Don't think so. There again, McKinley could be using anyone. Sherlock knew about them, and you know what a big mouth he's got. He coulda—"

"It was a rhetorical question, you donk," Pete berated him. "I know you didn't tell Bent Benny."

"You mean historical."

"I forgot, English was never your strong point. Kev, we have to ask ourselves where he found out about the DVDs."

"Johnny and Jimmy Tate?"

"I dunno," Pete admitted, "and until I find out, I'm saying nothing to him. That five grand is as good as ours, pal, once I can open Wilcox up a bit further, and I don't wanna let a berk like McKinley screw it up for us."

"So what are you gonna do about Wilcox?" Kevin asked.

Pete shrugged and poured boiling water into four cups. "Apply some pressure." He grinned. "In fact, I think I'm gonna enjoy it."

Kevin picked up two cups, Pete brought the other two and they joined Scepter and McKinley at their table by the computer set-up.

But a barrier seemed to have opened up between the two sets. After her disagreement with him in the attic, Pete sensed that Scepter preferred the company of McKinley. Telling himself she was doing it just to annoy him, Pete dropped the two teas on their table and joined Kevin across the aisle.

"Pete," Kevin whispered, "now that you know Wilcox is behind it all, why aren't you doing something? You know, going to the filth or beating him up?"

Pete cast an envious glance across the aisle at Scepter and McKinley's tête-à-tête. Answering Kevin, he kept his voice down. "Because Wilcox *isn't* behind it. He's only the crankshaft, not the engine. It's this Jay character. He organized the theft."

"And you reckon that this Jay character exists, do you?" Kevin sounded doubtful.

Pete shrugged. "How else would Wilcox know about the DVDs and where to get his hands on them? Look Kev, Wilcox is a two-bit gangster. Pushing dope, flogging iffy booze, running gambling rackets, loan-sharking. Those are Wilcox's fields, not flogging pirate DVDs. Even if he knew about them, he wouldn't be interested, other than maybe selling the information to a third party. He admits he took them, but it had to be for cash. He was transport and storage, nothing more."

Kevin accepted Pete's analysis. "And you reckon Wilcox was telling the truth, do you? That he really doesn't know who Jay is?"

"No, I think he was lying, but only time and a good, old-fashioned stakeout will prove that." Pete grinned with avarice. "Once I know who Jay is, I can wrap the whole thing up, deliver Bilko's killer to Locke and pick up the five grand from Tate."

⁕

Across the table, Scepter eyed the close discussion between the two old friends and felt a stab of jealousy rush through her at the thought that Kevin and Pete had something to discuss which excluded her.

"Why do you bother with these two bums?" asked McKinley.

His question irritated her. "I told you before. Both Pete and Kevin were very good to me when I first moved to Ashdale. They gave me a roof over my head and offered to help me with my work."

McKinley was dismissive. Keeping his voice really low to ensure Pete could not hear him, he said, "You owe them nothing, and they'll hold you back. Keeley is a crook, and my experience of Brennan is that he helps those he thinks will let him help himself later on." He narrowed his eyes at her. "In the same way you wouldn't let me help myself earlier tonight."

Scepter recalled their passionate embrace and the way she had stopped him. "I told you, I'm not that kind of girl."

McKinley stared pointedly at her blouse and Scepter recalled, with a blush, the way it had been open when she returned to her body. "You sure came on like that kind of girl upstairs, and you were almost advertising like that kind of girl when Brennan saved your life."

Maintaining a stern, almost matriarchal face, a trick her mother had taught her many years previously, she said, "And you wonder why I bother with Pete and Kevin? Having my blouse open came about because Pete was saving my life. He's reliable, Mike, and so, too, is Kevin."

Leaning even closer to her, he ignored her mild reproof and pressed his argument. "Scepter, you and I could be a winning team. They're a pair of losers, but I'm not. I'm a respected investigative reporter, and I think we could really hit it big together. The reporter and the medium. We could expose the cons, follow up the real hauntings, put out stuff that would really make Joe Public think twice about spooks and stuff. Take the world by storm."

"In the *Ashdale Evening Chronicle*?" Scepter was still smarting from his inane comment on her advertising like that kind of girl.

"No, not the *Ashdale Evening Chronicle*. I can freelance. I have contacts—"

"Shush."

The instruction took McKinley by surprise because it was not whispered. She had raised her voice so that Kevin and Pete could hear too, and they all fell silent, listening to the night.

Outside, the wind had dropped, but there was a faint rasping, like someone breathing in and out. Kevin began to sweat, the glisten of perspiration lighting his forehead in the dim glow of their lamps. Pete and McKinley held their breath, listening.

The voice came in faint at first, but gradually gained in strength and volume, coming from all directions, enveloping them, the words spoken through hissing, labored breathing, its message clear.

"WIGJAM... WIGJAM... WIGJAM..."

⚜

"I told you I'd heard it!" Kevin cried. "Wigjam!"

"Quiet," Pete ordered, and they listened once more to the voice. He stood up and began to wander around the room, head cocked first to one side, then the other, trying to locate the source of the sound.

At the table, Scepter made no effort to keep her voice down. "Fishwick?"

"Modom?" The voice of her butler sounded in her head.

"Fishwick, is the source of that sound on the spirit plane?"

"Not to my knowledge, Modom."

"Not to your knowledge? What is that supposed to mean?" Scepter was positively indignant over her butler's response.

Fishwick did not react to her tone, but answered matter-of-factly. "None of the spirits haunting this house are making that sound, but there may be other spirits here not native to the house which I have not noticed."

"So, it isn't Steven Bilks?" she demanded.

"No Modom. He is in the background, sulking after his failed attempt to possess you." Once again, Fishwick's reply was factual and unemotional.

Coming back to her fellow investigators in the cafeteria, Scepter passed on her butler's remarks. Kevin breathed a sigh of relief, Pete scowled and continued his efforts to locate the sound.

McKinley laughed. "You really believe all this guff, don't you?"

She frowned. In that instant, whatever efforts McKinley had made to ingratiate himself with her were negated. "I speak the truth. Nothing more."

"And I don't need her ghostly butler to tell me it's nothing to do with ghosts," Pete declared.

"What do you mean?" demanded Scepter.

"How many ghosts do you know that know how to use a PA system?" Pete gestured vaguely at the four corners of the room.

In each corner, set high up, near the ceiling, were small, discreet speakers.

"Not very big, are they?" commented McKinley.

"Size isn't everything," said Kevin with a pointed stare at both Pete and the reporter. "They may be tiny, but they could still push out a coupla hundred watts per channel."

Pete looked satisfied, Scepter crestfallen. With the noise of the voice providing a backdrop, Pete said triumphantly, "I told you someone was taking the mickey with us all along. Now where will this be operated from?"

"I haven't a clue," said Scepter miserably. "We've checked the entire house and the stables. There's no one here but us."

Light dawned in Pete's eyes. "No. There's one area we've never checked." A slow smile crossed his features. "The private apartments." He glanced across the grand hall.

"Pete, no," urged Scepter. "We were told we couldn't go into the private rooms. Jonathan Melmerby could withdraw permission if he finds out."

Pete dismissed her with an angry, backward wave and strode out of the cafeteria, into the entrance hall, where the noise of the rasping voice was even louder. Across the hall, the paneled door to the apartments was roped off. Pete marched to it.

"It's locked," Scepter protested, hurrying to his side, "and we don't have a key. You'll have to break in and... "

She trailed off as Pete removed the rope, turned the doorknob and pushed the door open. Once inside, they found that the noise from the entrance hall diminished into no more than a muted, indecipherable mumble.

The private apartments were just as lavish as those open to visitors, but the furnishings were more modern. Two doors led off in different directions, one to the dining room and kitchen, the other to a narrow hall and the bedrooms. Pete checked them all quickly. In the final room, a small, windowless apartment, he found what he was looking for.

"Now, tell me it's Bilko," he said, gesturing at a modest, computer-driven PA system.

Kevin came in, and cast his expert eye over it. A small control board held marked switches for speakers all over the house, and every one of them was in the "on" position. The computer screen was lit, its screensaver running. When Kevin hit a key, it disappeared, replaced by a sight familiar to him: the display of an active media player. In the center of the screen in its own window sat a view of the cafeteria where their own computer monitored the house.

Kevin sat before it, his fingers dancing over the keyboard. In the far distance, all sounds in the hall ceased. He fiddled once more with the keyboard, redirecting the audio output, then restarted the track. From the computer's built-in speakers came the sound.

"WIGJAM... WIGJAM..."

"Did they use the manor's CCTV security system too?" asked Scepter, pointing to the image of the cafeteria.

Kevin made a study of the links. "Curiously enough, no. Probably couldn't trace the line from the cafeteria back to here." He tapped the screen. "This view comes from a webcam, or some camera in there that they've used as a webcam, and they've been driving the whole thing over the Internet. Whoever's linked to this machine simply sends the sounds. While the PA speakers are switched on, it'll play all over the house." He called up the file list and found a track entitled *Breath*. He played it, and from the machine's speakers came the sound of breathing he had heard earlier. "They saw me alone in the cafeteria earlier," he grumbled, "and took advantage."

"Can you find out who's behind it?" McKinley asked.

Again Kevin hit the keys, his fingers darting across the keyboard with unerring accuracy.

"One or two tracking cookies," he muttered, scanning through the Internet Options menu, "but they're probably from the ISP. Nothing that I recognize. Ten to one they were watching over the camera and cut their connection when they realized we'd rumbled them."

Behind him, Pete fumed. "Whoever it is, they've been watching us all the time. That explains how they knew when to play ghosts the other night."

Kevin was doubtful. "Could be, but how would they have known to watch the café the other night?" He scowled at McKinley. "After his rag printed reports about Bilko's drum a few nights back, they might have twigged that they could watch us tonight, but not two days ago. Even the way news spreads in this town, they couldn't have moved that quickly." Abruptly, he switched the subject back. "Pete, this has to be one of Bent Benny's set-ups. He's a wiz at putting these things together, and as far as I know, he was the only other person in Ashdale, apart from us, who had heard the wigjam thing. He listened to that tape we took him, and as we know—" Again he looked at the reporter. "—he made at least one copy."

Pete mulled over the information. "It makes a sort of sense. The noise we've just been listening to is an enhanced copy of the tape you took to him, but why would Bent Benny try to scare us off?"

McKinley chuckled. "He may be trying to scam *me*, not you. As you've guessed, he was the one who tipped me off to the connection between this place and the missing DVDs. Maybe he was trying to persuade me the Melmerby ghosts took them."

"No," Scepter argued, "it doesn't make sense. How did Benny get in to set this all up?" She gestured around at the house. "He would need keys to this place and there's only the one set as far as I know, and they have been with me, apart from the time the police had them. Pete, could one of your former colleagues have—?"

Pete cut her off. "No way. I told you before, Locke is an honest cop. A pain in the ass, but an honest pain in the ass. This was a murder scene and he would not have let those keys out of his sight."

Scepter nodded. "Then there's more to this than meets the eye."

"I agree," Pete said, "but I still don't believe it's anything to do with ghosts. As for getting in here, Benny wouldn't have too much trouble. He's like Kev. Got more contacts than the printed circuit board in that computer. I'll see Benny in the morning. In the meantime, Kev, shut that thing down and let's see if we can find the camera in the restaurant."

Kevin busied himself for a moment with closing down the computer, and they retraced their steps back to the cafeteria, where Kevin once more took center stage, ambling round the servery, carefully studying the walls above it.

"It must be somewhere here. The angle clearly showed the windows." He waved at the panoramic view.

Scepter flicked the restaurant lights on. "Then we should be able to see it."

"Don't bet on it," said Kevin. "These things can be the size of your little finger. Smaller, even."

They all settled on the area around the ranges as the most likely spot for the camera to be secreted and began looking.

"Modom," said Fishwick, "there is a curious device like a tiny black billiard ball above the ranges, next to the cooker ventilation hood."

"Thank you, Fishwick," said Scepter and reported his findings to the others.

The moment she guided them, Kevin spotted it. In deference to Pete's greater agility, he allowed his ex-policeman chum to climb onto the frying range, pick up the device and yank the wires free.

Jumping down, Pete tossed it to Kevin, who took the tiny camera back to the table where he studied it under the close lighting of their lanterns. It was the size of a novelty pencil sharpener, round and bulbous, its fisheye lens bulged out of a black, polymer casing. On the back was a tiny label.

"There you go." Kevin tossed the thing back to Pete. "Supplied by B. Stringer Electronics, Chapel Road, Ashdale. Told you it was one of Benny's."

"Right" Pete dropped it in his pocket. "I'll want a word or five with Bent Benny tomorrow. In the meantime, Kevin, you're in the frame again. Check tonight's video footage, will you? See if that message on the attic wall was there when we turned up."

Kevin transferred his attention to their computer system and searched out the footage. Using a lens similar to the webcam they had just found, their camera gave a distorted view of the whole room, and on the back wall, the message, *WGJAMW*, could clearly be seen. At the bottom of the screen was the timer strip Kevin had set up, and it read 17:23:37.

Pete laughed in triumph. "See? It was there at half past five yesterday afternoon." He sneered at Scepter and McKinley. "Some ghost hunters you two are. How could you miss it?"

Scepter blushed and McKinley coughed to hide his embarrassment.

Pete scowled his disapproval. "Oh, I get it. You were distracted. With each other. Scepter, how could you? With him? Especially when I'm so close."

"Pete, I—" Scepter began.

"I mean I thought you had better taste than a scumbag like McKinley," protested Pete. "Even Kevin would have been easier for my bruised ego."

"I'm sorry. I don't know what came over me."

"'What,' being the operative word," said Kevin with a pointed stare at the reporter.

McKinley took instant umbrage. "Are you calling me some kind of animal, Keeley?"

"If the cap fits," said Kevin and left his words hanging.

McKinley took in the frank envy in Pete's eyes. "Come on, guys. She said she wasn't an item with either of you."

Scepter gave him a withering stare. "I object to being described as 'she' and I'm not 'an item' with anyone. I am a woman, not a thing, and I am not a possession." To Pete, she said, "Forget about Mike and me. Were do we go from here?"

"You go on with your ghost hunt. I'll see Bent Benny in the morning."

15

Sylvie nudged Wilcox in the back. His eyes opened and he stared at the green LED display of his alarm clock registering 4:00 a.m. It took a moment for him to realize he was in his own bedroom, in the living quarters above the club.

"There's someone downstairs."

Wilcox grunted. "Do you know what the bloody time is?"

"There's someone downstairs, you twit," Sylvie urged. "Burglars."

The word snapped his brain into overdrive. He threw off the duvet, dragged open the drawer of his bedside cabinet, and took out an automatic pistol. Cocking it, he marched out of the room and onto the landing, where he met Groom and Lawson, both carrying baseball bats.

"Someone downstairs, Ronnie," said Groom.

"Tell me about it." Wilcox hurried on down the stairs and through the private access into the clubroom. "Lemmy," he barked, "Check the front and side doors. Tommy, you do the cellar. Come on. Move your asses. And don't overdo it," he shouted as they split up. "I want them alive."

"Don't overdo it?" queried Groom. "Who was it that put Bilko's lights out?"

⁓⁂⁓

Lawson made his way carefully down the cellar steps. He was tired, and when his sleep was disturbed, it made him angry. Angry enough to damage the scroats who had the nerve to break into Flutter-Bys.

He cheered himself up with the thought that it might that pig, Brennan. He'd love to give Brennan some serious GBH.

The cellar was quiet. When the club was open, there would be the occasional hiss of compressed gases from the beer feeds, or the click of a pump switching on, and there would be the muted sounds from the main room up above, but at this hour, it was silent but for a light buzz from the cold store.

He reached the bottom of the steps, baseball bat at the ready, and turned sharply to his left, looking under the stairs. Nothing. No one. He padded across the stone floor and checked the cage where the spirits, expensive wines and tobacco products were kept. All secure.

A glance around at the crates of bottled beers, packs of canned drinks and cases of wine told him he was the only one there.

Finally, he turned his attention to the cold store. He gripped the handle to open it—and paused. Was that a whisper?

He cocked an ear, his brain editing out the sound of the cold store motor. There it was again. A faint, distant whisper. Almost inaudible. Almost like...

"Wigjam."

It was clearer this time. Coming from somewhere behind the cold room. But there was nothing behind the cold store other than a brick wall.

"Ronnie?" he threw the question into the cellar.

He stepped to the side of the giant fridge and looked around. Nothing. No one. Again.

He decided that his tired mind was playing tricks on him. Fatigue and all that fooling around up at Melmerby Manor was tricking his hearing.

He returned to the cold room door and gripped the handle again.

"Wigjam."

Anger consumed him. "You're dead meat, whoever you are," he shouted and yanked the door open.

A blast of foul-smelling methane struck him full in the face. "WIGJAM!" The roar almost deafened him. Something rushed past, hurling him across the cellar. He picked himself up groggily, looked around for his dropped bat. An empty, galvanized metal beer barrel hurtled through the air and clanged onto the floor next to him. He stood and ran. A bottle of wine sailed through the air and smashed into the stairs as he reached them.

"WIGJAM!"

Lawson fled in terror.

⚜

Fishwick arrived to find the spirit of Steven Bilks wreaking havoc in the cellar of Flutter-Bys.

"Take it easy, me old china, or you'll have a heart attack." The nonsense of such a statement struck Fishwick. "Bin over here all these years, and I'm still talking to 'em as if they're alive," he reproved himself.

"WIGAM," roared Bilks.

"What about wigjam?" Fishwick wanted to know.

"WIGJAM."

Bilks flew off through the astral plane, and Fishwick was left to ruminate. "I don't even know what a bleeding wigjam is." He made his way to Melmerby Manor and hovered above Scepter's sleeping form in the cafeteria. For a moment he considered reporting the events, but changed his mind. "Let her sleep. There's always tomorrow."

In the clubroom, Wilcox passed Lawson a shot of whiskey. The thug took it in shaking hands and gulped it down.

"So you didn't see him?" Wilcox demanded.

"I'm telling you, Ronnie, there wasn't anyone there."

Wilcox dismissed the idea. "He was well hidden, you mean. And he probably got out through the beer trap while you were running away." He picked up a bottle of Old Sporran, recalled that it was mostly water, and instead reached for a half empty bottle of Jack Daniels. Pouring himself a generous slug, he sipped on it, his face beaming with pleasure. "Better than that witch water Keeley dumped on me." He turned to face his two thugs. "I'll bet it was that toerag, Brennan."

"Ronnie, I tell you—"

"I don't wanna hear it, Tommy," the boss cut him off. "Tomorrow, the pair of you can get the word out. I wanna know who broke in."

At Melmerby Manor, the night wore on with no other significant events. Their equipment picked up the occasional orb, traveling wispily across the floors or through the air, their microphones and tapes collected the odd noise, but there were no other major manifestations.

At just after six-thirty, with the first, pearly light of dawn showing through the cafeteria windows, Scepter checked on everyone. Kevin and McKinley were dozing, Pete stood by the windows, staring moodily at the coming day.

For her, the entire night had been a disaster. Brought to the brink of death, her life saved by a man dead for 90 years and another man who was fixated with the idea of her becoming his girlfriend—whether she wanted to or not—and as if all that were not enough, she had foolishly let her guard drop and let passion overtake her with yet another man whose bona fides she was already beginning to question. She took a crumb of comfort from the fact that she had stopped McKinley in time, but that was the only relief in a night of discord.

Moving quietly so as not to disturb the two sleeping men, she left the table and crossed to the window to join Pete.

Outside in the crystal clear air, a third quarter moon lit up the sky, just above a bright, steadily shining star.

"Venus," she whispered. "The goddess of love. Brightest planet in the sky. Beautiful, isn't it?"

Pete grunted.

On the ground beyond the windows, a crispy white coating of frost covered the faded lawns and barren tree branches. The windows of Pete's car, McKinley's car, and Kevin's van were iced up, and it would be another hour before the sun rose to thaw them out.

She tried again. "So beautiful, and so peaceful."

Pete still said nothing and Scepter began to feel guilty again.

"Look, Peter, I'm sorry. McKinley and I were alone, and I suddenly found him—er—attractive."

"What?"

It was as if he had just registered her presence and the way she used his full Christian name rather than the more common, abbreviated form.

"I thought you were bothered about McKinley and me," she explained.

"What?" He repeated. "Oh, I see. No. I was just thinking about the last few days and how odd it's all been. We could be in serious trouble, if we don't watch ourselves. I told you, Locke probably doesn't believe it's anything to do with us, but he can make life difficult, and as a private eye, I rely on my reputation for honesty." He looked down at her and shrugged. "Besides, you and McKinley are nothing to do with me, are you? Your life's your own."

"Nothing happened... well, we kissed and then he got a bit physical." She gave a murmur that could have been a cynical laugh. "Octopus hands. But that's all." Scepter wondered why she was bothering to explain the situation. Was she taking care to ensure Pete did not think less of her, or was she simply rationalizing the non-event to herself?

He confirmed his apparent lack of interest. "I just said, didn't I, it's nothing to do with me. Just watch him, though. I know him. He doesn't care about anyone but Mike McKinley. He'll use you, get the copy he wants from you and then dump you. I know. I've seen him do it before."

Her intuition pointed her towards the core of his warning. "Your business with the prostitute?"

He nodded. "The general details were never meant to be made public, but he was dating a policewoman. She let slip secrets in bed, and the next thing we knew, it was all over the *Chronicle*. The editor dressed it up in moral outrage, but it didn't fool anyone. That rag is all about digging dirt, and McKinley did a good job digging it on me. What's worse, to sweet talk his way out of a potential lawsuit for publishing the story, he named the woman who told him the tale, and she lost her job, too. Trust me, he'll do it to you if he has to."

Scepter gave a sad little laugh. "I have no real job to lose, have I?"

"Probably not, but you have your reputation, and by the time McKinley has done with it, it will be in tatters. He's scum, worse than the Wilcoxes of this world. At least you know where you are with them."

Silence took hold again. Scepter watched a fox emerge from the trees bordering Melmerby Manor's retaining wall and amble across the lawn.

"Going home after a night's hunting," she commented. "A bit like us, really."

"Except that the fox knows what it's looking for."

"So do we," Scepter assured him, "if only you'd open your mind."

"Let's not start that again, eh?"

She smiled up at him. "Fishwick finds your skepticism easier to deal with than I do. Apparently, he was like that in life. But think, Pete, I told you where to look for that camera, didn't I? Fishwick told me where it was."

"Or you spotted it and you *think* Fishwick told you where it was."

"What would it take to convince you?"

He shrugged. "Fishwick would have to materialize in front of me... and even then I'd swear it was booze or fatigue tricking my eyes." His brow knitted in perplexity. "You told us your butler was killed on the Somme."

"And so he was," Scepter agreed.

"Then how would an old git like that recognize a webcam?"

"Pete," Scepter said patiently, "Fishwick has been watching the real world for over 90 years. Just because he is a ghost, doesn't mean he's lost the capacity for learning. Besides, his description to me was of something like a billiard ball, not a webcam."

He sighed. "Always an answer, isn't there?" He checked his watch. "Six-forty. Nearly time we were wrapping it up."

They walked back to the table.

A question occurred to Scepter. "Pete, what would Benny Stringer stand to gain from that computer set-up?"

"Nothing. Bent Benny is like your boyfriend here." Pete gestured at McKinley. "He only gives a damn about himself. If I go to him and pay for information, I'll get it, but if Wilcox goes to him and pays for information, *he'll* get it. Benny works for Benny. No one else."

"And will you pay him?" she asked.

"No," he promised. "I'll persuade him. Don't worry about it; Bent Benny will tell me all I want to know. Now hadn't we better wake up Sleeping Beauty and Rip van Winkle here? We've an hour's work taking the equipment apart."

Scepter nodded. "You're probably right. It'll be daylight soon, and I don't think we'll get anything else now."

McKinley was slumped in his chair, his ankles crossed on the seat opposite. Pete kicked the second chair from under his feet, and he awoke with a start. Across the table, Scepter tapped Kevin gently on the shoulder and he awoke slowly, groggily.

"Why couldn't you wake me like that?" complained the reporter.

"If I tapped you, it would be with a hammer," Pete assured him, "and I'd get a round of applause from most of Ashdale for doing it." He clapped his hands together like a market trader about to offer a deal. "Okay people, we have to get our gear dismantled. Kev, me and you will take the attic rooms; Scepter, you and the git here can deal with the first floor landing."

❦

In the corridor outside the master bedroom, Scepter disconnected the jacks connecting the camcorder to the mains supply. At her shoulder, McKinley looked back, watching Kevin and Pete disappear up the attic staircase.

"You should watch Brennan, you know," the reporter warned.

Carefully removing the camcorder from its tripod, Scepter was not listening properly. "Hmm?"

"He's bad news to women," McKinley grumbled on. "Sent out to arrest a woman and he jumped her in exchange for not running her in."

Scepter had heard this time but did not immediately answer, preferring to ensure the camcorder was packed properly in its box, a minor distraction which gave her a few more seconds to formulate a reply.

At length, she looked up from the task. "Pete has told me all about it, and you are editing the tale for your own purposes, aren't you? The woman concerned was that kind of woman, wasn't she?"

'Well... " McKinley trailed off and gave here a silly lop-sided grin. "All right, so I'm trying to eliminate the competition."

Putting the box on the floor, Scepter turned her attention to the tripod, folding the legs together, unfastening the butterfly nuts that held the extended, telescopic legs in place.

"There is no competition," she declared, sliding the legs up and locking them in their shortest position. "I'm not interested in Pete, I'm not interested in you. And where you find the nerve to criticize him, I do not know. You jumped to the wrong conclusion about me last night, didn't you?"

"Okay, okay. I did. I admit it. But hey, you're such a good-looking woman, I just got carried away." He smiled. Scepter did not.

McKinley backtracked along the landing, pulling the cables free of the wall so they could be wound back onto their drums. "Why not let me make amends. Have dinner with me."

"I don't think so," said Scepter, collecting the camcorder and the tripod and following him along the landing.

He paused at the head of the stairs and turned to face her. "Oh, come on, Scepter. Doesn't everyone deserve a second chance?"

"Did you give Pete a second chance?" she demanded "Or the young female officer who told you the tale?"

"I was arrested," he howled. "And I'll bet Brennan never told you that, did he? Don't you believe in telling the truth when faced with the cops? They demanded to know who had given me the information and I had to tell them. I did run a piece afterwards in which I said their treatment of her was too harsh." He softened his approach. "Come on, Scepter. Have dinner with me. All right, so I've given Brennan some stick in the past, but tonight has shown me that he has considerably more assets than I ever gave him credit for. It's a damn good job he was with us last night when you had your seizure, or you'd have been a goner."

At a nod from her, he began to make his way downstairs, pulling the cables clear of the wall as he went. At the bottom, they worked as a team, Scepter drawing the cable slowly towards them, McKinley winding it onto the drum. When it was done, they stacked everything up by the door, ready for loading into Kevin's van.

She had used the time to contemplate his last words. Ignoring his earlier flattery, she decided he was right. Everyone did deserve a second chance, and it occurred to her that Pete and Kevin might be wrong about him. His job inevitably meant invading someone's privacy, and it was impossible to be both objective and please everyone. By the time they were finished with the cables, she had relented.

"All right," she said. "I'll have dinner with you, but that's all I'll have. And there's one other condition."

He grinned broadly. "Name it."

"You give us a good write-up," she demanded.

The grin settled to a smile. "You've got it."

⁂

Even with the manor's lights all switched on, there were still dark shadows lurking in many corners. Kevin felt his nerves rising again and stuck close to Pete all the way up the attic corridor, where Pete pushed open the door of the nursery room.

"You get the camera from Aggie's drum, Kev."

Kevin's color drained. "What? With wigjam written on the wall in there? Not likely. You get it."

Pete shrugged. "All right. You take this room."

"Fine. Pete?"

Pete paused at the door to Aggie's room. "Yes?"

"Leave the doors open," Kevin suggested. "That way I can hear you."

Grinning to himself, Pete moved on, and Kevin entered the nursery.

Although dismantling the equipment was not a complex process, there was a considerable amount to carry once it was done. Cables had to be unplugged and carefully coiled to avoid tangling before being traced back to the socket drums, the tripod had to be folded away, sensors had to be collected and put back into their cases.

Bending over the tripod, unfastening the butterfly screw, releasing the digital camcorder from its seat, Kevin could hear Pete working just a few doors along, and it brought him comfort. Nothing would happen while Pete was there. He could scare off the Argyll & Sutherland Highlanders, never mind the local spooks.

Something struck him lightly on the back of the neck. Intent on releasing the tripod screw, which was supposed to be only hand-tight but offered considerable resistance, Kevin did not look up.

"Stop mucking about, Pete." He concentrated on the butterfly screw again, and heaved at it. "I do wish you wouldn't tighten these things up so much. Great, ham-fisted git."

It happened again. Something stung him lightly on the neck, but this time, it fell to the floor. Already looking downward, Kevin watched it roll away and under the rocking horse. It was some kind of glass bead. Where did Pete get glass beads?

"Pete? That you, Pete?"

Another struck him on the neck and fell to the floorboards under the tripod.

"P-p-p-p-pete?"

"I'm busy." Pete's voice was muffled by walls separating the two rooms.

Kevin began to tremble. "Not again."

Almost the moment he uttered the thought, he was showered with glass beads. With a cry of "WAAH" he ran from the room.

⋘❧⋙

"I'm telling you, someone threw them at me."

All four of them had crowded into the nursery and were staring down at the beads scattered across the floor. In the face of their obvious disbelief, Kevin, his courage restored with their very presence, was beginning to lose his temper.

"What do you think I was doing with a load of glass beads?" Kevin persisted. "Making junk jewelry so I could open a market stall?"

Scepter handled the cardboard box where the beads had been stored the last time she saw them. "You're sure you didn't disturb them?" The look on his face answered her question, and Scepter hastened to explain her thinking. "You had your back to them while you were pulling the tripod apart; you could have knocked the box over."

Kevin looked down his nose at her. "And hit myself on the back of the neck with them? Talk sense."

McKinley cleared his throat. "Well if you ask me—"

"We didn't," Kevin interrupted.

"Her explanation makes more sense than yours," the reporter persisted.

Kevin stared. "I told you once to shut it." He looked to his oldest friend. "Pete, you believe me, don't you?"

Pete shrugged. "Sorry mate, I'm with them."

Kevin leaned huffily on the rocking horse. "I'm sick of this. Every time we come here, these spooks have a go at me, and no one believes me."

Scepter sympathized. "And this time, you'd already shut the camera down, so we don't have it on video."

"I know. I'm telling you, these ghosts have got it in for me. And what have I ever done to them?" Kevin gave a fat shrug. "Aside from Bilko, I didn't even know them when they were alive."

Scepter leapt on the idea. "It's possible that you did, you know."

The three men stared at her: Pete and McKinley were amused, Kev astonished. "I'm 27, not 327," he complained.

"Yes," Scepter agreed, "but Kevin, in a former life, you may have worked with or for them."

Kevin's flexible features registered outrage. "I have enough enemies in this life without dredging up more from a previous one. Get your butler to tell them to leave me alone or I'll … I'll … I'll be seriously fed up."

⁂

Once home and with Kevin's van unloaded, while the other two went to bed to catch up on some much-needed sleep, Pete made a quick phone call and then drove down to police station, where he met Detective Sergeant Bob Phillips, an old friend.

"It's Saturday," complained Phillips, "and supposed to be my day off."

"Just do me this favor, Bob," Pete begged. "It might help keep Locke off my back."

Phillips took the sample from Pete and placed it under a microscope. "I heard about that," he said, placing his eye to the lens. "I'm sure he doesn't really suspect you, but he never forgets that time you thumped him."

Pete was happy to hear it. He relied upon his reputation as a hard nut. "Most people don't forget."

Phillips adjusted the eyepiece, studied it for a moment and then leaned back. "I'll have to run some more tests, analyze it properly, but for my money, it's paint. Take a look."

Pete looked into the microscope and found himself studying a grainy red mass. It meant nothing to him.

"Blood is more cellular in appearance, and red blood cells refract so you get the impression you're looking at little red doughnuts," said Phillips as Pete straightened up and raised his eyebrows. "I'll run a few more tests and get back to you. Still on the same mobile number?"

"Yep."

"I'll let you know by lunchtime."

"Cheers," grinned Pete. "It's one I owe you."

From the police laboratory Pete drove out of town and down to Chapel Road and parked outside Bent Benny's shop.

The shop was empty. Benny's only customer, a young man seeking an electronic top-up for his mobile phone had walked out as Pete entered. Somewhere in the background, a radio played sixties music at a low volume, but aside from that there was no other sound in the place, and the noise of passing traffic barely penetrated the windows.

One of Benny's less endearing habits was continuing to read his newspaper when customers approached the counter. It gave *him* control, let them know they were secondary in importance to the latest football reports or racing tipsters. When Pete's dark shadow fell across the counter, cutting off most of the morning light, Benny continued to study form for long seconds.

Pete did not move, he did not cough, he did nothing at all to draw attention to himself, but waited patiently for the pressure of silence and his persistent refusal to go away to get to Benny.

Eventually, Benny folded the newspaper shut, tucked it to one side and looked up into Pete's smiling face. Benny's weasel features paled.

"Pete. Long time no see. What can I do you for?"

Pete tossed the tiny camera on the counter. "You can tell me how that found its way to the cafeteria at Melmerby Manor, and was used in conjunction with a computer, the Internet and recorded sound that Kevin had you copy the other day, to scare the living Hell out of Kev and Scepter."

Benny gave a nervous laugh and reached for a bottle of Scotch at his elbow. A dangerous glare from Pete stopped him. Clearing his throat, he said, "I'll bet it didn't scare *you* though. I've always said it takes a lot to scare Pete Brennan."

"If you were female and in your twenties, flattery would get you a long way, but you're just a rat-faced old git, so it won't work. Now what are you playing at, Benny?"

Benny picked up the camera and turned it over in his hands. "Who's to say this came from me?"

"It's got your label on the back."

The shopkeeper's ears turned red. "Ah, well, anyone could have got hold of one of those and stuck it... "

He trailed off. Pete's features had not shifted, but his eyes had narrowed slightly.

The shopkeeper continued to play innocent. "Whatever happened at Melmerby Manor had nothing to do with me, Pete. Honest."

"Everything that's happened over the last 24 hours has to do with you, Benny." Pete insisted. "First off, you sold us out to that scum, McKinley."

"I was only trying to make a few bob," Benny squealed.

His pleading, like the squeal of a piglet taken from its mother, pleased Pete. "I'll bet you were. As it happens, McKinley is just as unreliable as you, and he told us you mentioned 25,000 missing DVDs. Now, that information was known to only a few people, so where did you get to know about them?"

"Kev told me."

"No, he didn't. I checked." Pete cracked his knuckles and Benny swallowed hard. "Now come on, Benny. Open up before I practice my surgical skills and open *you* up."

Benny's weasel-like face puckered into a frown, and sweat broke out on his upper lip. "Now, you just cool it Pete. Don't go losing that temper of yours."

"Persuade me not to lose it, Benny. Talk to me."

"All right. I'll tell you what I know, but whatever happened to you guys last night had nothing to do with me. I swear." Nervously, Benny cleared his throat. "Yesterday, after Kev and that bint left, a certain party, who will remain nameless for now, called on me and wanted to know what your mate wanted with me. By then, I'd already rung McKinley and tipped him off to the voice. This party—"

"By whom you mean Wilcox and his crew."

Benny shook his head vigorously, but it was not a denial. "I ain't saying nothing, see? Let's just call him Mr. X. Well, Mr. X and his friends wanted to know what Kev and that tart wanted. I'd already given the spiel away to McKinley, so I didn't see a problem with giving it to Mr. X, so I told him."

"What you mean is, Wilcox and his goons, Lawson and Groom, threatened to splatter you all over your shop unless you told them."

"You're getting the picture," Benny agreed. "When I told them, they asked me for a copy of the message your pal had got on his radio. I played it, and then they asked me for the gear to set up at Melmerby. Speaker, Internet connection, and all the rest of it. They wanted to be able to drive the computer from their place, so I sold them the software and everything."

"And they paid you?" Pete was astonished.

"Well, not in cash, you understand."

"In other words, they paid you by promising to lay off if you kept your trap shut."

Benny gave a nervous laugh. "You're really picking this up quick, aren't you?"

"I follow it all so far, but where did you learn about the missing DVDs?"

"Wilc... I mean Mr. X asked me whether Kev had mentioned them. I told him I didn't know what he was talking about. He believed me, which was good of him considering one of his mugs had me pressed back against the wall and was threatening to slice my throat."

"And from that single reference, you put it all together and then sold it on to McKinley?" Pete's sounded unconvinced. "Stop fooling around before I lose it."

Benny's face fell. "Honest, Pete. That's how it happened, but I already knew about the DVDs. I was talking to Bilko in the Mare and Foal the night before he went missing. He told me about them. He told me the filth didn't even know they were nicked. When Wil... Mr. X mentioned them, I figured it was a good enough tip for McKinley, so when our favorite hack came to see me about the tape, about an hour after Mr. X and his chums had left, I passed it all to him."

Pete mulled over the information. If Benny had seen Bilko the night before he died, would that hold any clues as to his next move? "Bilko. When you spoke to him, what was he doing with the information?"

"Sitting on it." Benny shrugged. "He bought me a drink. Said he was on an earner if he could confirm where the DVDs were. He'd heard about them from someone, dunno who, but he had to check the tale before approaching Jimmy Tate."

Pete nodded. Given Tate's reputation for not suffering fools at all, let alone gladly, it was a wise move. "Right, Benny. We've done quite well. All we need now is confirmation that Mr. X's full name is Ronnie Wilcox."

"Come on Pete, you know better than that. If I tell you and he finds out, which he will because you'll go see him, he'll torch my shop with me in it. I can't confirm that."

Benny reached again for the bottle of scotch. Pete stopped him and picked up the bottle, studied the label. *Old Sporran*, he read, and his face split into a broad grin.

"Thanks Benny, that's all the confirmation I need. Oh, by the way, don't drink that whiskey. It's Scotch-flavored water from Latvia."

16

It was 3:00 when Kevin finally crawled out of bed and ambled into the front room to find Scepter poring over the computer video and audio files of the previous night.

"Where's Pete?" he asked.

Scepter looked up from the computer. "He went to see that friend of yours. Benny Stringer."

Kevin nodded. "Oh yeah, I remember." He watched Scepter's nimble fingers dancing across the keyboard for a moment. "Scepter. Why did you do that to Pete last night? Y'know, with McKinley? You must know Pete fancies you."

She replied reluctantly. "I don't fancy Pete. He's a friend, and I don't date friends. Come to that, I'm not really interested in dating anyone at the moment."

"I know, but—"

"Kevin, I don't want to talk about it. We're flat mates, friends and business partners. That's it. My private life is my own affair, no pun intended. Besides, like I said to Pete this morning, nothing happened. Well, nothing serious."

Kevin snorted. "Your private life? Not with McKinley. Any woman going out with him doesn't have a private life. He's real scum, you know. Don't be surprised if your little interlude makes the front page of next Thursday's *Chronicle*. I wouldn't trust that bloke further than I could throw you, and you don't weigh half what he does." He reached into his pocket and came out with a piece of paper. "Anyway," he went on, "let's forget that. I've finally come up with a name for us. This was my idea for the business card."

He passed the sheet of paper over, and Scepter studied it. *Spookies*, read the heading, *Paranormal Investigators*. Beneath the announcement were their home telephone and three mobile numbers.

'That's very clever, Kevin, but where did you get the idea?"

"From you. I—" Before he could explain, the telephone rang, and he reached for the receiver and with an insouciant grin at Scepter, announced, "Hello, Spookies?"

"Who?" demanded Pete from the other end of the line.

"Spookies is the name of our team," Kevin explained. "I was just about to tell Scepter. I dreamed it up this morning after you left us. I got it from our initials. Scepter, Pete, Kevin. S-P-K. Spookies. Good, innit?"

"Sounds bloody silly to me," grumbled his best friend.

"Well, I tried our surname initials, B-R-K," Kevin sneered, "and all I could get was Berks. Didn't have the same ring about it."

"I dunno, that sounds about right, especially if you put "clueless" in front of it."

"What are you moaning about?" snapped Kevin. "The Post office paid millions for someone to come up with Consignia."

"Yes, and everyone still called it the Post Office. Eventually, even *they* went back to calling it the Post Office."

"Just shut up about it. Scepter likes it, and so do I. Anyway, why are you ringing?"

"I've seen Bent Benny," Pete reported, "and I'm on my way to see the Tates and then Wilcox. I'm gonna try put the wind up him. While I'm out, you can get onto that scumbag McKinley and ask if he's managed to trace that mobile number yet. The one sending you all the text messages."

"Roger dodger." Kevin gave Scepter a withering stare. "I'll get Scepter to do it. She's well in with him. What's happening after that?"

"If I've got this right," said Pete, "we can wrap it all up tonight. I want you and Scepter at Melmerby Manor for about half seven, and I'll meet you there. I'm betting that Wilcox and his crew won't be far behind. By the way, the message in the attic? Paint. Like I said."

"Paint? Not blood?" Kevin managed to sound both relieved and disappointed at the same time.

"Not according to my contact," replied Pete, "who is much more reliable than any of yours. At least he's qualified."

Kevin ignored the slight on his contacts. "What's this about Wilcox? I don't understand."

"I'll explain later. You just make sure you and Scepter are out at Melmerby Manor for half past seven. The fireworks begin soon after."

The line went dead.

Scepter raised her eyebrows. "Well?"

"Pete. He's going to see Wilcox—again. Wants us at Melmerby Manor no later than half seven."

"I should be through here by then, but I'm supposed to be meeting Mike at nine, and I hadn't planned on spending another night at Melmerby Manor." She gave Kevin a wan smile. "We all need a little time off."

"I agree," said Kevin, "but Pete doesn't. Who's Mike?"

"Mike McKinley. You know. The reporter."

Kevin sniffed disdainfully. "Oh. Mike now, is it? *That* serious."

"Oh, stop being childish, Kevin." She reached across the table and touched his hand. "If it's any consolation, I'd *never* have gone out with you."

"Let alone stayed in with me? Well, thanks, Scepter. You sure know how to make a bloke feel good. Couldn't you have broke it to me more gently?"

"Like what? Write you a Dear John letter?" She smiled to show she was only teasing.

"Pete figured you were seriously pigged off with McKinley, yesterday," Kevin ventured, "so how come you're suddenly dating him again?"

"Everyone deserves a second chance."

He sniffed disdainfully. "Except me and Pete. We don't even get a first chance."

Scepter was about to argue further, but the bleep of Kevin's mobile stopped her.

He took it from his pocket and checked the menu window. "Text message," he muttered. "Wigjam again. By the way, Pete's just asked me to get you to check with McKinley and see if he's traced that mobile number yet." He deleted the message. "What's it supposed to mean?"

"I told you," Scepter said. "It's the name of the man who killed Steven Bilks."

"But it doesn't make sense." Kevin studied the message again. "Who has a name like wigjam?"

Scepter picked up the phone and dialed. Moments later she was chatting with McKinley. Kevin expected her to be gooey and lovesick, but he was surprised to hear her businesslike, almost severe.

He did not understand women. Pete did. He had that happy knack of being totally at ease in female company, and making them feel at ease too. No woman, Kevin reflected sadly, ever felt like that when she was out with him. The secrets of technology were an open door to him, but the secrets of success with women were a complete mystery.

Scepter put the phone down.

"Well?" he asked.

Scepter was triumphant. "The mobile belonged to Steven Bilks."

Kevin stared, blank faced with astonishment. "But... but... it can't be. Bilko's dead."

"Yes he is, but his phone isn't."

"So someone else is using it?"

Scepter shook her head and drew on her reserves of patience. "No, you don't understand. The spirits are able to manipulate matter. I've seen Fishwick do it, you've seen other souls do it—the milk and sugar, the beads early this morning? Remember? As I understand it from Fishwick, it takes time to master the art, but any ghost can do it if he tries hard enough. Now, Steven Bilks knows where his mobile is. He can manipulate the keypad. If you recall, I said I'd got the impression of a keypad last night. That was it. Wherever the phone is, Steven is using it to send text messages to us and the message is the name of his killer."

"So we've come full circle. No one has a name like wigjam," Kevin repeated.

Scepter picked up his mobile.

"Hey. Get your own phone," he demanded.

"It's in my bag, and I can't be bothered looking for it."

"Yes but those calls are expensive," he protested.

"I'm not going to make a call. I'm going to show you something." Scepter pointed to the keypad. "When you put a text together, how do you do it?"

He shrugged. "You go into text mode and press the keys."

"True," she agreed, "but look at key number two. It has a, b and c on it. How do you get b? Or c for that matter?"

Kevin was still puzzled. "Easy. You press they key twice for b and three times for c. But you have to look sharp. Leave it too long and the phone assumes you want an a."

"Correct." Scepter took a pen and blank sheet of A4 paper on which she wrote WGJAMW. "W is on key number nine. Suppose he doesn't mean w, but x, y or z? He's pressing the keys once, but in some cases, perhaps all cases, he should be pressing them two, three or four times? Remember, he's a new spirit. He hasn't yet familiarized himself with his abilities, his memory of life is clouded by anger at his murderer, and so he may have forgotten how to do it."

Kevin took the phone, pen and paper from her. Looking from the mobile to the word WGJAMW, he wrote out the corresponding numbers from the mobile's keypad and moments later he had 945269. He showed it her. "So all we have to do is work out what names we can get from that series of numbers?" he confirmed.

She nodded.

"Great," he sneered. "There's a haystack just down the road. Shall we go find the needle hidden in it?"

"Don't be so defeatist, Kevin. If we work at it, we'll get there." She retrieved pen and paper and after a moment's work, studying the mobile keypad, she said, "See? I've already got Yikboy."

"But that doesn't make any more sense than wigjam," he complained. "Whoever heard of someone called Yikboy?"

"Then help me, Kevin," she urged. "Work with me on it. We'll crack it."

With an exasperated sigh, Kevin, too, took up pen and paper and lit a cigarette. Together, they began to work. They quickly dispensed with Zhlamx and Xljcoz, and Kevin's idea that Whlbny sounded Russian was soon dismissed by Scepter.

They worked on in silence, the time passing, no nearer a solution, Kevin constantly complaining that there were better things he could be doing—like sleeping, eating or drinking—Scepter insisting that they carry on.

Many different combinations of letters appeared on their separate sheets of paper, but none of them made much sense.

"Modom." Fishwick's voice rang in her head.

"Yes, Fishwick?" she said, causing Kevin to look up and smirk.

"I should have mentioned this earlier, Modom, but Steven Bilks' spirit left the manor early this morning and created havoc at the place you know as Flutter-Bys."

"He did?" Scepter was both surprised and interested.

"Yes, Modom. If he has no earthly ties there," her butler speculated, "it might be an indication of where he met his death."

"Thank you, Fishwick."

With this fresh information in mind, Scepter returned to her study of the telephone number pad. If Bilks had been at Flutter-Bys, could it be that the mysterious message spelled out... W... I... L...

Long before she finished, she knew she was right. She checked her watch and saw that it was 6:30. Then she checked her answer—and checked it again. "Oh, my God!"

Kevin looked up. "Huh?"

"I've got it! Kevin, ring Pete immediately. He's in terrible danger."

❧

Pete's first port of call was the Tate brothers' estate.

Pulling into the drive, he looked up at the dark, turbulent clouds threatening snow as the evening temperature dropped. He shivered as he walked to the door and rang the bell. The dark clouds pleased him. This was a dark business, and gloomy weather was ideal for bringing it out in the open.

Johnny let him in. Pete noticed that his left arm was bandaged. "Been hassling a Girl Guide, have you?"

Johnny scowled. "You know, if I slapped you, plod wouldn't be there to help."

Pete chuckled. "By the time you're big enough, you'll be too old. Now be a good boy and get me a beer while I talk to your brother."

While Johnny disappeared into the kitchen, Pete moved through to the lounge where Nicky sat curled in a corner of the settee reading a magazine, and Jimmy snoozed in a recliner chair close to the fire.

"Pete Brennan," said Nicky seductively. "Again. We really must see more of each other."

"I've seen all of you, remember," Pete riposted. "And it wasn't worth it." He grinned at Jimmy Tate's sleeping mass. "Hey, tubby," he called out, "you dropped a tenner."

"Huh? What? Where?" Jimmy was instantly awake and alarmed, and it took him a second or two to realize that Pete was ragging him. His face fell. "Oh, it's you Brennan. What do you want?"

"I'm getting close, Jimmy. I've got enough leads on this business to wire it up to the national grid, but I need some gen from you." Pete took a seat at the opposite end of the settee as Johnny brought a tray of beers in for them. Pete took a can and eyed the bandaged wrist again. "Broken?"

Johnny shook his head. "Sprained. Some idiot tried to run me off the road the other night."

"Snap," said Pete. "Maybe they're getting worried that we're close."

"Never mind him and the nutter in the jam jar," objected Jimmy. "What do you know and what do you want to know?"

Pete sucked down some beer. "Bilko overheard something and shot his mouth off. He was killed for it. The cops are onto that."

"You told us this the other day," Jimmy reminded him. "So what's new?"

"Well, Locke's so busy trying to railroad me as being involved that he's missing he obvious." Pete hoped his disdain for Locke showed through. It would help convince Tate that he was playing a straight game and not simply interested in the reward. "I *know* who did it," he went on. "I'm hoping to bring him out into the open tonight, but I don't think he triggered your robbery. He was in on it, certainly, but someone put him up to it. Someone he knows as Jay. Does that name mean anything to you?"

Jimmy shrugged and nodded at his brother. "Our Johnny used to call me Big J when we were kids, but other than that, nothing."

Pete frowned. "In that case, we're snookered." He drank from his can again. "How many people knew about the shipment?"

Jimmy was about to answer when Pete's mobile rang. With an annoyed, "tch," Pete took it from his pocket and checked the menu window. Kevin. Pete switched it off and dropped the phone back into his pocket. "Sorry about that," he excused himself. "You were going to tell me how many were aware of the shipment."

Jimmy raised his eyes to the ceiling as he calculated the number. "Half a dozen, at the most. There's me, Johnny and Nicky, natch, then there was the transport company. They were supposed to come to my lock-up with the container the day after the stuff was nicked. Naturally, I cancelled it. So who else?" Again he fell silent, think of the people who might have known.

Pete took the opportunity to redirect his enquiry. "Jimmy, you produce your gear here." He waved a hand to indicate the front room where Tate produced his pirates. "So who shipped the cartons from here to your lock up?"

Jimmy nodded at his brother. "Me and Johnny. I own a 7-ton van."

Pete stared again at Johnny's injured arm. Suspicion clouded his mind. Could it be? He caught Johnny's eye, but the younger Tate did not appear unduly worried or perturbed. Keeping his thoughts to himself, he asked, "If you own you own van, how come you were waiting for a container lorry to pick them up?"

"That's the way the system works," Jimmy said. "You can't just go trundling into Hull docks with these things. They have to be containerized, and I don't own a container truck. So I produce them here and ship them to my lock-up, then the container comes for the shipment and takes it to the docks where it's loaded onto the cargo ship... speaking of which, the shipping clerks at the docks would have known about the consignment too."

His tones still guarded, Pete commented, "Yes, well, their idea of security is to put the door key under the mat."

"Well obviously, the guys on the dock didn't know what was in the cartons," Jimmy pointed out. "As far as they were concerned, it was simply printed matter."

"Kevin was right about you," Pete commented. "You shouldn't be left in charge of a fruit stall. But this time, I don't think the guys in Hull had anything to do with it. This was someone closer to home."

Jimmy leapt on the suggestion. "There was that Sherlock character. The security boss."

Pete dismissed the idea. "No. It's not Sherlock's scene. He might turn a blind eye while someone rips you off, but he wouldn't get involved in the actual robbery. Doesn't have the bottle." He toyed with one or two thoughts. "Tell me something, between me, you and the gatepost, where do you get the originals to make your copies from?"

"You've been told all you need to know, Brennan."

"I'm not gonna bubble you, am I?" Pete protested. "I want the five grand you're offering. Come on, Tate, Wilcox doesn't have your DVDs, and if you want them back, you've gotta help me."

Jimmy sighed and nodded at his shapely wife. "Nicky?"

"You know I used to be an actress," she said to Pete. "I still have contacts in the business, and they're happy to make a few bob supplying the originals. Strictly in the back pocket, mind. They could get worse than fired if anyone rumbled."

"And this Jay wouldn't be one of your contacts?" Pete asked.

Nicky doubted it. "What would he stand to gain? If we found out that he'd stolen from us, we'd bubble him to the owners of the movies—anonymously, natch—and he'd go down for handing the originals over in the first place."

"But that would leave you with no contact," Pete protested.

Nicky smiled seductively. "You think I couldn't cut another one, Brennan?"

"I'm wasting my bloody time here." Pete finished his beer and stood up. "Looks like I'll have to beat it outta Wilcox and his boys." He cast another glance at Johnny, but once more the younger Tate did not bat an eyelid.

"That's twice you've used that name," said Jimmy. "If Ronnie Wilcox is up to his eyes in it, I'll come with you and sit on him."

"No. Don't do that. Leave it to me. If you get anywhere near him and the law turns up, they'll twig everything, and if that happens, I'll never see this reward you're offering." He grinned. "Not that I'm simply after your money, Jimmy."

The fat man was not interested in Pete's motives. "Whatever you want. What's your master plan?"

Pete checked his watch. "I'm going from here to see Wilcox and tempt him out to Melmerby Manor." For the third time, he glanced at Johnny. Too calm, was Pete's private analysis. Inscrutable. Impossible to read. "I'll have one or two surprises waiting for him when he gets there." He turned to leave. "I'll be in touch."

He stepped out into the encroaching night, where the threatened snow had begun to fall. Here in Ashdale, under the hills, it would settle as a slippery, wet film on the pavements, and tire friction would keep the roads clear, but up at Melmerby Manor, out on the moors, it would be centimeters deep before midnight, which did not help his cause. He would need the police out there before the night was through and the last thing he wanted was Locke whining that he couldn't make it because of the weather.

As he drove down to Ashdale, he considered the things he had just learned.

Tate owned a large van, similar to the one owned by Wilcox. Wilcox had already admitted that he shipped the DVDs out to Melmerby Manor on the night of the robbery, but he denied having taken them away again. What price Tate junior had done it. But if he did, what would he stand to gain from ripping off his own brother? From all accounts, Jimmy looked after Johnny financially, so the younger brother would have little incentive to steal from his elder sibling.

"You're missing something here, Brennan," he told himself as he parked at the side entrance of Flutter-Bys, and checked the time. 7:00 p.m. Kevin and Scepter should be on their way to Melmerby Manor. Once he had seen Wilcox, he would join them and wait for things to happen.

He rattled the door. Groom slid open a view slot and gave him the evil eye. "Not you again, Brennan? Why don't you take a short walk off a long pier?"

Pete shook his head good-humoredly. "I always said you were an idiot, Groom, and now you've confirmed it. Short walk off a long pier." He laughed. Beyond the door, Groom's eyes narrowed in puzzlement. As quickly as it had materialized, Pete's laughter died off and his irritation returned. "Open the door before I rip your head off and kick it up and down the street to see if I can get any sense out of it."

"Wait there."

Groom slammed the slot shut. There was a considerable delay before the bolts were slid back and it opened.

"Checking with your boss, were you?" Pete asked.

Groom said nothing but stood back to let him pass.

The club was due to open at nine and preparations were in well in hand, but Pete was surprised to find no one but Wilcox, his brutal wife and his two minders there.

"Bar staff turn up at half eight," said Wilcox, disinterestedly. "I thought we'd seen enough of you, Brennan. What do you want this time?"

Pete smiled. "Social call, Ronnie. Just called to say thanks."

Wilcox frowned. "Thanks?"

"That name you gave me," said Pete. "Jay. I found him. I've just come from Jimmy Tate's drum and he fingered him right away. I'll be nicking him when he turns up at Melmerby Manor later tonight."

"Nicking him?" Wilcox sounded outraged. "You can't do that. You're not the law any more."

"No, but I can hold him until the filth get there, can't I?" Pete dropped his tones to casual and friendly. "See Ronnie, I figure he topped Bilko, and even if he didn't, he'll tell me who did. You know what I'm like at getting information from bodies. Just thought I'd let you know. When I pick up the reward from Jimmy Tate, there's a drink in it for you. See ya."

With a cheerful wave, Pete ambled back out of the club and climbed into his car, certain that he had tempted Wilcox out of his complacency. Even if he was off base about the murder, Wilcox would not be able to take the chance that the non-existent contact might squeal.

As he fired the engine, two shapes appeared ahead of the car. Groom and Lawson. He killed the engine once more and got out of the car. "What do you two want?"

"Not us," said Groom. "Ronnie. He wants a word."

"You tell Ronnie I'm busy. I'll get to him when I've a minute. Tomorrow maybe."

Lawson cracked his knuckles. "He said if you didn't come, we had to persuade you. Both of us this time."

Pete relaxed. The day hadn't come when he couldn't take two goons like these. "So persuade me."

In the background, Sylvie Wilcox turned the corner to join them. "If they can't, I will."

Pete laughed. "Why, what are you gonna do? Threaten to strip and turn me to stone?" Her frown suggested Sylvie was struggling to understand, so Pete explained, "I'm saying you remind me of a Gorgon."

Her manly features turned more gorilla-like. Angrily, she snapped her fingers. "Lemmy, Tommy, sic him."

Head down, Lawson charged like a bull; Pete sidestepped and Lawson flew past him.

"Olé," Pete called as Lawson's head connected with the car's headlamp.

Groom came, threw a punch; Pete caught the fist and twisted. "Your mate," said Pete, "has dented my headlight. I'll have to hammer it out again... with your head."

Reaching across, he took Groom's head and brought it down on the bonnet. With the two pugs reeling, Sylvie came and threw a right; Pete caught it and glared into her offset eyes. "I've warned you before not to mess with the big boys," he said. He head-butted her, and she, too, staggered back.

Pete chuckled at the groggy threesome. "Tell your boss if he wants to see me, he comes himself."

"No sweat, Brennan, I'm right here."

Pete turned to find Wilcox behind him, bringing a bottle down through the air. Pete put up an arm to protect himself, but the bottle cracked on his forehead, and he sank to the ground.

Wilcox grinned and looked at the bottle of *Old Sporran*. "I always knew this junk would be good for something."

⁊⁊⁊

In the reception area of Ashdale police station, Scepter was negotiating with Locke. "Chief Inspector, we can't get in touch with Pete, and he's in terrible danger."

"Good," said Locke. "Maybe it'll keep him outta my hair for a while."

Scepter struggled to keep her patience. They had been trying to ring Pete for the last half hour. His mobile had rung the first time Kevin tried, but it was not answered and since then, it had been switched off. In desperation, they had come to the police station, only to find Locke in a bad mood brought on by a manpower shortage after trouble at a football match.

Scepter tried to assert her authority as an aristocrat. "Listen to me. Wilcox murdered Steven Bilks; Pete has gone to see Wilcox, and he could be next if Wilcox realizes he knows the truth."

Locke eyed her; from one side, Keynes gave Scepter and Kevin a sympathetic shrug.

"You know for sure that Wilcox killed Bilko, do you?" demanded the Chief Inspector.

"Yes," retorted Scepter.

"And how do you know?" he asked.

"Steven Bilks told me," Scepter declared.

Locke snorted. "Oh, I forgot you're psychiatric, aren't you?"

"Psychic!" she snapped.

"Same thing, in my book." Locke wagged an angry finger at her. "Well, listen to me, lady: Scepter and specter are spelled using the same letters, and so are stupid and sod off—"

"No, they're not," interrupted Kevin.

"Don't get technical Keeley, just do it." The Chief Inspector's voice rose in proportion to his color. "Get out of my hair and my life. If you expect me to go chasing after Brennan, you've got another think coming. If Wilcox tops him, he'd be doing me a double favor. I get Wilcox walled up for life and I get rid of Brennan."

Racked with frustration, they came out of the police station.

"Now what do we do?" asked Kevin.

Scepter chewed her lip. "Try Pete's mobile again."

Kevin recalled the number from his phone's memory and clicked the connect button. He put the instrument to his ear and listened. After a moment, he cut the call.

"Still switched off." He clucked impatiently. "Do we have a number for Melmerby Manor?"

"Of course, but what's the point of ringing it? Or did you imagine that the spirits can manipulate matter well enough to answer the phone?" Immediately she said it, Scepter regretted her sarcasm. "Kevin," she went on more gently, "if Pete was out at the Manor and found we're not, he would have phoned us, wouldn't he?" From the glum look on Kevin's face, Scepter guessed he agreed. After a moment's thought, she said, "What about those other two. The Tates?"

Kevin checked his watch and shook his head. "He wants us out at the manor within the next half hour, and he was on his way to see the Tates when I spoke to him on the phone. For him to meet us out there means he must had done with Jimmy and Johnny and been to see Wilcox." He looked at her as if seeking inspiration. "You got any ideas?"

Scepter shrugged. "We could go see Wilcox ourselves?"

"Why don't we just swallow a couple of hundred morphine pills?" Kevin suggested. "As a way of killing ourselves, it's less painful than going to see Ronnie Wilcox."

She frowned. "What are you talking about?"

"If we go to Flutter-Bys," Kevin explained, "we let Wilcox know that we know and he'll do the same to us as he did to Bilko." Kevin took out his mobile and dialed Pete's number once more but received only his voicemail. "Scepter, we have to face it, if Pete has faced them out, they may have already killed him."

The notion filled her with alarm. "Fishwick?" she called out, and then listened in silence to her butler.

"There are no new spirits in this locale, Modom," he assured her. "Well there are, but most of them have gone straight through The Light, and if Mr. Brennan had come over, I'm sure he would be angry enough to stay on this plane."

"Thank you, Fishwick." Scepter came back to the world of the living. "Fishwick assures me that Pete is not dead."

Kevin snorted. "Oh, well, that makes everything tickety-bloody-boo then, doesn't it? I mean if Fish 'n' chips says Pete's fine, let's go home and watch TV."

"No. We're not going to do anything of the kind." Scepter chewed her lip in desperate thought. "You don't suppose he could have gone out to Melmerby Manor already, do you?"

Kevin became even more agitated. "I just suggested that, and you said he would have phoned us first." He unwrapped a stick of gum, popped it in his mouth and let his jaw work on it. "Scepter, I have a bad feeling about this. If Wilcox has him, he'll want to know exactly what Pete knows, and Pete's idea was to tempt Wilcox out to the manor. Ten to one, that's where Wilcox will take him to bump him off, just like he did with Bilks."

"According to Fishwick, Bilks was killed at Flutter-Bys, not the manor."

"Oh well, we must get these things right, mustn't we." His frightened eyes looked into hers. "Wherever Bilko was killed, wherever they decide to ice Pete, we'll be next."

Scepter became decisive. "We need help." She retrieved her mobile, flicked through the address book until she found McKinley's number, and dialed it up. A moment later, she was connected. "Mike? Scepter. We have a problem. We think Wilcox may have Pete, and we believe we could be the next targets. We're on our way out to Melmerby Manor, and we could do with some support."

"Melmerby Manor? Scepter, I thought we had a date." McKinley sounded aggrieved.

"We do. I'm simply switching the venue. Now will you help us deal with Wilcox and his crooks?"

At the other end of the line, McKinley hedged. "Well it's a bit difficult. I'm not generally into... good grief is that the time? I have an interview at eight with Chief Inspector Locke."

Scepter struggled to contain her disappointment and anger. Making an effort to keep her voice even, she said, "Strange. I've just been with Locke, and he said nothing to me."

"Did I say Locke? I meant the Chief Constable."

"Oh? And what about our date?" Scepter began to tap her feet.

"Rain check," begged McKinley. "I'll get back to you after I've spoken to him. Catch you later."

He hung up on her and Scepter stared at the telephone as if it had betrayed her.

Virulent rage pumped the blood through her veins. "You ... you ... COWARD!"

Shivering in the snow, his brain idling, Kevin jumped at her final, shouted word. "What?"

Scepter did not answer. She stomped to the van, and leaned her forehead against it, fighting down the disappointment. "Charming and persuasive," she hissed, "and it's nothing but a thin coat of paint to hide the truth."

"What are you on about?" asked Kevin.

She turned to face him, her face suffused with fury, and held up the telephone. "I should have listened to my head last night, rather than my heart. I will never trust another man as long as I live."

From the look on his face, Kevin guessed what had happened. Softly, he reminded her, "You can trust me and Pete."

Scepter tried to calm down. "Yes. I was generalizing, Kevin. I didn't mean Pete and you but the male sex as a species."

Kevin's brow furrowed as he tried to sort out her meaning. He opened his mouth to speak, but Scepter brought the debate to an end before it could properly begin by changing the subject.

"Right, partner. It's down to you and me. What are we going to do?"

He shrugged. "Go home and wait for Pete to ring us?"

Scepter shook her head. "And leave Pete at the mercy of these gangsters? I don't think so. Like you said, he wanted us out at Melmerby Manor, and that is exactly where we will be."

"Now, hang on, Scepter, let's not lose our heads. Chasing ghosts is one thing; hassling Wilcox and his goons at Melmerby Manor is an entirely different bottle of aspirin. That guy can seriously damage your health."

"So you're happy to leave Pete to their brutality, are you?"

"Like I said, Pete could already be dead, and before you say it, I don't trust Fishwick on this one. People snuff it all the time, and do they carry ID cards into the next world? No they do not, and Fishy can't spot them all."

Scepter folded her arms and tapped her foot irritably on the ground. "Nevertheless, we are going to Melmerby Manor."

"Look, I don't wanna stand out here in the snow, arguing the toss with you—"

"Good. Then let's get in your van and go." She moved to the van.

Kevin hung back. Scepter waited by the passenger door. Once again, she tapped her foot impatiently. Reluctantly, Kevin followed her. A minute later, they drove out of the police station yard and into the snowy streets.

Behind them, Keynes started her engine and followed at a discreet distance.

⚜

Pete came around slowly. His back ached, he had a storming headache, he felt cold and, when he tried to move his hands, he found they were tied behind his back. He shook his head to clear it and took in his surroundings.

The room was small, cramped and poorly lit, filled from floor to ceiling, wall to wall, with cartons, packed in so tightly that he would have to go outside just to change his mind. Pete recognized the cartons immediately. He had last seen them at Melmerby Manor when they filled the floor of the stable warehouse. They were Jimmy Tate's pirate DVDs.

He rolled first to his knees, then, pressing his back against the nearest of the cartons, struggled to a standing position and looked around for some means of cutting the rope biting into his wrists. All he could see were cartons. Behind the boxes containing the DVDs were other cartons of butter, bacon, ham, and other cooked meats. He could make out catering-sized pots of yogurt and cream, and two liter containers of milk, but there was nothing on which he could get any purchase.

He cleared his head and thought about his likely location. Wilcox had taken him by surprise in the alley outside Flutter-Bys. At seven on Saturday, even a bitterly cold, snowy Saturday, the streets of Ashdale would be packed with people out on the razzle, and he reasoned that they would not risk taking him anywhere but inside the club until very much later. So he was in Flutter-Bys, but where exactly?

The room was cold. Not freezing, and perhaps as many as five degrees above: the kind of chill that, with his overcoat, would not get to him for some time. He searched his memory for those occasions when he had raided the club as a police officer. There was a cold store in the cellar, next to the cage where Wilcox kept his spirits and cigarettes. That was it. He was crammed into the cold store of Flutter-Bys' cellar along with the cartons of stolen, pirate DVDs, and there was barely room to swing the proverbial cat.

He faced the door—a thick, heavy-duty affair designed to keep the chill in rather than others out. There was no handle on the inside. He kicked it—and instantly wished he hadn't. The only effect was to send pain lancing along his leg to his knee, and he doubted that the sound could even have been heard out in the cellar.

He perched his backside on the corner of a carton and took the weight off his feet. The situation was one of his own making. Like his best friend, he had suddenly become obsessed with the money—Jimmy Tate's £5,000—and he had stupidly decided to play a lone hand.

Still, all was not lost. They would have to come down here and move him at some point, and he would not go without a fight.

17

Behind the wheel, Kevin peered through the heavy snow into darkness as his ancient van plodded along Melmerby Lane.

"I'll tell you what we've never tried," Scepter said suddenly.

"There's hundreds of things *I've* never tried. Swimming with concrete shoes on, for instance, but that's something Wilcox will put right if he catches us tonight."

"I'm talking about our current situation," Scepter responded irritably. "We've never tried ringing Steven Bilks' mobile."

Kevin snorted. "You reckon he'll answer? I didn't know your butler and his chums had a mobile network over there."

Scepter ignored his sarcasm, reached across and picked up his mobile from the drinks tray. She recalled Bilks' number from the incoming text menu, and dialed it. "Wherever it is," she said as she waited for the connection to be made, "it must be switched on or you would not have been receiving text messages from it. If so, we can contact the police and get them to put a GPS trace on it."

"And do what?" Kevin demanded.

Impatience got the better of her. "Are you being deliberately obtuse?"

"I can't be." He objected. "I don't know what it means."

"Kevin, you are our tech head. GPS tracking will lead them to the phone's location and, hopefully, Bilks' killer." She became excited. "It's ringing."

Kevin wiped condensation from the windscreen with his sleeve. "Good. If you get through to Bilko, tell him to stop texting me."

Scepter sniffed disdainfully. "I didn't expect an answer." Taking out her own mobile, she transferred Bilks' number to her address book, and then dialed the police station. "Chief Inspector Locke, please," she asked when the call was answered. "Tell him it's Scepter Rand."

There was a delay of about a minute, during which Kevin stopped at the gates of Melmerby Manor and climbed out to open them.

"I'm sorry, Ms. Rand, but the Chief Inspector is too busy to speak to you," said the desk officer.

Scepter puffed out her cheeks. "All right. Take a message for him. I'm going to give you a mobile telephone number. It belonged to Steven Bilks. The phone is still switched on, and it's probably where Bilks dropped it when he was murdered. If Locke gets a GPS trace on it, it may lead him to Bilks' killer."

❧

Pete had relied upon his physical strength for much of his life, and he had the idea that if he tugged at the bonds around his wrists, he might be able to stretch the rope enough to loosen it. One tug, however, sent a stab of agony through his wrists, and he realized immediately that he was not bound with rope. Instead, fine wire, about the same thickness as that used to make paper clips, had been expertly twisted and looped round his wrists so that no matter which way he tried to free himself, it would cut into his skin.

With an effort, he struggled to bring his fury under control and bring his logical processes into play. Wiring his wrists together like that, they must have used pliers to twist the wire into place, and if he could hook it over something—anything—he might be able to undo it.

But he was crammed into a tight space, hemmed in by the cartons and the steel door, none of which was any use to him.

In a further paroxysm of fury, he kicked the nearest box.

As if taking a cue, a mobile phone whistled the theme tune to Laurel & Hardy. Pete cursed again. It was in his pocket, and he couldn't get to it to answer...

"Your phone doesn't play the theme to Laurel and Hardy, you berk!" he cursed himself.

He cocked an ear. The ringing was coming from one of the upper shelves. If he could get to it... but how?

He looked around. Nothing to see but the boxes. A slow smile crept across his face. The very manner in which the cartons had been packed into the cold store provided the perfect answer. They were so tightly packed that they formed a near-solid wall, strong enough to bear his weight. Pressing his back to the door, he jacked himself up with a foot against the nearest carton and twisted his head to the right. The phone was there. Half-pushed behind a catering pack of pure orange juice.

Pete leaned over, nudged the carton of orange juice away, gripped the phone with his lips and tried to pull it towards him. It slid away. He repeated the process. The phone slipped from his mouth once more. Praying that whoever was ringing would not ring off, he tried—and lost it a third time. His legs ached. His calf muscles screamed for release. The weight of his back pressing his bound hands into the door made the wire bite into his wrists. The phone was tantalizingly close.

Summoning every ounce of strength, he lifted himself a fraction higher. "Don't ring off," he urged the phone. He locked his knees to keep him there, ignored the pain in his wrists, and craned his neck over the shelf. *Got it!* Filled with triumph, the phone locked firmly in his lips, he dragged it towards him. Then, in a sudden flurry of activity, two things happened.

First, the phone stopped ringing. Pete shelved his disappointment and considered ways in which he could get the thing into his hands, but then the door suddenly opened and he fell backwards, out into the cellar of Flutter-Bys, dashing the mobile phone to the floor of the cold room.

He cursed audibly.

Ignoring the pain in his head, back and especially his wrists, he opened his eyes and found himself looking up at a pair of chunky female legs and, beyond the footballer's thighs, beneath the folds of a skirt, a living nightmare—a pair of boxy white cotton panties. He closed his eyes to ward off the terrible sight. All his life he had dreaded waking from a drunken stupor to be greeted by a sight like this.

Sylvie Wilcox leaned forward and looked down at him. Pete decided that the view under her skirt was preferable to the one above it. She raised a leg and rested one blocky heel on his chest, then gave him an evil smile.

"What are you playing at, Brennan?" Without waiting for an answer, she glanced into the cold store and down at the cell phone. "What's this? I thought Ronnie had taken your mobile." She stepped over Pete, picked the phone up and examined it. "Well, well, well. Bilko's phone. We've been looking for that, and you had it all the time. Handy when the law finds it on you, though. After we've put you to sleep for good, obviously." She laughed and crossed the floor to the bottom of the stairs. "Okay Ronnie. He's cool," she called up to the clubroom. She looked into the cold room and laughed. "Literally."

❦

Fishwick was keeping an eye on Bilks' livid form when Scepter called him. He rushed through to her location on the upper landing of the manor. "Yes, Modom?"

"Fishwick," Scepter ordered, "I want you to go down to Flutter-Bys, and check the place to see if Mr. Brennan is being held there."

The butler's tone, respectful as always, nevertheless conveyed his concern. "If I may make so bold, Modom, Bilks is here and if I were to leave, he may give you trouble."

"Fishwick, this is important." Scepter put greater urgency into her voice. "I need you to check on Flutter-Bys. Don't worry about Bilks. If he tries anything, I will deal with him."

"But Modom—"

Scepter cut him off. "That is an order, Fishwick."

He capitulated. "Very good, Modom."

As the communication with Scepter was broken, Fishwick returned to the far end of the house, where Bilks hovered in the background, away from other spirits in the vicinity. He made his way over to them. It was all very well Modom saying she would handle Bilks, but Fishwick preferred to hedge his bets.

"Now then, Sir Henry," he addressed himself to the former incumbent, "I'd like to ask a favor of you."

"Tha gets no favors from me. Tha's naught but an interloper. Now git outta my house."

Fishwick persevered. "I'd like to get out, but for the moment, I can't. See him?" Fishwick's form gestured at the fiery ball that was Bilks. "If I leave, he'll give my mistress some trouble. I wondered if you might help keep him at bay."

"I'll do naught of the kind. If it gets him and thy mistress outta my house, he can do as he pleases with her."

Aggie joined them. "Take no notice of him. He was a nowty old sod when he were alive and he's a nowty old sod now."

Sir Henry's form wavered from white through blue to red. "Don't talk to me like that, woman."

"And what's tha going ter do about it?" demanded Aggie. Her glow settled to a cooperative indigo. "I'll keep an eye on yonder," she said, indicating Bilks. "You be about your business."

Fishwick performed a twisting maneuver, the spirit equivalent of a bow. "Thank you, Miss Aggie."

Sir Henry gave a loud laugh. "Tha don't need her anyway, lad. Yon feller is away with himself."

Fishwick turned urgently to see Bilks zooming off. "Now where the blooming heck are you going?"

༄

The muted sounds of Flutter-Bys' clubroom reached Pete's ears as Wilcox, flanked by Groom and Lawson, came down the stairs. For a moment he considered shouting for help, but he knew that the club members would be too engrossed in the drinking and gambling to hear, and the staff would have been warned off.

Two other people followed him down. For a moment, Pete could not see who they were, but, shortly, the glimpse of a bandaged wrist told him the identity of one.

"Get him up." Wilcox's words were directed to his two thugs, who yanked Pete to his feet.

If the confirmation of his earlier suspicions about Johnny Tate satisfied Pete, he could do no more than gape for a moment as he took in the woman at Johnny's side—Nicky. But even as he stared, everything fell into place. "Now I see it all," he said at last. "An estate car running you off the road, Johnny?" Pete gave them a good-natured laugh even though he felt no humor. "It was the other way round, wasn't it? *You* tried to run *us* off the road."

"Just shut it, Brennan," Wilcox growled.

Pete swiveled in his direction. "Loosen the wire round my wrists and then we'll see if you have the bottle to say that."

Wilcox shook his head. "It's not gonna happen."

Pete ignored him and faced Tate. "I guessed it was you earlier, when Jimmy told me he owned a van like Wilcox's. So what was it all about, Johnny? Sick of playing gopher for big brother?"

Tate smiled. "Something like that, only a bit more complicated." He winked at Nicky.

Pete let out a false laugh. "You didn't just want his money, you wanted his wife, too." Pete put on a disapproving face for Nicky. "I'm surprised at you. Sleeping with a cop is one thing, but your husband's younger brother?"

Judging by her easy expression, she was not unnerved by the charges of serial adultery. "Do you know what it's like being married to the fat man?" she asked. "Watching him eat like a pig, listening to him fart like a gorilla, having to look at him when he gets out of the shower, having to deal with the other when he wants it? I may as well be trying to jump on top of a beached whale."

"I can guess. So, why stick with him? Oh, of course, the money." Pete again laughed humorlessly. "And there I was thinking it was true love. I thought Jimmy would let you have anything you wanted."

"You think I like being a kept woman? I want money of my own, and I want Johnny. The 50,000 we'll pick up for the DVDs will give us a fresh start in another country. Right, Johnny?"

Johnny nodded "Right, Nicky."

"50,000? You have buyers lined up for the stuff?" Pete's surprise registered in his voice.

"Natch. The minute Jimmy ducks out on his delivery commitment, *we'*ll ship them out. And get this: Jimmy financed all the production and incidental expenses, so we have minimum overheads. The whole 50K is ours." Greedily Johnny rubbed his hands together.

Pete's brow creased. "I thought you were Jimmy's partner?"

Johnny snorted. "Partner, nothing. Gopher was right." He jerked a thumb at Nicky. "You might say the way she's a kept woman, I'm a kept man. But not after we ship those DVDs, I'm not."

Pete looked at Wilcox. "You're not getting a cut?"

It was Tate who answered. "Mr. Wilcox is making amends for a series of cock-ups earlier in the week."

"Like murdering Bilko?"

"Enough chitchat," Wilcox cut in. "Let me tell you what's happening, Brennan. We're going for a little drive in my van—"

"Shut up, Wilcox," Pete shot back. "I'm talking to the organ grinder, not his monkey."

His face flushed with anger, Flutter-Bys' owner snapped his fingers at Groom. "Teach him a lesson." He pointed to Pete.

Groom took a step forward. Pete looked him in the eye. "Think you can, tosspot?"

The thug stepped even closer. Pete head-butted him, and he sank to the floor. Lawson came forward with a baseball bat. He swung it overhead, aiming at Pete's shoulder. Pete sidestepped and kicked out, landing his foot hard between Lawson's legs. Tears coming to his eyes, Lawson sank to his knees.

"You should get tougher minders, Wilcox. Try the old folks' home on Mersey Road. They have some D-Day vets there." While Wilcox stared at his prone thug, Pete turned his attention back to Johnny and asked, "Why have Bilko killed?"

Tate's features darkened, and his eyes fell slowly on Wilcox. "I didn't. I just asked someone to shut him up." He faced Pete again. "I was in the bar here a few nights back, talking with Wilcox here, and Bilko was earwigging. We were joking about Jimmy offering two grand to get the DVDs back, and I think Ronnie said something like, no one would ever find them at Melmerby Manor. Bilko must have overheard, and you know what he was like for playing it close to the chest. He rang Jimmy, told him he thought he had some info on the theft but wanted to find out if the two grand was pukka before he went to the trouble of following up his lead. When Jimmy said it was, he said he'd get back to Jimmy when he'd checked it out himself. We figure he must have gone out to the manor to check it out and taken one of the discs to prove his claim. He called Jimmy again the next night to say he'd found the DVDs and had one in his possession to prove it, though, of course, he wouldn't say where without seeing the two grand.

"Jimmy told me about Bilko's call when I got home and, of course, said it was my job to handle it. And I meant to. I belled Bilko and agreed to meet him here to exchange the DVD and the information for the reward. But I also belled Ronnie and told him Bilks was coming and to shut him up. What I meant for them to do was to show him the wisdom of keeping his mouth shut." He gave an open-handed shrug and indicated Wilcox and his thugs. "These clowns went too far."

Wilcox, still smarting from the easy manner in which Pete had flattened his minders even though his hands were bound, grunted. "Nobody misses a scumbag like Bilko. Come on, Johnny, let's get this done." He gazed at his minders, both coming groggily to their feet. "Move it, you two." He shook his head. "When will you ever learn how to take someone out?"

"One last thing," Pete said as Groom and Lawson came behind him and gripped him by the upper arms. "Why'd you run me off the road?" He nodded at Tate's bandaged arm. "It might have scared Kev and Scepter away, but not me."

"I wasn't trying to frighten you. I was trying to kill you." Tate grinned. "Nothing personal, you understand."

Pete controlled the urge to rush the younger Tate. Deep inside, he yearned for his hands to be free of their bonds so he could tear out Tate's heart, rip off Wilcox's head, and use both to beat the two minders into an unrecognizable pulp. Outwardly, he smiled and nodded his understanding. "I understand, Johnny, and I hope you won't take it personally when I break you in two for it."

Johnny smiled. "'Course not."

Pete was calmer now, more in control of himself. "Wilcox, what's your angle on this?"

Wilcox reached into his pocket and pulled out an automatic pistol. Nonchalantly checking the clip, he said, "The trouble with you, Brennan, is you don't know when someone's telling you the truth. I told you the other day. I was simply hired to deal with transport and storage. I was on a good earner for helping Johnny out. Simple enough job. Get the cartons into my van and ship them out to the manor for safekeeping. Safe there because no one goes near the place in winter. After Bilko opened his mouth, Johnny said we needed to move them back here. We didn't know how many people Bilko had spoken to. That went doubly so when your mate Keeley shot his mouth about you spending the night there ghost hunting. So we went out there, took them back and left Bilko instead."

"And that was one of you in the woods that Kevin saw when I told him to close the gates before the DVDs had been moved."

Wilcox nodded. "We sent Tommy ahead to case the joint, see what you were up to. He told us you almost caught him. He just got out the back gates in time. When he reported back that you hadn't set up any gear in the warehouse, it was easy for us to keep you occupied while we got the cartons out and left Bilko behind."

"Keep us occupied by fooling around as ghosts."

"You were perfect as patsies for Bilko. The timing had to be right, and yes, we created the ghosts. Well, some of them, anyway. We made a few noises slamming doors, and we managed to trip one or two of your sensors by tossing stones through the beams."

"And the lettering on the attic wall, and playing with the PA system in the private rooms?" Pete wanted to know.

"That was the second time around. Tommy has a set of lock picks, and that back door, the one into the Long Gallery, is so easy. We painted the message on the wall and then we watched you on the webcam and cut the Internet line when you rumbled it."

"So Kev was right after all," muttered Pete. "That must be a first." He queried Wilcox again. "Benny really didn't do the Internet hook up?"

"He supplied the equipment, that's all. We're not total idiots, you know. We do know how to hook up a webcam."

"I'll reserve judgment on your stupidity." Pete slotted the information into the theory that had already formed in his mind. "So what's the text message all about?"

Wilcox was puzzled. "Now, that wasn't us. *I* kept getting it, too, and it came from Bilko's number. We couldn't find his phone after we topped him, you know. But Bent Benny told me your mate, Keeley, was receiving it on his phone and that he also got it over the radio. I figured I could scare you with it." He laughed. "At least we knew how to spell it when we wrote it on the attic wall."

Pete's looked baffled, but he spotted a way in which he might just divide his opponents. "Well, considering I just found Bilko's phone in your cold store, who *did* send the texts?" He indicated Groom and Lawson. "One of them?"

Doubt crossed Wilcox's face. "What?"

"You heard. I just found the phone in there." Pete nodded at the open cold store.

The owner of Flutter-Bys passed a rapid, angry and suspicious glance at his two cohorts. They both shrugged.

"Don't look at me," Groom said.

Wilcox stared at Lawson. "You were down here this morning, when we had that disturbance."

"Yeah," grumbled Lawson, "but we've been getting the texts for days, and I didn't know the phone was in there." He, too, nodded at the cold store.

"Ooh," said Pete as if he were worried. "Bilko's ghost come back to haunt you, Ronnie."

Wilcox spat at him. "Watch your mouth. Where's the damn phone now?"

Sylvie held it up. "I have it."

Wilcox's anger dissipated rapidly and he laughed again. "Whoever sent those messages, it don't matter. When the filth find the phone on you, they'll figure you were trying to scare off Keeley and the la-di-dah tart so you could have the reward for yourself. They'll also figure that those two killed you for it, and then fell out and killed each other."

"You're taking it for granted that Locke and his team are that thick," Pete said.

"You should know. You used to work for them."

Pete racked his brain for further argument. Anything to gain time, give Kevin and Scepter a chance to get to Melmerby Manor, work out that something had gone wrong, and call the law. "Kev and Scepter have already called the filth, you know," he bluffed.

"I doubt it," said Nicky. "I know you, Brennan. You're the big hero type, and you'd wanna crack this on your own, shove it under Locke's nose, and gloat. You've probably ordered your pals to keep schtum."

Wilcox cut in. "Here's the deal, Brennan. We're going up the stairs and out the side door of the club, where you'll be jammed into my van. Be a good boy, and you'll live until we get to Melmerby Manor. Hassle us, and Tommy here will blow you away right where you stand."

"One last thing, Ronnie," said Johnny Tate.

Wilcox raised his eyebrows. Tate took a pace forward, his right fist clenched, and whipped it into Pete's gut. "God, that felt good. I've been wanting to do it for years."

<hr/>

The snow was coming down more heavily when they bundled Pete out of Flutter-Bys and into the badly lit street behind the club, where Wilcox's van stood. Pete's car had been moved alongside it, and a debate broke out amongst Tate, Nicky, Wilcox and Sylvie.

"Nicky and me were going to get out of the way," Johnny whined.

"Not likely." Wilcox growled. "If you want Brennan iced, then you come and help us. That way, if it goes wrong, you go down with us. Take his car out to the manor. We'll follow in the van."

Pete was impressed with Wilcox's control of the situation. He'd underestimated Flutter-Bys' owner. "I need you out there, too, Johnny," he called out as Tate and Nicky capitulated and headed for his car. "I'm gonna beat your brains in when I've done with these clowns."

Tate climbed back out of the car and took two paces towards Pete. He looked annoyed, but behind the anger, Pete detected a hint of amusement.

"Will you never learn to shut your trap, Brennan?" Johnny clenched his fist, but Wilcox stopped him.

"Just let it go," Wilcox ordered. "He's only shooting his mouth off."

Tate's fist relaxed. With an open palm, he tapped Pete twice on the cheek. "I'll have the last laugh." He walked away.

Pete watched as his car was driven off, and then Groom and Lawson bundled him into the van, while Wilcox stood at the roller shutter.

"Word of warning, Brennan. I wasn't joking when I said Tommy and Lemmy would blow you away, but just in case you get fancy ideas," he waved his automatic pistol in the air, "Sylvie and me will be up front, so just behave yourself."

Pete grinned. "See you up there, then, Ronnie."

With a scowl, Wilcox rolled the shutter down and slammed it shut.

❦

To the more experienced spirit, movement from place to place was as simple as thinking about it, but newcomers like Bilks literally traveled through the ether like a low-flying aircraft.

"You'll learn, my lad," said Fishwick to himself as they crossed the snowy landscape below.

Fishwick was concerned. His mistress had given him a direct order, and in following Bilks, he was disobeying her. He recalled those early days when he was a boot boy at Rand-Epping Castle, and later when he served as Lord Rand-Epping's butler and batman in the army. Following orders was something that had been drilled into him ever since he first went into service with the Rand-Epping's and, of course, no soldier would dare contemplate disobeying orders.

"Thank God you're not in the army anymore, Albert," he muttered to himself.

Flutter-Bys was not a large place and checking it out would take only a matter of minutes. After Bilks' efforts in that same place in the early hours of yesterday morning, Fishwick was more interested in what the furious spirit was up to.

Fishwick was not as concerned for Scepter as he had been. If Bilks' slow departure were a feint, designed to get Fishwick away from the manor, it served only to underline Bilks' lack of experience in the astral plane. Fishwick could get back to his mistress' side from the moon in considerably less than a second. If Bilks decided to double back to the manor, Fishwick could still be there ahead of him.

He was surprised when Bilks swooped down on Flutter-Bys.

"Two birds and a single stone," Fishwick chuckled as he followed the angry ball of fire down.

He noticed a large van pulling out of the rear yard as he dropped through the roof. The driver looked like the gangster Wilcox.

Dropping into the clubroom, Fishwick found it full. A strictly male membership sat around the tables. Some were dining, others playing cards, shooting craps, playing the roulette wheel. In direct contravention of recently passed anti-smoking laws, a thick haze of cigarette smoke clung to the ceiling; on the tiny stage, a young, scantily-clad woman writhed and wriggled in a lewd dance to background music. Occasionally, men would throw five or ten pound notes on the stage, and she would turn her attention in their direction, as if she were dancing specifically for them.

"Nought like that in your day, Albert," Fishwick muttered.

Bilks was nowhere to be found in this room. Fishwick ducked into the cellars. As he did so, Bilks' furious form hurtled from the cold store, blazing scarlet with anger.

"WIGJAM!" he roared.

"All right, me old sparrow. Try to calm down." For days now Fishwick had tried to calm Bilks without success, and Fishwick suspected he would do no better now.

He was right. As he suggested it, Bilks roared again and again aimed at the cold store . Instead of passing through the door, he hit it hard. It shook violently. To Fishwick's mystification, Bilks struck again and again and again, and still nothing happened.

"What are you trying to do?" asked Fishwick. He waited to see if the tremors produced by the repeated battering of the larder would be noticed upstairs. No one came to investigate, and Fishwick decided that they were too busy with their eating, drinking, gambling and ogling to notice.

The penny dropped. He understood Bilks' activity. "You want to open it? Let me show you how."

The ball of energy backed off its color, settling into an irritated orange.

"If you calmed down, you'd learn," Fishwick said as he positioned himself in front of the huge door. With a deft movement of his arm, he flicked the handle and the door opened. Bilks' color shot up the scale to crimson, and he rushed past Fishwick into the room. He tore at the cartons of DVDs, he ripped cartons of foodstuffs apart. In seconds, the floor of the cellar in the immediate vicinity of the cold store was covered in a mess of milk, butter, yoghurt, and DVDs.

Fishwick was puzzled. "What are you looking for?"

"WIGJAM!"

"Wigjam?" Fishwick mulled on the word for a moment and then his entire energy form brightened. "I get it."

<hr>

At Melmerby Manor, Kevin and Scepter worked quickly, hooking their computer into the PA system and running secreted cables up to the attics. Once in the old nursery, Kevin set up his own laptop and booted it up to test the links.

"The cables are not that difficult to spot, and they'll lead Wilcox and his people right to us," he complained.

"Good. If they do, we'll be ready for them, won't we? Now, are you sure you can drive the system from here?"

"If Wilcox can do it from his club, I can do it from here," Kevin boasted, "and we'll test it in a few minutes. But it's not gonna scare them, Scepter, because they'll know we're scamming them. They set it up in the first place."

"It's not supposed to scare them," she told him. "It's supposed to bring them upstairs, and we will be ready for them when they get here."

"How?"

She smiled secretively. "You'll see. Fishwick?" The call to her butler was greeted with stony silence. Scepter's face fell. "Oh dear. He's not there."

Kevin snorted. "He wouldn't be, would he? It's not so long since you sent him off to Flutter-Bys."

Scepter shrugged. "He'll be back. I'm sure he will."

Kevin was not impressed. Bent over the keyboard, he muttered to himself. "A spook for support? On the whole, I think I'd rather have the Marines."

The computer screen came alive. Hooking his mobile phone into the Internet connection, Kevin booted up the media package, ran through the various direct links to the Melmerby system and hit "play". Somewhere far below, in the house, they hear the sound of heavy breathing interspersed with the strange word.

"WIGJAM... WIGJAM... WIGJAM..."

Kevin shuddered and shut down the connection. "There you go. Works like a charm."

Scepter rubbed her hands with un-aristocratic glee. "Then we're ready. All we have to do is sit it out here and wait for Wilcox and friends to turn up and Fishwick to come back to help us."

Kevin swallowed hard. "I prefer *people* on my side. Especially when they're called Pete Brennan."

Scepter ignored him and switched on her flashlight. "Right, come on, let's shut the lights down."

Again Kevin swallowed. "And we'll be in the dark too? I don't think I wanna be a ghost hunter anymore."

⚜

As the vehicle began to move, Pete took in his surroundings. There were no windows in the back of the van, and the only light came from a tiny, overhead bulb. The metal interior walls of the van were lined with metal support struts running from floor to roof, spaced about half a meter apart, each one ten centimeters wide. When carrying items of furniture or heavy cartons, the struts could be used to anchor securing straps.

The set-up confirmed his opinion of Wilcox. An idiot. By spreading his forces so thinly, he had given Pete the chance of escape. An organized mobster would have stayed in the back of the van himself instead of leaving the job to two hopelessly inefficient goons like Groom and Lawson.

Sitting to one side, as soon as they moved off, Pete began rubbing the wire binding his wrists against the blunt edge of a single strut. The movement was unobtrusive, and to Groom and Lawson, it looked as if Pete were simply being jerked around by the unsteady movement of the van on the roads.

With no windows in the van to let him see their progress to the manor, he could only guess where they were, and the weather did not help. The journey usually took 20 minutes, but a dusting of snow in Ashdale would mean several centimeters on the moors, which would slow them down.

While he worked at the bindings, he turned over his precarious situation in his mind. He needed to be free of the wrist bindings, he needed to take out Groom and Lawson, and he needed to attract attention so he could lure Wilcox into opening the back door, so he would have the opportunity to fight his way to freedom. But he was hopelessly outnumbered, and they were armed. If he escaped in an open area like the moors, they could easily gun him down. To have a chance, he had to let them get all the way to the manor, with its multiple rooms and its dark wine cellar, before he tried to escape.

The timing, however, would be critical. Once out of the van, he would have to get to cover on foot. If he left the vehicle too early, even if they had made it to the Melmerby property, it would be too easy for them to bring him down before he could gain the shelter of one of the structures. And if they gave up on him, he would not be able to get there in time to prevent Wilcox murdering Scepter and Kevin.

The bumps in the road began to get worse. They were out of town on the less well-maintained highways of the moors now. The vehicle slowed down. Pete guessed that the deeper snow was causing Wilcox—and Tate up ahead—to take it more slowly. The last thing they wanted was to have two vehicles stuck out here with three dead bodies lying around.

If they were on the moors, then even at a slower speed, they would reach Melmerby Manor in a matter of five or ten minutes. Over the course of their journey so far, which he guessed to be about half an hour, ignoring the cutting pain in his skin, he could feel his bonds thinning and beginning to stretch. The wire was a long way from breaking, but that no longer mattered. It had to be now.

Pressing his back to the van wall, he began pushing himself up into a standing position.

"Siddown," growled Groom.

Pete glared. "I'm stretching my legs."

"I said siddown."

"And if I don't? What you gonna do? Kill me?"

Groom leapt to his feet... just too late. Pete was already upright, and as the thug came at him, he sidestepped. Groom hit the sidewall of the van and turned, in time for Pete to bring up a well-aimed knee into his breastbone.

Groom crashed to the floor, clutching his chest. From the corner of his eye, Pete saw Lawson raise his pistol, and in that second, Pete knew he was lost.

❧

Fishwick followed Bilks from Flutter-Bys back towards the manor. Crossing the moors, he noticed the large van making its slow way through the snow.

"I wonder," he muttered. He watched Bilks' form moving away from him. Fishwick experienced a moment of indecision. Bilks represented a danger to the mistress, but this van had come from Flutter-Bys, and that, too, could mean danger. He decided that the mistress and Miss Aggie could handle Bilks, and that whoever was in the van was probably the greater danger, and Modom would be more grateful for the reconnaissance. He swooped down to hover in front of the moving vehicle.

It was a tricky maneuver, hovering in front of the windscreen so he could check on the occupants, he moving backwards while the vehicle continued on its way, but Fishwick had not been on the spirit plane for 90-odd years without learning a trick or two.

Wilcox was behind the wheel, while his hideous wife sat in the passenger seat fiddling with the radio. Fishwick was puzzled. It seemed unlikely that a gangster like this would come here with only his wife for company, so where were their henchmen? Ahead of the van, he noticed a car. He rushed after it. Before he got there, he realized it was Pete Brennan's. Curious. Surely Mr. Brennan had not gone over to the opposition.

Fishwick dropped into the car and took the rear seat. Johnny and Nicky Tate. So, like Wilcox's minders, Pete was AWOL. Where could they all be?

Logic answered the question. The back of the van, of course. If it was loaded with pallets of goods, Pete was probably hidden amongst them waiting to spring a surprise when he got to the manor. Fishwick smiled at the notion. He liked Pete. There were times when he wished the mistress would take to him as well.

He was about to zoom off to Melmerby Manor when he realized that his mistress would be most displeased if he had not confirmed his suspicion. He shot back to the van, through the cab and into the rear in time to see Lawson pull out a pistol and aim it at Pete.

The van was lurching from side to side. Pete had just floored Groom and was hampered by his hands tied behind his back, whereas Lawson was leaning against the van wall, quite steady on his feet, and from a range of three meters, he could not miss.

Fishwick had a split second in which to act. He rushed Lawson, knocked the pistol from his hand, and then flew out of the van into the night. Turning quickly, he rushed at the vehicle again and, taking a leaf from Bilks' book, hammered into the side of it. The van rocked, its rear end lurching to the right before Wilcox righted it again.

Dropping back into the van, Fishwick took in the scene and saw that Pete was now in control of the situation. Time to get back to the mistress. Fishwick left the van and took off for the manor.

Pete was expecting nothing but the pain of a bullet tearing into him when two things happened so quickly that he was not sure of the order in which they occurred.

It seemed to him that Lawson dropped the pistol and then, a second later, the van lurched to the right, causing Lawson to lose his balance.

The sudden movement threw Pete too, slamming him into the side wall. He twisted away from the reeling thug and lashed out a foot, barking Lawson's shin.

With the vehicle throwing them around, Lawson stood groggily. Pete tucked himself into a corner to maintain his balance, summoned his strength and launched himself. He landed a foot in Lawson's midriff. Groom was up, coming at Pete head down. Pete sidestepped and, as Groom passed him, kicked out. His boot propelled the thug into the forward bulkhead. Groom's head collided with a loud bang. And the vehicle came to a sliding halt, throwing Pete back to the floor. Lawson was crawling across the van floor reaching for his pistol. Pete rushed, kicked the gun away and brought his boot down on Lawson's hand, crushing it and dragging a scream of agony from the thug. To silence him, Pete kicked him on the jaw.

Catching his breath, Pete chuckled. "I always said I could beat you two with both hands tied behind my back."

Pete heard the cab doors slam as Wilcox and Sylvie got out.

With the babysitters temporarily out of commission, Pete's concern switched to Wilcox and his gun.

"You're still tied up, buddy," he said to himself.

He scooted to the rear of the van. He could hear Wilcox manipulating the locking mechanism of the sliding rear door. He lay on his back, his legs bent, muscles tensed.

"I'll shoot that Brennan right here and now if he's causing grief," he heard Wilcox curse.

As the shutter came up, Pete lashed out with both feet simultaneously. He caught Sylvie square in the face with his right boot. She went down. His left foot kicked the automatic from Wilcox's hand and sent it spinning into the road. Pete flung himself out, landed feet first, then dropped and rolled on hard-packed snow between Wilcox and the pistol. Half-crouched, Wilcox reached across him for the gun, clearly visible in the illumination from the rear lights of the van. Still prone, Pete kicked the pistol away and, tensing his neck muscles, raised his head to butt Wilcox. Behind and above him, he could see a dark shape launching from the back of the van. Groom or Lawson? It didn't matter. Pete rolled away; the unidentified thug landed in the snow, slipped and sat down unexpectedly. Gathering his wits, Pete forced himself up and ran.

"Get after him," he heard Wilcox yell.

You're running in the wrong direction. The thought smashed into his brain. He looked over his shoulder as he continued to run. It was pitch dark. He could see nothing but the van's rear lights, and movement in their dim glow.

"What the hell's going on?" he heard Tate ask, as if he had just arrived.

"Brennan's out," he heard Wilcox reply. "I told you to get after him, Tommy."

Lawson's reply was lost as Pete slipped in the snow and rolled off down a steep gully.

They must have heard the rustle of bushes as he rolled through them, for the next thing he heard was Wilcox urging, "He's over there. Get him."

Pete staggered to his feet and ran along the bottom of the gully. It was pitch dark. He could see nothing other than the snowflakes falling just in front of him; all he could hear were Lawson's footsteps padding along the road above the gully. Pete stumbled again and rolled into a thicket. Lawson was getting nearer. The red lights of the van were now fifty meters away, but he couldn't make out Lawson's figure. Pete smiled to himself. If he could not see Lawson in the darkness, then Lawson could not see him. He lay stock still, holding his breath. The footsteps passed and faded. Soon they returned, going the other way, and then there came the noise of conversation.

"I can't see him, boss. He could be halfway to Ashdale by now."

"On foot? In this weather?" snapped Wilcox. "All right," he sighed. "Let's just get up to the hall and deal with the other two."

"But if he calls the cops—"

"How many phone boxes do you think there are out here in the middle of nowhere, you idiot?" Wilcox interrupted. "Anyway, I know Brennan. He'll come to the hall to rescue his pals, and we'll get him then. Come on."

Pete heard more commotion as they climbed into their vehicles, and soon both the car and the van drove off. Frantically now, Pete struggled to his feet and felt around for a stout branch in the thicket. Anything to help free his wrists of the wire bonds.

After suffering many scratches on his hands, he found a suitable branch, hooked his bindings over it and began to work. It hurt: every movement sent spears of pain lancing through his wrists. The wire bit ever deeper into his skin, and the thin cuts, already sore, began to bleed. Several times, the bite of cold and the wire brought him to the brink of agonized tears, but he persevered. He had to move quickly. If he did not, Kevin and Scepter would soon be joining

Fishwick... and although he did not believe in Fishwick, he would rather argue with his two friends about it than send them across to prove his point.

Then, suddenly, the wire gave and he was free. Blood ran down his wrists. More than he would have expected, but not enough to bring him to a dead faint. He fished in his pocket for a tissue, pressed it against each wrist in turn to stem the flow of blood. He dismissed his minor injuries and released the anger that had been bottled inside since the confrontation in Flutter-Bys' cellar. It was time to bring his specialist skills in mayhem to bear on Wilcox and his team.

In a crouch, he climbed up the embankment, slipped once in the deepening snow, and tried again. He slipped yet again. This time, he pressed himself flat to the ground, ignoring the freezing temperatures and the damp soaking through his coat to the shirt beneath, and crawled up to the road. In the darkness he could not see which way he needed to go. He paused a moment. The gully had been on his left when he ran, so that meant the manor must be to the right. He turned and ran. He had no idea how far it was. A kilometer? Two? Three? Would he be in time? If they got to Kevin and Scepter first... He closed his mind to the thought.

Lights came from behind. Pete stuck out a thumb. The car rushed past, splashing him with slush and snow. He cursed. Twenty meters on, the vehicle stopped. He hurried along, yanked open the passenger door, and, leaning in, looked into a pair of smiling, china blue eyes.

"Fancy meeting you here," said Andrea Keynes.

"Thank God," Pete said, climbing into the passenger seat. "You'd better get a move on or Kevin and Scepter are dead."

Keynes pulled off, peering through the heavy snow into the darkness. "The manor is about a kilometer."

"You got backup?"

She shook her head. "I overheard your buddies at the station. Locke showed them the door. I figured I could do worse than tag along. I've been parked down the road for the last hour. Then your car came past, followed by Wilcox's van. Trouble was, I'd been parked there so long, I was bogged down in the snow. It's taken me ten minutes to get out of it."

"Just as well," said Pete. "Wilcox is armed."

She tutted. "I'll bet his van isn't insured either."

Pete laughed. "Have I told you I could be the best thing that ever happened to you?"

18

At the sound of Fishwick's voice in her head, Scepter emerged from a disturbed reverie of the way the coming events might play out. "Yes, Fishwick."

"Modom, Wilcox and his friends are quite close and Mr. Brennan is with them. He was in some difficulty, but he got out of it with my assistance."

Scepter smiled. "He will not thank you for it, Fishwick. He doesn't believe in you."

"No, Modom, but I believe in him. He has the same selfless dependability my father had."

"Thank you, Fishwick. How long will it be before they get here?"

"A matter of only a few minutes, Modom."

"Then we must prepare. Can you arrange reinforcements amongst the other spirits here?"

"I shall try, Modom. There is one other matter."

"Yes?" asked Scepter, her interest aroused.

"I have to confess, Modom, that I disobeyed your orders." Fishwick sounded almost embarrassed. "You asked me to check out Flutter-Bys. A moment or two later, Bilks flew off so rather than obey you, I followed him. As it happens, he was going to Flutter-Bys. When he got there, he tore all the contents from the cold store in the cellar. It's quite a mess, I'm afraid, and the missing DVDs are all over the floor, mixed with the foodstuffs he scattered everywhere."

"I see." Scepter considered the information. "That should be useful to the police, but tell me, Fishwick, why did he do it?"

"I believe, Modom, he was looking for his cell phone," replied her butler, "which has been hidden in that cold store since he died. I also get the feeling that he was beaten almost to death in the cellar and left in the cold store, where he probably expired. Before he did, however, he hid his cell phone in there. It would be one way of hinting to the police, that he had been there."

Scepter immediately agreed. "That sounds likely, Fishwick. Thank you for the information."

❧

Kevin shivered in the chill and looked worriedly around the attic nursery. "Why did it have to be this room?"

Over by the window, Scepter gazed down onto the rear courtyard. "Because we can see the stables from here, and that's probably where they'll come in."

Kevin's mind was occupied with the room, not the view. "Yes; we can see the rocking horse, too, and the writing on the wall." His eye traveled around the room to the dripping, crimson message, WGJAMW, on the wall. "Scepter, you never told me how you worked out it was Wilcox."

"Fishwick suggested it. Bilks paid Wilcox a visit in the early hours of the morning."

"Good old Bilko. He was probably trying to rob the safe." He toyed idly with the mouse pad on his computer, his eyes darting everywhere, his hands shaking.

Scepter looked at him, a sympathetic smile crossing her lips. "Kevin, what's wrong?"

"Nothing. I was just asking—" His face, already showing his agitation, now reflected his full-on fear. "All right, I'm scared. We've got a house full of spooks who've had it in for me since we first came here, and a shed-load of gangsters on their way to put us out of it for keeps, so I'm a bit jittery."

"There is nothing to be afraid of," she tried to assure him.

"How about death?"

"Since none of us really understands death," Scepter pointed out, "you can't be afraid of it. It's *dying* you're afraid of."

"Oh, well, it's important to get these little details right, isn't it?" Kevin's voice dripped sarcasm. "I'm a young man, Scepter. I don't want to die yet. There's so much I haven't done. Got married, had kids, won the lottery, been to Brighton. See, I've never been to Brighton and I think everyone should go to Brighton at least once in their life, don't you?" He played with the computer again, moving the mouse pointer around the screen. "I mean, what would my old mum say if she knew I was sitting here, in a spooky old house, waiting to be murdered by a gangster? I know what she'd say. She'd say, 'Don't be silly, Kevin, and eat your rice pudding'. That's what she'd say, cos she was sensible, my mum."

Scepter returned to the window and looked down. Once she realized he was prattling to soothe his nerves and would keep talking whether she listened or not, she tuned him out. She, too, was afraid, but she was only afraid of failure, not death. She had visited death once, 24 hours ago, and whatever terrors it may have held for her before were gone.

"They're here, Modom," Fishwick said suddenly.

Scepter snapped from her thoughts and looked through the window, down into the rear courtyard where the gates had been opened and a large van nosed through them.

She turned from the window and cried, "Come on, Watson. The game's afoot."

"Watson?" Kevin said in complete befuddlement. "Who's Watson?"

Stopping his van in the stable yard, Wilcox climbed out and slammed the driver's door. He walked to the rear and rolled up the shutter to let Groom and Lawson out. Groom was still groggy from his encounter with Pete while Lawson worked at his hand where Pete had crushed it. At least nothing seemed broken.

Leaving Pete's car outside the gates, Nicky and Johnny walked into the stable yard as Wilcox began to marshal his forces. "Lemmy, you stay here and look out for the van. If Brennan tries to get in this way, stop him, and if Keeley or that bitch tries to get out, deal with it."

"I can deal with them two," Groom agreed, "but I'm not sure about Brennan."

"Just do it." Wilcox drew Tate and Nicky into the briefing. "This is a big house. They could be anywhere inside, so when we get to it, we split up. Johnny, you stick with Nicky; Sylvie, you can stay with me."

Unable to speak because her jaw was swollen where Pete's foot had connected with it, Sylvie nodded.

"What about me?" Lawson asked.

"You're watching the ground floor, Tommy. Just keep an eye out for any of them trying to leg it and for Brennan turning up."

"Now listen, Ronnie, I don't think I can take Brennan on my own."

"You've a shooter, haven't you? If he shows up, just blow him away." Wilcox took out his automatic pistol and cocked it. "Remember, all of you. No prisoners. We ice them all."

"What about plod?" asked Tate. "Brennan could have already called them."

Wilcox rolled his eyes, as if praying for patience. "You're as bad as these two." He gestured at his henchmen. "We're in the middle of nowhere. There are no phones, and I've got this." From his pocket, Wilcox took out Pete's mobile. "Besides—" He gestured at the falling snow "—the filth would never make it in this lot. Talking of phones, Sylvie, you still got Bilko's?"

Sylvie dipped into the pocket of her anorak and brought it out. She tried to smile, but it hurt where Pete had kicked her, so she contented herself with a grimace.

"Great," said her husband. "We leave it on one of them as evidence, and don't forget to wipe everything down after we're done. Don't leave any prints. All right, let's get to it." He crossed the courtyard to the rear doors and tried them. "Locked. Tommy?"

Lawson dipped into his pocket and came out with his lock picks. He bent to the door and, in the space of a few seconds, had tripped the lock. He stood back as Wilcox opened the door and led the way in.

He felt around for a light switch and flicked it on. The Long Gallery was promptly illuminated, although dimly, the free-standing exhibits casting long shadows into dark corners. They became aware of the heavy breathing.

"*WIGJAM... WIGJAM... WIGJAM...*"

Lawson began to quake. "Oh crikey, there really are ghosts here!"

Wilcox snorted. "Ghosts, my foot. They're using that PA system, same as we did with them. Tommy, get into the private rooms and shut it down."

"On my own?" The thug found his courage seriously on the wane. "With Brennan knocking about somewhere?"

"You want someone to hold your hand?" Wilcox sneered. "Just get in there."

They emerged into the grand entrance hall. As Lawson made off to the private apartments, Tate spotted the cable drums and lines leading up the stairs. "They're waiting for us, Ronnie."

"Then let's not disappoint 'em, eh?"

<hr/>

"I shall do nowt of the kind."

Fishwick sighed at Sir Henry's refusal to help. "Sir," he said with great respect, "my mistress and her friend are in great danger from these intruders. If we do not help, they may be killed."

"If yon wench were around in my day, I'd have saved her all right—for myself," declared Sir Henry. "But if they can get her outta my house, it'll do for me. I'm off to my room."

"He's got a one track mind," muttered Fishwick as the old squire moved off.

"Pay him no mind," said Aggie as she approached Fishwick. "He's a miserable old bugger. I'll help where I can." She cackled. "I can make that rocking horse do things a real horse couldn't."

"Thank you, Miss Aggie."

<hr/>

Lawson's hands shook visibly as he opened the door to the private apartments and made his way stealthily along to the control room.

His mind was still full of the strange events in Flutter-Bys' cellar in the early hours, and the manor gave him the willies. He had been all right when Groom was with him. Now, alone, with Lemmy left behind at the gate looking after the van, Lawson was afraid. Reaching the control room, he yanked the wires from the computer, then sighed in relief as the room fell silent.

Then the breathing returned, deeper, heavier, more rasping—and closer. Lawson froze, his eyes fixed on the computer screen. In the blank screen, he made out a dim reflection of his terrified features and something else: a huge shape forming somewhere behind him.

"WIGJAM!" The voice bellowed in his ear, the furious roar of an enraged lion.

Visions of Flutter-Bys' cellar filled his mind. With a cry of sheer horror, Lawson turned. Before him was a huge, monstrous form—a man but larger than a man; a bear, but larger than a bear. His heart leapt. His limbs trembled. He could not even decide what it was. Gripped by a dread he had never known in his life, he ran blindly from the room.

Hurtling through the apartments, he came out into the entrance hall, the shape and voice following him. He glanced frantically to his left and the front door, then to his right and the Long Gallery, and then up the stairs. Deciding that discretion was the great part of valor, he ran for the front door and yanked it open.

An even more fearsome spectacle met his eyes. Blood-scarred wrists bared and held forward, eyes blazing with fury, ham-like fists clenched, the terrifying figure towered over Lawson... and the thug's eyes rolled back as he collapsed.

⚜

Out by the stables, Lemmy Groom leaned against the front of the van, where the radiator was still warm from the drive out. It would warm his back, he decided as he lit a cigarette.

He was still light-headed and seeing occasional stars after the pasting from Brennan, but he looked forward to Wilcox, Tate and Lawson bringing out the three bods, and he hoped that the ex-cop would still be alive when they did. He wanted to press that pistol against Brennan's head and squeeze the trigger. The ultimate payback.

Smiling at the thought, Groom drew in a lungful of smoke and expelled it with a hiss into the night.

There was a rattle from the ground a few meters away. Groom looked to the left of the van where a stone skidded across the snow. He looked down the offside, to the right of the van, and saw nothing, no one. Next he checked down the nearside. Still no one. He crossed to the stone, bent to examine it. Nothing special, nothing spectacular.

"Just a boring pebble," he muttered. He looked up at the manor towering above him. "Probably fell off the roof."

He turned and found himself looking into the smiling eyes of Detective Constable Keynes.

She winked. "Hello, Lemmy."

Groom reached under his arm for his pistol. Keynes brought her knee up between his legs and he sank to the ground. While he concerned himself with trying to pull in a deep breath so he could control the pain, she searched beneath his arm and removed the revolver.

"Tsk, tsk, tsk. Ex-con carrying a firearm. You're looking at a long stretch, Lemmy." She gripped his wrist and slapped her handcuffs around it, then dragged him to the vehicle, where she forced him to stand up, and then snapped the other manacle over the tubular arm of the wing mirror. Left with his arm high in the air anchored to the lorry, Groom could do nothing except hang there, gasping in agony.

Keynes removed the ammunition from the pistol and slipped the weapon into one pocket, the bullets into another. She moved to the driver's door, opened it and took the ignition keys from the lock, then, with a smile at Groom, entered the house.

⸙

Keynes moved quickly through the Long Gallery to the entrance hall, where she found Pete standing over the unconscious Lawson.

"I hope you didn't hit him too hard," she commented, taking another pair of handcuffs from her coat pocket.

"I didn't hit him at all," said Pete. "He took one look at me and fainted. I seem to be having that effect on people just lately. Day before yesterday, even Kev was bowing to me." He smiled at her. "Will you be that submissive for me?"

Keynes scowled. "Knock it off, Brennan. We have business to attend to." She nodded at Lawson. "Is he armed?"

"He *was*." Pete held up a revolver, now emptied of ammunition. Dropping the pistol back into his pocket, he rolled the inert Lawson over onto his abdomen and pulled both hands behind the gangster's back while Keynes handcuffed him.

"So, where's the party?" she asked.

Pete nodded at the cables. "Looks like it's upstairs. Shall we join them?"

⸙

"Excuse me, sir."

In the middle of compiling a report on the afternoon's football hooliganism, Chief Inspector Locke was not happy to be disturbed by PC Robb. "What is it?"

"Well, sir, we had a call from Scepter Rand about half an hour ago."

Locke groaned. "Not again."

Robb grinned. "You've met her, sir? Only I have too, earlier in the week..." Locke scowled, and Robb wiped the smile from his face. "Well sir, she gave us a mobile telephone number, saying it belonged to Bilko—er—Steven Bilks, that is, and she told us to get a GPS track on it."

"And you took her seriously? Bilko is dead and—"

"Yes sir, I know that, but being as it's a murder investigation, the Sarge thought it best to check, so we contacted the mobile company and asked them to verify the details, which they did, and we asked them for a GPS location."

"Yes? And?"

"Well, it's odd, sir," said Robb, "so we thought you'd better know. The thing is switched on, and it's on the move."

Locke suddenly became alert and interested. "Where?"

"Along Melmerby Lane, sir. Towards the manor house."

Locke stood up and reached for his overcoat. "Right. Where's DS Keynes?"

"Dunno, sir," Robb admitted. "She went out a couple of hours ago."

"Tell Sarge to get me a team together," the chief inspector ordered. "We're going out there."

"Yes, sir. Only—er..."

In the act of putting on his coat, Locke paused. "Something wrong?"

"Well, it's snowing quite heavily."

"Snowing?" Locke demanded indignantly. "Who gives a damn about snow? Where would we be if Monty had told Winnie that he couldn't face Rommel at El Alamein because it was snowing? Get that crew together and move it."

"Yes, sir. Sir?"

"What is it, man?"

"Did it really snow in the desert, sir?"

❦

"They're up in the attics. Look." Tate pointed to the cables disappearing under the door to the attic stairway.

Wilcox tutted. "It's easy to see why Jimmy uses you as a gopher. You haven't got the brains for nothing else. Running the cables like that could be a dupe." He waved vaguely at the doors along the first landing. "We have to check these rooms too. You and Nicky see to them; me and Sylvie'll go up to the attics."

Johnny huffed. "Well, running the wires up the stairs from the ground floor could be a trick, too. They might be down there."

"Which is why I left Tommy there and Lemmy out near the van. Now get on with it. Come on, Sylvie."

Wilcox and his wife disappeared up the attic stairway; Tate and Nicky carried on along the landing and into the master bedroom.

Nicky perched herself on the edge of the four-poster, while Tate took a look in the wardrobe.

"No one here," he declared.

Nicky smiled up at him. "Nice bed, though."

Tate took the hint, sat next to her, placed his hands on her shoulders and half-turned her to face him, then pushed her gently back onto the mattress. He followed her, and their lips met in a passionate kiss.

❧

Sir Henry looked down on the couple. His irritable orange to red drifted to scarlet fury. "Not on my bed, tha doesn't." He made for the dressing table.

❧

The couple were oblivious to anything but each other, lost in the throes of passion. Suddenly, it began to go wrong.

First, a wood-backed hairbrush on the dresser flew at them and hit Tate in the back. He broke the kiss and looked sharply at the dresser just in time to duck away from the comb flying through the air at him. The corner of the antique bedspread rippled, then flipped up and over their heads. Something pummeled Tate in the ribs. He threw the bedspread off in time to see one of the pillows rise into the air and batter Nicky around the head.

"What the... ?" he gasped.

If Tate was puzzled, Nicky was terrified. "Never mind the questions," she yelled. "Let's get out of here!"

They ran from the room, out onto the landing—and straight into Keynes and Pete.

While Keynes tackled Nicky, Pete squared up to Tate with a smile on his face.

"Hello, Johnny. Fancy your chances now, do you? Now that I'm not wired up?"

Trapped, with nowhere to run, Tate threw an accurate right at Pete's jaw. Pete blocked it. He lashed his own right into Tate's abdomen. Winded, Tate doubled up. He wrapped his arms around Pete's waist, locking his hands and pushing forward, slamming both of them back into the oak-paneled walls. Pete clasped his fists together and brought them down hard on the back of Tate's neck. At the same time, he brought his knee up into Tate's chest. Tate gasped; his grip slackened. Pete grabbed his hair and pulled back. With a yelp, Tate let go of Pete's waist and reached up for his own hairline. Pete straightened him up by the hair, smiled again and landed a head butt on Tate's forehead. Johnny Tate crumpled and fell to the floor, where he lay still.

"God, *that* felt good," said Pete with a satisfied smile.

⁎

Fishwick was impressed with Sir Henry's intervention. "I thought you weren't going to help."

"They can do as they like with yon strumpet of thine," declared Sir Henry, "but I'll not have them defile my bed."

⁎

"You okay?" Keynes came to Pete wringing her right wrist with her left hand. On the floor lay Nicky Tate, not moving, aside from the even rise and fall of her chest as she breathed. Keynes gestured down. "Tough cookie."

"A pussycat." Pete nodded with satisfaction. "Hurt your hand?"

Keynes shrugged. "It's nothing."

"We've run out of handcuffs," Pete advised her.

"There must be something we can use," said Keynes.

He eyed Tate's belt, a stout leather affair. Exchanging a glance with Keynes, he unhooked it and removed it. Crossing to the two women, while Keynes turned Nicky round Pete clasped her hands behind her back, then ran the belt round her wrists and tightened it. He dragged Tate along, sat him back to back with Nicky, and tied him, too, with the rest of the belt.

"That should keep them quiet until we get back." He nodded to the attic door. "Shall we?"

Keynes nodded.

"Ladies first."

She grinned. "Oh, no. Age before beauty."

⁎

"There's been a bit of a do in the master bedroom, Modom."

Scepter tutted at her butler's vernacular. "A bit of a do? Explain yourself, Fishwick."

"Well, Modom, two of our visitors were about to use Sir Henry's bed for –ahem– unseemly purposes and the old man got a bit miffed over it. He threw a few things at them, and they ran for it."

Scepter smiled. "So can we count upon his help after all?"

"I doubt it, Modom. Sir Henry was only annoyed because they were using his bed. However," Fishwick pressed on more optimistically, "Miss Aggie is close by and has promised to do what she can."

Scepter remembered her manners. "Make certain you thank Aggie and Sir Henry for us, Fishwick. Where is everyone?"

"Right now, two of the enemy are making their way along the attic landing, Modom. I'm ready for them." Fishwick's tone suggested that he was standing to attention and saluting.

Alongside Scepter, Kevin was shaking. She tried to sound encouraging. "We'd better get ready. They'll be here any minute."

They listened in silence and heard a door open and close again, just along the landing.

"Arm yourself, Kevin," said Scepter, checking a box of toys and picking up a bag of glass marbles. "These will do nicely."

Kevin, too, checked the box and came out with a child's pinwheel on a stick.

"What are you gonna do with that?"

"I'll think of something," he said with a shiver.

"Jam it against your backside and see if you can make the sails turn," suggested Scepter, and promptly wondered why she had delivered such a crude comment. "I'm sorry, Kevin. I shouldn't have said that. I must have been channeling Pete instead of Fishwick for a moment."

Kevin quaked even more and gave out a nervous laugh. "That's what comes of living with a couple of ratbags like me and Pete."

The door burst open. Wilcox and Sylvie came in; Wilcox raised his pistol at Kevin, but before he could squeeze the trigger, it was dashed from his grip by Fishwick's unseen hand. While Wilcox stared in disbelief, Scepter began to throw marbles at him.

Sylvie threw herself at Kevin, who began to beat her about the head with his toy. She backed off and threw a punch; Kevin ducked and broke wind with a loud raspberry. Sylvie screwed up her nose in disgust. Perfectly accustomed to such a reaction, Kevin had anticipated it and took the opportunity to poke her in the eye with his stick.

Wilcox fought through the rain of marbles and struck out at Scepter. She crashed to the floor, and he slipped on one of the marbles and fell upon her. Automatically, his hands went around her throat.

Scepter was taken by surprise. She had anticipated some help from Fishwick as soon as Wilcox attacked. "Kevin," she croaked as she struggled, "Fishwick, anyone. Help!"

Kevin lashed out and flattened Sylvie. He turned to the others, wrapped his arms around Wilcox's throat and yanked him back. Wilcox lammed out a single punch. It did little damage but knocked Kevin sideways and to the floor, where Sylvie leapt upon him. He poked at her with the pinwheel stick, but, enjoying the advantage of her superior position, she avoided the stick and rained blows down on him.

Across the room, Wilcox's grip tightened around Scepter's throat again. She sucked in her breath with loud whoops. Her vision was beginning to blur. She knew she had lost. The idea did not so much frighten as disappoint her. For all his powers, Fishwick could not help her.

Similar thoughts occupied Kevin's mind. His consciousness began to fade under a flurry of blows from Sylvie's hard fists, and the thought crossed his mind. "Pete, you've let me down." He knew it was selfish to blame his best friend, but he could not help it. Pete had been there all his life, and now, when Kevin needed him most, he was not.

⌘

When Bilks rushed towards the struggling figures of Scepter and Wilcox, Fishwick's first thought was that he was after Scepter's body again, so he put himself between his mistress and the furious spirit. Bilks collided with him in a shower of light. Fishwick was knocked to one side, and Bilks bounced off obliquely and through the wall onto the landing.

Across the room, Aggie's spirit arm extended and began to rock the rocking horse back and forth, giving it a harder strike with every oscillation. As Fishwick watched, she set the toy into frenetic motion until finally, its front legs left the floor altogether, at which point Aggie shouldered it slightly to the right, aiming it at the fighting bodies of Kevin and Sylvie.

As Bilks came back through the wall, Fishwick heard Scepter's strangled gasps and, turning quickly, launched himself at Wilcox.

⌘

Above Kevin and Sylvie, the rocking horse began to rock. Then, without warning, it reared up as if its legs had broken free of the rockers. Sylvie caught the movement from the corner of her eye, turned, and looked up in terror as the heavy toy came crashing down on her. The rocker caught her on the shoulder and threw her off Kevin, who, though just as terrified as she, had the presence of mind to roll quickly out of the way. Spotting his opportunity, he jumped at her and sat on her abdomen. With a sly grin, he let rip and deliberately forced out the wind. From beneath him came a satisfying "ugh".

Fishwick collided with Wilcox and knocked him from his position astride Scepter. The mobster rolled across the floor, unable to comprehend what had happened. He stopped within reach of his pistol. Gripping it, he got to his knees, leveled the gun at Scepter and smiled evilly.

"You lose." He squeezed the trigger.

Scepter stood her ground, expecting nothing but death.

❦

"WIGJAM!" roared Bilks and rushed at Wilcox, dashing the pistol from his hand.

The furious spirit scooped up the marbles and began to throw them at the mobster, the glass balls hurtling at Wilcox as rapidly as the ammunition of an unseen machine-gun.

Fishwick, aware now that he had misread Bilks' earlier attack, kept his distance, permitting Bilks' absolute fury free reign.

❦

Wilcox threw his hands up to protect his face. When the supply of marbles was exhausted, other toys flew from the box. A teddy bear, dolls, farm animals molded from lead: all attacked the gangster.

"WIGJAM!" They all heard Bilks' roar.

His mind a whirl of frightened confusion, aware of nothing other than the need to be out of this madhouse, Wilcox fled the room. The rain of toys followed him. He burst onto the attic landings—and rushed straight into Pete and DS Keynes.

The collision knocked the Detective Sergeant to the floor. Pete grabbed Wilcox, who lashed out with a flailing arm. They hit the deck, rolling and tussling across the bare floorboards. Pete got the upper hand; Wilcox threw him off, stood and ran. Pete stretched out a hand and, with a superhuman effort, grabbed Wilcox's ankle. Wilcox crashed back to the floor. Pete leapt for him. Wilcox struck out with a foot, caught Pete in the midriff and knocked him to one side.

Leaping to his feet again, Wilcox ran for it.

Pete checked on the dazed DC Keynes. "You okay?"

"I'll be all right," she gasped, clutching at her ribs. "Get after him."

"He'll be in that truck and away before I can catch him."

Digging into her pocket, she held up the ignition keys and grinned. "Not without these, he won't."

Pete smiled and ran off after Wilcox.

❦

Wilcox fled down the stairs, through the Long Gallery, the terrible voice following him.

"WIGJAM... WIGJAM... WIGJAM..."

It filled his ears and his mind. He did not understand it, but he knew it meant something dreadful, and if he did not escape it, that dreadful something would take his life.

He dashed out into the stable yard, where he slipped on the icy ground and skidded under the front of his lorry. Ignoring Groom's pleas for release from his handcuffed position at the passenger door mirror, Wilcox picked himself up, leapt into the driver's seat and reached for the ignition key.

"WIGJAM... WIGJAM... WIGJAM..."

The voice was there with him.

No keys.

He dived out of the truck and ran to the rear gates, out onto the snowy moorland. The electric blue lights of several police cars lit the landscape. Scared half to death, Wilcox looked frantically out at the woods. He would never survive. Not in these freezing temperatures. He turned back into the courtyard and hurried to the truck again.

"WIGJAM... WIGJAM... WIGJAM..."

As he opened the driver's door, it slammed shut again. Once more, Wilcox stared around in terror. The warehouse.

He hurried into the stables and looked around. He needed somewhere to hide. Somewhere they'd never find him. He made for the racks and the narrow alleys between them. He could hide where they had left Bilko's body.

The engine of the forklift truck roared into life. The shift slipped into forward and the machine roared at the racking.

"WIGJAM... WIGJAM... WIGJAM..."

When the forklift struck, the whole structure rocked and folded. Wilcox had time for one last scream before the tangle of steel and palletized goods crumbled and crushed the life from him.

❦

Wilcox looked down upon his crushed body in astonishment. He did not understand what had happened. One moment, he was suffering terrible pain as the metal grid structure collapsed upon him, and the next, something had dragged him from under it and the pain had vanished.

"That lot could have killed me," he said aloud.

There was something wrong. He knew he had spoken aloud, but he had not *heard* his voice. He had *felt* it.

"It *did* kill you, chum," said Fishwick.

Wilcox looked around and could not believe his surroundings. It was dark, the sky crystal clear, yet there were no stars. When he looked down, he could see the forklift truck and hear its chugging engine. He could see the mangled wreckage of the warehouse racking, a tangle of steel and wooden pallets, with a hand protruding from underneath. It looked like his hand.

He looked away, unable to comprehend. Opposite him was a bright light, as dazzling as the sun, but white. An attractive light, it seemed to be beckoning him.

"I'm dead?" he asked.

"Afraid so," said Fishwick. "Your life weren't saved, matey. It's over."

Wilcox took a moment to let the fact sink in. He looked around. "So what's with the spotlight?" Wilcox's energy form gestured at The Light and the steady stream of other forms passing into it.

'That's the way to the next life, mate," Fishwick explained. "That's where you will learn to atone for your sins before you're born again."

Wilcox sounded dubious. "So how come you're here?"

"I don't want to go to the next life," Fishwick replied simply. "I haven't finished with this one."

The form that had been Wilcox gave the impression of a malicious grin. "Let me get this straight. I don't have to go through The Light unless I want to. I can choose to stay here and carry on hassling nurks like Brennan?"

"You can," Fishwick agreed, "but you'd only end up fighting me most of the time, and trust me, I've been a here a long time. I know what I'm about."

Now Wilcox laughed. "You think I'm impressed. Think again."

A white-hot blur hurtled towards him. "WIGJAM!" it roared.

Suddenly, Wilcox understood that message. He knew that he *was* WGJAMW and WIGJAM, and that the roar came from the deceased Steven Bilks.

"Now Bilko, that's no way to speak to your betters." Wilcox's form wafted as if he were goading Bilks.

Bilks roared and rushed. Wilcox quickly learned that by an effort of will he could avoid the oncoming spirit with little effort. He laughed. "You were never quick enough to take me when you were alive, Bilko."

Bilks looped and came at him again from a narrow angle. Wilcox waited until the last second and ducked back.

"Olé, toro, toro, toro." He laughed again.

Once more Bilks swooped, and once more Wilcox ducked back, getting closer to The Light. Again and again Bilks came, and each time, Wilcox laughed and got closer to The Light, without realizing he was being shepherded.

He was almost on top of The Light when Bilks shot straight at him. Wilcox flinched for the last time, tottering on the edge. Fishwick gave him a nudge, then looked away, calmly whistling to himself as if he had had nothing to do with it. With a cry, the gangster disappeared into The Light.

The raging spirit of Steven Bilks calmed instantly. The blaze of energy settled, took on the more human-esque form Fishwick was accustomed to in other spirits.

"What... How... wh-where am I?"

"The Other Side, my friend," said Fishwick, emanating waves of friendship. "You've squared the circle, and you're at peace now. It comes to us all sooner or later." He looked down on his disheveled mistress in the attics of Melmerby Manor. "Well, almost all of us."

Understanding dawned on Bilks. "He killed me, didn't he? Wilcox? I remember."

"I'm afraid he did," Fishwick tried to send out waves of sympathy.

"Funny," said Bilks, "I don't feel sad. I'm not happy, but not sad."

Fishwick understood. "At least you're not angry anymore."

Bilks looked around, took in his strange surroundings. "Where has he gone? Wilcox? Somewhere peaceful? I hope not."

Fishwick gave the impression that he was rubbing his chin thoughtfully. "Now, there's a thing. Truth is, me old china, none of us really knows. Some say it leads straight to the next life, some say it leads to a place of judgment and then onto the next life, where we'll pay for the sins we committed in this life. What we do know is that once you go into The Light, you can't come back. Wherever it leads, wherever he's gone, Wilcox can never bother anyone again."

Bilks' form wavered slightly back to an angry red, but he brought it quickly under control. There was, nevertheless, a good degree of indignation when he spoke. "So Wilcox, who's been a hardened criminal for most of his life could start afresh, with the slate wiped."

If he had been human, Fishwick would have shrugged. "We don't know." He waved vaguely at the whole spirit plane. "The Universe has a way of ironing things out, my friend, so it's likely that in the next life, Wilcox will be born into poverty." He tried to sound more encouraging. "It's time for you to stop worrying about Wilcox, and consider yourself."

It was as if Bilks had just been reminded of it. His voice was shocked, filled with awe. "I'm dead. But what about Angie and Damon? What will they do?"

Fishwick looked down on Scepter and her friends. "Get on with their lives, mate. That's what the living do."

"And what about me?" asked Bilks. "Is it time for me to go through The Light?"

"That's up to you," Fishwick explained. "If your work is done, you can go through, or you can stay here and hang about with me, keep an eye on your wife and child."

Bilks disappeared. In a second he reappeared. "It's no good. Like this, I would only frighten them. I think I'd better move on."

Fishwick glowed a little brighter. "Just as you wish."

"Thank you," said Bilks, drifting slowly to The Light. "Thank you for your help."

Fishwick watched him drifting further and further back until The Light had him in its grip and he disappeared into its welcoming brilliance. "My pleasure, me old china."

19

It was 10:00 on Monday morning when Andrea Keynes visited Scepter, Pete and Kevin at their flat. They had all been questioned and released on Saturday night, and she had come to give them a clean bill of health.

"We've been out at the manor all weekend," she reported, "working under floodlights at night, getting that wrecked racking out of the way, piece by piece, so we could shift Wilcox's body. Trouble is, no one's come up with a convincing explanation as to who drove the forklift truck."

Pete had had the whole weekend to think about Wilcox's actions. "Since you took the keys out of his truck when you handcuffed Lemmy Groom, Wilcox must have figured he could do a runner on the forklift truck."

Keynes laughed. "Leg it on a forklift truck? And do you think we wouldn't have noticed as he passed us and plodded into town on it?"

"Knowing your men, they'd have held up the traffic and waved him through." Pete thought about the devastation again. "He probably rammed it into the racks by accident, then ran for it, but he was so confused, he ran the wrong way. Or maybe he believed there was a rear exit."

"Locke had it figured another way, Pete. Like you came after him and rammed the racks. That makes it manslaughter at least. Possibly murder."

"Well in that case, I'm glad I was with you."

Keynes stared through the windows at the gray light of a grim Monday morning and a heavy sky threatening more snow. She glanced back and smiled. "Be thankful for your fairy godmother. Me. Groom swears that there was no one in that warehouse but Wilcox, and I told Locke it wasn't you."

Pete was satisfied, but Fishwick knew otherwise and had already imparted his knowledge to Scepter, who passed it on. "It was Bilks who drove the truck, Bilks who killed Wilcox," she insisted. "He was getting his revenge for his own murder."

No one believed her, although Keynes did confirm that they had officially cleared up the murder of Steven Bilks. "Groom and Lawson admitted that it was Wilcox. Smashed Bilko with a baseball bat in an effort to keep him quiet, and went a bit too far."

"It was cold-blooded murder," Pete grunted, "and Wilcox got just what he deserved. So we're officially in the clear, are we?"

"On all fronts," Keynes confirmed. "We did find a hell of a mess on the floor of Flutter-Bys' cellar. Butter, eggs, yogurt, and in amongst it all were thousands of pirate copies of *Mind Games III*. Johnny Tate said they belonged to his brother, but Jimmy is denying it. Do you know anything about them?"

"Me?" Pete put on an air of virginal innocence. "Would I have anything to do with pirate movies?"

Keynes gave a throaty laugh. "All right. I won't push it, but you have one last thing to do, Pete."

He was mystified. As far as he was concerned, everything had been covered. "What's that?"

Keynes grinned. "Buy me dinner."

With an eye on Scepter to see if it provoked any reaction—it didn't—Pete agreed and showed the Detective Constable out. When he returned, he found Scepter in good form, expounding her own theories to Kevin.

"Wilcox heard the ghost of Steven Bilks in that nursery, it terrified him, he ran for it and Bilks chased him down to the warehouse, where he drove the forklift truck into the racking."

"I must say," Pete commented, rejoining them at the table, "he's very versatile, our Bilko. He's been sending text messages to Kev ever since he died, he's been through you once—which is one more time than me or McKinley—and now he's driving a forklift truck. If he were that clever, he could have made an honest fortune when he was alive, instead of passing his time breaking and entering."

"All right," Scepter bristled, "who threw the marbles at Wilcox?"

"You did," Pete declared.

Scepter promptly disagreed. "No, I mean after I'd run out of them. He had me on the floor, choking me. Someone threw marbles at him to get him off me, and it wasn't Fishwick."

Pete gestured at his best friend. "Kev, then."

"No," Kevin denied, "I was busy poking Sylvie in the eye with my pinwheel."

"We've had this debate before," Pete objected, "when Kev got the milk and sugar and forgot. I think it's happened again. He thinks he was poking Sylvie in the eye, and in reality he was chucking marbles at Wilcox."

Scepter gazed calmly at him. "You're just afraid that I may be right."

⁂

"Pay you? Have you gone completely mad, Brennan?"

Opposite Jimmy Tate, Pete fumed. "We had a deal, Tate. Find your DVDs and you pay us five grand."

Jimmy nodded. "That's right. But you didn't find them, did you? The filth did … in Wilcox's cellar. If you'd told me that when you came earlier and left it to me to pick them up, I'd have paid you, and plod would have been none the wiser, but you didn't."

"I didn't know they were there until Wilcox walled me up in his cooler," Pete yelled.

"Irrelevant. You hadda play the big hero, didn't you? Finding Bilko's killer and all that, and where's it got us all? Johnny and Nicky are walled up, and when they get out, they're gonna clear off together, and Trading Standards have impounded all the DVDs, and I'm out several grand. Not only that, they're investigating me, which means I've had to trash all my gear, wipe all the hard drives, get rid of written records and stuff. It'll be a year before I'm back in business."

"Jimmy," said Kevin, "we showed you that your missus was having an affair with your brother."

"You think I didn't know about that? Get real, Keeley. What woman in her right mind is gonna find *this* attractive?" Jimmy swept his podgy hands down from shoulder to waistline.

Scepter tried to reassure him. "Mr. Tate, there are remedies for chronic obesity. You could have your jaw wired and your stomach stapled."

"Ugh," was Jimmy's response.

"All right then, how about a few classes in self-esteem. There *are* those women who find intelligence attractive."

He dismissed her with a snort. "I don't have intelligence, lady. I'm streetwise, but I'm still a blimp, and women like Nicky find my bank balance the most attractive thing about me. I knew about her and Johnny months ago."

Scepter was amazed. "And you did nothing about it?"

"Yes, I did. I kept my trap shut." Jimmy swallowed a large swig of beer. "He was my brother and she was my wife. As long as I played dumb, they stayed here."

Pete reared angrily. "They were going to walk out on you, with your money."

"Yes, and if I'd known, I could have talked them round. Instead, you dragged them into the Bunfight At The No Way Hotel, and they're nicked. Now, they'll never come back." Jimmy glared at the team. "You get nothing."

They emerged from Tate's house and climbed into Kevin's van.

"You have to feel sorry for him," said Scepter, settling between her partners.

"Sorry for him?" Pete slammed the door. "If we ever meet again, I'll kill him."

"He's lost everything," she pointed out.

"Not quite. He's still got his money." Kevin fired the reluctant engine and ground the gears into reverse. "And look on the bright side, Pete. You've shut down Ashdale's biggest dealer in porn and pirate movies, and you've helped rid the town of one of its gangsters. Wilcox. Admittedly, we didn't earn on it, but you can't have everything."

"Kevin?"

Kevin dropped the van into first and drove off down the drive towards the gate. "Yes, Pete."

"Shut up and lend me 50 quid," ordered Pete.

"Yes, Pe—What?" Kevin was so shocked, he braked hard and the van skidded into a small tree, smashing one of his headlights. "Now look what you've done."

"I think the tree's okay," said Pete as Kevin drew away from it.

Scepter laughed and Kevin boiled. "What about my van?"

"What about that 50 quid?" asked Pete.

Kevin dropped the van into gear again and drove to the junction where the drive met the main road. "Pete, give me one good reason why I should lend you 50."

"I'm taking Andrea Keynes out tonight," Pete reminded him. "Come on, I'll pay you back when things pick up."

Kevin shook his head. "You shouldn't have agreed to taking her out when you didn't have the money."

"I was banking on Tate paying up," Pete explained.

Scepter smiled. "Lend him the 50 pounds, Kevin. You must owe him that for the number of times he's saved your hide."

Kevin pulled out of Tate's drive and into the afternoon traffic. "I'll want a receipt."

Scepter handed Pete a small notebook and pen. He scrawled *"IOU fifty sovs"*, signed it and passed it to Kevin. Pulling up at a set of lights, Kevin checked it.

"Hey," he protested, "this is signed Donald Duck."

Pete smiled innocence. "Must have been Bilko's hand guiding the pen."

❧

Ten minutes later, as they pulled the car park of the Crown & Anchor, Scepter's telephone rang. She took it from her bag and made the connection. "Hello, Spookies."

"Spookies now, is it?" McKinley's voice came down the line. "How you doing, sugar? Just wanted to know how you got on the other night."

Climbing out of the van, Scepter covered the mouthpiece and reported to her two partners. "McKinley."

"Tell him where to get off," Pete suggested, leading the way into the bar.

"Better yet," said Kevin, "tell him where the railway station is and what time the next London train leaves, and tell him to be under it."

She ignored them. "What can we do for you, Mr. McKinley?"

"I want to apologize for Saturday night," the reporter confessed.

Scepter smiled to herself. More soberly, she announced to the mouthpiece, "Your apology is rejected by a majority of three to none."

"Come on, Scepter," begged McKinley. "I bottled out. It isn't the first time. Heroes, like your pal, Brennan, are thin on the ground, and I don't reckon to be one. Let me make it up to you and buy you dinner tonight."

"I'll think about it," she said, and hung up.

Following her partners into the bar, Scepter bought a bottle of wine, and they retired to a corner table.

"So what did the scumbag want?" Pete asked.

She poured three glasses from the bottle. "He wants to take me to dinner."

Pete was aghast. "You're not thinking about it, are you?"

Scepter pushed a glass to each of them and took the third for herself. "Why not? You have a date with that detective."

Pete thought about it for a moment, then said, "Yes, but McKinley is probably only after the bottom line on the police investigation. He'll get what he wants and dump you."

"Pete," Scepter said, "someone once told me that there is no such thing as bad publicity. McKinley may be a creep, and he certainly won't get what he *really* wants, but he may be useful to us in the future."

"The future?" Kevin swallowed hard. "I've had it with ghost hunting. My future is in buying and selling."

"We were extraordinarily successful at Melmerby Manor and *that* is our future." She raised her glass. "Gentlemen, I give you a toast."

Mystified, her partners raised their glasses too.

"I give you... Spookies."

∗

BRITISH
CULTURAL REFERENCES

BRITISH BEER—In most areas of the world, beer is beer, but not in the UK. What Americans call beer, e.g. Coors or Budweiser, is more like the drink we sell as lager. In Britain we have several types of ale: mild, bitter, stout, and when sold in bottles or cans, there will be light ale, pale ale, or brown ale. In addition, breweries have their own labels, such as Newcastle Brown Ale, McEwan's Export, Watney's Red Barrel. Tradition has it that beer is also ordered by the pint (even though these days it is sold by the half litre). Although lager has gained in popularity over the last 30 years, a customer ordering in a pub would not simply ask for a beer. He would specify the brand and amount. "A pint of Ashdale Mild," "a half (or glass) of John Smith's Bitter." At the very least, he would ask for a pint of bitter, a half of lager, and so on. In the home, however, things are different. A householder would grab a beer from the fridge.

DRINKING & DRIVING—The drink drive (equivalent to US "drunk driving") limit for the UK is similar to the newly-adopted universal limit for the US: 80 mg. of alcohol/100ml. of blood. There are plans to cut it to 50 mg., which would bring it into line with many other countries in Europe, some of which have a legal limit as low as 10 mg. 50 mg. would result from drinking about a half pint of strong beer or 175 ml. (about 6 ounces) of wine. If stopped and breathalyzed, anyone over the limit faces a mandatory driving ban of 1 year and a heavy fine. Drinking and driving is now considered so antisocial that drivers are becoming more and more wary of committing the offense. Most drivers, if they suspect they are over the limit, leave the driving to a partner.

BRITISH HUMOR—Brit humour is often self-deprecating, invariably cynical and politically incorrect, but it's not meant to be taken remotely seriously. To call someone, for example, a soft tart, is not a slur on their sexual mores, but a reflection on their lack of courage, or "bottle" as it is known in the UK.

BRITISH POLICE—Forces are arranged by county, and there are two main division to each force: uniformed and CID. Uniformed handle routine policing, traffic, and minor offenses. CID stands for Criminal Investigation Department, and they deal with offenses ranging from theft and burglary to murder. There are other, specialised divisions, e.g. anti-terrorism, but they rarely impinge on everyday life.

POLICE RANKS:
Constable
Sergeant
Inspector
Chief Inspector
Superintendent
Chief Superintendent

These are the lower and middle strata of policing in the UK. Other, higher ranks tend to be more administrative. A CID officer is differentiated from a uniformed office by the addition of the title "Detective" before his rank, so we have Detective Constable, Detective Sergeant, Detective Inspector and so on. That distinction ends with Detective Chief Superintendent.

Police and other emergency vehicles in the UK have blue flashing lights, not red.

There are several slang terms for the police—the old bill, the filth, john law, the scuffers, the bobbies, but perhaps the most entertaining is PC Plod. This derives from a children's character created by Enid Blyton. Noddy lives in Toytown and the local constable is PC Plod.

Police officers are responsible for their conduct both on and off duty. At one time, a British police officer needed his station commander's permission to marry and the force would vet his bride before granting permission. A police officer may not marry a person who holds a liquor license; a police officer has a duty to discharge his debts, and he is accountable for any relationships in which he is involved, therefore PC Robb's relationship with the unnamed woman on Cranley Estate could be called into question if it became general knowledge.

SCENE OF CRIME TEAM—also known as SOCOs (Scene Of Crime Officers) this team is the first to arrive after any serious incident such as a murder. They are usually ordered out by the senior investigating officer, who will follow them and take early reports from them.

EDUCATION—Compulsory education in the UK begins at age 5 and runs to age 16, with brighter pupils going on to the age of 18.

- *Primary*—Also known as infants for the younger classes; ages 5-16

- *Comprehensive*—ages 11-16, leading to General Certificate of Secondary Education (GCSE) at Ordinary level (O levels)

- *Sixth Form*—ages 16-18, leading to General Certificate of Secondary Education (GCSE) at Advanced level (A levels)

Higher education is voluntary, and can begin after the age of 16.

- *College*—either academic or vocational, ages 16+, leading to business, trade, or university entrance qualifications.

- *University*—ages 18+ leading to degree level qualifications.

HORSE RACING—The handicapper decides what weights the horse will carry.

MULTI-STORY BUILDINGS—In the USA, the street level floor of any building is the first floor. In the UK, this would be the ground floor, and the next level would be the first floor.

PAPER SIZES—Great Britain works on European paper sizes, A1, A2, A3, A4, etc. A4 and A5 are the most common sizes used, A4 being approximately the same size as quarto (or letter paper: approximately equivalent to the US 8 ½"x11") and A5 being half that size.

SOCCER REFERENCES—In the UK, soccer is known as football and has the biggest following of any sport. There is fierce rivalry amongst the fans. The four biggest teams are Manchester United, Chelsea, Arsenal and Liverpool. In the English Premier League, they usually comprise the top 4 teams at the end of each season. The season runs from August to May.

Even more virulent is the rivalry between fans of different teams from the same city. In Manchester there are two Premier League teams; Manchester United and Manchester City. Over recent years, since Sir Alex Ferguson became head coach in 1986, United have been in the ascendancy, winning every club trophy, some several times, in the past 21 years. It means that City, despite their professionalism and classy style of play, are often the butt of United fans' jokes.

In general, no United fan would stand in favor of City, Arsenal, Chelsea or Liverpool, but he might cheer other teams as long as they were not playing against United.

- *Own goal*—An own goal is a goal scored by a player into his own net (so he has scored a goal for the opposition). Therefore, if the score is 0-0 and a player scores an own goal, then the score becomes 1-0 in favor of the opposing team. Scoring an own goal as a colloquial term means that a person has done or said something that is to his own detriment.

- Bloomfield Road is the home ground of Blackpool FC. Stanley Matthews, arguably the greatest English footballer ever, known as the

Wizard of the Dribble, and Stanley Mortensen played for Blackpool in the late 40s and early 50s.

- The 1957 Manchester United league championship team took part in the 1957/58 European Cup (known as the European Champions League these days). On February 6, 1958, they were returning from a match with Red Star Belgrade and landed at Munich for refuelling. The aircraft crashed on take-off. Seven of the team died in the crash, another died later of his injuries. In all, 23 of the 44 passengers aboard the flight died. The tragedy is still marked by Manchester United fans today, and 2008 is the 50th anniversary of the accident.

TELEPHONE NUMBERS—In the UK, landline telephone numbers all begin 01, followed by an area code. Mobile telephone numbers all begin 07. Toll free numbers and local rate, non-geographical, local rate numbers begin 08 and premium rate numbers 09.

VEHICLES—Like anything else, the Brits tend to complicate descriptions of vehicles. An ordinary car is known as a saloon. A small saloon is usually a hatchback, a station wagon is an estate car. Where commercial vehicles are concerned, the term "van" is used to describe a panel sided box vehicle regardless of its size. They can range from small, car-sized vehicles up to 44 tonne articulated trucks, and they all would still be described as a van. Many vans use a roller shutter to close the rear doors. It can be thrown up as far as is necessary: a few centimetres to let the driver pull parcels from the rear, or all the way to let the driver climb in. The shutter's securing mechanism can only be operated from the exterior.

In the UK, we drive on the left, and the left hand side of any vehicle is known as the nearside, while the right hand side is called the offside.

BRITISH
VERNACULAR

AGGRO— a contraction of aggravation (more like US "assault"). It can be either verbal or physical. Anyone looking for aggro is looking for an argument or a fight. Not to be confused with agro, which is a prefix, as in agro-chemicals, meaning agricultural.

AUNT AGGIE AND DESPERATE DONALD— Desperate Dan is a character in a children's comic, The Dandy, and he's looked after by his Aunt Aggie. Kevin is simply playing on words.

BENT— an indication that the goods have been acquired in suspicious circumstances, possibly stolen or bootlegged. If a person is hooky or bent, it means he has criminal tendencies.

BERK— an airhead. Someone who thinks or acts in a dumb manner. This kind of low-level insult is common amongst British working people, and it is rare that it is meant or taken offensively.

BOD— person, individual.

BOTTLE— courage. Conversely, it can be used to indicate when someone chickened out by saying, "he bottled out."

BRIEF— as a noun, this means a lawyer. The British legal system utilizes a two-tier system, beginning with solicitors, who handle low-level litigation, and barristers, who act as advocates in higher courts. The term brief comes from the need to "brief" a solicitor or barrister.

BUBBLE— to bubble someone is to grass them up, inform on them.

DABS— fingerprints. Fingerprint officers are frequently referred to as "dab men."

DIPSTICK— See Berk

DOLE— unemployment benefit, welfare.

DOSSER— an idler, usually, but not always, unemployed.

DRUM— house, flat, apartment, living space.

EARNER— backhand payment for unofficial services rendered.

EARWIGGING—eavesdropping

ELECTRICS—anything electrical, quite distinct from electronics.

FELL OFF THE BACK OF A LORRY—See full explanation at Bent

GAFF—site, location. Distinct from "gaffe," which means a mistake.

GBH—violent assault. Legally, the term stands for grievous bodily harm, but as slang it is often used to indicate committing violence on another.

GEN—information

GIT—See ratbag

HOOKY—See full explanation at Bent

JACK JONES—See Todd Malone

JAM JAR—car

JIFFY—See full explanation at Bent

KEEP SCHTUM—Keeping quiet, not letting on about known information.

MAINS—electricity which comes from the main supply as opposed to battery generated.

MINDER—a bodyguard.

MOB HANDED—coming in with a mob in support, especially when numbers are out of proportion to the perceived threat. Any organisation, including the police can come in mob handed if there are enough of them

MOBY—cellphone usually known as a mobile phone or simply "mobile" in the UK.

MODOM—a very old, standing British joke. When putting on airs and graces, working class people would often address customers or people of a higher social class as Modom rather than the more correct Madam.

MONEY—English money consists of the pound, which is comprised of 100 pence. Denominations are 1, 2, 5, 10, 20, 50 pence coins and the £1, £2 coins. There are also £5, £10, £20, £50 notes, but the £50 note has been the subject of such levels of counterfeit that few establishments will accept it. There are numerous slang terms for money, including: moolah, spoolah, spondulicks, bread, cabbage, sovs, ackers, notes, dabs, nicker, quid. There are a number of other terms denoting actual sums of money:

- Grand = £1000. Can also be described as "k", for example 10k is the same as £10,000

- Monkey = £500

- Ton or century = £100

- Pony = £25

- Score = £20

- Tenner = £10

- Skin diver = fiver = £5

- A guinea is an old term for £1/1 shilling, or £1.05 in modern money.

NO NAMES, NO PACK DRILL—a British army expression meaning those concerned remain unidentified.

NODDY—See British Police above

NOUGHTY—bad tempered, mean spirited. Probably a medieval corruption of "naughty"

NUMPTY—See Berk

NURK—See Berk

NVQ—National Vocational Qualification. Low level, employment based qualifications, often attached to careers that require no specialized skills, such as Administration or Customer Service.

ON THE RAZZLE—Out on the town, making merry.

PENNINE FOG—The Pennines, often called the backbone of England, are a range of hills stretching from the Midlands to the Scottish border. We have no proper mountains in the UK, and these low-lying hills tend to generate much mist and fog, and also account for the sometimes-startling changes in weather between the east and west of the country. The author lives on the edge of the Pennines, northeast of Manchester, and can drive from thick fog, to gin-clear skies in a matter of a few miles.

PLOD—See British Police above

PROVERBIAL—anything that can be derived from old sayings. For example, "he'll get my boot up the proverbial," means a kick in the backside.

PUKKA—genuine, real

RATBAG—low level insult, not intended to be taken seriously or literally.

RUMBLE—Understand. In another context, someone who is "savvy" would be a person who is clued up, in the know, but in general to rumble, tumble or twig something is to suddenly understand what is being said, or what is happening

SAILING CLOSE TO THE WIND—coming near to the thin red line, or getting close to the line between legal and illegal.

SAS—Special Air Services. Elite commandoes of the British army, reputedly the toughest soldiers in the world.

SADDO, SADDOES—People who are perceived to follow a nerdy hobby or occupation, or people perceived as pedantic. Often also known as anoraks.

SAVVY—See Rumble

SCROAT—See Ratbag

SIR COWARD DE CUSTARD—someone who is chicken. Children often call such an individual a cowardy custard, presumably because custard is yellow, which is where this phrase derives from.

STUDYING FORM—A convention in British betting is the study of form, which simply means reading the racing pages to decide which horses to bet on.

TAKING THE MICK/MICKEY—taking a rise out of someone.

TART—slang for a woman who appears or is believed to be of easy virtue. Again, it is not usually meant or taken offensively. To call a woman a stupid tart is usually an irritable response to a woman who has acted foolishly. To call a man such a name indicates that he is behaving like stereotypical woman.

THE CITY—The City is the financial heart of the UK and is located within the square mile that is the City of London, but in order to distinguish it from its geographical location, it is known by the title "The City" in much the same way as New York's financial HQ is known simply as Wall Street. However, in football related conversations between Pete and Kevin, it means Manchester City football team.

TODD MALONE—Alone. Can be contracted to "on my todd," meaning on my own.

TOPPED, ICED, SNUFFED—although topped originally meant execution by decapitation, it has now come to mean anyone who is killed whether by due legal process or otherwise. Iced and snuffed mean murdered.

TOTTY, SKIRT, TAIL, BIRD—a chick, a woman, a single girl out about town, someone a man would hit on in a bar.

TRAMP—A woman of easy virtue, one who sleeps around, not necessarily a prostitute, often used as a name-calling device against a woman but not meant not be taken literally.

TUMBLE—See Rumble

TWIG—See Rumble

DAVID ROBINSON is a former adult education teacher, trained hypnotist, freelance writer, novelist and humorist. An avid fan of classic science fiction (Asimov, Wells, etc.) he writes in two main genres: dark thrillers and more light-hearted mysteries, bringing an extensive knowledge of the paranormal into most of his works. Mr. Robinson is extensively published in small press and on the Internet, and published two comedy novels in 2002. He has an odd, often cynical sense of humor, a passion for classical music, brass bands and 60's beat music. David is married with 4 children, 9 grandchildren, and lives in the North of England where he enjoys walking his dog, a West Highland White named Max, on the moors. When not writing he researches the paranormal, everything from UFOs to ghosts, and supports his favorite football team, Manchester United.

Printed in the United Kingdom
by Lightning Source UK Ltd.
135217UK00001B/310-354/P